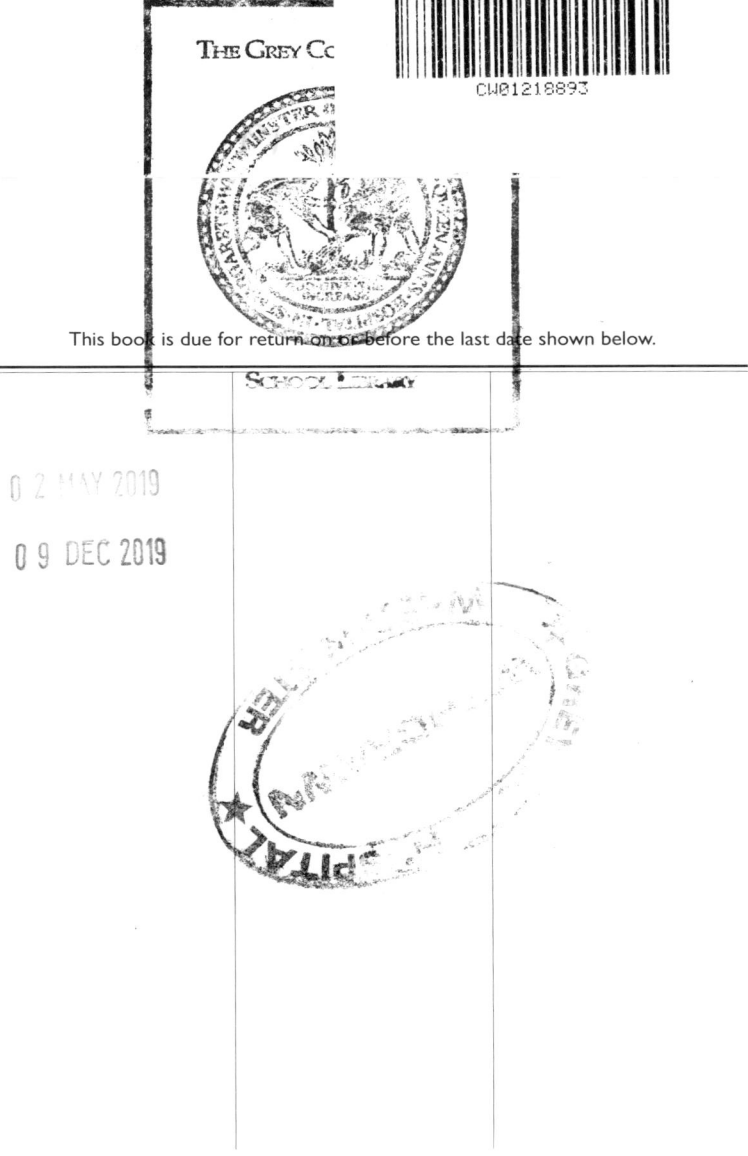

This book is due for return on or before the last date shown below.

0 2 MAY 2019

0 9 DEC 2019

WILD FIRE Copyright © 2017 by Anna McKerrow. All Rights Reserved.

All rights reserved. No part of this book may be reproduced in any form or by any electronic or mechanical means including information storage and retrieval systems, without permission in writing from the author. The only exception is by a reviewer, who may quote short excerpts in a review.

Cover designed by www.bookollective.com

This book is a work of fiction. Names, characters, places, and incidents either are products of the author's imagination or are used fictitiously. Any resemblance to actual persons, living or dead, events, or locales is entirely coincidental.

Anna McKerrow
Visit my website at www.annamckerrow.com

Printed in the United States of America
ISBN: 9781973309222

Prologue

August 2047, Tintagel

I hold the lame rabbit in my hands. The girl - Gilly, she says - looks up at me with wide, round eyes.

"Can you fix him? Can you mend my Huxley's leg?" she asks, with all her hope in those round eyes like she's never known disappointment; lucky, cossetted, innocent little girl with parents that probably love her. She's grown up all her life with witches being able to do this shit. She trusts us. She trusts in my magic. She shouldn't.

"Yeah. Just be quiet," I frown at her and feel along old Huxley's leg. Unlike Gilly, he's rightly terrified, his liquid cute-bunny-eyes shading over with a dim, matte resignation to the pain. I locate the break; fortunately it isn't bent in a weird angle, just a fairly clean indenture in the bone. I close my eyes and visualise it as clearly as I can. A small, white rabbit bone with a crack like a hair running through it, and a tiny bone chip separated a millimetre or so into the flesh. Not a fatal wound, not even a nasty break, but even the smallest fractures can hurt like hell: especially when you're small and sweet and you never asked for any of the pain that life seems more than willing to hand out.

Holding my hand around the leg I say a prayer to Brighid, patron Goddess of the Greenworld. Healer, among other things. My Goddess. My girl. (Though "girl" is completely reductive; there's so many patriarchal elements of our language we're working on changing, Greenworld generation by generation. Brighid's a gigantic, all-powerful, intense-as-shit GODDESS, lest we forget).

Blessed Brighid of the healing springs, Blessed Brighid of the silver moon,

Tending every wounded thing, deep inside your fiery womb,

I command and direct your healing power; Help me in my healing hour.

The heat in my hands grows and radiates. I imagine the energy wrapping the rabbit's bone like a bandage, sealing the break. Huxley Bunnywugs lies pliantly in my hands, either resigned to his fate in some kind of primal fear-state, or accepting the energy, knowing in his rabbity animal way that I'm helping him; that he doesn't have to struggle. I smile at Gilly.

"It's working?" she breathes, watching my hands. I nod.

Huxley's eyes start to refocus and I feel his heartbeat thrum more regularly than the panicked, injured rhythm of a body when it's injured. There's a mild ache in my own leg; sometimes your energy feels the shadow of the pain in the other person - or rabbit, in this case. I can feel his bone knitting; that's why you have to make sure a broken bone's set right before you get going healing on it. Otherwise you'll knit it at the wrong angle or something and you'll end up with a rabbit with a leg at a right angle or a dog with an amusingly backward paw all its life.

I close my eyes as the healing energy intensifies, coming through me from everywhere around me; in nature, in the trees, in Lowenna's garden; coming from Brighid herself, Queen of Nature, Queen of Fire, Celtic Goddess of all living things.

Unexpectedly, in my mind's eye I see a map, a globe: a crisscrossing of lines of light across the world, and I'm flying, I'm seeing it from above. Other lands; mountains, rivers, cities like the Redworld across the border from us. But there are some places without the industrial sprawls, without the electric lights that flicker on and off. And on these greener, remote areas, as I fly, I see small groups of folk lighting beacons. Lighting fires, all over the world, uniting the night and dawn and the midday sun. And in my vision I know that they're like us. Resistance groups; living in harmony with nature, saying no to war, to pollution, to corruption and violence. And as I open my eyes I hear their call in my mind as if for just that second, it resonated around the earth. *For Earth. For life. For our children.*

Weird. I blink and hand the rabbit back to Gilly. But it's easy to slip into this kind of vision sometimes; especially when the moon's near full. It's all part of the joy of being a witch, a protectress of the folk, a healer, herbalist, cartomancer; seer, oracle, bard. Witches do everything. Birth, death, healing, government, agriculture and being scary bitches when the need arises. The need doesn't arise very often, but it seems that it might, now, more and more.

"He'll be fine now," I say, and old Huxley jumps out of my hands and straight into a bush. I say a short prayer to Brighid, thanking Her. Gilly smiles shyly and thanks me.

I could always heal animals, but I never told anyone. Some things were better kept secret when I grew up, especially from my dad.

CHAPTER ONE

A quilt is a web of time, a document of the Greenworld, stitching life to life, season to season, memory to eternity.

From: Tenets and Sayings of the Greenworld

BAH-buh-buh; BAH-buh-buh. The drums thump low and heavy, a rhythm of three repeating beats: One heavy beat, a slight pause, then two lighter beats that follow, BAH-buh-buh; BAH-buh-buh, reverberating off the tall stone Cornish cliffs as if the earth's making love to the sea, a gigantic mythical tryst, a love song, primal and beautiful in the night air. BAH-buh-buh: drawing power down from the moon and up from the earth into the circle traced in the wet sand, lit with flickering torches; focusing our minds, attuning our bodies to the same heartbeat.

I half-close my eyes; feel the reverberation of the deer-hide drum in my hand, hitting it hard with the ash beater, its end covered in a soft leather pommel. Both were made for me: just for me, now that I'm a witch here in Tintagel; me, Sadie Morgan. I still can't believe it. For so long I was just a villager, just a messed up girl, trying to get through the freezing Greenworld winters in the horrific wool dresses and the knitted leggings that's all that keeps the wind from slashing your legs. Being just another girl to work the fields and watch at the solstice and equinox celebrations, on the edges, mind, on the boundary, being like everyone else; I never thought I would be a witch.

The drum face's painted with the triple moon: two crescent moons with their rounded edges facing off a full moon. The triple moon: symbol of our goddess Brighid, and my tattoo, my witch-brand. Only a few of the witches have them at all, and only Lowenna Hawthorne, Head Witch of the Greenworld, has the same one as me. I self-initiated, something no other Greenworld witch has ever done, apparently. Here it's always at someone else's hand; a High Priestess that confers your witch-ness upon you. But me, I had to do it different, right? I went out to the stone circle near my village, Gidleigh, over in Dartmoor and did a ceremony the best way I knew how, and woke up with the brand. I'd observed the witch in my village, Zia, my whole life. Fascinated and scared by her. And there was my dad, of course. The witch who went bad.

The drum beats get louder; the power builds in the circle. Love. That's what power is, ultimately, creative and destructive at once. *The great universal force of love thundering through us all, if only we can feel it, if only we can listen*, so

Lowenna says. She's the High Priestess here. We're on the cold beach (did I say it was cold? It's bloody cold. It was always cold at home on Dartmoor, but being on the coast's worse. There's a wetness in the air that clings to you) next to Tintagel village, under the rocky island of Tintagel Head. It's the monthly full moon esbat of the witches. Sabbats are the seasonal festivals, esbats are the private meeting, not the public one for the village, thanks. Here's where the real magic gets done.

But back to love. Not twee or small or frilly: raw, bigger than all of us, wild, wider than the cold waves. Love is power, power is love, direct and overwhelming, like being burned whole. Or swept away by the sea, maybe. That's how I think of it. Great and terrible and dramatic.

And there's the love in the power of the circle, of the witches, but there's also the love of one woman for another. The greatest love, so they say here. And in the book of love, in my book, page one, there's me and Demelza Hawthorne, eye to eye and heart to heart and the fire between us could engulf the whole world.

If only she knew I liked her.

I don't care about that sounding as soppy as it does. I DON'T CARE. I'm an unashamedly-over-the-top kind of girl about these things. Rhapsodic. Symphonic. Sapphoerotic. It's a crazy-ridiculous-faerie-enchantment kind of crush, admitted. Yeah. And yeah, if you were a tiny bit more well-adjusted and, you know, more *normal* than me, I know you might say *well, Sadie, it's clear to me that you're purposefully avoiding a close attachment by forming a crush on someone unattainable and finding a familiar perverse comfort in the resulting heartbreak and sadness because you don't know what love is anyway* but a) that's old news, and b) knowing it doesn't make it stop, unfortunately. So am I a romantic? Or am I a fantasist? And are they the same thing?

Anyway, I'd rather protect myself from the disappointment of an average person and all their irritating quirks and farts, or, worse, their violent and terrifying rages, by living in fantasy's warm and rainbow-sparkly sunshine, thanks.

Fortunately/unfortunately, Melz has no clue about my overpowering crush/admiration/minor obsession. So I'll admire her from the sidelines and say nothing, because she'll never want me anyway. And no, I don't like thinking about why that might be, because if I do, everything unravels and the emptiness at the centre of me swallows up everything. I don't want to be that girl with daddy issues, anyway, I mean, how dull's that? Blahblahblah nothing of interest here, move on.

I open my eyes and look across the circle at Melz; her eyes closed, head nodding to the drum beat. She's sitting opposite the circle to me and through the spiralling smoke of the fire between us, I watch her, pale lips parted, cheeks flushed, long throat graceful and willowy under the heavy wool collar of her long cloak. Watching Demelza Hawthorne, a witch since she was eight, a priestess of the dark and terrible goddess Morrigan, when all her being's totally enmeshed in making magic, is a moment of pure beauty. Like Cleopatra entering Rome on her barge, that kind of beautiful. *The barge she sat in, like a burnish'd throne, Burned on the water: the poop was beaten gold; Purple the sails, and so perfumed that/The winds were lovesick with them.*

Mum had all the books. People in the village used to come to our house to borrow them. I read everything, even the non-Greenworld-approved ones in the hidden cabinet in the kitchen. Shakespeare was approved, though. What kind of animal would you have to be to burn Shakespeare? Though they burned others when the Greenworld started.

Usually, Melz is guarded as hell. But all that's gone when she's in magic, within it, whatever: she *is* magic, she glows like the moon and the stars. She doesn't have to know how I feel, and in moments like these it's enough just being close to her. The perfect witch, the beautiful enchantress.

Witches: the patriarchy's worst nightmare. Probably that's why we're down here cut off from the rest of the country with a mile-thick barbed wire border filed with attack dogs and armed troops. They don't want us getting out anytime soon and spreading our "you're powerful" propaganda to the general populace any more than we can be arsed to have to deal with their thundering ignorance. Hence the Greenworld and the Redworld. Us and them. Self-sustaining ecopaganism one side; corruption, poverty and pollution the other.

I close my eyes again and rise up on the beat of our drums, my energy circling the fire, my consciousness half in it, half in my body. Ten witches now, in Tintagel. Five of us in training, the rest the older and more experienced: Lowenna, in charge, our High Priestess; Demelza, her daughter, a witch since she was eight; Merryn, Beryan and Rhiannon. And us, the trainees.

Tonight, it's Imbolc. February 1st, Brighid's festival of Spring where the fires are lit again, where the first crocus peeks its white head out from the recently frozen ground. It's a time of healing, of returned warmth and hope and light. Tonight, we're healing the Greenworld itself. Knitting the communities back together. Mending the fences that can't be fixed with wood and wire, so Lowenna says. No better time to do it.

First, we raise the energy with drumming. BAH-buh-buh, BAH-buh-buh. The energy in the centre of the circle builds; pours from my hands, from the drum, which has a power of its own, into a cone of power. That becomes a sphere of golden yellow light that surrounds us, over and above and through the sand and the earth under us. The tide's out and the beach's small and the spectacular waves still crash hard and loud on the cliffs, echoing our beat.

In witch training there's loads of chants and songs to learn, By Brighid. It's essential to tag that on the end of what you say, by the way, *By Brighid*, here in the heart of the covenstead, the beating breast, as it were, to make sure you fit in, like a verbal camouflage. You have to read, you have to study. *The Common Herbal*, *Prayers and Songs of the Greenworld*, the thick version, not the one you get in school. *The Book of Brighid*, *The Book of the Morrigan*.

We chant as we drum. *Fiery Goddess Brighid of the earth and sun; Come, goddess of the waters too, and see our work is done.*

"Knit the Greenworld back together, Brighid. Lend us your healing. Drape your green mantle over this land again. Make us whole. Reunite us and heal the divisions in our community," Lowenna calls out to Brighid, and her eyes flutter closed.

Being a trainee witch. It's SO much less exciting than I expected. I'm in the background, doing the grunt work. Tonight, us lowly trainees are keeping the power raised in the circle by drumming and singing. It's just like school. No teacher ever picked me to lead the goddess-awful community acapella singing or the storytelling or be a part of the seasonal festival plays, not that I wanted to, it was all lame.

Then, when there's enough energy raised, we lay down our drums and Melz opens a large carved wooden box, taking out a quilt; a circular cloth of green, white and gold pentagons, trimmed with red and black. Red for the blood that was sacrificed in the battle for Tintagel a year and a half ago. Black for magic, for binding and wisdom; green for the land, our beautiful south-west England Greenworld; white for the moon, gold for the sun. Five points in each patch and five sides. Five fingers on a hand, five points on the holy pentagram: Earth, air, fire, water and spirit. Five witches that used to protect Tintagel, once, before more were needed. *A quilt is a web of time, a document of the Greenworld, stitching life to life, season to season, memory to eternity,* so says the Greenworld tenet.

We've stitched this quilt together most nights over the past two weeks since the new moon, using the two weeks to the moon's fullness to harness that energy of growth and wholeness. Sitting in Lowenna's big kitchen, singing prayers and chants to Brighid; squinting over tiny stitches and stabbing ourselves with the needles, rubbing our blood into the cloth when we pricked ourselves, red for blood given in the service of the Goddess. But the quilt still has one seam still loose; one line to be completed. Melz puts in the first few stitches: small, neat tracks that start to bind the felt and wool, then passes the needle and thread to Catie, one of my fellow trainees.

We'll each contribute a few stitches to the final seam; each of our energies meshing into one, into a symbolic restored Greenworld union. That's what we'll all visualise, anyway, when the quilt comes to us. But we know that we need powerful magic, big big magic, to do that, because the Greenworld's dividing more and more every day. Lowenna will make the final stitch, as the Goddess herself. She'll channel the power of Brighid, take on Her voice. Her face. Bring Brighid's blessing to our task.

I take the quilt when it's my turn and concentrate on the magical image I've prepared before now. I've spent a week building it up in my mind, making it real and three dimensional and full of colour and detail. I push the needle through the thick green felt and into the white patch below it, the black thread thick and final. I imagine that the land of the Greenworld - Cornwall and Devon, it was once - is a number of little islands floating in the sea: broken apart, loose on the water.

I imagine the rough rock edges of the islands; in some places, the rocks have parts of houses on them, torn apart from the division, gaping into the freezing, black-grey British Channel, their pulled-apart rooms gaping like mouths. And I imagine the pieces floating back to each other; rejoining each other. The broken houses become whole again and the rock hinges back together with rough crashes. The land becomes bigger and bigger as I pull the black binding thread through the felt, joining one side to the other. Pulling the Greenworld back together, whatever our differences. It's that or sink.

But try as I might, as I put my last stitch in, I can't make one stray piece of the Greenworld rejoin the mainland in my meditation. It repels from the edge like an eel, eluding my grasp. I can't find the satisfactory feeling of a neat union in my mind's eye. Guiltily, I hold out the quilt to Lowenna to put the last stitches in.

She takes the quilt and bends her head to sew, and starts singing a gaelic chant – *Teigi ar bhur ngluine, agus osclaigi bhur suile, Agus ligigi Brid bheannaithe isteach*: Be on your knees and open your eyes, and let blessed Brighid in. We repeat the chant softly as she sews. Melz picks up her drum, nodding to all of us to do the same. We resume our hypnotic beat as before, this time chanting over the top. BAH-buh-buh, BAH-buh-buh. *Teigi ar bhur ngluine, agus osclaigi bhur suile.* BAH-buh-buh, BAH-buh-buh. *Agus ligigi Brid bheannaithe isteach.*

Lowenna's supposed to become Brighid in this process. Take on her form, her spirit. I've heard about it but I haven't seen it before, so I'm watching her like a hawk, waiting for it to happen. But as the drumming and the chanting fill up my head and my heart and my whole body, I feel more and more as if I were in a dream: a strange, fast dream where suddenly I'm racing across the land, fleet-footed, faster than any human could run.

I'm still in the circle, still on the beach, but I'm not there, too. I'm somewhere else.

I find myself on the top of a grassy hill, rising softly from the green fields around it like a pregnant belly, the sun baking into my skin. I can see a town on one side of the hill, at the bottom, dark and broken, but on the other side, the fields stretch to the horizon and the far hills beyond are dappled with sun and cloud.

Glastonbury Tor. I know it from Melz's descriptions and from books: in the Redworld, but not too far from the Greenworld border. It was Avalon, the faery kingdom, once, so legend has it: ringed in mists, home of Morgan Le Fay and her priestesses who made magic there. And the energy portal here, on the soft green hill that I stand on ni my vision, that's the one that Melz unblocked when she was here. Before that, the dead had nowhere to go. Their way to the next world, the land of death was blocked. That's what portals do: these massive energy centres that only witches know how to operate; no-one else even knows they're there, like. They pour energy into our world, they connect us with the universe, and provide us with our pathways into the next world; they're our passage between life and death. Tintagel Head has a portal. And its existence is less of a secret than it used to be.

And there, on the top of the green hill, is Brighid. Or, rather, she is the hill. The whole thing is the skirt of her dress, and she towers above me, a vast and ancient power.

Being this close to her is overwhelming and peaceful and joyful all at once. Maybe you never get used to it, this all-encompassing heat and chill and awe, peace and giddiness, just like when She came to me at Scorhill stone circle when I self-initiated.

I open my mouth to speak, but coral-pink butterflies fly out instead of words. Yet I can hear myself talking somewhere else, as if in another room. I'm saying *Blessings to you all, priestesses*, and I can feel Brighid speaking through me to the circle as I stand here, watching the butterflies form the words of my conversation with Her.

My Lady, Highest Blessings to you, the words flutter in the air, changing and flowing with the flip of one pink wing and another, changing colour iridescently to a lapis lazuli blue for her answer: *And to you, my Priestess*. Her answers are accompanied by sound: everything in this place resonates with Her; everything is Her, and everything responds as Her.

Where am I? My question pulses pink again against the blue sky, immediately graduating to lapis at the edges again: changing as soon as formed.

At the place where I am her voice fills the sky like a bell, and now her words are written larger in the wings of the butterflies; each letter the size of a tree.

Glastonbury? I ask.

Yes and no. Her reply is evasive, turning around and about in the wind.

Why am I here? The pink butterflies alight on me, now. Soon I am covered in them.

Are you ready, Sadie Morgan? Brighid reaches forward and I feel the earth move under me as her fiery touch traces a circle over my third eye chakra; I concentrate on standing. *You are Love. You are Healing. You are Fire. Nothing is more incendiary, nothing more liberating.*

The Glastonbury portal opens, then, and undulates around me; I spread out my hands so I stand like a star, and feel the energy beating strong through the hill and my heart and out through the top of my head and I laugh with the joy of it, inside the Heart of the World; it's like being inside love.

Love heals, this is your path, this is your role within the

Three. But love is also healing and forgiveness her voice says; the wind breathes it and the trees rustle Her words. And suddenly, I look up and my dad's standing opposite me on the Tor; bruised and slumped and broken. The opposite of love. I turn away. *No. No. No.* The butterflies disappear; the sun goes behind cloud. *No.*

I come to with my face in the wet sand, with Melz's hand on my shoulder. The witches are humming quietly, holding the space. *No, No, No* I'm muttering, spitting out sand. I stare wildly at her, not knowing where I am for a minute.

"Okay?" Melz looks concerned but I come to my senses and sit up, plastering a smile on.

"Uh,… sure, fine. I'm fine," Reflexively, I look behind me, in case somehow he's there, my dad, like I've brought him back with me from the vision.

"You're sure?" her stare's direct but full of concern too. I nod.

"Sure I'm sure. Really," I smile shakily and she nods, and Rain, another trainee, tucks a blanket around my shoulders. I don't talk about him, not ever, my dad, and I'm not going to start now. "What happened? I zoned out.

Sorry,"

Melz frowns.

"You didn't *zone out*. You channelled Brighid. You spoke to us. You wore her face,"

"What?!"

She hands me some ritual wine in a ceremonial chalice - green glass, made in the village - and puts a piece of bread in my mouth. Her touch is gentle; her fingertips brush my lips.

"Thanks. I mean, sorry, what?!" I can't think of anything else to say. I'm also very aware of her soft touch.

"Eat your bread," she smiles. I chew and swallow obediently. "She came through you. She blessed us all. Didn't say much, just that love was in the circle, and love was the key to healing the land. Your face, though, took on the goddess. And your hair reddened even more," Melz smiles softly and touches my hair gently. "It was beautiful,"

I smile goofily back at her. *It was beautiful, or I was beautiful?*

Lowenna says nothing, and now that properly back

in my body I can feel an atmosphere in the circle. Lowenna is the Priestess of Brighid. Lowenna is the one that was supposed to become the Goddess in the ritual. She's obviously not happy, but she doesn't say anything. She picks up the quilt.

"A quilt is a web of time, a document of the Greenworld, stitching life to life, season to season, memory to eternity." She quotes the Greenworld tenet, her voice level and unemotional, finishing the ritual. "Blessed Brighid, lend us your power to heal the rift in the Greenworld. Let us all feel your resolve and energy in making this happen. We will heal our land. We will heal our people." She looks at me, unreadable. "We will grow strong again. So mote it be,"

"So mote it be," I repeat, and close my eyes. But I know it'll take more than stitching a bloody quilt together to repair the divisions in the Greenworld - and a lot more to protect us from the raw wound of the land, the creeping apocalypse (really, "creeping apocalypse" isn't even overstating it) that threatens to be the end of everything, the end of peace, the end of these fertile times: a Redworld war for the last scraps of fuel, far away in Russia. A Redworld that's fracked and drilled, poisoned and tortured its land for fuel so badly that we're feeling the results here, even though we're separate - earth tremors, less birds, fewer bees. Because we might be a self-declared island, but what they do to their part of Mother Earth - to Brighid - affects us too.

I imagine the yellow sphere of light protecting us draining back into the earth, and as I do, the beach returns to normal: I focus back on the sound of the waves, the salt in the air, the grit of the sand clinging to my wool dress and inbetween my toes. Taste the wine and the bread in my mouth, feel the food grounding me.

Brighid spoke to me about healing in my vision. Brighid might know that I need to heal. I might even give it lip service, the power of healing, but I don't want it. I know what healing does. It makes you fall apart, explode, face what you don't want to face. I can't fall apart. Not now, when I'm training to be a witch. I don't want to be the ruined girl anymore. I just want to forget.

I get up quietly like the rest, and watch as Lowenna folds up the quilt, putting it back inside the carved wooden box; as Rain and Catie help Melz close the circle. Lowenna looks up and catches my eye as the others file back over the rocks to climb off the beach.

"Sadie," she makes me wait until the rest have

gone. I meet her eyes on the beach, in full darkness now without our lamps. "That was quite something," she says. "Has that happened before?"

"No," I feel really awkward. "I didn't do it on purpose, it just happened,"

"Hmm," she doesn't comment either way, just eyes at me speculatively.

"I heard myself, on the outside. I knew I was talking, but I don't know what I said. I was... with Brighid. On Glastonbury Tor. Kind of,"

Lowenna holds the folded-up quilt to her as if it could protect her from me. I've really rattled her. And I don't want to do that, because she's my High Priestess. The one that can finish my training as a witch.

"I serve Brighid, and She has never shown me that. And you... you just *became* her. So quickly, so effortlessly. You did the full transformation. It took me years to master that. You stood in the centre of the circle and prophesised," she makes me look her in the eye, then. "That's not your job, Sadie. It's mine. I'm the High Priestess,"

"I'm sorry," I don't know what to say. *It wasn't me,*

it was the Goddess. I wouldn't have done that on my own. Both make me sound like a child making excuses.

"Don't be sorry for your gift," Lowenna snaps. "Others train their whole lives to have what you have," and I know by *others* she means her.

"I'm so-...," I stop myself apologising. "I don't know what to say,"

"You've said enough," she says. We walk up the beach and up to the piled-up boulders that you have to climb up to get to the path above.

"I hope it works. The quilt,"I offer the wish quietly, shyly, as some small apology for my apparent taking over and pissing Lowenna off.

"Goddess willing," she says, tersely, her back to me.

"So mote it be," I murmur. Not for the first time, I wonder what Brighid's will really is - and whether anyone's listening.

CHAPTER TWO

And it was not in our name that the Redworld burned.

From: Tenets and Sayings of the Greenworld

I want to forget him, my dad, but I'm not allowed to.

I lie down on the padded table on top of the clean sheet and Lowenna covers me with a patchwork quilt; not one used for magic, this time - a simple one for warmth and cosiness. Faded reds and blues and grees, interlocking circles. Comforting, or so you'd think.

"Warm enough?" she asks and I nod, closing my eyes and fighting the wave of dread I always get when I come for healing. "All right. Same as before. Let it happen; breathe through any crises. I'm here with you," she pats my shoulder, but she's definitely not being as warm as she was before the ritual at the beach. "It's all right to cry. Tears release stress hormones,"

I nod. I have to heal, Lowenna says, to be able to access all my power as a witch. My first week in Tintagel, she sat me down and insisted I tell her everything about my childhood. She knew it'd been bad, but she didn't know exactly what she was dealing with when she took me in to her covenstead; when she took in Roach's estranged little heller of a daughter.

She took me in because I have the witch-brand and that makes me special. Worth the risk, apparently. Roach, my dad, he was a branded witch too, once. Here, in Tintagel, at the very start of the Greenworld. Then he *went bad* and became the head of the criminal gangs that roam the space between barricaded Greenworld villages. And decided to make life a living hell for me and my mum. Hence the healing.

Lowenna knew the more recent stuff too: the reason I was here at all. My mum, Linda Morgan, stabbed Zia Prentice, Danny's mum, a witch of the Greenworld, through the heart. We'd lived alongside each other all those years, but that didn't count for anything in that moment, when Mum stood there with the knife in her hand. She saw us working magic together. She hadn't known I'd become a witch. She picked up the athame off the tree stump we were using as an altar in the middle of the garden and just... did it. Snapped.

I know why she did it. When you're brittle enough to snap like that, it's because pain has stolen your flexibility, over time, like an ageing bone. What he did to her - Roach, my dad - hardened her. She became more and more rigid, shielding me, protecting herself. And, that day, suddenly, everything shattered. There was no bend left anymore.

After we buried Zia, something in Danny boiled over. And right there in the middle of the village green, where we'd played as kids and ran around the maypole with our ribbons at Beltane, he used dark magic against Mum and me. Would have killed me if Melz hadn't stepped in. And the thing is: I understood that too. I didn't blame him, and I didn't blame his little sister Biba when she attacked me before then, full of her own grief. She threatened to kill me and mum. Said she'd make sure the doors and the windows of our house were locked before setting fire to it with us inside. Because we'd taken her mother away.

Zia training me as a witch had led to her death, and Biba witnessed it firsthand. Dad's abuse of us ended up ruining so many lives. *Community, family, covenstead. All one and none separate*, so the Greenworld tenet goes. But the truth is, the community knew what was happening to us in those early days when dad still lived with us, and no-one intervened. No-one did a thing. Abuse doesn't happen in a vacuum; a community allows it to happen. And, finally, the community became the victims of that same abuse. Mum contained everything for as long as she could, rigid and afraid. And when she broke, the community shook with the force of the explosion.

Let the healing fires of Brighid burn through you. Let Brighid transform you, dear, was what Lowenna said before we started that first session. I don't think she was expecting what happened, but I wasn't really surprised.

I'd lain on the table that first time, clenched, tight as a board, resisting the energy pouring from Lowenna's hands as hard as I could, because when you're wound tight, when you've worked so hard to keep your walls up around the shapeless dread inside you, you're terrified when someone comes to pull those walls down. Well-ordered, well-tended walls made of memories. If some of the memories are jagged and dangerous, then you made sure they got cemented hard into the wall a long time ago. Because if just one stone comes out of place, the whole thing goes, and you die.

Despite the wall, sometimes I feel like I might fall apart: dissolve, lose my togetherness, be invaded by everything else. Sometimes I feel so thin, so badly woven and weak, that I'm afraid of birds and insects, even the chaos of falling leaves, because they might enter me, get too far into my space, without me wanting them to. It's like I'm not sure where my outline is anymore. I can't keep myself whole, and that's why I never talk about it to anyone, even in the Greenworld, because I know how nuts it sounds (though, thank Brighid I'm where I am, because pre-Greenworld, someone would have fed me so many chemicals I wouldn't need the psychedelic effects of a magical practice). But fear isn't rational. Even though I know the witches understand healing and holistic health, even though I know they can help me, I'm still terrified of anyone making this worse.

That first time, I tried. I wanted to please Lowenna. So, as the energy flowed around me, I breathed a little looser and relaxed a bit. I let it in, just a little: the goodness of the universe flowing from her wide, work-callused palms. But as soon as I did, I felt the familiar panic blooming from my middle, from my damaged solar plexus, full of yellowed nightmare heat, like a sick yellow dog biting my heart and stomach out. I gasped and Lowenna put a firm hand on my shoulder and told me to *breathe, just breathe and let it go,* but I couldn't *just breathe.* I couldn't breathe at all. I felt like I was drowning; the taste of salt water filled my mouth. Panic gripped me and I lunged off the table and cowered in the corner of the room, shaking, with an overwhelming sense of horror, as if something terrible was just about to happen. Wide-eyed, I waited for the room to crumple, for that well-ordered wall of memory to cave in and kill me, to end it forever.

Ruined girl, ruined girl, ruined, spoilt, wasted; that familiar wave of disappointment in myself washed over me then, and I thudded onto my heels, leaning against the wall, weeping, wishing I could cry hard enough for my heart to explode, so I could die and be done with all of this, just walk into a calm white room forever and close the door behind me, to not come back, and what a relief that'd be.

Lowenna had knelt next to me and held me, rubbing my back, not saying anything, until finally I stopped crying and stared at the wall blankly. *This is going to take some time,* she'd said, *but we have to continue, and every time it's going to get a bit easier. You have to let the pressure out slowly. But once you start, it will never hurt as much as it does now. I know it was terrible, what he did to you. But you can only become a true Priestess of Brighid by going on your own healing journey. You can't keep this inside you anymore.*

All that means that every time it comes time for my healing session with Lowenna, I get more and more stressed about it, and every time I cry and every time I try to push away the thing I won't remember, but it comes, every time, and I sit up and push her hands away and say *that's enough*. Every time, she gives me a glass of water and a biscuit and listens to whatever I have to say. Sometimes she asks me about dad. Sometimes I answer, and as much as she tells me *I'm here to listen, I'm here for you, Sadie,* I don't believe her. I just don't.

But today as I pull the quilt over myself, I feel resigned. I don't have any option to stop the healing sessions; it's all part of my training. You can't be an effective witch with this level of neurosis/psychosis/crap, because so much of your energy's being used up dealing with it, day to day (dealing with it in the sense of ignoring it and trying to get on with your life, not *actually* dealing with it). Lowenna says the further we go with the healing, the more energy I'll have for my witch work. I can still heal others while I do this - *if we all waited to be perfect to be witches, we'd be waiting forever,* she says to me once. *But at the same time you have a responsibility to yourself and to the covenstead to deal with what Brighid has given you.*

I sigh as I close my eyes.

Because of my witch-brand, Lowenna initiated me into Brighid's service at that same beach, the one that lies in the shadow of Tintagel Head. She lit a sacred fire and the flames and shadows rippled on the still water like the spirits of birds. I stripped naked and walked into the freezing water, her behind me; when I was up to my waist she gently pushed me under, in over my head in the freezing salty Cornish sea, leaving my old self behind. She pulled me up out of the water and took me, shivering, to the beach where she dried me and dressed me in a white gown and green, blue and gold robe. She took the role of Brighid.

I had my lines prepared: *Great Goddess Brighid, I am your daughter, contemplating your mystery. Grant me entrance into the River of Death, that it may cleanse me and the womb of my rebirth.*

In whose name do you ask? Lowenna's voice was loud on the beach, owning it.

I said, *I ask in the name of the Goddess of the Blue and Green and Gold. In your name, Blessed Brighid, Dark Mother, Bright Mother, Fire of the Sun, Water of the Moon, Warrior, Poet, Smith, Eternal Flame. Tender Mother, Strong Daughter, Loving Sister, Mediator of disputes. I ask also in the name of the Morrigan, whose feet are in the River of Death, who cleaves flesh from bone, soul from body, in Your name as Brighid the Healer and Consoler, Liberator and Inspirer. Brighid of the poets, initiate me. As You loosen the grip of the coldest season, so loosen and liberate me. Breathe life into me this Imbolc as You breathe life into the mouth of the dead winter.*

She embraced me. Asked what I pledged to Brighid.

I pledged myself to fire, poetry, magick and healing. *If I should break faith with you, may the skies fall upon me, may the seas drown me, may the earth rise up and swallow me,* I said. I think I meant it.

I lit a candle inside a storm lamp. Promised to always keep Her light burning in my heart.

But some days, it's hard.

"Maybe we'll get through a whole half hour today," I joke nervously. Lowenna doesn't say anything; she's definitely still pissed off about what I apparently said at the ritual, but the clean, purifying smell of copal and pine fills my nose as she sprinkles some loose incense on a lump of smouldering charcoal in a bowl.

"Just relax," she says and I feel her hands hover

above my middle, and feel as she traces the healing symbols into my aura.

Behind my eyes, colours flash for a moment and then settle on pink and green, the calming and loving colours of the heart chakra. The green colour gets more intense; I feel as though I'm lying in a bright green grassy field, the sun shining hard through the chlorophyll in the plants and into my eyes, full of that pure, wholesome goodness that sunny plants have (not all plants - some live in the shadows and have different powers). And the more intense the colour gets, the more I can feel the pressure building in my chest. Silently, I start to cry, but not the same as I usually do. This isn't panic; it's sorrow, bittersweet and sad.

With my eyes still closed, in my mind's eye I see myself as a little girl, playing with my dolls in the garden one summer's day. I'm pretending that the bushes are faerie houses. Mum's reading, lying on a blanket on the long unkempt grass, smiling over at me occasionally; the sun shines and I can feel the pleasurable tightness of sunburn across my nose and cheeks. The metallic smell of the black earth and the feel of it, thick and hard, cracked around the stems of the lavender bush, so vivid. The lavender drones with bees, redolent of other summertimes, of summer nights when I smelt that sleepy sweetness in my bedroom, windows open onto the soft blackness of the moor. And I weep for that moment, for its loveliness, and for knowing that I can never go back there, to my mother's garden. And I weep because I lost that mother. That smiling woman, reading. Not dead, but disappeared, changed, hardened. She changed a long time ago.

And in the vision, as I feel Lowenna's hands move to hover above my head, I see his shadow block out the sun, and the world goes from green to yellow. He stands over mum as she lies on the blanket, and she holds her arm over herself, but it won't be enough. It was never enough. His hand, his big, flat hand follows its inevitable arc. She's lying there reading when she should be cleaning. *Smack*.

Breathe, just breathe through it, comes Lowenna's voice, but I can't. I sit up, pushing the quilt away.

I'm not sure if it's inside my head, at first: a glassy, clinking sound, like little bells. It gets louder and less regular. Weird phenomena can materialise as part of healing - voices, vivid images, forgotten memories, sounds, the sense of other folk nearby. But Lowenna steps over to catch a chalky green glass bottle filled with dried rosemary before it falls off the shelf.

"That was…" *odd,* she was going to say, *that was odd*, but before she does, the bottles start rattling again, all of them this time, and she holds out her hands ineffectually to catch them all but there are too many and they fall and smash on the slate tile surrounding the Victorian fireplace. I clamber off the table, quilt still wrapped around me, and grab her hand, pulling her away from the broken glass.

"What was *that*?!" I yell, and then I realise I'm yelling, and I'm yelling for a very good reason. Because now the whole house's shaking. Books, candles and goddess figurines topple from shelves onto the floor. Panicked, I stamp out the lit candle that reels towards the quilt I'm wrapped in. The little occasional table that was next to the bed I was lying on rolls drunkenly on its castors towards the window and the door creaks as the doorframe splinters. Lowenna and I cling onto each other; she smells of freesias. I hold my hands over my head.

"No, no, no, no, no… no… n-" I'm muttering *no* like a spell, but it's powerless.

There's a kind of grinding, tearing noise and I realise white dust's falling on her shoulder. I look up, stupidly, and the ceiling plaster gets into my eyes. As I try to rub the sting away, that familiar heat in my middle spreads up my whole body. It isn't Brighid's steady, incendiary healing fire, but the other type: sick heat, far more familiar. It spreads into my head and behind my eyes and makes my heart race. Total fear overcomes me like a blade of sickness opening me up, stomach to throat, peeling me back, open and unprotected like meat, like a carcass, and suddenly that's all I am, meat and fear, and I want to die.

"No... not... no, no..." But it isn't stopping, the panic or the house shaking, and it's the same lack of control I always had with him, he'd never stop, just hit and smack and scream at us and mum always tried to put herself between him and me, and somehow that was worse. At least when it was me - when he was shouting at me, *useless, ruined girl*, when he was beating me, I could be inside the pain instead of having to watch it be inflicted on the only person in the world I loved.

"The ceiling!" Lowenna cries out, and pulls my head down into her chest, instinctively shielding me with her body. Time slows down. There's a part of me that knows I'm in shock and that's what the brain does in moments of panic, slows your perception of time, and I should just breathe from my belly - but that's almost impossible. I can hardly breathe and I feel like I'm going to black out, crouching there under Lowenna's long cardigan like a tent.

I roll into a ball at her feet; she crouches above me like she's in labour and I'm the bloody, glistening baby bird she's birthed; wet and defenceless and unable to fly. I lie there and shake and want to sick up every part of myself like the diseased horror I am.

It might be an hour or a minute later when it stops. Lowenna stands and looks up cautiously. Everything's still, broken, completely quiet, as if the house has raged all it needs to.

"Sadie. Sadie. Get up. It's okay," she says, but I don't want to get up; I want to stay here in the ball, my arms over my head; I need so desperately to feel safe, but I feel as though there's a pit I'm falling into, teetering on the edge and it's all I can do to stay on the ground. And then when this happens, when it takes over like this, the darkness and the hot sickness, it wipes me out, leaves me as ruined as this room, broken glass and upturned furniture.

"Sadie! Lowenna kneels down next to me and the

next thing I know she has her hands on my shoulders and I can feel the warm rays of healing break over the dark horizon, and I start to cry. "Sadie. It's all right. We're safe. It's stopped," she says, her voice like a boat in a black sea and a black sky that I can hold onto, a life raft. "Sadie. It's all right. I'm here. Just breathe. Just breathe," she says, and I lie there and breathe, and every breath's an achievement and a rung on a ladder I pull myself up on, out of the blackness, heavy with the saltwater in my clothes, wanting to pull me back in to drown.

"What was that?" I manage to croak out as I lie there, the tears running down my cheeks and onto the floor dusted with crumbled white masonry from the ceiling.

"I think it was an earthquake," Lowenna says, her hands remaining where they are, on my shoulders.

"But we don't have earthquakes here," I mumble, trying to breathe.

"We do now," she says grimly.

CHAPTER THREE

Badb and Macha, greatness of wealth, Morrigu--
springs of craftiness,
sources of bitter fighting
were the three daughters of Ernmas.

From: Lebor Gabála Érenn, or Book of Invasions

"What a bloody mess," Demi stops sweeping and holds onto her broom, pulling her long straight black hair into a high ponytail and tying it with a strip of green cotton. She leans out of the front door and smiles at two gardener boys as they walk past the end of Merryn's garden with a wheelbarrow piled high with rubble from the house next door. She's unstoppable. Whenever there's boys, there she is, smiling her false megawatt smile and standing in that weird side-on posture, all hips and tits.

"Bloody Redworld. They've done this. We didn't frack. It's unfair that we have to pay for their mistakes," Rain complains, crouched over on in the hallway, picking up books and broken ornaments from the carpet.

"Pretty shitty," I agree, and place a box of broken glass on the bottom stair.

After we were sure the earthquake was over, and

that was indeed what it was and not some otherworldly event, Lowenna and I ventured out of the house and onto the street. Fences broken, trees down; some had fallen into windows, onto roofs. Folk disoriented, upset, crying. Later in the day we found out that one of the elders had tripped over a stone flag that got pushed up from the kitchen floor, hit his head and died. A wardrobe fell on two kids playing in their bedroom and broke one of their arms. "Lowenna says with the amount of fracking they've done over the past ten years, it's amazing this hasn't happened before now," I add.

"I don't want another one. D'you think there'll be another one?" Rain looks scared.

"Probably," I say, deliberately not looking up because I want to seem cool and unbothered and casual but actually it's taking massive amount of willpower to be here, wiping surfaces clear of tiny specks of broken glass and pottery and not making a run for it. My heart's beating so hard it's making me want to pant. It's hard to talk normally.

I didn't want to come back here. It was like all my fear made real; in a panic attack, you feel like the world's ending. Like you're dying. So when the world actually does fall apart, it's not exactly helpful. But Lowenna sent me on purpose. *You can't avoid it,* she said. *When you go in you'll see it for what it is. A house that needs repairs. That's all. No hidden monsters.* And she'd given me that High Priestessy stare like *Sadie, I hope you're smart enough to understand this very basic metaphor about broken houses and broken selves needing repair otherwise I might have to seriously rethink your training.*

So I came, I tried not to tremble, I mostly succeeded. *Veni vidi vici.* Only that's more about conquering and winning (and - ugh - the patriarchal Latin). No-one won. There was an EARTHQUAKE. The Greenworld is not home to earthquakes, as a rule.

"You know when Melz was in the Redworld? When the tower on Glastonbury Tor collapsed?" Rain pushes her long blonde fringe out of her eyes - the rest of it shaved short - as she re-shelves some well-thumbed paperback books. We've got the tall rattan bookshelf back up against the wall with some effort, mostly because it's been repaired so many times it isn't so much a bookshelf as a vague association of sticks and string; the bastard thing keeps falling apart and losing the general will to be a bookshelf at all.

"Yeah?"

"Was that an earthquake too, then?"

"I don't think so. I mean, no-one said it was," I go back into the kitchen for another wooden box we've borrowed from the gardeners; a not wholly unpleasant smell of apple and damp wood fills the kitchen as I walk in. I take a few deep breaths, taking advantage of being alone for a few seconds. I don't want the other girls to know being here's making me feel so wobbly.

"It might have been, though? She just didn't realise it at the time? I mean, there was a landslide. That whole fracking site got buried, she said," I hear Rain say to Demi.

"It didn't really happen like that," I can hear the sneer in Demi's voice and frown at her as I come back out. "I was there, remember?"

"You weren't there right as it happened. You were just in the general area," I counter. "Melz told me. It was the portal reopening that did it,"

"Well, she would say that," Demi sneers. No love lost between her and Melz. Something from when Melz was in the Redworld. "She's just trying to make herself sound powerful,"

"She is powerful. If Melz said it was the portal,

then it was the portal," I argue, though it's hard to look authoritative holding a large fruit box awkwardly in front of you.

"Have a day off, Sadie. You don't have to defend her every time," Demi pushes past me into the kitchen.

"What? I'm just saying, she doesn't lie," I call after her.

"Nor does your face," she says, returning from the kitchen, eating an apple.

I blush.

"Dunno what you're on about," I mutter.

"Nah. Course you don't," she rolls her eyes and picks up her cardigan from the hook by the door, grimacing at the homely handknitted green wool with shell buttons. Not what she was used to in the Redworld, I guess. "I'm off. Catch you losers later," and she sashays out of the front door to where one of the boys is waiting for her, presumably having picked up her scent of constant availability in his nostrils and appearing wordlessly like a man possessed.

"You're supposed to help us until we've finished!"

I call after her, but she holds up her middle finger, the rest curled down, without looking back.

"Bitch," I mutter, ignoring Perfect Pixie Rain's shocked expression. Witches don't call each other bitches.

I can make an exception for Demi.

Untitled poem, excerpt from Sadie Morgan's notebook

Somewhere, when I sleep, there is an upside-down castle
and a bread maze guarded by sugar-and-salt lions.
I my dreams I am the Red Queen; you are the Black Queen
And we sit at opposing ends of a crystal table,
Staring into each others' eyes, making a new world.

All day I take your gaze and you absorb mine;
Salt water erodes rock, and fire and earth shake and reform
as another world builds and falls: mountains, ice floes, villages, cities.

In that world, we search for each other across the moor.
And every day we push the pieces of our small selves
just a little bit further together or apart,
Depending on how cruel or kind we feel.
We experience much hardship: frostbite, dogs,

loneliness.

    And when the sun has set over the upside-down castle
    We close our eyes, and the world crumbles into black
sand on the table.

    As Black Queen and Red Queen, we walk
    in the moonlit bread maze. All night we walk,
    talking of everything, holding hands, eyes closed,
always closed,
    navigating the maze by the smell of smoke.

    When we reach the fire, we strip off
    our armour and robes and cast them in,
    where they burn runes into the coals
    under the moon. And we tell the fire
    our doubts and fears and many-edged truths,
    Paper scrolling out of our mouths,
    Taking our words to be burnt.
    And when midnight has passed, we walk
    back out of the maze, eating it as we go.
    By morning we have returned, naked, to the crystal
table
    and retake our thrones.
    You open your eyes. And my story begins again.

CHAPTER FOUR

Ornamental clouds
compose an evening love song;
a road leaves evasively.
The new moon begins

a new chapter of our nights,
of those frail nights
we stretch out and which mingle
with these black horizontals.

Evening Love Song, R M Rilke

"Concentrate, Sadie!" Melz's low, rounded Cornish burr snaps my meandering attention. She's circling the five of us like a mother duck. No, a black swan. Black hair in a long plait; triskele painted in blue woad on her forehead. A black dress, as ever, and a brown woollen cloak to keep out the cold. Black cowboy boots, worn at the toes.

"Sorry," I mumble, but she catches my eye and smiles, and my legs go weak. Just as well I'm sitting down. Melz doesn't smile much, but when she does, the sky opens right back to the stars, and I feel as though I could lose my footing on the earth altogether. (Ick romance novel territory but still: true). There were romance novels at home. *Wuthering Heights*, that was a favourite of mine: *"He's more myself than I am. Whatever our souls are made of, his and mine are the same."* I read them all. Straight man-woman romances: happy endings. Doomed (pre-Greenworld) woman-woman romances: sad endings. And the Greenworld-approved feminist romances: happy endings where victorious lesbians kiss against the backdrop of a dismantled patriarchal discourse.

All new witches, all in training. Six months, so far, and still so much to learn. Me, Demi, Catie, Rain, Macha. Catie and Demi came from the Redworld, part of the stream of refugees that have been arriving here for months, desperate, starving and looking for a better way of life for themselves and their families. Though I have to say that Demi in particular never looked like she was starving, even when she arrived. Rain and Macha came from other Greenworld villages to be trained. Local girls with promise. And me, the branded daughter of two murderers.

Everyone has their eyes focused on the middle of this windy, grassy rock we're standing on: Tintagel Head, an island only connected to the mainland by a tiny strip, a series of treacherous steps. *Disrespect the way to the sacred space at your peril*, Melz said before she led us up them, our leather boots slipping on the sea-splashed wood, the stone underneath. *Approach the portal with respect or go home.* I hear my stomach grumble, and a stifled giggle from someone in the group. We get another sharp glare for that.

We're standing on Tintagel Head at the end of February, in the brave new year 2048, and I've just turned eighteen. The salty air's moistening our cheeks. I hate the winters. I hate the cold, the washing in icy water, hardly being warm under five blankets, and waking to frost inside the windowpanes. It'd be warmer with someone sharing my bed, but no-one does. I dart a furtive glance at Melz at the thought, and feel myself blush. I'm in her sister Saba's old room, since she left to stay with her auntie at Boscastle, not far away ("left" doesn't really convey the drama - *flounced out and abandoned the covenstead* might be more accurate) - but I think of Melz every night when my hand traces the curve of my own breast, imagining it to be hers; when I imagine kissing her, touching her, imagining long afternoons where we have nothing but privacy and a rumpled bed, our bare skin warmed by the sun slanting through the windowpanes.

When the Goddess Brighid appeared to me at my self-initiation, back at Scorhill stone circle last year, she told me my life would change. She told me I should be ready for upheaval, for change, for doing things I'd never have thought possible. She told me that only my true self, my deepest self, would be allowed to progress as a witch. That being the most authentic me would be my key to... something. Something great and wonderful and *ye epic winds of change*, but I don't know what, yet. I wish the great and wonderful thing was me and Melz ruling the world as two impassively beautiful queens, making love every night on a bed of furs in some kind of inexplicable return to medieval times, but that MAY possibly be not really what the Goddess was on about. Sadly.

Still, this is pretty epic. We're here to experience the energy portal for the first time. We're deemed ready, but it niggles at me slightly that even if we weren't ready we'd probably still be here, because the Greenworld needs more witches. Things aren't going well. Gidleigh village on Dartmoor is rebelling against witch rule. Danny Prentice, its rightful witch (a branded witch, too - him, me and Melz) and therefore ruler of his village, is in prison. Danny Prentice, my friend, once.

"Open your eyes," Melz's sharp voice cuts through my thoughts and I try to look as though as I've been meditating, tuning in with the Brighid energy up here, instead of thinking about her. We have these invisible ties between us, somehow. Lines of shadow braiding the ether, pulling at the elements between us: a little earth here, a little fire there, giving life to strange undercurrents; crooked lines of destiny. Ah, well, maybe that's the poetic crush talking - but, what I'm trying to say is, there's definitely something there.

My eyes sting as I focus back on the circle; the wind blows smoke from the censer into them. Frankincense, dried rosepetals, pine resin, the sharpness of orange peel and the underlying smokiness of the black charcoal. These days my clothes always smell of smoke. I try not to think about the earthquake, but I can't help it. I'm expecting one all the time, now. I visualise my mental wall keeping the anxiety away and feel slightly better.

Melz looks around the circle at our apprehensive faces.

"Right. Now I'm going to show you how this works," she speaks clearly and loudly into the wind, her voice competing with the deep green waves crashing on the black cliffs below us. I wish she was mine. I'd wear her on my sleeve, I'd climb inside her, nestle in the recess of her lungs, be her breath, and I'd listen to her at night and in the morning, rolling in her soft rounded vowels. I'd read to her every night so that she fell asleep in my arms listening to love poems. We'd write love poems to each other, in fact. Every week. And when we died, there'd be a lifetime of them for folk to find and marvel at our love.

I'll admit this crush is kind of intense. *Focus, Sadie.*

"It's a series of symbols that you trace into the dormant portal here. The symbols will open the portal. Then we'll work on entering and exiting it. But you're not going to need to do that very often. The symbols to open and close are the most important, so that you learn to check in with the energy; make sure it's running smoothly if Lowenna asks you to. Any questions?" eyebrow raised, she looks around the circle: we all avoid her gaze like it would cut us to ask anything. No-one wants to be a novice. "Good. All right. Watch closely,"

Melz's long fingered white hands cup and circle the air as if it were clay; I watch as the energy flowing from her hands leaves an impression on the sky, like reversed-out colour; I watch the magic bounce between her fingers. I follow the shapes, my hands tracing them along with her. The meditation was meant to focus us on bringing the energy through, and I feel it buzzing in my hands.

Melz pushes one last symbol into the air and a large dark orange-red flower of light bulges into being, engulfing us all. I gape up at it like an idiot, then catch my expression mirrored in the other girls' faces, and snap my mouth shut. The light swirls in a gentle spiral, like water in a plughole, but expanding upwards and outwards, then dissolving into air again at the edges. All in all it's probably twelve feet high and about the same wide. I start to feel out of breath, and take in a few long breaths to compensate.

"The open portal will make you feel dizzy and breathless. Try and centre yourselves and breathe slowly," Melz shouts. Rain squats down on her haunches instinctively and lowers her head onto her knees. Melz touches her short blonde cropped hair gently and I feel a flare of jealousy. *Nonononono, get your pretty head out from under her hand, bitch.*

"Try and stay focused on the portal," she calls out to all of us, her hand on Rain's shoulder. "It will help," she kneels down to be able to make eye contact. "All right?" she says, and I see that same caring in her eyes as when she first brought me to the village. "Yeah," Rain's voice wavers, but she stands up again. Melz holds her arm, and I wish I'd faltered. I wish she was supporting me, touching me. *I'm weak too! I'm the ruined girl. Didn't you know?*

Melz looks across the circle at me.

"Sadie. You seem to be adjusting well. You can be first to enter the portal. Just keep breathing, but focus on becoming less solid. Your body. Imagine it losing definition. You're entering an energy source and a between-place. You can't just walk into it in your solid body. You have to defocus,"

"Like astral travel?" I'm getting better at it, but it takes years to really master unless you're one of those rare folk that can naturally slip out of their body on a whim. Lowenna says that Danny can do that. It would be hard to imagine Danny Prentice doing anything magical, if I forgot the last time I saw him. The last time, he was a very different Danny from the one I knew, growing up in Gidleigh where we used to muck about in the woods. The last time I saw him, he tried to kill me.

"Kind of. Not as far as that. Just try and merge with the portal energy. Go in slowly. You'll find yourself in a corridor. Just observe how it looks and feels. You'll feel the pull from the other end. Don't go too far into it. And don't try to go through any of the doors, if you see them. Just look and come back, okay?" she looks at me with those piercingly beautiful black-lined eyes, and I nod.

"Of course," if she's asked me then of course I'll do it, I'll do anything she asks and I'll do it better than these novices.

"All right, then. Watch, everyone," she says, and I walk in slowly.

It works the first time. I'm inside a strange tunnel where my feet aren't quite touching the ground and my body isn't quite a body anymore: it's something less and more at the same time. I'm a presence, but not completely whole.

The end of the tunnel telescopes away from me – it's long, and I can't see the end, but I can feel it immediately. That pull from the end, the call of death and disintegration. I want to go that way, but at the same time, I'm feeling faint and woozy. Colours start to flash in front of my eyes, and now it isn't just the lights of the tunnel. I feel myself sway, and then it's like the floor shifts, and I'm falling.

Falling a long way, feeling my stomach clutch desperately for grip on the world, and then nothing.

CHAPTER FIVE

Knowledge comes from the earth more than any book. Listen to the songs of the trees, the beat of the soil, the caress of the wind on wheat if you would be wise.

From: Tenets and Sayings of the Greenworld

I open my eyes and feel the familiar wind on my face; slowly my body regains its solidity, and I feel the pull of death from inside the portal lessening. It feels horrible being inside the portal. I don't want to do that again in a hurry: I don't like that feeling of being out of control. Dissolving on purpose isn't good for someone as generally broken as me.

I gaze out to what should be the Cornish sea, seeking Melz's eyes again. Only, she isn't there.

Shit. *None* of them are there.

Instead of windy Tintagel Head, I'm on top of a snow covered mountain.

My breath's tight and the air's thin up here; my lungs pull deeper, stronger, to get what they need, but I have that same feeling as being inside the portal; a little dizzy, a little fuzzy. Lightheaded. Only, it should have worn off by now.

The sun's shining and the glare off the hard-packed snow's so bright I shield my eyes. Snow? *Where in the holy goddess' realm of all existence am I?*

"Ayukii, traveller. Welcome,"

Behind me there's a girl sitting cross-legged on a small woven mat, warming her hands on a crackling campfire. She smiles up at me and points to the ground, where there's another empty mat waiting.

"I've been waiting for you," she says, and smiles, presumably at my expression because I can feel my mouth form an O of idiocy. "You are confused. It is natural when you have travelled through the portal. And the sun is bright but the cold is strong,"

I reach out my hands carefully towards the fire, looking at her. She's dressed in leather and furs: a deep hood lined with grey fur, long soft brown leather boots that strap her legs and tie at the side. Her hair's long and black, in two glossy plaits, and her skin's deep brown. She has some kind of symbol that I don't recognise tattooed in the middle of her forehead. She touches it and bows her head to me.

"Welcome," she repeats, smiling.

"Err... alright?" The hard snow crunches under my feet. "Where am I? I mean, sorry if that's rude, but I...I was just in Tintagel, I went into the portal for the first time and I came out here. That's not supposed to happen. Where is this?" I feel sick. I take in some deep breaths and try and ignore the impulse to retch into the snow.

"*Wyeka*. In English, Shasta Mountain. A sacred place,"

"What language's *Wyeka*? Where am I?" the cold air helps the nausea a bit; I take some more deep breaths. In through the nose, out through the nose. I try and alternate nostrils like Merryn teaches us in yoga but I can't do it unless I close one side with my finger and then swap, but I don't want to do that in front of this girl because I'll look strange but more to the point *what the hell's happening? Oh my goddess oh my goddess oh my goddess.* I can feel the familiar rise of the yellow sickness starting to bloom in my solar plexus and I try to focus and not let it take over. I swallow back the salt water taste.

"*Wyeka* is a Shasta word. English is the invader's language. Shasta is the language of my ancestors. We resist the capitalists, the corrupt, the godless, by speaking our traditional language to each other here. But everyone speaks English too," she shrugs and makes a face. "I try not to unless I have to,"

"Where's *here?*" I peer around me at the mountains. I could be anywhere.

"America. Wyeka is in California. On the west side,"

"America?! But that's..." unimaginable. So far away it would take months on a boat that we don't have. "That's impossible!"

"Possible for you," the girl warms her hands on the fire. "This is a magic place. A sacred place. Odd things can happen,"

I hold out my hands to the flames, and their warmth combined with the cold mountain air helps. I feel calmer and more centred. I sit down cautiously.

"Sacred like there's a portal here, sacred?" I ask, looking around.

"Yes. My family are its guardians. We've looked after it for centuries," she offers me a drink of something hot in a clay cup. I take it and sip gratefully - in for a penny, in for a pound, that's what Mum used to say - apparently pennies and pounds were units of money before the Greenworld did away with it altogether.

"So I must have…" I frown, and punch myself in the arm. "Sorry. But, you know. This is weird. I'm checking I'm awake,"

She smiles over at me.

"And are you?"

I rub my arm which feels about as sore as it should after a thump.

"I seem to be. So I came through the portal? From Tintagel to here?"

"Seems like it. The elders have been expecting you," she rubs her gloved hands on her arms.

"Goddess be praised," I say half ironically and half with a certain kind of reverence. "So you live here?"

"No. Below the tree line," She points away down the mountain – below the drifting cloud I see a thick evergreen forest, with tall pines packed together. "The mountain's too magical,"

"Oh," I think of the portals I've heard about from Melz in the Redworld and how Glastonbury Tor was blocked for ages until she renewed it. I've learnt about the Book of Portals and how there's a global network of these natural energy sources, magical places that're the gateways between life and death. Modulating the natural energy of the world.

"But you were waiting for me? You knew I'd come?" I wrap my arms around myself against the fresh cold that blows across the mountain. I remember the vision I had when I was healing the rabbit. A network of communities, lighting beacons across the earth.

"As surely as the wolf hunts," she smiles.

"How?"

"I told you. The elders have seen it. We know of you, of your…" she clicks her tongue in frustration. "What, now. The stewardship, you do, of your holy place by the sea? The rock?"

"Tintagel,"

"Yes. They have seen that. Felt the energy of that centre along with ours, here. Shasta is a Master Centre. There are seven, and then many lesser centres. Yours is a lesser one, but very powerful,"

"A Master Centre?"

"The seven big energy vortices of the world. Here is the Base of the World, pure life energy." She counts them off on her fingers. "Lake Titicaca, Peru, the second, the Life of the World. Uluru, in Australia, the Stories of the World, the third. Glastonbury, in your country, the Heart of the World, fourth. Fifth, in the Eqyptian desert, the pyramids house the Voice of the World. The seventh is another mountain. Kailas, in the Himalayas. The Roof of the World. It channels our spiritual destiny,"

"You missed one. The sixth?"

She nods.

"One is damaged. The war has taken it almost beyond repair,"

"In Russia? That war?"

"Yes. The sixth vortice, the sixth Master Centre – a portal, you call it. It sits in the middle of the fighting. And next to last natural gas field left in the world. Mount Elbrus. The Fire of the World. The connection to the new Aeon,"

"What does that mean?"

"The start of something new. Heavenly fire; creation of new possibilities," she looks at me shrewdly. "You have hair like fire. Are you a fire mistress?"

"Ummm. A Priestess of Brighid, so kind of, I guess," I say, and touch my hair, only grown midway to my shoulders. It used to be long, but I hacked it off. In the time I try not to think about.

"Brighid is a spirit of fire?" she says, and takes my hand.

"Kind of. A goddess,"

"Ah, even better. So this makes sense. The one that gets sent to us to heal the Fire of the World is a Priestess of a Fiery Power. The elders will like that,"

"But I didn't… I didn't do this on purpose. It just happened,"

"Nothing just happens, Priestess. This is one of your powers, then. To travel between holy places. This is your Goddess showing you, just like our spirits showed our elders you'd come,"

"I s'pose, I… I didn't know,"

"You do now," She looks piercingly at me and I start to feel really wavery and odd. "But your place is pulling you back. You aren't meant to stay long."

I can feel the pull from the portal on me, even though I'm not inside it. It's a different feeling – not the inexorable pull of death, but something else. I'm on the wrong side of it, where I shouldn't be. The polarity's wrong, or something. The girl stands up.

"I'll tell my people about your visit; from my people, this is a gift. And a tool, perhaps," I take what she hands me; a rolled parchment, tied with a leather strip, "It is time for you to go," the girl holds out her soft leather-mittened hand to me. I take it to steady myself; her grip's strong and the suede of her glove's padded and worn. The portal yawns behind her, fully open again; she's silhouetted against it, already becoming a memory.

"What's your name?" She takes my other hand in hers.

"Ki'putska. In English it means Fox,"

"Sadie Morgan." I rack my brains. "Sadie means Princess, I think. Morgan in our land was Queen of the Faeries," Morgan's mum's name. She refused to let me take dad's.

"Faeries?" she looks blank.

"Oh. You know, like… like nature spirits. The spirits of the trees, the plants, the rocks," I explain, and her face lights up.

"Ah! Yes. I understand. So you're a shaman too. The Princess of Spirits,"

The odd feeling of being on the wrong side of the portal intensifies, pulling at my stomach.

"I guess so. I have to go," I start to feel faint: the tips of my fingertips go white.

"Go back to your people with our blessing," she says, and kisses my cheek.

"Blessed Be," I sway on my feet; I feel like I've drunk a whole bottle of ritual wine.

She guides me into the swirling red light again, and I black out.

CHAPTER SIX

Nach doiligh domhsa mo chailín a mholadh,
Ní hé amháin mar bhí sí rua,
Bhí sí mar gha gréine ag dul in éadan na ngloiní,
Is bhí scéimh mhná na Finne le mo chailín rua.

Isn't it hard for me to praise my red-haired girl,
Not only because of her red hair,
She was like a ray of sun reflected through glass,
And she had the beauty of the Finne women.

From: Na Cailin Rua (The Red Haired Girl), a traditional Irish song, in Greenworld Prayers and Songs

"But, mum! This has to be important!"

Shakily, I walk into the kitchen and find Melz, Demi, Merryn and Lowenna sitting at the table, looking at the yellowed parchment I recognise from Mount Shasta. Melz looks up at me and beckons me over.

"Sadie. You okay? You shouldn't be up,"

"I'm all right." All I remember is feeling really faint, going back into the portal on top of the mountain and falling out of it onto Tintagel Head, whereby I collapsed and blacked out and woke up just now in bed in my underwear, thinking basically *oh crap what happened,* though at least here I can't be much chagrined by being seen by someone in these faded and stained cotton knickers. In the House of the Witches at Tintagel, no underwear's yours, it just all goes into the same wash every week and there's definitely a few pairs no-one wants to get because they've been the unlucky bystanders in some particularly heavy menstrual flows.

Blood's sacred, I mean, of course it is. But forgive me if I'm not overjoyed at looking at the ghosts of other flows when I get dressed in the morning. (Mum told me about all the phrases there had been, in the Redworld, where women were shamed about their menstrual cycle. All the slang. *Having the painters and decorators in. Aunt Flo's come for a visit. On the rag. Carrie at the Prom* - mum had to explain that one; *On the blob, the Crimson Wave, Leak Week*). All of it a signal of the social awkwardness the patriarchy made women feel about the natural functions - the sacredness, in fact, of their bodies. Thank Goddess we don't have that problem. We all menstruate at the dark moon, because we're witches and we're girls and we all live together, so we're all powerful sexy bitches and blanket-hugging fragile flowers on the same days, near enough.

Still, I don't love the fact that we don't seem to have anything strong enough to get bloodstains out of underwear. I mean, we use washable cotton pads too, but at least those are vegetable-dyed brown to start with.

I sit down gingerly and drink some tea and eat some buttered bread, and tell them what happened. About the girl, Ki'putska, the Fox. How she was waiting for me, how her folk knew I was coming. That the parchment's a message.

"What message?" Merryn traces her finger over the symbols. "I've never seen anything like this before," she looks up at Lowenna and Melz.

"It's some kind of way to connect, I think," I saw, tiredly, remembering my dream of the lit beacons again, feeling that it needs to be said. "There're other portals. We always knew that. Dunno if we knew about these other Master Centres, though. Did we? And that there are so many resistant communities, around the world? Like us?"

Lowenna's expression is guarded.

"My sister Tressa's the expert on that. I know there are other places, yes. And the Master Centres, I'm aware of them. But not the communities so much, I mean, who and what they are. The longer we're separated, the harder it is to know. Even with Omar's information; every now and then he hears of somewhere else, in another country; other folk that are holding out against the Redworld. But you never know how much of it is rumour," she brings the parchment up to her face again. "But all these symbols. I don't know what they are," she looks at me sceptically. "And this girl, the Fox - she didn't tell you?"

Omar's an ex-gang member that visits sometimes. He was Zia's lover; I remember him being around when me and Danny were kids back in Gidleigh. A huge, hulking black man with blacker tattoos all over him. People didn't like him much - basically because he was ex-gang and he was black, and they were racist - but Danny said he was cool. And he's helped the Greenworld out of more than one tight catastrophe, including bringing Danny and Melz back from the Redworld.

"No, there wasn't time. I was fading, I felt really weird, suddenly... like, I was in the wrong place,"

"You were," Melz says, pushing the cup towards me, smiling. "Drink your tea,"

"Come on. We don't know that she didn't make this herself. Trying to impress you," Demi interjects, turning the parchment over dismissively in her hands.

"You two are way too close. You're supposed to be training her. Training her in what, I'd like to know. Meaningful looks? Holding hands?"

Shamelessly, I search for a clue in Melz's eyes. But her expression's a mask.

"There's nothing between us," Melz snaps dismissively at Demi. "I'm training Sadie just like I'm training the rest of you. Which you'd know if you ever showed up at circle. You're supposed to be on herbalism as well as psychic protection and we've had to cover for you twice. I know you've been off shagging the gardeners' apprentices,"

Demi glares at Melz.

"I've got a right to my opinion," she says, huffily; I think we all notice that she doesn't comment on the gardeners.

"You've got a right to shut up and stay out of what doesn't concern you," Melz flares back.

"Girls! It's not the time for your squabbles," Lowenna glares at them both. "And, since Demi's brought it up, I'd like to think that Demelza and Sadie understand that, if at all possible, the witches in the covenstead do not form romantic relationships with each other, especially when one is mentoring the other. I turned a blind eye to it before with Danny and Bersaba, and look where that got me. Chaos. D'you hear me?" she stares around at us: Merryn, sweet, caring and looking uncomfortable; Demi, fuming, Melz, expressionless, and me, blushing furiously. I couldn't look guiltier if I tried. Mum always said I couldn't hide what I was feeling.

"Right, then. Can we focus, please? Now. I'm going to call a meeting of the covensteads to see if anyone recognises anything here," Lowenna taps the parchment with a yellowed fingertip: she smokes a pipe in the evenings.

"You don't need to do that," Melz says. "I've seen them before. The symbols," she reaches for her bag, a green and cream woven one slung carelessly under the table, and pulls out her Greenworld Journal. She opens it to a page in the middle, dated months ago, and places it next to the parchment on the table. "I don't know what it means, either. But when I was at Gidleigh, after Zia died, I woke up and I'd drawn these out in my sleep. It happened a few times, the same every time."

Merryn peers down at Melz's scribbles.

"Why didn't you say anything, sweetheart?" her rounded Cornish vowels caress Melz's tense shoulders and I see them relax a tiny bit. Merryn's a healer, and her whole being - her voice, her presence, her body, is soothing.

"I don't know. I didn't know what it meant. I thought it was a Morrigan thing, like, something just for me. But if this girl gave Sadie the same message, then it isn't,"

"What did you dream before they appeared?" Lowenna asks, taking Melz's book and peering at it.

"Nothing. It was a blank dream. But then, one time, this came too," Melz flips over the page. Scrawled in the same charcoal is a series of lines of words. "It's a poem of sorts. A chant, maybe. But the funny thing is that part of it is the words in Danny's witch brand. And Roach's," she says, looking at me.

I start to get a really weird feeling, like déjà vu. I pick up the book and read aloud.

"I am the spear, the slingshot, the smith,

The poet, the warrior, the magician, the gift;

The trunk of the tree, the arrow of war,

WILD FIRE

The movement of time, the lover at dawn.

I am the sun, the heat of the day;

The might of the land; the great bird of prey.

"I am the Lady, the joy of the Land,

The green in the meadow , the gardener's hand,

The moon in the trees and the tide on the shore;

The light and the darkness, the balance restored.

I am the plant, the harvest, the corn

I am the future waiting to be born.

"I am the crow, the raven, the battle,

The sacrificed hero's final death-rattle,

The blood that is split on the ground to make life,

The end of the suffering, the glint of the knife.

I am the Power, the Channel, the Dream,

The seer, Prophetess, the magnetic stream.

"Three to bind, to open, to see,

The power in one as within three,

From life to death and death to life,

One brings the moon, and one, the knife,

One brings the sun and the song, the key –

The power in one as within three."

"That last part. When I got my witch-brand, She sang that to me. Brighid. She said *The power in them as in thee*, or something," I say, feeling weird. I'm still new to being a witch and this kind of dream-connection freaks me out, even though I'm frankly *vag-a-hoop* (to reclaim a more feminist *cock-a-hoop*) to have any connection with Melz, dream or otherwise.

"Yes. You told us when you got here. I remember," Lowenna takes the book from me. "Demelza. Is there any way you might have just made this up yourself? You've already heard the first and the last sections. Perhaps you just filled in the rest,"

"I'm no poet," Melz frowns. *Hm. That's our lifetime love poem exchange down the pan.*

"Well, the subconscious is a powerful thing. We all know that," Lowenna muses. "You have a strong ability to channel, like me, and the Morrigan develops psychic abilities in Her priestesses,"

"What about the other symbols? The stuff we don't understand? What about Danny, too?" Melz looks calculatingly at her mum – it's a sore subject. Since Danny got imprisoned by the villagers, after freaking out and trying to kill my mum last year, there have been shockwaves running through the Greenworld.

Lowenna's refused to make a decision about what to do - about either Danny or the village. Go to Gidleigh and take over – reassert the divine right of the witch to rule the covenstead, or let them have their little victory and hope it stays contained in Dartmoor. We also have the problem of the Redworld refugees to deal with. Maybe Lowenna's still in shock that her best friend, the other Greenworld visionary, Zia Prentice, died.

"But he's not here. And he won't be until we figure out whether go and get him, or let them keep him in prison. Just to keep the peace," Melz's voice is dry with sarcasm. Lowenna raises an eyebrow.

"Don't think you can lecture me on leadership, Demelza. Don't let your feelings for the boy cloud your judgement," she hisses at her daughter, and her eyes flick back to me. "You can't have them both, you know. Pick a side,"

Ouch. I'm learning that the easiest way to get slapped down in the coven is question Lowenna's judgement. Maybe it's an effect of channelling the Goddess so much. Maybe some of Her lingers, and makes you act like an unreasonable, all-powerful, heavenly sword-wielding Bringer of Fate from time to time. I better watch that, since Brighid seems to prefer me now.

Melz looks furious, and balls her fists up, hidden in her skirt, then releases them slowly.

"I don't have feelings for Danny apart from friendship. However, I get the *feeling* that we should be looking after a branded witch, not leaving him to rot in a cell whilst the good folk of Gidleigh try and forget witches ever existed. Worse, while they let the gangs take Scorhill circle in return for a quiet life. We need to get in there and take control, mum. Fast,"

"It's not that simple, Demelza," Lowenna snaps, but there are clouds in her eyes. Fear. She's afraid to look at the dissent square in the face. To look at the faces of the Greenworlders that feel she has failed them. And maybe she has. Maybe we all have. "I want to wait until the girls are trained. Then we can take Gidleigh back. With more power, more magic, we'll be in a stronger position,"

"We can't wait that long, mum. And I don't think forcing witch rule on Gidleigh's really feasible at this stage, is it?" Melz fires back. "What are we going to do? Spend all day every day psychically restraining the whole village? We can't do that. You know we can't; everything you've ever taught us was about understanding the flow of energy and working with that. Run with the tide, not against it, that's what you said. And the tide in Gidleigh turned a long time ago,"

Lowenna shrugs.

"We can take it back. We're witches; witches turn tides if they need to,"

"But we don't need to, mum. Let's just go and get Danny and let Gidleigh get on with whatever it wants to do!" Melz is trying to keep her temper under control, I can tell - but it's hard.

"No!" Lowenna gets up and starts banging the books on a wicker bookcase back into the shelf with the side of her hand, hard. "I have the power in the Greenworld. In *all* of it!" she yells.

"I saw what happens with absolute power, in the Redworld. The refugees are here because absolute power didn't work. People defect, they leave, they suffer. You'd win more hearts by admitting you were wrong," Melz argues back.

"Admitting we were wrong? About what?" Demi scoffs. "Honestly, Melz. Bran Crowley must have shagged all the common sense out of you. Making more witches isn't a bad thing. There are more people in the Greenworld now because of the bloody pr-... refugees. So we need more healers, more psychic protection. More herbal expertise," *Proles*, is what she almost said; the Redworld name for the poor: far more of them than the rich, like Demi was. We don't approve of her past, but Lowenna says now we're witches, the past's gone and shouldn't be talked about. Which suits me fine, frankly.

Melz narrows her eyes at Demi.

"First, *Demeter*," Melz calls Demi her full witch name: Demeter, Greek mother goddess of the harvest.

You couldn't find a less appropriately named witch if you tried. If anything (and I know that Melz doesn't think Demi should be a witch at all; she's yet to show any aptitude for anything, or, in lieu of a natural talent for something, a willingness to put the hours in to learn) Demi should be Inanna or Aphrodite; one of those pouty, selfish sex goddesses. "I think it's a little premature to include yourself in "we". You've only been a witch five minutes so don't think you can lecture me about the balance of power in the Greenworld. Second," she glares at Demi so hard that even she flinches "If you ever say Bran Crowley's name to me again, I'll kill you,"

Bran Crowley. I know he and Melz were lovers when she was in the Redworld. He turned out to be a pretty nasty piece of work in the end, but I think she still has complicated feelings for him. Naturally, I'm glad he's dead.

"Girls! Enough," Lowenna gives the books one final whack and turns back to us at the table. Melz just looks away and I see her balling her fists again. "Danny Prentice is a threat to Sadie. While he blames her for Zia's death I can't have him here, or free anywhere else. He's unpredictable. And you know how powerful he is," Lowenna says, looking at me, and I direct my gaze down at the rough stone slabs of the kitchen floor. He tried to kill my mum, Linda, out in front of everyone, on the village green in Gidleigh. I was looking in his eyes when he called the dark magic down to torture her. There was nothing left of the Danny I used to know, then.

"He was mad with grief," Melz protests. "He didn't know what he was doing. He's one of us. Why don't we go and get him, talk to the villagers at Gidleigh. Make peace. If they want to be autonomous, let them, but they can't have Danny. And instead of training up these new witches to control the villages, let's use them positively." She picks up the parchment, and her book with the scrawled charcoal symbols, the lines of verse. "I don't know what this is, but Danny's a part of it, just like Sadie and me. *Three to bind, to open, to see.* I think it means us three branded ones. Sadie just travelled to another portal in another place. What if we could... I don't know. Travel to more portals, across the world. Learn from other cultures. Bond with them. Fight the Redworld,"

"This conversation is over," Lowenna pushes the chair she's been leaning on firmly under the table, and grabs Melz's face in her wide, hard hand. "We are not on some half-arsed mission to change the Redworld. Hear me, Demelza? The trainees are to be instructed in the traditional methods. We will maintain the Greenworld. The Redworld can fall into the sea for all I care. We do not have the resources to help anyone else. It's us or nothing. Got it?"

Melz pulls away from her mother's grasp.

"No. I don't agree with you," she enunciates, her dark eyes blazing. "We should go back through the portal. Find out more,"

"No. I forbid it. You dn't have to agree. But you'll obey me, Demelza, as your mother and your High Priestess. Your oath as a witch demands it."

Melz regards her mother for a long time.

"I won't break my oath, unlike some," she says, finally, and I know she's thinking of Saba, who, in a fit of fury, destroyed the secret witches' measures on the day I arrived, pulling the symbolic hanks of red wool apart - lengths of wool taken on each witch's initiation, traditionally held by the High Priestess - that knitted the covenstead together. Because when she told Lowenna it was her or me, that she'd leave if I stayed, Lowenna chose me. "I'll always do what is best for the covenstead," Melz's eyes are flat and unreadable.

Saba is with Tressa, Lowenna's sister, at the Archive in Boscastle, just along the jagged coast; Tressa keeps the Archive, all the magical paraphernalia of our past, reaching back across the centuries. From the hundreds of years of witchcraft in the south west of England, before we decided to close off what used to be Devon and Cornwall and make our ecopagan utopia.

The night Saba left, I remember the wool strewn across the floor and Lowenna weeping, slumped on the stained wooden floorboards. She'd looked up at me, eyes full of tears. *I hope you're worth it, Sadie Morgan,* she'd said. *You better be the one.*

Maybe I am the one, whatever that means. I managed to make contact with Ki'putska

I don't want to disappoint her. I want to be trained as a Priestess of Brighid; there's no doubt in my mind about that. But I also doubt Lowenna's judgement, because I know Melz is right. We can't leave Danny locked away somewhere in Gidleigh. He's one of us. We can't sacrifice him on the altar of Lowenna's fear.

CHAPTER SEVEN

War is not for the Greenworld. We leave war to those that have not found peace.

From: Tenets and Sayings of the Greenworld

Dreaming, I watch the envirowarriors form a stumbling line. They're starving and thin and missing limbs, limping, leaning on each other. It's all they can do to put one foot in front of the next. They have been told they can leave. That the war is over.

I'm standing behind them. I'm breathing in their exhaustion and dying a little more with every breath, feeling their hopelessness, hearing their wandering thoughts. *Will I ever see home again, will I die here on the return journey? How will my feet, my hips and legs, my shattered back, make it all the way home? And what will be waiting for me when I get there?*

The rain soaks me as I shamble along with them. A long stream of bodies ahead of me, an incongruent snake of men and women, following each other's shadows, bent coathangers for limbs, ripped brown and grey-black uniforms against the mud and the sludgy snow. We're walking past a vast mountain; in the dream, I know it's

Elbrus, the damaged sixth Master Centre. One of the enviros walking near me says something about it, but I don't catch it; I know his words are dream-words, linguistic nonsense, but I know whatever he says means *that is a place of power.*

I feel a hand in mine and look around, surprised; Melz stands next to me, dressed as if she was playing the Morrigan in a ritual; black leather armour embossed with crows; long leather boots, her hair plaited against her head with black feathers tucked into them. A long silver sword hangs at her belt. Basically: looking awesome.

"So this is where they've been," she says. I nod, looking back at the mountain.

"They're all so exhausted. Injured, ruined. And for what?" I watch the heavy tread of the enviros ahead of us.

"Nothing worth having," she says.

A soldier in front of us turns around. He's gaunt and tired and dressed in the same tattered envirowarrior uniform as the rest.

But he isn't a soldier. It's Danny Prentice. He stares at us.

"Great," he says flatly, to himself.

"What are you doing here?" I ask, and note how I actually hear my own voice as it really is, which isn't a very dreamlike experience. "In my dream. This is…" I know I'm dreaming, and to test myself, I imagine Danny turning into his dog, Gowdie, but nothing happens. And he's far too realistic-looking. I reach out and prod him on the chest. There's a definite resistance.

"Stop it. I'm not in your dream. You're in mine," he says, pushing my finger away.

"No. You're both in mine," Melz says, looking around her. "This is weird,"

"No! This is my dream. Isn't it?" I stop and hold up our linked hands. "See? I'm moving our hands. I'm deciding what to say next. I'm going to make you breathe fire now." I visualise it, but Melz looks at me with her not-impressed expression and very definitely does not breathe fire.

"What am I, a dragon?" she opens her mouth and points in with one very realistic dirty-fingernailed Melz hand. "No fire, Sadie. Though that is random enough for it to be some kind of dream suggestion,"

"This isn't a normal dream," Danny interrupts. "I've never dreamt of you both like this before. This vividly. Here," he holds out his hands to us both. "Take them." His hand feels real in mine. I can feel his untrimmed, jagged fingernails, his long palms, his thin fingers. The soldiers spill and stumble around us as if we're rocks in a river, but unlike Danny's hand in mine, I can't feel them as they pass me. I peer at Danny up close; the black beard on his brown skin; the lines and shadows around his piercing green eyes. I know his lips, his cheek; I've kissed them many times. I know his smell; warm, boy-musky.

"What then? Are we co-dreaming?" Sometimes, witches appear in each other's dreams - we call it "meeting on the astral". But co-dreaming like this; I've never done this before. Melz and Danny are so clear, so hyper-real. The untidy column of envirowarriors in front of us fades away. Still holding hands, the landscape blurs briefly and we're transported away from the long dirt road and I find myself looking down from the mountaintop. Elbrus.

"How did we get up here?" I ask, looking around like an idiot.

"I thought of it. I actively thought about standing

on top of the mountain, and here we are. The dream is meldable. But we… we seem real, somehow," Danny says, crunching his feet in the snow. "I can feel my feet. I can both feel your hands in mine. But I can bend the rest. Like I would in a vision or a dream,"

Danny is incredibly good at visualisation. Melz told me how Roach - my dad - dream-kidnapped him once when he'd just started training to be a witch, tried to torture him in the astral realm. As the more experienced witch, Roach should have been able to keep Danny there. But he couldn't.

I pull my hand away from him but he holds onto me tightly.

"No. I feel like we need to keep together, otherwise this won't work,"

"What won't work? I didn't know this was going to happen at all," Melz snaps. "Did you pull us here somehow? I'd like to be consulted on this kind of psychic interference, for future reference,"

"I didn't do it on purpose. I was dreaming of the enviros, then I heard your voices and looked round. There you were. I had this - have this - instinct, that's all," he says, gripping both our hands tight. He looks so gaunt and thin, and I remember that outside of this dream, he's imprisoned somewhere in Gidleigh. I can feel how awful he feels: how weak and defeated. And he's angry too. I can feel that. Angry at being put there; angry we haven't come for him. Grieving for his mother.

"If we're really here together, what does it mean? And why are we on this mountain in Russia?" The gathering clouds imitate the thick snow under our feet.

"It's an energy centre, a portal. It's been blocked, though. Because of the all the fighting and the mining" Melz says.

I feel its power under me. Different again, its own natural frequency. And damaged, like Melz told me Glastonbury was.

"The war's ruined it," Melz brow furrows in concentration. "It's big, but something like this - all these years of digging, drilling for oil, for gas, all around it, plus the war - the death, the death.." she breaks off and a look of horror covers her face like a sheet. "It's too much. I can't…" she pulls her hands away but I hold her tight.

"No! Don't break the connection!" I shout, but

now I can feel Danny pulling away from both of us; his outline wavers, and suddenly I can't see his dry, split lips in as much detail or feel the sweat on his skin.

"Help me, Sadie," he whispers, as he disappears, just for that second, his anger gone, and I feel the desperation in him. "Please…"

"Danny. Hold on. We're coming for you1" I shout. I reach out for him with my whole being, but it isn't enough; he's weak; his body pulls him back.

Then it's just me, in the dream, holding both of Melz's hands; Danny's disappeared, and Melz and our surroundings start to dissolve. Without his power we can't hold it together. I open my eyes, back in bed, and know that we have to save him, or he'll die there, wherever he is in Gidleigh: cold, hungry and alone.

CHAPTER EIGHT

Respect Nature, for She has no respect for you.

From: Tenets and Sayings of the Greenworld

The black sky cracks and spits out lightning, urgent, unpredictable.

"We shouldn't be here," Melz says, looking back over the crashing Cornish sea to the village.

It feels like the lightning cleaves the world in two for a while: past and present, future and dream, real and hyper-real; it's something to do with the light and the way it makes you half-blind every time it flashes, leaving the negative on your eyes like a map of the underworld. The hit tree burns even in the rain; time was, we never got storms like this in April. But the Redworld's messed up the climate so badly that we get weird weather all the time now.

We build a fire up on Tintagel Head even as the rain patters around us and the storm rages on above. If we're going to stay up here for a while we'll need some warmth and shelter, what with the wind wanting to blow us to kingdom come (queendom for us though, obviously).

We build it next to one of the ruined walls of an old chapel they had up here, those old medieval kings and their abandoned bearded-old-man god.

Melz stares into the fire as it crackles under the darkening clouds, the moon just a dim grey smudge and the wind moans around like a banshee, but we have peace with banshees - the bean-sidhe, in gaelic - and the spirits'll leave us alone unless we reach out to them. *We are but skin about a wind, with muscles clenched against mortality* like Djuna says in *Nightwood,* one of my favourite Greenworld-approved books.

"He was so weak," I frown. "I could feel it, the cold, that kind of dank cold you can't get out of your bones. He's suffering, Melz. We have to help him,"

"I know. And the co-dreaming. What was that about? I mean, I've had dreams about Danny before, precognitions, visions. And dreams about you -" she breaks off, and fiddles with her cloak clasp. *Dreams about me? Excuse me?*

"Oh. Er…" all sense of language leaves me. What do I say to that, especially when she's so clearly regretting mentioning it? That I dream of her almost nightly? Mostly dreams where Melz sits me down in a caring yet distant fashion and tells me she knows I have a huge crush on her but that her destiny lies elsewhere blahblahblah, and I wake up, defeated, but still wanting her? And, occasionally, vividly erotic dreams full of kissing and tongues and my legs entwined in hers and her skin in my mouth?

"I know. It must be something to do with our witch brands. We can actively dream together," I pull it together and make a sensible comment.

"So it would seem. But, Danny. I mean, I know he did a bad thing by your mum. But we can't leave him there. And he needs healing for his own demons,"

We know the truth. A demon's no more and no less than the deepest shadow inside you. Everything has shades of light and dark. The challenge is to love the dark, here and now, not, as the erstwhile bearded-man-god would have it, banish it to a fiery hell and hope you never get sent there. Though, obviously, that's easier said than done, especially for a ruined girl like me. I've got my share of shadows.

"I know. But he didn't kill mum, he just threatened her. And I understand why. Melz, he's suffered enough,"

"I know," her face is earnest in the moonlight. "I

want to get him back and I want the three of us to follow these symbols, these words, wherever they're meant to take us. Mum doesn't want to see it but the only way we can stop the Greenworld fragmenting even more is find a permanent solution to stop all the refugees coming here. Not because I don't want them, but we can't cope for much longer, we just don't have the resources. So we need to... I dunno. See if we can make things right in the Redworld so they don't have to leave,"

"But we can't tell Lowenna if we go to rescue him?"

"No. She told us not to. We just have to do it and bring him back with us as a fait accompli. She won't turn him away if he's there on the doorstep. I hope," she frowns. "We're talking about Danny Prentice." She pokes me in the chest. "Your friend. Your boyfriend, once. He's a witch, he's one of us, and he was Zia Prentice's son. There's no way I'm leaving him to rot while those bloody witch-hating, racist villagers decide what to do with him,"

Danny's mixed race. As a brown kid in an almost-totally white village, he didn't have the easiest of times growing up. Nor did his little sister, Biba.

I'm divided because I agree with Melz, but

Lowenna's my High Priestess, inducting me into the secret ways of the Fire Priestess, the mysteries of Brighid and all that. If I disobey her, I'll be betraying her confidence. I might as well tear up my witch's measure just like Saba did. But I know Melz is right.

"Lowenna's afraid for me. What he'd do if he was here. Because of mum," I pick at my cuff. "I'm afraid, too," I'm afraid because Danny has power, a huge power, and I've seen what happens when he decides to use it negatively.

But I know that Lowenna's also afraid for herself. Because she knows, she must know, deep down, that we're right; that we can't carry on like this. And if Danny was here, if the three of us were together, she knows something would happen in the balance of power in the coven. We've got some kind of bond with each other: that's obvious. And she knows that's a threat to her, because she's the last of the first generation of the branded ones. One's dead; the other banished, destroyed in darkness. We're the three now.

And Brighid has chosen me above her once already. This will just make it worse.

"You can't be afraid of him, Sadie. He's not a bad

person. He's in a bad place, that's all. He's mourning. Healing is what he needs. Inclusion is what he needs, not banishment," she takes my hand and squeezes it. "Trust me on this, okay?"

"Of course I trust you; I just…" my heartbeat quickens and my hand tingles with the unadulterated pleasure of being touched by her; at her index finger curling into my palm. "Lowenna. If we go - will she let us come back?"

"I don't know. We'd be disobeying her as High Priestess. You know how she is," Melz broods.

"We still have to go, though. Don't we?" I say, resigned.

"Yes," she says. "Yes, we do,"

I know she's right, but I don't have to like it. But then she takes my face in her hands and I'm so surprised for a moment that I forget to breathe.

"I'll protect you, if you need protecting, but you're so much stronger than you believe you are," she looks deep into my eyes. "You told me a bit of what your dad did to you, when we came here from Gidleigh. You must have been so frightened. But you're transforming, Sadie.

You're stepping into your power more every day. You can protect yourself against whatever Danny Prentice might throw at you. You're a witch and a Priestess of Brighid," her hands leave my face and she leans in and kisses my forehead. "You burn with Her incandescence. Nothing will touch you,"

I stare at her, feeling the kiss like a brand on my forehead. She smiles a small, secretive smile and looks away shyly. "Sorry - perhaps it wasn't the moment,"

"No, I… No, it's fine," I stammer, unconsciously putting my palm to my forehead and then pulling my hand away again as soon as I realise what I'm doing. But I want to capture that kiss and press it into my heart, make sure I never lose it.

"I…" Shit, I want to say something. Tell her how I feel. She's just kissed me - I mean, in a sisterly way and on the forehead, but it's something.

"What?"

"Oh… nothing," I lose my nerve.

"No, no, come on. It's just us here, hiding away from the rest of the coven. We're already breaking the rules," she raises her eyebrow and grins unexpectedly at me, stoking the fire with a long stick. As she leans away from me I catch a glimpse of the blue triskele witch-brand at the base of her neck.

What can I say? That if she's leaving Tintagel then I want to be on that boat and not left behind waving disconsolately from the shore like a sailor's widow. That I love her and would follow her anywhere? *"I love you without knowing how, or when, or from where. I love you simply, without problems or pride: I love you in this way because I do not know any other way of loving but this, in which there is no I or you,"* my favourite Rilke love sonnet plays in my mind.

"I know there's... something between us. Remember the dream? At Scorhill?" I'm boldened by not having to look directly at her and so I speak those words to her back, which stiffens as I mention the dream I know we both had of being in Scorhill stone circle before we even met and how good it felt to be together. That we did nothing but hold each other in the dream, but that was more than enough. That was the moment I started falling for Demelza Hawthorne, and I hadn't even met her yet.

And then she saved me from Danny and brought me here. She defended me when no-one else would. She listened to me calmly when I told her the darkest things in my mind and she didn't judge. And as I watched her, her quiet ways, her magic, that indefinable troubled shadowiness, I fell for her. Hard.

There's a silence and we both listen to the wind and the receding thunder roll back across Cornwall, blowing the storm that started over the ocean inland.

"It's final. Fire. You can't un-burn something. Once it's done, it's done," she doesn't answer me directly, but sits back on her heels and looks at me, running one fingernail under another, as if she was trying to clean out dirt from under it. "And it's unpredictable. It can get out of control. Quickly,"

"What does that mean?"

"I remember the dream, Sadie, but both times I got involved with someone it ended really badly. I don't want that again," she says. "I like you. And I... I find you..." she looks away, but her potential words hover on the grass between us like smoke. *Attractive? Vaguely decent? Repellent?* If I was in any way attractive to her, surely we'd be rolling across this hard earth, lost in an ecstasy of togetherness by now *(ecstasy of togetherness*: this is what you get for reading romances instead of ecology). "But it's just too hard. And I'm your mentor, your teacher. I don't think it'll go too well if we complicate things, do you?"

I know she's thinking of Tom as she stares back into the flames, the one that died on the battlefield, and Bran, the one that she believed she could change; but I want to turn that gaze onto me, feel it pierce me, fill me, go straight to my heart.

I want to grab her and kiss her, tell her that this is the moment and the past's gone; that fire destroys but it's also passion, and that memory's a cold stone library. A brief image of my own stone wall of memory, the wall I keep up against chaos, comes briefly into my mind, but now is no time for actually having to deal with my own crap.

Her eyes flicker to me.

"It doesn't matter. What I want doesn't matter anymore," she snaps, and looks away, into the night.

I reach out and catch her hand, feeling her rough bitten nails in my palm. She has faint traces of dried mud in the fine cracks of fortune crisscrossing her hand. Her patterns are there for anyone to see: loss and sacrifice, power and vulnerability. She shifts her gaze to me then and I'm shocked at the sorrow in it, but I hold that look anyway.

"It does matter," I say and hold her palm to my lips. Without breaking my gaze, I screw up my courage and kiss it gently.

"What are you doing?" her voice is low, but she doesn't pull away.

"I don't really know." I say, honestly, and then as if it's another person and not me - surely I can't actually be doing this? - I kiss her again, on her wrist, this time. She stares at me. I kiss the inside of her elbow, feeling the softness of the skin there and she watches me with those piercing eyes but doesn't tell me to stop, so I lean in to kiss her neck but she holds me back gently then, her hand on my shoulder.

"You don't know what this means," she says, but I've come this far and I can feel the fire in my blood, in my heart, and the wild fire burning strong in the core of my body telling me exactly what it means.

"Yes, I do," I breathe and lean in to kiss her, all caution thrown firmly to the wind, as they say - whoever made up that saying obviously lived on the Cornish coast - but she pulls away.

"No, Sadie. Please, don't. You don't know me. You don't… you don't want me," she says, and the aforementioned savage wind gusts suddenly and blows the fire almost out between us, leaving glowing embers at the base of the blackened wood.

She stands up and wraps her arms around her as if for protection. "Come on. Let's go back. The storm's getting worse," she says, abruptly.

"But…" but she's already striding away in that brisk taking-no-prisoners walk she has, so I've got no choice but to follow her back across treacherous Tintagel Head. The waves deafen me from below, their ceaseless buildup crashing onto the sharp rocks.

I'm mortified. What now? I don't know if I can ever look her I the face again.

I kissed her, and she said no. I feel sick.

Oh, Brighid. Take me now. I'm ready for the hereafter.

Untitled poem, excerpt from Sadie Morgan's notebook

I watch you, hands raised high; my vision tilts
up at your lips as you sing, half-shadowed
Damn you, my heart can't take this -
As you sing, transporting me to faraway hills,
My blood does unexpected shifts, longing,
Segueing from one cut-off limb
to another, slowly filling
with a rapturous, fearful lift;
Daring to open, to be part of a world of
seismic shifts and love paradigms and
hallucinogenic romance; this is it, this is love.
I watch you, pacing the circle, my heart,
How corruptible it is, repeating beats
that merge into the tone of your voice.
In shadow, in dream, those are the thoughtful
self-effacing lips that I think of kissing
At the most inconvenient times -
Damn you, my heart can't take it -
This love is bent out of my rib, plaited from my hair;
Feathered with black, hungover from dream,
With the astral still under my nails, in my head, on endless repeat:

How wet and corruptible my heart is

as your thoughtful lips sing and cry, ignorant of my

even existing. There are few things as bittersweet as this.

I dream of kissing your thoughtful lips.

Damn you. I can't do this.

CHAPTER NINE

Nervine relaxants /sedatives inc. Motherwort, Valerian, Rosemary, Chamomile, Mistletoe, St John's Wort. Valerian, Skullcap and St Johns Wort - also analgesic (reduces pain).

From: The Common Herbal

We sneak out after everyone's gone to bed.

It's a week after our secret assignation on Tintagel Head where I thoroughly embarrassed myself with the whole kissing thing; Melz hasn't mentioned it at all since and that makes it worse in every single way. I mean, it was probably sexual harassment, (*something just overcame me, you were too beautiful*: the cry of the harasser throughout history, note I definitely said *history* and not *herstory* there, thank you so much). I won't be making that mistake again in a hurry, By Brighid.

I meet Melz in the kitchen as arranged, furtively, earlier, on the way back from herbalism class at Beryan's house, hanging back from the group and looking suspicious like clichéd villains (I haven't been exposed to many villains - only my parents - so this is one of those odd occasions where you go to the cliché without even stopping to think about your actual experience which makes you far better informed about the subject. My parents, both murderers and one a notorious criminal, never seemed "suspicious" to anyone else until it was too late).

I collect up as many herbal remedies as I can imagine we might need; herbs for cleaning wounds and leaves to bind them, herbs for pain, relaxants, food to give us energy, and pack them into a tin in a fabric bag with a long strap. Melz carries her own bulky bag.

"Ready?" she whispers and I nod, and we tiptoe down the hall towards the front door. We're just putting on our long wool cloaks and knitted hats when we're lit up by the creamy light of a candle like a small sun at the top of the stairs.

"What're you doing?" Catie's voice whispers.

"Go back to bed," Melz hisses, but Catie pads down the wooden stairs, the worn blue cloth in the middle of each stair tread threadbare between her toes.

"No. What are you up to? It's past midnight," she looks at our cloaks and hats. "Where're you going?"

"None of your business. And don't tell anyone

you saw us," I whisper, but she doesn't budge.

"You're going to get him, aren't you? Danny?" she hisses.

"We can't tell you," Melz says, which is as good as saying *yes we are*.

"I want to come too," Catie says, already pulling on her boots. "He's a branded witch. He shouldn't be stuck in some prison or wherever they've got him,"

"Catie! You can't come!" I whisper to her, and, if I'm honest, maybe just a small sliver of me is saying that because I want this to be just me and Melz, in the night, on the moors, perhaps her holding my arm for steadiness in the dark, perhaps lighting a campfire and sitting by it together in the night like old friends, telling the truths you can only tell in the dark. But Melz looks at Catie appraisingly.

"All right. Come. But only if you're ready now. We've got everything we need, you don't need to go and get anything except warm clothes," she whispers, looking cautiously up the stairs, checking for any other movement.

I must be pulling a face - I've still not mastered the knack of not displaying every emotion I have - because

Melz looks at me and shrugs.

"We might need some more power on our side. We don't know what we're walking into," she says. I raise my eyebrow at Catie's bent back as she's pulling on her walking boots. Melz knows what that look means. It means *Catie can't do bugger all*. She's a trainee, not even a branded witch like me. Melz ignores me.

"Brilliant. The thing is, Demi told us about the argument you had with Lowenna, and Rain and Macha and me all thought you might go and get him. Because that's what we'd do. And we all said we'd want to come if you did," Catie stands up, swathed in her cloak and a long scarf, hat and mittens but avoids my expression which could roughly be described as a *fuck off and leave us alone* kind of look.

"It isn't a day out. This is serious," I glare at Catie.

"I know. It's just that... We feel like all we do is chanting and meditating and reading. We want to do some real magic,"

"That *is* real magic," Melz says, but there's the ghost of a smile lingering around her lips. "Fine. Go and wake them up. But do it quietly, and I mean silent. And fast. We don't have any time to waste," She holds her hand up to my face dismissively as Catie tiptoes back upstairs. "I can feel your look. I could do with more bodies on the ground, that's all. And just because you've got the brand, don't think you're more experienced than you are. I'm in charge here. Okay?" she turns her kohl-rimmed eyes to mine for emphasis.

"Fine. Fine. It's your plan," I know I sound grumpy and I can't help it.

"Yes, it is," she gives me a bemused smile.

Rain and Macha tiptoe down the stairs, dressed hastily in long jumpers and heavy work trousers; Macha's hair tied up in a scarf, Rain as irritatingly pixie-like as usual even though she's just woken up, with a brown knitted hat pulled down over her ears. Melz opens the front door and the cold Cornish night blows in as if to replace us inside the house. Briefly I think of those old stories where faeries swapped their babies for human children. We're gone on the wind tonight; how long will it take for the others to realise we've gone?

CHAPTER TEN

Love the land; share its bounty; grow with love; harvest well.

From: Tenets and Sayings of the Greenworld

Gidleigh village stinks. I never realised how bad it was (I mean, was it always like this?) until we get close enough to be upwind of it on the moor, but damn, it's disgusting. I can see the others' faces crinkling in disgust as the fog of human compost insinuates itself up their nostrils.

Tintagel's on the coast, so maybe that blows a lot of it away, but even so I'm sure it's a lot cleaner there and this has got way worse than it was when I left, and that's only been months, not a year yet. I fish out my Celtic knot design perfume locket on its long bronze chain and take a good whiff, which doesn't really work and now the shit smell just has lavender overtones. Lovely.

"This way," Melz calls in a low voice. We're tired and short of leg in some cases (Macha, that short, fat ponyfaced excuse for a witch) and we trail after her like one long grass snake through the ankle-breaking lumpy moor where long tufty grass disguises deep holes. I hear several *owws* and muttered swears behind me as those sea witches navigate my home turf, and the Greenworld tenet *Respect Nature, for She has no respect for you* rings hard and clear in my head, alongside the conversation we had in the firelight in our brief camp last night.

"But think about what it means. If we can travel to other portals across the world," Macha's chubby little face had glowed in the leaping orange of our campfire. "It means we can connect with other communities. And not just that. There are portals around the world that're blocked, unhealthy. Melz cleansed Glastonbury Tor,"

We'd started talking about my weird portal travelling; Melz was refusing to say exactly what she thought about it but the girls were dying to know more. Could we make it happen again, could anyone else do it, was it something special about me, blah de blah. I mean, not that I'm dismissing it - it was an intense experience, but in a way I could do without being the centre of attention because of it. I just want to learn how to be a witch. I don't always want to be the special one. It reminds me too much of dad. That's what he always used to say about me, that I was special. Being special didn't protect me, or mum.

"It's dangerous," Melz said in the end, but it was a rote teacher reply and not what she really thought. "Sadie only did it by accident. If we're going to do it again I need to go in. I'm the most experienced. I need to go back to Mount Shasta and meet the girl you met, Sadie. I need to find out more about her and her people. How did she know we were coming? How can they help us? They can explain the scroll she gave you. How to use it, what it means,"

"I should go with you. She gave the message to me," I'd said stubbornly, and this time it wasn't only because I wanted to be with Melz at every available opportunity. Perversely, even though maybe I don't want to be the special one, singled out for attention, I kind of do because Ki'putska was my connection. It was my experience. If anyone was going to go back it should be me. She'd nodded.

"Fair enough. When we get back to Tintagel, Sadie and I will go. The rest of you will hold the circle around the portal until we get back. But this is secret, is that clear? No-one tells Lowenna or any of the rest of them until I say so. Okay?"

They agreed; they're all in bad enough trouble

being here anyway; a bit more won't hurt.

We pass Scorhill stone circle on the moor and I clench my fists as home starts to get real for me; Zia's funeral and what came after is still a hard memory. The fear and isolation after mum had killed her and I was still there alone and I didn't know what to do; all that's like a ghost that lives here, just waiting for me to reappear so it can attach itself to me like a hibernating parasite and resume feeding.

But I'm not the uneducated, scared kid I once was, so, now, as I walk, I pull up strength and power from the earth through my feet and into my solar plexus like a green rope, a root through which power flows like moisture; and I pull down light from above, from the stars and the sun and the great unknowable infinity of space and all the molecules that make it and make us and everything else. Because it might be frowned upon to know too much science in the Greenworld, but I know that I'm made up of the same things as stars are, as grass is and rock is and the great blue wide ocean is. In the Greenworld we just call it another thing, we say *as above so below, as within so without,* but all that means is that microcosm and macrocosm are forever swirling in inevitable and infinite echoes of each other, and you can't have one without the other, right?

Right. Science and magic. Pretty similar in some ways, as it turns out.

To be on the safe side I close my eyes briefly and imagine throwing a heavy indigo cloak over my shoulders and wrapping it around me. Psychic protection. It feels better to be grounded and protected.

We get closer to the village and I slow down when we get to where the energetic boundary should be, the magic circle that protects the village. But there's no slight shimmer at the edge of my eyes, no rough heat haze baking off the ground even on a cold day; it's all gone, and I guess that makes sense with no witch at Gidleigh anymore. That circle's something that has to be maintained, like human pee keeps away foxes. I exchange looks with Melz who knows this village too and I can see she can sense where the lack is, she can feel the shadow on the grass like me.

We're going to walk straight past the top of the gravel path that leads to my house. Inside the village but not central, like mum couldn't bring herself to move us in any further, to commit any further to the Greenworld than she had to. I didn't think I'd want to go back but I do: it's where I grew up, after all, it's my home, even though Biba,

Danny's little sister, might've burnt it down by now like she said she would. The villagers might've looted it or crapped in the hallway or something out of sheer disgust for me or mum.

"Just going in quickly. Need to get some stuff," I call softly over to Melz, but I don't look back in case she says no. She can't shout as we're supposed to be stealthy here, and I'm going in, like it or not.

I walk up the path. The flowers haven't been tended so are wilder than they used to be, but otherwise the outside of the house looks normal. No front door kicked in, no messages painted on the door. I mean, Gidleigh's a good village but things have changed a lot since I've been gone. You don't know what's in folk's minds and what they'll do, especially now there's no witch in charge.

My door key's hanging on my necklace. I pull it over my head and open the door as quietly as I can. Not sure why I do it quietly; it's unlikely anyone's there waiting for me. I walk into the long hall cautiously. The house is musty. I walk into the kitchen and find deserted piles of unrecognisable food which has gone past the infested-by-flies stage, reverting back into organic matter.

I go upstairs to my room: it's exactly as I left it. I slide my hand under my mattress. They're still there: my tarot cards, a clear quartz pointed scrying crystal on a chain, both Zia's. I don't feel good about having taken them, but she was my High Priestess, my teacher, once. I know she would've wanted me to have something of hers. It was easy enough to get them in the confusion after she died and before Danny got home.

I reported Zia dead, in the end. Biba, Danny's little sister, had seen what happened but afterwards she went into some kind of shock and wouldn't speak; couldn't remember anything about what had happened for a week or two. So I did it, just with the most basic of details. But I told them, the community elders, I told them it was mum. There was never any doubt about that, but they didn't do anything about it for ages. They were shocked. Gidleigh had been governed by a witch for so long that once she was gone, they didn't know what to do.

I'd given mum a days' grace to get away; I thought she'd gone, and then she turned up that day on the village green. Looking for me. *I can't leave you,* she'd said. *Everything I did, I did it for you. Come away with me now. I'll protect you, please, we have to leave, we have to leave now.* She'd pulled at my hand as we stood at the edge of the village green, but I refused. I didn't want to run. This was the only place I'd ever felt safe, because of Zia. And now she was dead, but I still wanted to stay, because *he* was outside the village, somewhere, like he always was. Circling, like a wolf, like a predator. Roach. My dad.

And then Danny had seen mum; there was an argument going on with him and the villagers, and suddenly the crowd parted like wind through a field of wheat and there he was, staring at us, and it was too late to run.

I shove the cards and crystal into my bag and go into mum's room. There are some things of hers I want too. A couple of keepsakes, a necklace, a photo. Old things from the grandparents I never knew. I take a last look around. I wet the bed most nights until I was 10 if I had to sleep alone, so I spent most nights in here; she never complained. She never made me throw away my dolls and stuffed toys even though I was too old for them. She never asked why sometimes she came in to find me kneeling up on my bed, asleep with red eyes from crying, hands still folded in prayer, she never asked because she knew why I'd been up all night begging Brighid to keep us safe.

But she's gone, and this house is gone for me

now; sacrificed for my new life as a witch. I pick up a pillow and hold it against my check, feeling its familiar soft pilled cotton, taking in the old smell of my childhood.

I hear Melz call my name softly downstairs. It's time to go. I shut the bedroom door after me, follow Melz out of the front door and pull it closed. I know I'll never go back there.

CHAPTER ELEVEN

Losing too is still ours; and even forgetting
still has a shape in the kingdom of transformation.
When something's let go of, it circles; and though we
are rarely the center

of the circle, it draws around us its unbroken, marvellous curve.

Losing, R M Rilke

They have him in the old castle at the edge of the village.

We scryed for him on the way; crystals on old chains held above a folded map of the village. Their jagged points stuck to the site of the old castle on the paper like magnets to iron. Mine floated around the page indecisively, though, knowing that I'm ambivalent at best about finding Danny at all.

It's still early: there's no-one around. The early sun casts shadows around the squat building; thick grey stone covered in ivy and moss. As kids we thought it was what castles looked like and then we saw other ones in books and learned that they were supposed to house hundreds of folk and all their servants and cooks. Ours in Gidleigh could just about hold a small stationary old woman and maybe a really arthritic old cat that wasn't really up to asking more out of life.

It seems odd they'd leave Danny here: it was just a ruin, not exactly secure; but as we approach warily, scanning the trees and hedgerows for villagers, the front's all been boarded up and a roof's been put on.

"That wasn't there before," I whisper to Melz, nodding at the door.

"He's definitely in there," she whispers back. "Stay here and keep watch," she hisses at Macha and Rain and fishes out two pistols from her bag. "Anyone comes, point these at them. Don't fire, just look scary," Melz is a good shot, but these girls didn't spend countless hours practising shooting bottles off tree stumps when they were kids like this wild heller; in fact, they don't look as if they know one end of a gun from another.

"The bang comes out that end," I mutter in a low voice to Rain as I walk past, annoyed by her beautiful blonde pixie-ness - and at the fact that Melz has smiled at her once or twice - I mean, does Rain have to be that bloody wide-eyed and innocent? *Rain*. Plain, more like.

I follow Melz; we creep up to the front door. She runs her fingers around the crack between the door and the stone wall, but it isn't wide enough to let light in, never mind a hand or a gun barrel. It isn't a door, even; it's just one massive wooden panel nailed shut across the doorway. No handle, no lock. She pulls her hand away from the door and frowns.

"What?"

"Touch it,"

I touch the stone cautiously and, *By Brighid*, pull my hand back as if I'd been burned.

"What the...?" we exchange looks. There's something else here, possessing its walls, giving it a sheen of impenetrability that's thick and slow to the touch, as if the castle was doused in oil.

"Hate. They're focusing all their negativity on Danny, here, outside the village. All those people are raising more energy than we ever could in the circle, and now they've got a focus," she mutters under her breath.

"That's horrible,"

"People are horrible," she snaps. "Come on. Let's

look around the back," I take the left and she takes the right, without having to tell each other that's what we're doing. I focus on the rough stone wall, not touching it, trying to feel a weakness in the energy, but there's nothing. We both turn onto the back wall at the same time: no window holes or gaps in the stone. Melz squints up at the roof.

"It's tiled. I think one or two of them have come off. I can pull a few more off, get in that way," She smiles that occasional, dangerous Melz smile. She drops her bag and black wool cloak on the ground and looks up at the wall.

"Boost me up," she says, tucking her trousers into her wool socks; I kneel down so that she can climb onto my knee and then on my shoulders. I stand up with her on me and feel her weight shift as she reaches for a handhold, then feel her step onto the wall, balancing on the tips of her toes on one of the stones.

As her foot leaves my shoulder, there's a scuffling noise from in front of the castle and Macha's voice, burring unsteadily in the clearing.

"Don't come any closer. It's loaded,"

Melz is clinging tight to the wall.

"I'm going in this way. Keep whoever it is busy until I can get him out," she whispers down at me.

"How long will that take?"

"I don't bloody know! He could be injured, tied up, whatever. I've got to get him out through the roof or find another way out from inside. Those guns are loaded and so's mine. It's in the bag if you want it," she says, climbing up carefully, not looking down. "Okay?"

"All right," It isn't all right but I don't have a choice. I crouch down and reach into the bag for the gun. As my fingers curl around its cold muzzle, a small voice replies to Macha's challenge. I pull the gun out, stand up and tuck it into my waistband, skirting the side of the castle lightly and peer around the side out at the clearing. As I do, there's a thump behind me as Melz climbs up to the roof and throws one loose tile onto the grass, then another.

I can only see half of the girl from behind Macha, but I know her. I know her voice, her poker straight glossy dark hair, her skin a darker brown than Danny's. She doesn't have her brother's green cat eyes but hers are warm and brown, filled equal parts with sweetness and sadness.

Biba Prentice stares at Macha, unafraid. It's like watching two tiny faery warriors in a standoff.

"Who the hell are you?" Biba frowns and looks Macha up and down derisively; at her well-meaning horsey face and muscular legs in mustard colour leggings, heavy boots caked in mud.

"No closer!" Macha repeats; Biba rolls her eyes.

"I didn't move. Come up with something a bit more original, why don't you? Come on. You can do it if you try,"

Macha glances at Rain, who I can see is trying to remain impassive, but panic is about her as clearly as a cloud of bees. The hand she holds out, gun aimed at Biba, shakes. Goddess, this is a thirteen year old girl, built like a bird. Nut maybe Macha can sense some of Biba's titanic inner strength: she exudes an air of substantial attitude and don't-mess-with-me shit that's new since the last time I saw her.

I feel sick when I remember the last time we spoke to each other, when she spat at me, threatened to burn our house down with me in it, because my mum had killed hers; but I also remember her voice, pleading with Melz not to leave her as chaos descended on the village. Melz had stepped in when Zia died, looked after Danny and Biba. But Melz chose me over them. And it hurt. I know it hurt.

"Biba," I step out and walk slowly towards her. I shake my head at Macha and she lowers her gun slowly. Biba's eyes widen when she sees me.

"I didn't know you were back," her voice is guarded.

"I'm not, really. I'm here with Melz,"

"What're you doing here?" her eyes flicker at the mention of Melz's name, but she doesn't say anything about her.

"What do you think? They can't keep him here any longer, Biba. It's cruel,"

"He's not... he's not the same. Not like he was," she says, and this time her eyes look away from mine. She doesn't want him here either, but someone's persuaded her that she should go along with it.

"They shouldn't have locked him up, Biba. Not here. It's horrible,"

"There wasn't anywhere else. He kept... getting out," her eyes fill with tears.

"I'm sorry, Biba. I know this is hard on you," I reach out my hand carefully, as if I were stroking a wild cat. "It's okay. I'll take him with me. No-one has to know you were here,"

"Don't touch me." She snaps, and I pull my hand back.

"Sorry... sorry. It's okay. Everything's okay,"

"Everything is NOT okay!" she yells, then, the blood rushing to her cheeks. Tears fill her eyes. I want to hug her, to make it better, but she hates me. "They say he deserves to be in there. He almost killed your mum. He should have. She deserves it. Not him. Not Danny,"

"Believe me, Biba. I understand that folk do weird shit when they're sad. I do,"

She looks at me now, all that grief on her shoulders.

"He'll be safe with me," I say, soft but purposeful,

but she looks through me, at the castle.

"I bring him food and water every day. They let me do that," I feel so sad for her. How conflicted she must be. How alone.

"Where d'you put it? Do you give it to him?" I ask, softly still, like when I heal an animal. Soft tones, not to frighten it. If Biba knows how we can get in, I need to get that information from her.

"I leave it in a special slot. Around the side,"

"Show me?" I try to make it sound casual.

She takes a few halting steps through the long unkempt grass.

"I …,"

"It's okay, Biba. It's okay," I keep my voice soft.

"I don't want to lose him," she turns her face to me, eyes wide and full of uncertainty. "Even though he's… here, at least he's close," a tear slips down her cheek. "Please. I can't lose Danny too. He's all I've got left," she wipes her face furiously with her sleeve, like she doesn't want me to see her cry.

"You won't, if you let us take him. You'll lose him if you let him stay here. He'll die here, Biba. You must know that," I say as kindly as I can. "You can come with us too. I won't leave you here with them,"

She looks at me distrustfully.

"I don't want to come with you. You're the last person I'd go with,"

I exchange a glance with Macha. We don't have time for this.

"Look, Biba. I get it. I know you'll always hate me, and that's fine. But I'm not leaving Danny in there, and I can't make you come with me, but I strongly suggest that you do. You're the daughter of a witch. These people don't want witches anymore. If you stay, you'll be a threat to them. Maybe not now, but soon. When you're grown up, they're going to watch you for any signs of magic. And if you have any talent at all in that direction, they'll put you in here just like they have Danny, or worse. And, honestly? Even if you don't turn out to be a witch, they're likely to want you gone anyway. You're Zia Prentice's daughter. You're just too much of a risk,"

I know it's too much pressure to put on her, but

we need to get Danny out. Now.

She breathes out, slowly.

"There's not much time. They come to check on him in half an hour. It's only a small hole. You won't be able to get him out of it," her voice is controlled, steady. I know it's taking a lot of effort to keep it that way.

"Leave that to us," I say, and usher her ahead of me.

She leads me around the side of the house Melz had been around. There's no hole in the wall that I can see but Biba hands the tray to me. Uninviting smells waft from it. Boiled vegetables; the high, sweet odour of cheese on a warm day.

"Here," she says and reaches in between two stones. Her forearm tenses and she pushes, and a panel I hadn't seen appears, moving to the right to create a small space just wide enough to fit a tray – maybe a foot across, six inches high.

"That's it?"

"That's it," she says sadly. I notice she leaves her hand in the gap after setting the food down. She catches me looking. "Sometimes he comes. Sometimes not," she says, and pulls her hand away.

"Nothing," I take her hand.

"I'm... I'm sorry, Biba. For everything. I didn't mean…"

"Yeah, whatever,"

"We both lost our mums," I say quietly. Mine might not have died, but she might as well have done. She's somewhere, a murderer on the run. Or at least, that's what I've assumed. Our house hasn't been lived in for a long time.

"Yours is still alive. Don't tell me about loss," she mutters.

"She's not here, is she? Mum?" I look back at the village, my heart suddenly pounding with a hope I didn't know I had. Mum. I close my eyes, think of her giving me a hug. My heart wrenches.

"No. Disappeared," Biba mutters, avoiding my eyes. "Good riddance,"

I open my eyes, rub away the tears that have sprung there without warning.

"Fine," I sigh. "Let's just get this over with,"

CHAPTER TWELVE

Brighid came and keened... At first she shrieked, in the end she wept. Then for the first time weeping and lamentation were heard in Ireland.

From: Lebor Gabála Érenn, or Book of Invasions

"I don't know how you're going to make the hole any bigger," Macha takes her small pudgy hands out of the gap between the stones. "It's solid. We'd need a day and some serious tools to crack the stones out around it, make a big enough space for a person to get through,"

"Arse," I mutter and shout through the small aperture into the castle. "Melz! Can you hear me? Melz!" my voice cannons inside the walls, calling my words back to me. I stick my hand through and feel a hand grasp it.

"I'm here. He's very weak. No light gets in here. He's thin. I don't think he's going to be much help," her voice echoes through the stone. "I don't think I can get him out through the roof. What's this?"

"Some kind of access hole. Dunno if the villagers made it specially or what, but they pass his food through here. It's solid our side, though. Can you see anything your side you could do? Any loose stones, enlarge the gap a bit?"

There are some scraping noises and I see a light flicker to and fro in the darkness; candlelight. I wonder briefly if Melz brought one or whether they let Danny have a candle in the gloom.

"Nope. If I had an hour I might get one of them loose, but…"

"We've got about twenty minutes until someone from the village comes to check up on him,"

"Shit,"

"Yeah,"

"This energy over the castle. It's holding him here. I don't think we'll get him out until it's gone," her voice comes through the wall, ghostly, dimmed by brick.

"So?"

"So, I'm going to need some help," she says. "Listen up,"

We circle the castle like Melz tells us; not enough of us to hold hands, but we stand at intervals, holding our hands out towards each other, projecting an energetic circle around the building and into the gaps; above us, below us, a huge sphere intersecting the ground, a dome under the earth and above it. Biba stands awkwardly to one side.

Melz has told us to perform the Lesser Banishing Ritual of the Pentagram, with me, Macha, Rain and Catie each acting as a cardinal point – North, South, East and West, and Melz in the middle with Danny, calling on the Goddess, the Morrigan, for help. Because when you're in strife, the Morrigan is most definitely who you need.

The Morrigan has three aspects – Badb, Nemain and Macha, and all three elements of Her are war goddesses in different ways. Badb the Battle Crow, sent to confuse enemies with her screams on the battlefields; Nemain, the frenzy of war, and Macha, the Sovereign One, the Battle Queen, cursing her enemies, giving favour to her chosen ones. Though I'm Brighid's priestess, I know some of the Morrigan lore, and I want to know more because it's such a big part of who Melz is.

Fortunately this is something we've practised a lot; the Lesser Banishing is something you can do on your own, to protect yourself from external shit, folk attacking you, stealing your power or whatever. On this occasion, we can use it to clear this hateful energy around the building in the hope that it'll help us get Danny out: whatever's binding the stones together wants to keep him here, it wants him to suffer. If we clear the badness, we might find a way to break into the building.

We each draw out the pentagram a little in front of us with energy – forehead, solar plexus, right shoulder, left shoulder, hands to prayer position. We visualise the star in white. Usually we'd do this individually, but Melz told us do it together as four parts of a greater banishing. This energy is too much just for one.

So, next, we each turn to the compass points and draw the banishing pentagrams. One way for invoking, bringing in the energy; one way for banishing it. When I finish tracing the last one in the west, I stamp my feet. There's a feeling of movement, but it's like pushing a very heavy rock off the edge of a cliff. We know we can get it to move, but it's going to take a lot of straining until we get freefall.

"Again!" Melz calls from inside the castle. We draw the banishing pentagrams again. The energy falters a little more.

Now we've banished - twice - we call in the power to our quarter. North for Macha, calling on her namesake who, as well as war, is the fierce protector of the earth; Catie invokes Lugh for the East, the god of Air; I call on Brighid for Fire in the South, and Rain calls on the Welsh goddess Ceridwen for Water in the West. The energetic signatures of the girls' pentagrams flicker in the air in front of them, and we assume the star pose - arms out to the sides, legs apart - and chant the declaration. *Before me, Macha! Behind me, Brighid! On my right, Lugh! On my left, Ceridwen! Around me flame the pentagrams. Within me shines a six-rayed star!* I call it out with as much certainty as I can. I feel the power rising inside the circle we've set. The hate-power is ebbing away, but very, very slowly.

Now for the addition to the usual banishing ceremony. I focus my thoughts on the castle. *Undo, undo, undo. Unmake, unmake, unmake. Freedom.* I imagine the tarot card The Tower, a stone building representing old thought patterns or emotions, being hit by lightning and falling away, exposing what was inside all along. I focus on the image of the castle splitting apart, falling apart stone by stone.

Nothing happens. We continue to hold the space, all concentrating on the building. *Shift one stone, the task begun; open up, our will as one. Shift one stone, the task begun; open up, our will as one* – Catie starts the chant and we take it up around the circle.

I focus back on the unmoveable stone, because matter isn't anything but an event in time. Nothing's eternal. I think about how we're not supposed to think about molecules, matter, physics, in that way, but I always have and that's just the way it is. I read the banned books under mum's bed and they prepared me for a life in magic as much as singing prayers under the full moon ever could.

From inside the castle I hear Melz's voice, singing to Nemain, singing to Badb and Macha, the three sisters, The Morrigan.

From all directions I call you, Morrigan, Queen of Battle, Mover of the Earth.
Cunning raven, bring strength to your priestess. Great Warrior, Mistress of Magic.
Hear me now, breaker of bonds, beserker, screaming banshee. Unmake, unmake, unmake.
Crows circle, ravens call. Unmake, unmake, unmake.
Nemain, Badb, Macha. Buildings shake. Unmake, unmake, unmake.
Crows circle, stone falls. Unmake, unmake, unmake.

We hold the circle. Melz's voice gets louder, and I

feel her power emanating from the building, building momentum, and her voice changes, becomes a shriek. I know Badb is upon her then: she's channelling the banshee, the screamer that terrified Her opponents in war. The shriek starts to shake the building, piercing the air and everything inbetween. Matter is only molecules vibrating at a certain frequency, after all.

The shriek enters the core of me, and the only way I can avoid being dissolved myself is to open my mouth and let loose the same noise, the same scream at the same pitch as Melz. Macha, Rain and Catie do the same, and the scream reaches impossible levels. I know our attunement to the same note absolves us of hurt or pain or broken eardrums, but I also know that anything that isn't with us is against us. Biba drops to her knees with her hands over her ears, but I can't help her. She has to endure this for now.

And when I look inside myself, I can see memories dislodging with the intensity of the scream, with the unmaking power of the Morrigan; and this is why you can't be an effective witch without doing your own healing. Because you're everywhere in the magic; all of you is in the thing you're doing, and that means all your shit's in there with you too. And you can't avoid that power attacking all of your carefully constructed walls. One way or another, it's going to bring the tower down.

My eyes dart to one side: underneath the wailing I sense folk approaching, a movement of feet on the path, hedgerows rustling. *Leave, go,* I try and will them, but I can't make them, they're too close and I need all my focus on dissolving this building, getting Danny and Melz out. *Unmake, unmake, unmake.*

A middle-aged man and a woman break into the clearing, faces dismayed, holding their hands over their ears, and I see blood trickle down the man's cheek. I know them both; they were our neighbours, in the same street as mum's house, but I can't feel any compassion. They took a witch and denied him sunlight or moonlight, denied his Goddess-given right to walk the earth. Worse, they denied him a trial. And these were the villagers that shunned me too, after Zia – in those days between her dying and Melz taking me away.

The woman, Claire Trelawney, a friend of mum's, once, runs up and grips my arm.

"Sadie! What are you doing? Stop it!" she cries, fear rippling her mouth, but I can't stop. None of us can. And she pulls away as if I'm hot to touch, as if I'm made of fire, and maybe I am.

"We're taking Danny, and you can't stop us. And if you know what's good for you, you'll let us go. Don't come after us," I cry, above the noise, above the screaming and the stones grinding against each other in the little keep.

And at that moment, I feel Brighid come fully upon me and stand between me and Rain, Catie and Macha, her nine red braids snaking over her green armour, fine leather plates made of leaf-shapes, and Morrigan's opposite her, black-haired, black-armoured, and her leather armour's made of intersecting feather shapes. And there's another figure, one I didn't expect: wide-shouldered, crowned with antlers, long leather boots and some kind of green and brown clothing that shifts in the sunlight; in one moment, like a cloak of leaves, in another, a flowing green river.

The three gods hold out their hands to each other over the top of the castle, and as they touch, the ground rumbles and shakes, and the castle explodes.

It doesn't touch any of us: the stones and rubble fly through the air and settle around the site of the castle in the shape of a pentagram. No-one's harmed, and Claire

Trelawney and David Boscawen lie unconscious on the grass from the blast of the energy; unharmed, except for the blood from David's burst eardrum. And Melz stands straight-backed at the centre of the ruin, Danny unconscious at her feet, magnificent as the Morrigan herself.

CHAPTER THIRTEEN

The witch heals herself to heal others.

From: Tenets and Sayings of the Greenworld

We're a day outside Tintagel and I know I'm looking forward to getting home. Home's where the heart is, after all, and Melz could take my heart out of my chest and wear it around her neck on a leather strip if she wanted to.

Danny hasn't said much to me or to anyone, mumbling to himself, and both mornings when we woke up I think we were all willing him to be okay, but of course, being a prisoner doesn't work like that. After a while, maybe you start to love the cage and fear what's outside it. These wide moors stretch from horizon to horizon; it isn't the easiest place to be straight after a dank cell, penned in, like a goat waiting for slaughter.

Biba's the only one he'll walk with; I look back several times and they're holding hands, not speaking, but walking slowly, their heads down. Danny always made out that she irritated him; they'd do all that older-brother-younger-sister horsing around, but I knew he adored her.

I didn't have many friends after he left for Tintagel to become a witch. It was usually just him and me, hanging out, getting drunk in the woods, skipping school. I didn't trust anyone much and I knew they all looked at me and knew what I was; they knew I was the ruined girl; they didn't want to be around me in case I ruined them. Danny was an outcast like me. The brown boy in the village. The witch's son.

They were afraid of him, sometimes, but it didn't stop them asking him for help at Samhain; he told me once how villagers that hadn't spoken to him or Biba or Zia all year would come to their house that one day and act like their best friends. *Cross my palm wi' silver my loverrr,* I mean, I knew Zia never said that, that was just Danny trying to make me laugh. *And they don't even wait to see mum. They ask me all kinds of shit when they're waiting to go in. Who's having an affair with their husband. Who hates them in the village. If their infections are gonna get worse, I mean, it's disgusting, Sades.*

So when Danny ran away to Tintagel, I joined Biba's Young Greenworlders group, because I didn't have anything better to do. It was all right; not really my kind of thing, if I'm honest, a bit too political, but I wanted the company. And, maybe, now that Danny was gone, I wanted another reason to be close to Zia. To be able to visit her house, even though I knew she didn't like me or mum. Even though she politely declined every time I asked her anything about witchcraft. Until one day, I turned up with the witch-brand and everything changed.

"I can't believe we made that happen. Broke the walls. That was... dunno. Intense as shit," I'm walking next to Melz but I can still feel the Morrigan energy and it makes her kind of unapproachable, although still as beautiful and desirable and, you know, all the usual things. So I find myself speaking respectfully, as if I was in circle or something.

"You've got such an evocative way with words, Sadie," she says it archly, eyebrow raised without humour. Full warrior goddess: Proceed with caution.

"You know what I mean. Did you know that'd happen?"

She looks back at Danny, following us, mulishly. Her eyes clear a bit and there's more of her in them now.

"No. That was... unexpected," she murmurs.

"It was like... wow. The power. I haven't felt anything like that before,"

"It's the first time the three of us have been in the same place to do magic. Imagine what would happen if Danny was actually conscious," she sighs and looks back at me. "That was his god, Lugh. We honour him in the Greenworld, but you and I know we don't actually see a lot of him. Our work is so much with Brighid and Morrigan we tend to forget about the masculine principle,"

I look back at Danny. "D'you think he's okay?"

Melz looks back over her shoulder.

"I very much doubt it," she says.

"I'm going to talk to him," I resolve. I have to try and be Danny's friend again.

She shrugs.

"All right, but be gentle. He's going to need a lot of healing and therapy when we get home. You don't just get over something like that. Being shut up in a mouldy castle and fed through the wall for months on end. It's inhuman. Not to mention poor Biba. Be gentle. She's lost her mum and Goddess knows what went on before we got there,"

"I know. I'll be kind,"

I stop and wait for the girls to pass me, waiting for Danny and Biba to catch up. Danny barely glances at me, but Biba stares at me aggressively.

"Go away, Sadie. We don't want you," she fires at me.

"I just wanted to see if you're both okay," I say, smiling hopefully. I try and catch Danny's eye but he looks away and stumbles.

"Bloody holes everywhere," he mutters, pushing himself off the uneven ground and shaking out his ankle.

"I'm sorry about Zia," I blurt out. He stares at me, a big long look full of nothing, not nothing like he's forgotten or like he doesn't care but nothing like he's drowning in a well of blackness, and it's almost eaten him up.

"You're sorry," he says it emotionless and flat.

"We don't care if you're sorry!" Biba shouts, and the rest of the girls stop and look around. "Go away! You caused all this! You betrayed us!" Her normally studious, serious face is replaced by the same one I remember when I tried to apologise before; full of hate, full of fire.

"I'm sorry. I didn't know mum was going to do that. To react... the way she did. I would have stopped her if I could,"

"You could have. You were there. You've got eyes. You could see what was going to happen, couldn't you? You can't be that useless," she spits at me; Danny just walks on, head bowed. Useless. Ruined, like he - Roach, my dad - used to say to mum. *All that power in her, and you're letting her just...* Just what? Be a normal girl? Go to school, have friends? *I'll educate her. She's an instrument. You're ruining her, not letting me...* I don't care what you want. *Slap.*

"It happened so quickly. I didn't know she was going to turn up. We were halfway through a ritual, I was concentrating on that. And then even when I did see her it isn't like I could predict she'd..." *Stab a High Priestess of the Greenworld. Kill my mentor, the only person who'd ever helped me start to unravel who I really was.* No, me neither.

"When I find Linda, I'm going to kill her," Danny still isn't looking at me. He's saying it to his boots. "I'm going to make her regret the day she burned mum's cards. That was what started all of this,"

"But it wasn't," I try to explain. "My dad. He was the one that started it. She... she did that because he gave her no choice. He blackmailed her. She was protecting me,"

"She didn't do a very good job, then, did she?" he kicks the long grass.

"Actually, she did," anger ignites in my solar plexus and travels up in a sudden fiery ball to my throat which aches, full of the truth I need to say. "She did what she had to do. She protected me from him. From beatings. Weird shit. Burning the cards – yeah, he told her to do it. But she was scared. She wanted to make sure I never became like him. She was terrified I'd become a witch,"

"That's crap. She knew Roach was bad. She knew mum was good. Witches are good. Everyone knows that," Biba shouts.

"The villagers that watched Danny try to kill her with magic don't know that. They're terrified of him," I argue.

"That was a misunderstanding. They're wrong and they know it," she says, her eyes welling up and it really is the last thing I want to do, upset her, but I have to tell the truth.

"I don't think they do know it, Biba. And if you're

honest, you know what he did was wrong," I say, as calmly as I can, trying to remember Melz's words, *be kind*, but it's hard.

"No. I don't. They tried to convince me, all the time, after he was in that... that place. And I had to say it, I had to repeat it every day. *My brother is evil. Witchcraft is evil.* But I never believed it. They took him away from me. I didn't have anyone," tears fall down her cheeks and my heart breaks for her. "No. Leave me alone. Leave us both alone," She pulls her hand away from his and walks off ahead of us. Danny stares after her and sighs.

"I was upset," he says quietly. He has the grace to look ashamed. "I was out of my head, I'd lost mum. I shouldn't have done it. Biba had to be alone because of me. Because they had an excuse then, to lock me away. I kept escaping at first. She helped me. We almost got away a few times, but they kept finding us, and ... in that place where they put me, I got weaker. I felt... hemmed in there, I couldn't get out. They shut me up there, no light, no air, and ..." His face hardens. "Whatever. I don't know why I'm telling you this, of all people,"

I sigh.

"I'm sorry. Thank the goddess that Melz said we

had to come for you," I watch her her strong shoulders and straight back as she walks; her black hair plaited around her head. He follows my gaze and his bright green eyes search my face.

"You want her," his voice is flat, but he laughs sardonically. "Demelza Hawthorne. Weird loner cowgirl turned seductress,"

"No, I don't," I say, but denying it feels horrible, like a betrayal, even though there's nothing to betray.

"You do. I know you. It's all over your face,"

"So what if I do?" I shrug. "It's none of your business,"

"I thought you liked boys,"

"They're all right. Not the same,"

"Could have fooled me all those times in the woods," he raises his eyebrow, and he must know that makes me feel uncomfortable, thinking about that, but it feels like a lifetime ago.

"Sex's one thing. Love's something else,"

He half-laughs, half-coughs, and has to stop while

he hacks away and tries to catch his breath. His lungs sound heavy with phlegm.

"Love? You love her?"

"Shhhh!" I don't want anyone hearing that, least of all Melz.

"Oh, fucking spare me the coquettish act. You're about as subtle as a falling tree. Believe me, if I know, she knows," he coughs again.

"You all right?" I offer him my water flask but he turns his head away.

"Yeah, I'm fine, can't you tell?"

"Suit yourself,"

He clears his throat and scowls into the distance.

"She's trouble," he nods at Melz. "Lot of anger. You think you could love that?"

"It's nothing to do with you who I can and can't love. She's… she's amazing. It just feels right. That's all," I refrain from trying to explain how my body feels right when I'm with her; that even just standing alongside her, I make sense. Whenever she's there, here's no-one else in the room but her; everyone and everything else's a shadow, a mist of echoing conversation.

"Whatever. You've gone ultra Greenworld then, since you've become a witch. You don't have to be a lesbian, you know. It's not mandatory. Oh, excuse me. Womandatory,"

"Shut up. It isn't like that,"

"That's what it looks like,"

"I don't care what you think it looks like,"

"Whatever. Another good one dead. Well, not a good one. Another one dead,"

I stop, hurt, and he keeps walking, past me, past Macha and Rain and the rest of them, who have stopped, waiting for us. Biba runs back up to him and takes his hand again, throwing me another I-wish-you-were-dead glare. As Danny passes Melz he says something to her but too low for me to hear. She doesn't reply, but stares at him as he walks past, holding Biba's hand, and I see her hands ball into fists at her sides.

"You okay?" she murmurs as I reach her, and strokes my hair away from my face.

"I was trying to make up with him," I hate how pathetic my voice sounds.

"It's too soon," she says, taking my hand. "We have to be patient,"

"But we have to work together – for the portals. How long is it going to take?" I sigh.

"For what? For him to forgive you? I don't know. But he will. He'll always mourn Zia, though," She squeezes my hand. "In the meantime, we have each other. We can do the work without him for a while,"

We have each other. I try not to blush, surprised by her hand in mine, but it's impossible. I look away, pretending to be squinting at the distant trees.

"Okay," I can't think of anything else to say. Why am I always struck dumb around her?

"Good," We walk on in silence. Her hand stays in mine.

CHAPTER FOURTEEN

Blessed be the witch's tools,

Cards and candle, wand and rune,

Sword and knife, crystal true,

Blessed be the witch's tools.

Chant for sanctifying ritual tools from Greenworld Prayers and Songs

"Read my cards," I whisper across to Melz as she shuffles her pack absently, not in preparation to read but to keep her hands busy. I've learnt this about her, that she fidgets, can't keep still, all that nervous energy zinging through her bones like fractures of light.

"Oh, I wasn't..." she looks startled.

"Go on. Read them for me. I could do with some distraction," I grin winningly at her. The other girls and Danny are asleep - or, at least, pretending to be - under blankets around the campfire after the long day's walking. We thought we'd be home in a few days but Danny's so weak it'll take longer.

She shrugs, hands the pack to me and I shuffle

them automatically.

"Cut the pack into three," she says. I separate the cards into three small piles.

"Are you scared?" I ask her, as she takes them from me.

"About what?"

"Danny. Maybe he'll never get back to normal. Maybe we've lost him. A branded one. We need him. Though, to be fair, dunno what for, yet,"

Melz raises her eyebrows disdainfully.

"What will be, will be,"she says, levelly.

"You're such a closed book, you know that?" *Stop hiding from me.*

She blinks, but doesn't reply, laying the cards out in a Celtic Cross pattern on the ground between us. I've studied tarot far less than her - I've spent more time with The Common Herbal propped up on my knees, copying out old correspondences into my herbal notebook, squashing leaves and seeds into pastes and extracting oils.

"A young man has just come back into your life,"

she says, glancing meaningfully over at the Danny's blanketed heap on the other side of the campfire. "He's impetuous and you have mixed feelings about him. See, Knight of Wands, crossed with 7 of Cups. But here, this..."she points to The Hanged Man. "You're not ready to do what you have to do yet."

She points to the card at the top of the cross. "Eight of Swords. You're sad and you won't open up or ask for help, even though you need it. Ah." She turns over the Eight of Wands. "There's a lot of action coming. But here…" She points to the top right hand card. "The King of Swords. And this, underneath it, what you do and don't want. Four of Wands. Reconciliation, that's what I'm getting. With an older man. Cold. Calculating," she looks up at me suddenly, panic in her eyes. "Sadie. Something's wrong. Do you feel it?" she looks around her, peering into the shadows.

"What? No, I…" I'm about to say, *no, it's fine,* when the fire goes out and the trees around us cut their shadow outlines on my eyes.

"Hello, Sadie," he says, and my world darkens, dread thudding hard against the wall of memory I've taken so much trouble to construct.

CHAPTER FIFTEEN

We reject the unchallenged authority of the Father.

From: Tenets and Sayings of the Greenworld

There he is, towering over me like he always did and I'm small again, a kid cowering from her father as his voice barricades me with threats and rules; when the walls bristled with ways to annoy him. Just one word out of place could mean a hit for mum and a cuff or a slap for me, and that cage I thought I'd never be in again is closing around me.

"I'm so glad to find you," he says. I try to forget how his voice is like a snake; how he can make you imagine you're less than nothing if you don't do what he says and think what he thinks. I stand up. I'm not so small now and I'm surprised, even though I can't see that well in the dark, that he isn't as tall as I remembered: he's hunched, paunchy.

The fire crackles back into a shy light and Melz stands next to me, taking my hand instinctively. If you ever want Melz's full attention, put yourself in some sort of perilous situation and *bang!* She'll be there like yesterday.

"What d'you want, Roach?" Melz squeezes my hand and I feel reassurance and strength flowing from her to me in the same way as when she brought me back to Tintagel from Gidleigh, when my spirit was broken. "She's not a child anymore. She's a witch. You can't hurt her anymore. Just leave her alone," Melz is using her magical command voice and I can sense that he's fighting it, but it's hard because she's very strong, especially with the slight shadow of the Morrigan still on her.

But when I reach out to him tentatively with my energy, it's weird because he's so different. He used to be plated in iron, my dad, you could never do anything to hurt him, not even if, like I did once, you tried to stab him with a carving knife. It just bounced off his chest. *I'm better with knives than you are, little girl*, he'd said, *but you could be even better than me, one day.* He was always trying to do weird things with me, stuff that used to frighten me to death. Make me see spirits, make me look into the crystal ball and tell him what I saw. I lied and said I didn't see anything, but I did, oh, I did, and it wasn't pleasant. Crows pecking at dead bodies, eating the red flesh. His body rolling down a hill, burning.

Mum tried to stop him, every time, as she watched me try to pull away from the ghostly forms that stroked my face and invaded my dreams. She cursed him every night I woke up screaming because they haunted me, waiting around corners, trying to possess me. I felt spirit hands on me, unwelcome, flocking to the new flame, the special little girl I was. He'd slap, punch, kick mum for getting involved. *She's special, you don't know what you're doing. I have to train her*, he said.

It wasn't training. The gentle arts of magic and herbs that I've learnt from Zia and Lowenna, even the fire priestessing, that's a world away from the crazy shit he tried to get me to do.

"I wanted to see you," his voice cracks; bow, he's an old man, suddenly. Weak, but it must be a trick. He uses everything to get what he wants.

"I don't want to see you. You promised. Never again," I stammer. The last time we saw him, he'd bribed me and mum: it was the only way we could finally get rid of him. Spy on Zia Prentice, sow the seeds of discord in the village, make trouble, and he'd leave us alone for good. And we did it, we were that desperate. I got hold of her tarot cards and mum burned them. Zia's magical tools, one of the things that made her powerful.

He looks at me thoughtfully for a moment.

"You have it now? The witch-brand?"

"None of your business," I glower at him, but he nods.

"Yeah. You do, I can tell. I can see its power in you. I'm glad," he says, but I get the feeling that whatever it is about the witch-brand that makes him happy, it's some nefarious reason of his own and not some newfound daddy caring he's earthed up in his worm-infested heart.

Mum was so scared I'd end up screwed up and twisted like dad - Roach, I can't call him dad, he was never a dad to me - that she freaked when anything remotely witchy came into our house, Danny included. And for me - I went along with the plan; what else could I do? But at the heart of it all I wondered. *What if I'm a witch really, like him, because I can feel something in me, I know I'm not like the other kids.* There were embers of the fire of magick in me from day one. It was always going to happen. Maybe mum knew that.

But in the end it was mum that stabbed Zia, her oldest friend. Fear for your children makes you do really crazy shit. She must've thought it was Zia now, abusing me, keeping me in a weird magical chokehold when in fact she was the one that set me free. It was Zia that made me know my own power and taught me how to protect myself. It was Zia that had started teaching me what power I had and how to use it.

"Sadie. It's... I'm... I'm different now. You have to believe me," Roach says, and he holds out his hand for me to take. I stand there looking at it like it's an exhibit from the Greenworld Archive.

At our feet, Melz's scattered tarot cards - I see Death, The Devil, Five of Pentacles, The Hanged Man - turn over and flutter in the night breeze. I look back at his outstretched hand and the shadows that move on it like snakes, and I keep my hands by my sides.

"I don't have to believe anything you say ever again!" I shout at him, and he steps backwards. I'm not seven. I'm not motionless in fear. His clothes hang on him like a scarecrow where once he was a ball of muscle, buzz-cut hair and rippling with a fervent, humourless obsession. I lunge at him and push him hard, and he falls over right next to the bonfire which leaps as if in victory. I can feel its euphoria in my blood, fire to fire.

I might be the ruined girl; I might always be, but I'm a witch now too.

"Shut up. Leave me alone. Leave all of us alone. Come any closer and I'll burn you," I lean in close to his face, seeing his scars. Melz told me what happened to him in the portal but I saw it happen years ago, in the crystal ball. Life's only just caught up. "Don't think I can't do it, or I won't, because I will, believe me," I hiss, right in his face.

The rest of the witches, awake now, gather warily behind Melz, and Danny comes forward and takes my other hand, and I look up at him in surprise.

"You heard her, Roach. Get out of here," he says, his voice still unsteady, still so thin, but still with power. Roach smiles.

"The second generation," he coughs and spits blood into the fire. "There's an offering for your Goddess. She's taking me, little by little," he strokes his cheek where the flesh's ruined, in white rivulets as if it's soft wax, and I look away, repulsed. "Fire and healing. That's yours, isn't it, Sadie? I tried to get you to work with the spirits of Fire, but you never wanted to. Strength, vision, that's him," he nods at Danny. "Same as me. And Demelza. She's the darkness. The unfathomable depths,"

He gets up painfully; I want to attack him, kick

him, pound his head into the stones around the bonfire, but I know I don't have to, because I have Danny and Melz and the power in the three of us. And I can hear their voices in my head saying *this is yesterday, this has passed. We are the now, we have the power of the moment. He's a shadow.*

Roach backs away from us, from the shining power of our interlinked hands and into the shadow of the forest.

"If you change your mind, Danny, come and find me," he calls back to us. "It's not too late to find the power that awaits you,"

Danny says nothing, watching Roach walk away through the trees, his expression unreadable. And I can feel an ambivalence in him, under the sorrow. A curiosity, and that frightens me. Because I know where Roach's magic leads, and it's not anywhere Danny wants to go.

When Roach is totally gone, Danny lets go of my hand. Without saying anything, he goes back to his sleeping bag and pulls it over his head. Melz hugs me.

"You okay?" her arms are strong around me.

"Yeah. Really, I'm all right," I hug her back. And I am okay. I'm strong. We're strong together. But Danny turns away from us, his back to the fire, and stays facing away until the morning.

*

When we get back with Danny and Biba we take them straight to Merryn's house for healing. They collapse on her sofa, a saggy three seater with a faded rose design. I'm amazed Danny made it at all, to be honest: he was so weak, and though Biba's presumably been living fairly normally, she's still small for her age, undernourished and obviously traumatised.

"What on earth?" Merryn follows us into her front room, drying her hands on a tea towel. "Where have you been? Your mum's been going mad with worry," she puts her hand on Danny's forehead. "Feverish. By Brighid, he's in a bad way,"

"Hello, Merryn," he smiles at her weakly. "Long time no see,"

"Still the same Danny Prentice," she kisses him on the forehead. "Good to have you back, anyway,"

"Don't ask. Well, do ask," Melz drapes a nearby blanket over Biba. "But later. We did what we could on the road but they need some intensive energy healing as well as nutrition. Danny's been imprisoned inside a cold, wet stone place for months with no windows and the most basic of food. He's really not good,"

"I can see for myself, my lover," Merryn kneels down next to Danny, scanning him with her hands above his body; he closes his eyes, detached from everything. "Bloody hell," she mutters and draws healing symbols straight into Danny's solar plexus, holding her hands there. She looks Biba over without moving her hands away from Danny. "And this one?"

"Grieving. Underfed. I don't know otherwise," I say, avoiding Biba's stare.

Merryn nods, both hands staying on Danny.

"Rain. Get the little girl a blanket and some food. You can stay and give me a hand,"

"I'm not a little girl," Biba objects, but not too harshly. Merryn smiles gently.

"Of course, sweetheart. Go with Rain, go and get something to eat. Then it's bed,"

"But it's daytime!" Biba protests. "I don't want to leave Danny,"

"He's safe with me, poppet. You need your sleep. Go on, now," she smiles kindly, and Biba follows Rain to the kitchen at the back of the house.

Merryn gives Melz an uneasy look.

"You shouldn't have taken the trainees, Melz. Lowenna's not happy,"

"I can't help that. Danny was in trouble and she wouldn't do anything about it,"

"She'll have had her reasons," Merryn says, her eyes flickering to me.

"He's not a danger to Sadie. He's just grieving and ill and weak. We can build him up again, given time. And we couldn't leave Biba there, either," Melz argues. Merryn raises one eyebrow.

"I hope you're right, my lover," she mutters.

"Just look after them, okay? I'll be back later,"

"You're welcome, by the way,"

Melz goes back and kisses Merryn on the cheek.

"Thanks, Merryn," she closes her eyes, and for a moment, something shadowy crosses her face. Maybe it's tiredness. "Come on, girls," she says. We let ourselves out and me, Melz, Macha and Catie walk along the street to her mother's house.

"This'll be interesting," she says grimly as we walk down the path to the front door, painted with the symbols of the covenstead: the triskele, the triple moon, the pentagram, and the Five Hands, the symbol of Tintagel: five hands holding the village within them.

The witch of the community always keeps a welcome for travellers, so they say, but that's just another saying that can be revoked as easily as a witch's measure can be destroyed.

CHAPTER SIXTEEN

God and Goddess, sun and moon,

Rising sap and witches' rune,

Join as lovers, dark and bright,

Celebrate this Beltane night.

Chant for Beltane, from Greenworld Prayers and Songs

"Where the bloody hell've you been? You can't just disappear like that. It's almost Beltane!" Lowenna roars at Melz as soon as she gets into the kitchen; the rest of us file in after her, heads bowed. "Sit down. All of you," she orders and we slide into the chairs around the large wooden covenstead meeting table with the carved pentagram in the middle; Macha with downcast eyes, Catie and me watchful, and Melz, poised.

"Before you say anything, mum, I know you told me not to go. But I had to. They would have left him to rot there. He was stuck inside some horrible mouldy castle thing they've got there. It was medieval. They can't treat a witch like that. By Brighid! They shouldn't be treating anyone like that," she holds her hands palm-forward to

Lowenna in an unconscious protection gesture but her mum slaps Melz's left hand.

"I told you. I told you not to go and you disobeyed me! And you took all this lot with you!" she shouts, but Melz stands up and faces her mother. When you see them together you see how alike they are; the same profile, same eyes, but it's more subtle than that too: the same regal bearing, the same absolute lack of respect for differing points of view.

"We brought Danny back. He should be with the coven," Melz argues. "And poor Biba. What was I supposed to do? Leave a thirteen year old girl to fend for herself, in a village that probably hates her? I don't think so,"

"Where is he, then?" Lowenna yells, still furious. "I notice he didn't come and face me himself. After all I've done for him!" she glares at all of us, apparently ignoring the fact that she really hasn't done anything for Danny for quite a long time.

"He's very ill. He's with Merryn. It's going to be a while until he's back to normal," Melz replies, calmly.

"He'll heal in due course. And the villagers would

have dealt with him in their own time. The point is that you should never, on any account, disobey me! Ever!" Lowenna shouts.

"So - what? You're just going to let them carry on? You would have let them punish Danny? He didn't know what he was doing when he attacked Sadie. He was mad with grief. And anyway, if he's going to be punished for trying to kill Linda," Melz's eyes flicker to me "Then we should be the ones to do it. Our way. If we're going to leave Gidleigh in such an uncertain state, then…,"

"I will deal with Gidleigh in my own time, Demelza! And how dare you question my authority in front of the trainees!" Lowenna thunders, interrupting.

"But you haven't told us what you are going to do about Gidleigh! Sure, we've done magic, but none of it's worked as far as I can see. There's no point working magically if you're not doing all you can to make that thing happen in the material realm, too. You told us that over and over again, mum," Melz stands there, hands on hips. I wonder what Lowenna can say to that, because it's true. I would have expected her to at least visit Gidleigh since Zia's funeral. But she's done nothing.

"It's not that simple," Lowenna insists, doggedly.

"You don't understand what it's like, being the Head Witch of the Greenworld. I can't be seen to negotiate with those villagers. And maybe I did want to storm in there and rescue Danny, yes, and Biba too, but I can't act without the permission of all the covensteads. That's the way we wrote the Constitution. Which, by the way, you've just disobeyed," she says.

"Well, I'm sorry. But I wasn't going to let them rot because of some bureaucratic Greenworld regulations," Melz flares back. "Brighid protects Her own. She wouldn't want a Priest of Lugh to be kept away from his magical duties and neither should you. And…" She breaks off and looks slightly unsure.

"What?"

"And, any High Priestess that puts box-ticking before someone's life and sanity isn't much of a High Priestess at all," Melz finishes.

Lowenna stares at her daughter for a long moment. Her favourite. Saba knew it, which was why she left. Lowenna chose me over her, but she might not have chosen me over Melz.

"I see," she says, narrowing her eyes. "Well,

Demelza. Don't think you can step into my shoes so easily. Because that box-ticking, as you call it, is what keeps the Greenworld together. Unity of purpose, togetherness, unilateral consent. That's what I manage, every day and every night. You think you could do a better job? You're seventeen years old. I guarantee you'd last a week,"

"I don't think I could do any worse sometimes," Melz snaps back and I can tell she didn't mean to say it because she immediately looks at her feet.

Lowenna smiles coldly.

"Thank you. What a lovely sentiment to hear coming out of your daughter's mouth."

"Mum, I'm sorry. That was - "

"Unnecessary and hurtful. Yes, it was. Girls, you're dismissed," she says to us. "Up to your rooms, please. Meditate on your actions for the rest of the day and I'll deal with you all tomorrow. Demelza, stay where you are,"

I reach over and press the back of Melz's hand with my fingertips as I get up, and follow Rain, Catie and Macha out of the kitchen.

They start shouting as I shut the door behind me,

and it doesn't stop for over an hour. Finally, I hear the doors to the garden bang against the wall of the house. I look out of my bedroom window and watch Melz as she stalks out through the garden and out of the flaking wooden door in the stone wall. She doesn't look defeated. She looks furious.

CHAPTER SEVENTEEN

Honour your Mother above all.

From: Tenets and Sayings of the Greenworld

Everything's gone quiet in the week since Danny and Biba came home. They've been at Merryn's the whole time, having intensive daily healing, eating and sleeping. Lowenna's been stomping around giving Melz the cold shoulder, and the rest of us have been keeping our heads down. As punishment, me, Melz, Rain, Macha and Catie have been off witch duties for a week, and that included Beltane. Lowenna made us sit with the villagers and watch the ceremony; we weren't allowed to jump the fire, or to drink any mead or have any fun at all, either. It was shit.

Instead of witch things, I've been on gardening duty with Melz and Catie; it's dinnertime when we get back from the greenhouses with mud all over our boots. Funny how quick I've forgotten the mud; as a witch, there's less of it than in the life of a normal village girl.

As we open the door of Lowenna's house, Danny pushes past us, tears streaming down his face.

"Danny! You're up…?" Melz reaches out for his

arm as we pass but it's all too quick and he pulls away, breaking into a run when he gets to the pathway at the end of the front garden. "Danny!" she shouts after him, but he's gone.

"By Brighid! What on earth?" she frowns at me.

"I didn't know he was up and about yet," Catie says, kicking her shoes off in the hall.

"S'pose he is, then," I peer up the road and watch him limp-run around the corner. "Don't think he should be running, though,"

We walk into the kitchen and Biba's sitting at the kitchen table next to a man that looks familiar, even though I can't place him for a minute. Dark brown skin, straight grey-black hair that needs a cut, grey-black stubbly beard. Deep shadows under his eyes, gaunt cheeks. A frayed and dirtied Envirowarrior uniform hangs on his thin frame, not that I've seen one for a long time, but I remember. I remember a gang of the dads leaving Gidleigh when I was about ten, being all hopeful and full of purpose, in the green-and-brown outfits mum had helped make out of jute and hemp, nice and strong against the elements. Stout brown leather boots that strapped all the way up the leg. This man's boots are scuffed and black with grime, and one of them's missing the whole toe area, showing his bare foot underneath which is just as grimy. His left leg's bandaged with dirty rags.

Lowenna motions to us to sit down.

"Girls. This is Sanj Nayar. Danny's dad. He's just back from the war."

"Welcome home," Melz shakes his hand; I nod, because I remember him now. He left long before that day when ten-year-old me watched the Enviros leave in their new uniforms, but I remember him anyway.

"Hello," I say shyly to Sanj. "I'm… I was a friend of Danny's,"

His tired eyes take me in blankly.

"I don't remember you, sorry. It's been a long time," his voice is quiet: a strange mix of soft Cornish with an overlay of something else. "You were just children then. He's… he's changed so much," he looks down at his hands and I realise that two fingers on his left hand are missing. "He grew up, and I missed it," he hugs Biba, who's sitting next to him and looking bewildered, but she doesn't pull away. "And this one, she was just a baby, really. Now look at her," he rests his chin on her head uncomfortably for a second and then moves away; she might be his daughter but really he's just hugging a strange child.

"You went of your own accord," Melz snaps, and Lowenna gives her a look. "No, mum. He went chasing glory like the rest of them. The Greenworld wasn't enough for them,"

"The Envirowarriors provided an essential resistance against the war. The Greenworld opted out of conflict, yes, but we also allow our citizens the right to express themselves and follow their hearts," Lowenna corrects her daughter but I know a tired party line when I hear one. None of the witches wanted them to go. Mum told me. They didn't like it that not everyone wanted to stay and live off the land in peace when the world beyond the border was in turmoil. Some people couldn't ignore the war. And Melz's dad was one of those, too. He left her and Saba. They were four years old. Only, her dad hasn't come back.

"They should have stayed at home and looked after us," Melz mutters and looks away for a moment, then back at Sanj. "So Danny wasn't pleased to see you, I take it?"

"No," he whispers.

Lowenna gets up and sits beside the broken man, even though he stinks. She gives him her half-full cup of tea and nods to me.

"Sadie. Get some casserole from the pot, would you? It's still warm," I get up and ladle some into a brown ceramic bowl and bring it to the table.

"Thanks," he picks up the bowl without waiting for a spoon and pours it into his mouth. We watch as casserole leaks around his chin and onto his beard. He slurps it down and we look away politely.

"The war's over," Lowenna turns to us. "The soldiers are being sent home. There's no fuel left in Russia,"

"Nothing?" Catie asks, wide-eyed.

"Nope. We knew it would happen one day."

"Goddess. What does this mean for the Redworld?" Catie looks worried. She's from there, so I suppose it's more natural that's her first thought; I don't personally give a bloodstained knicker elastic for the suffering of the Redworlders, but there you go.

"Things'll get worse, again. Over the border, most of the forests have been cut down. Most of the shale fracked already, what there was, and that's destroyed the water sources in most places. More and more earthquakes. That'll affect us too, in time," Lowenna sighs deeply. "And the refugees. Word's spreading fast in the Redworld. That we have food. That we have order," she shakes her head. "Though we won't do for much longer with so many people coming in. I suspect it's the Redworld guards. They don't want the poor; they're probably waving them through. They're not going to want an influx of maimed soldiers, either. Their soldiers as well as the Enviros are likely to end up here. More mouths to feed,"

"Then we'll feed them. We can't turn them away," Melz interjects.

"I'm not saying we should turn them away, Demelza. But it's going to get harder to keep the Greenworld on an even keel," Lowenna gives her daughter a tired smile. "We didn't factor in mass migration when we created all this," she gestures around her: the glass roof, the trailing plants, the open hearth, but she means the Greenworld. An idea as well as a place.

"But it was always supposed to be a haven. A

green utopia. Now it just has to be a home for more people than we expected. That's all," Melz counters.

"It's a lot more complicated than you make it sound," Lowenna snaps. "You're young. Everything's black and white to you. When you get to my age, all you see is grey. Believe me, nothing's straightforward. Much as we might wish it to be," she turns to Sanj, who drains Lowenna's teacup in one go and wipes his mouth on his sleeve.

"Sadie, would you?" she takes the empty crockery from him and gives it to me. I refill the bowl with casserole and pour another cup of the slightly bitter tea from the stained rose-painted pottery teapot, setting them both in front of Danny's dad.

How must Danny have felt, seeing him after all this time? After probably thinking he was dead? I try and imagine, but all I can think of is that I wish my dad had gone off to war and not come back. Died a hero's death, maybe. Maybe then I could forgive him.

"So you went to Gidleigh first?" Lowenna probes as Sanj drains the second cup of tea.

"Yeah. Got the feeling I wasn't welcome. Not that

I ever was,"

"So you know about Zia?"

He stops eating and nods slowly but without expression.

"Yeah."

"I'm so sorry," Lowenna's voice cracks. "It was so sudden. I… I didn't see it coming. I'm sorry," she looks down, avoiding his stare. He regards the top of her greying yellow-haired curly hair for a long moment.

"Not your fault," he says flatly and looks at me. If he's been to Gidleigh he must know what happened. "Linda Morgan. She and Zia never got on. There was always bad blood."

Lowenna catches my eye and I know what she's thinking. That Sanj doesn't know I'm Linda's daughter. She's wondering whether to say anything.

"I saw it happen," I say, quietly. "She's my mother. Linda. She saw Zia and I doing magic. It all happened so quickly. I couldn't stop it," I turn around, gripping a tea towel in my hands. "I'm sorry,"

He stares at me blankly then starts eating again,

clearing the bowl quickly.

"I've seen too much death. Zia feels like a lifetime ago," he shuts his eyes. "I just want to sleep,"

Lowenna gets up and goes over to her medicine cabinet.

"Melz. Start boiling water for a bath for Sanj. Sadie, help me with this," she starts pulling out her glass jars, going for the sedatives. "Just relax, Sanj" she calls over to him. "We'll look after you now,"

He stretches his arms out on the table and lays his head on them, saying nothing, and Biba sits next to him, staring furiously at the back of his head; I can't tell if she's angry or glad he's here. Maybe she doesn't know either.

CHAPTER EIGHTEEN

*...and this solitude surrounds me
as something vast and unbounded,
when my feeling, standing on the hills
of my breasts, cries out for wings
or for an end.*

From: Girl's Lament, R M Rilke

We find him down on the beach, sitting on top of the rocks, his legs steepled like a spider's. The huge boulders underneath him must have been there for thousands of years.

"Danny!" Melz calls down to him from the path above, the one from the village down to the beach, but he ignores her. "Danny! Come up. Let's talk!" she shouts, but the wind carries her voice away, over the choppy green sea. He turns his head away.

"Danny Prentice," Melz mutters darkly. "Goddess, he's always such a pain in the arse," Her earlier compassion for him seems to have left her.

"I'll go. Stay down here," I say, and start climbing down the slippery rocks.

"Sadie! Don't…" Melz cries after me but it's too

late, I'm like a goat, I can climb anything. "Be careful!" I wave one hand back at her.

"I'm fine!" I call back. Because he's my friend; he always was. This is up to me.

"Go away," Danny calls when I'm a few metres away from him. He doesn't look like he wants to move anytime soon, the stubborn little bastard. You can't get Danny to do anything he doesn't want to. Only, I could, sometimes. Once.

I sit down cautiously next to him.

"Nice evening," I venture; my hair blowing in the savage wind.

"Bugger off, Sades. I don't want to talk to you. Seriously,"

"Charming,"

"Charming as I'm ever going to be. Go home," his eyes are turned to the sea.

"I can't go home," I hug my knees; I can at least keep him talking and he might warm up to me a bit.

"You know what I mean. Lowenna's," he says.

"That's not home for either of us," I try to catch his eye but he avoids it.

"It is for you. Well and truly in the heart of the covenstead now, aren't you? Cosy in the nest," there's a sneer in his voice but I don't respond to it.

"You know you're welcome too. You trained there. That's where you became a witch," I say, levelly.

"Lot of good it did me," he picks a pebble out of a smooth recess in the boulder.

"Stop feeling sorry for yourself. Anyway, shouldn't you be back there, spending time with your dad? You haven't seen him in, what? Ten years? Don't you have stuff you want to say to him?"

"Do you have stuff you want to say to Roach? Nice chat brewing, is it? A few hugs, show him all the cards you made him at school that you never got to give him? Eostre, Midsummer, Yule. *I miss you, Daddy; blessings of the season*," his tone's hard and hurtful but I try not to let it show.

"It's different and you know it. Sanj never hurt you," I watch him turn the pebble in his long fingers.

"How do you know? Of course he did. He abandoned me and Beebs. He thinks he can walk straight back in and pick up where he left off like nothing happened. What a prick. He can sod off,"

"You don't mean that. He's your dad,"I say, softly.

"No he isn't. Omar's the closest thing I've got to a dad," he picks up a larger pebble from the pile and tosses it into the approaching tide below.

"Your real dad, then. Omar's great, but…"

"But what? Biology doesn't mean shit. Ten years is too long,"

"It doesn't have to be. You've lost your mum; don't you think…"

"What? Don't I think what? That he can just step in and replace her? Go to hell, Sadie. That's never going to happen." He looks out at the grey-blue waves pushing inwards, the tide coming in. "I hate him," he says, his voice quieter.

Melz hovers on the pathway above us, looking down anxiously, but she knows this is up to me.

"You don't hate him. Not really,"I try to take his

hand but he glares at me and pulls it away.

"Don't tell me what I feel. You'll be saying I don't hate you next. Your witchy perception skills leave quite a lot to be desired," he snaps.

"You hate me."

"Yup,"

"I don't think you do."

He sighs.

"Don't be thick, Sadie. You got mum killed. Yes. I hate you," he refuses to look me in the eye, though.

"That wasn't my fault! You know it wasn't. Don't let's go over all that again,"

"Stop telling me what I know and what I feel. I know what I know and I KNOW it WAS your fault," I pull back as if he'd slapped me. "Yeah. You little slut. Was it really worth it, conning me, pretending you wanted me? Even going to the trouble of sleeping with me once or twice? That must have been an effort, since you're into girls," he glares at Melz on the path, her face a white mask of anxiety in the dusk. "Don't mind me. Lovergirl's waiting for you,"

"I'm not leaving you here like this," I feel responsible for Danny. I can't leave him here alone.

"Fuck off and leave me alone," he snaps, throwing another large pebble.

"Come on. Come back with me. Talk to Sanj. He wants to see you,"

"Have you heard anything I've said? Make it up with Roach if you're so bothered about dads. Slut,"

"Don't call me a slut again," I feel the fire of Brighid rising up inside me. I understand that he's upset, but I haven't done anything wrong and I know he knows that. And he's jealous. Jealous of Melz and me.

"I told you. Don't tell me what to do!" he stands up and I do too, defensively, because there's anger in his green eyes and he's unpredictable, and I don't trust him anymore like I used to. He pushes me away and I fall back onto the rock, holding out my arm to support myself. I slip, banging my knee.

"Leave me alone. I told you!" he shouts; Melz's climbing down to us now, fast, slipping dangerously.

"Take it back!" I raise my voice. I tried to make

friends, but no-one calls me a slut.

"Go away. Fuck off back to your woman. Whatever. I don't care,"

"TAKE IT BACK! NO-ONE CALLS ME A SLUT!" I scream at him then, and he looks briefly surprised, maybe he didn't think I had that much rage in me, but I'm sick of being blamed for Zia's death when all I did was try and be a witch. But his look darkens again as Melz gets to us and takes my hand.

"Are you all right?" she asks protectively, and I nod; I know the balance of power is firmly back on my side with her here. Goddess knows I never want to be the recipient of the expression of pure black fury she lashes Danny with.

"You need to go away and calm down. I think we've all had quite enough of this *poor me* act," she snaps. "Do you think you're the only one with shit to deal with? Do you think you're the only one that feels grief and regret and abandonment? All of us have lost parents. You've got no idea what Sadie's going through. Your dad's alive and in one piece and he wants to see you. I suggest you go home, put your ego aside and talk to him."

"Leave it, Melz. I'm not in the mood for a lecture," he mumbles, and turns away.

"Nah. I've had enough of this. Sitting alone on the rocks like a princess. *Oh, save me, feel sorry for me, my mummy died*," - even I'm surprised at that part which's uncharacteristically harsh, even for Melz; she must be REALLY pissed off.

"Grow up. Deal with it. And don't you ever. EVER. Call. Sadie. A. Slut. Again," and with these last words she grabs him by the shoulder, turns him around and stabs his chest with her finger, emphasising each word. "Apologise,"

"No," he turns away again.

"APOLOGISE!" she screams at his back, and three crows plummet down from nowhere, screeching straight into his face. Instinctively he crouches down and holds his arms over his head and they fly over his head.

"All right! I'm sorry! I'm sorry!" he cries out, and she nods grimly.

"That's better," she says, and turns to me. "Come on. Let's go,"

Blood runs down his cheek; a scratch runs from his nose to his ear. A crow's beak's scratch.

"Melz, he's hurt," I go to him, but she holds my hand firm.

"Leave him. He'll be fine," she says. "We're going home,"

She leads me up on the rocks carefully. At the top, my boot slips on some moss and I look down: he's still crouching, his hand to his cheek, and I know he's crying.

"Danny? Please come with us," I call and hold out my hand, but he turns his back.

"It's his choice," Melz mutters grimly. "If he wants to be a prima donna, let him. We shouldn't have bothered going after him,"

"I care about him," I say, and a look passes over her face that for just one second looks a lot like jealousy.

"You shouldn't," she mutters. Then the mask falls back down and she says nothing more, and we walk back to the house, shivering, and some of me's in shock and some of me's stressed and some of me's shamefully, brightly exhilarated at the memory of Melz screaming at

Danny, making him apologise for the outrage of calling me a slut.

When you have Demelza Hawthorne in your corner, nobody gets to insult you twice.

CHAPTER NINETEEN

The Greenworld is comprised of thirteen regional covensteads, all of which have their own witch. Each regional witch reports to and accepts governance by The Head Witch of the Greenworld, who holds executive power.

From: Greenworld Governance: Rules for Utopia

It's two days later and Danny hasn't come home. Lowenna, sitting at the big wooden kitchen table, looks up from a letter that's just been delivered. It's unusual; witches in the covensteads usually either wait for a covenstead meeting to communicate, or communicate psychically if they're able to. Bush telegraph, Lowenna calls it. She could do it with Zia: they were both strong senders and receivers.

This letter came by messenger from Zennor. All I really know about Zennor is that we used to have to listen to the radio programme from there at school - *Bull's Greenworld Gardener's Guide*, which was so utterly boring that Danny and I would frequently either pretend to be ill to avoid the long school afternoon listening to the broad oooh-arrr of the presenter, Bull (I mean, what sort of name was that anyway?) or just not even turn up to school in the first place.

We spent many afternoons in the woods on *Greenworld Gardener* day. We'd take black market Redworld booze and occasionally other things that could be relied on to heighten the senses and alleviate the incredibly muddy-minded tedium of the Greenworld. Having Omar going back and forth into the Redworld meant Danny could always find substances of dubious origin around their house. Now that I'm a witch, life's far less tediously boring, but I miss the days when Danny was my friend and before everything got so complicated. I kind of miss the boredom.

"Bad news?" Melz asks her mum; there's a cautious tone in her voice, presumably because Lowenna's staring at the pulpy Greenworld paper with a look bordering on horror (and I'm not even being dramatic here).

"Read it for your bloody self," Lowenna crumples up the letter, throws it at Melz and stalks out. I pick it off the floor and smooth it out.

"What was that all about?" Melz holds out her hand and I pass it to her without really reading it first: my eyes skim over spiky ink handwriting: beetroot dye, it has this pinkish-brown colour on the paper. Quite pretty really, although you could say that it does bear a passing resemblance to dried blood.

"Blessed Brighid," Melz breathes as she reads down. "Now Zennor's opted out of witch rule,"

"What?!"

She hands it to me so I can read it in all its politically independent glory. A letter from the newly elected community ruling panel in Zennor, signed by them all: five ordinary men and women, no witches. There's been a coup. The witch in charge there, Bella - I don't know her, but I've never met any of the witches outside Tintagel - has been, the letter says, "deposed".

"What does that mean, deposed? Knocked her off?"

"I bloody hope not," Melz starts pacing up and down.

"That sewing-the-Greenworld-together thing's not really going so well, eh?" I say.

"Not really," she makes a clicking noise with her tongue, thoughtfully. "They've followed suit. I told her this would happen. One village does it, then it's just a matter of time until another one does. With all the refugees, and the gang's attack on Tintagel last year, they don't believe in witch rule anymore,"

"Don't blame them, really," I sigh.

"No. Me neither," she puts the letter down on the table and looks calculatingly at the kitchen door, following Lowenna's wake. "I don't think she's going to do anything to stop it, either. Or, I don't think she can. I think…" she goes to the door and closes it quietly, then comes back to stand next to me. "I think we need to do something," she whispers, and my whole body thrills to the feeling of her breath in my face.

"What?"

"Go over her head. Go to the Redworld, even. I don't know," she's giving me her intense stare, which some folk would find offputting - bordering on psychotic, maybe - but to me it's all part of her gothic allure.

"What?"

"I've been thinking about it for a while now. We have to do something differently. Otherwise I can see this going very, very wrong,"

When we got back from Gidleigh with Danny and Biba, and Melz questioned Lowenna's authority, it crossed my mind: *What happens if the coven disagrees radically about something, and one side refuses to back down?* I didn't know the answer then and I don't now.

Melz takes my hand and looks imploringly at me.

"Sadie. Listen. I know you don't agree with the stance she's taking with everything. Head in the sand, pretending it's all going to disappear as soon as she can train you all up and dispatch you to all the rebellious villages so you can put them straight. We both know that's not going to work,"

"No, I know. But…,"I trail off. I don't have any clear point to make, except I'm cautious of where this conversation might lead.

Melz presses her lips together nervously.

"Everything's different now. The war's over. The refugees. The earthquakes. Things are at crisis point in the Redworld, Sadie. We don't have the luxury of being able to ignore them anymore. We can't pretend we're separate. We're not - what happens there affects us. But I think we have to be the ones that extend the olive branch. Only we know about the portals and what they can do,"

"But we don't know all of what they can do," I reply.

She lets go of my hand; I regret being negative immediately.

"I know. So we need to try and find out," she paces the stone flagged kitchen floor in her wool socks.

"But we don't have Danny," I say, worried for him. Two days, he could be anywhere. He could be dead.

"Okay, so we try without him. Come on, Sadie. Aren't you at all curious? Don't you want to find out what Ki'putska meant? About the three of us? The other communities around the world?"

"Of course I do," I watch her pacing, my heart beating in my ears. "But we'd be betraying Lowenna. She told

"Now we're back, we need to find a time to go up to the portal. The girls'll hold the circle and we'll go through again. Just like we agreed. See if we can get back there, together,"

Together. The magic word. She smiles wickedly at

me and all the angels sing, all the trumpets trumpet, all the spirits dance in their spiritish way.

"All right," I hear myself say the words, devil-may-care. *Together* with Melz? Impossible to resist.

"Okay. Let's talk more later. After esbat," She grins that wild grin again and it lights me up inside, every chakra point, ping ping ping. Rainbowwwws. "The future's in our hands, Sadie. Don't you feel it? Something's coming. Something big,"

She holds out her hand for mine again, and I take it, grinning up at her like a fool, which I am. Damn right I feel it. I don't know about the future of the Greenworld, but in moments like these I let myself imagine a future with Melz. A future where her hand, her gaze, her touch is on me. I shiver.

I never knew that the future could be so full of magic.

CHAPTER TWENTY

Mistress of Magic, hear my call:

You who are one, who are many, who are all –

Give me wisdom, give me sight,

Lend me your vision in the sharp moonlight.

Scrying chant, from The Book of the Morrigan, Greenworld Prayers and Songs

"Where's Danny? Still not back?" Lowenna barks. "He didn't say anything to me about missing tonight," She frowns as all the girls trail in and take their spaces in the community hall; it's raining again and not even Lowenna makes us go up to Tintagel Head when it's torrential.

Melz and I exchange glances. We haven't told anyone about what happened on the beach. I thought he was off somewhere sulking, but he longer it goes on, the more worry starts to creep into my mind. The girls are unforthcoming. No-one else has seen him. Melz sighs.

"Bloody Danny Prentice. He's a complete liability. I suppose we were the last to see him, then. Me and Sadie went to the beach and we saw him there. He had quite the attitude. I had to make him apologise to Sadie for insulting her,"

Demi raises an eyebrow.

"Isn't she lucky to have such a protective girlfriend," I hear her murmur to Rain, who stifles a giggle.

Melz glares at her and Demi returns it, unblinking, but shuts up at least.

"Attitude about what?" Lowenna asks, her tone icy.

"Sanj, I think. He wasn't happy about him being back,"

"And?"

"And, Sadie tried to talk to him about it, he insulted her, I made him apologise, and we left him on the beach,"

"Shouldn't we go and look for him? He might've had an accident. Could he have drowned?" I start to panic. Danny might be a dick sometimes but I've known him my whole life. I don't want him to die.

"He's alive," Lowenna sets out the altar at the north end of the circle. "I'd know if he wasn't. But he might still be in danger. It tends to follow that boy," she comes back to the outside of the circle and looks at all of us beadily in that way she has of making us all feel horrendously guilty even if we haven't done anything. "As if I haven't got enough to worry about without teenage boys disappearing," she mutters.

Melz and I haven't mentioned the letter from Zennor to the others, and Lowenna hasn't, either. Suddenly I wonder if she will at all. It isn't really in her interests to share something like that with the wider community of Tintagel - and even though these girls are witches in training, I wouldn't trust most of them with a secret. They'd blab as soon as they got out of the circle. *Ooooh, you'll never guess, Zennor's gone independent! NO witches! Can you believe it*, etc etc, not once thinking how that might affect us. Not to say that I agree with keeping it a secret. But I understand, that's all. I understand the position this news puts Lowenna in.

But I also understand that things are coming to a crisis point, and Melz's right. It needs something bigger than our old ways now.

"All right, everyone. We'll scry for him once we've opened the circle, and see if we can find him with some meditation. No need to panic just yet. Now, who's going to cast the circle today? Macha, I think. Remember the incense this time,"

Melz's face is unreadable as she watches horseface Macha draw the circle successfully around us with earth, air, fire and water. I remember the way Melz taunted Danny. She went too far in mentioning Zia, and I was surprised at that. Melz can be cutting and caustic sometimes, but that was just cruel.

As I watch, a shadow moves over Melz. Just for a minute, I tune into her aura, and something's hanging on to her; something sticky and purplish; I feel the energy of it briefly; terrifying, dark, brutal. Then Macha passes me, carrying the terracotta censer we use for incense, the cloud of resins and herb smoke with the burning charcoal obscuring my sight for a second, and when the smoke clears, the feeling has gone and Melz is just Melz again.

I close my eyes as Lowenna asks Rain, tersely, to call the quarters - north for earth, east for air, south for fire and west for water, to protect the circle, our sacred space, and our magic. Rain's little voice is tremulous as she calls them.

"Louder, please, Rain. The guardians won't hear

you. Make it worth their while," Lowenna admonishes. Rain tries again with more oomph and apparently to Lowenna's satisfaction as she lets her complete all four.

Lowenna, as High Priestess, calls Brighid to the circle. I recite along with the Charge of the Goddess in my mind for practice.

Listen to the words of the Great Mother, who was of old also called Artemis; Astarte; Diana; Melusine; Aphrodite; Cerridwen; Morrigan; Arianrhod; Isis; Brighid; and by many other names.

Whenever ye have need of anything, once in a month, and better it be when the Moon be full, then ye shall assemble in some secret place and adore the spirit of me, who am Queen of all Witches.

There shall ye assemble, ye who are fain to learn all sorcery, yet have not yet won its deepest secrets: to these will I teach things that are yet unknown.

I can feel the power building in the circle. Lowenna finishes the Charge.

"Now, to business, girls. Danny's gone missing, we can assume," Lowenna spreads out some large maps of North Cornwall out on the scuffed wood floor of the hall.

"Get out your crystals and let's have some scrying practice," her tone's forced-jolly, but my feeling is that actually she doesn't really care about Danny at all.

Melz says he was her great hope once; a saviour of the Greenworld. But everything's so messed up now. The Greenworld has definitely not been sewn back together at all. That's not Danny's fault; one eighteen year old boy can't save an entire society. But perhaps Lowenna thought he would. And she hates to be wrong.

"All right. Concentrate. Focus in on Danny. Spirits, we are looking for Daniel Prentice. Please show us where he is," she calls out as our crystals hang above the worn, brownish maps. Mine - the one that was Zia's - is clear quartz with a point at one end; Melz has the same shape but hers is a smoky quartz, full of flaws and imperfections. When the light hits it, it looks as though a little forest's inside: some kind of faery realm. *Mistress of Magic, hear my call: You who are one, who are many, who are all – Give me wisdom, give me sight, Lend me your vision in the sharp moonlight.* Melz sings the scrying chant from *The Book of the Morrigan*.

Some of the girls have other crystals - amethyst,

jasper. Lowenna's is a large green jade pendant. Ours have mostly come over the border with Omar by request, or been gifted by other witches. Crystals they already had when the Greenworld started.

As I hold the quartz over the paper, I sing softly along with Melz and close my eyes to ask for help from my spirit guides. Everyone scrys differently; I know that my crystal will move from left to right for no, in a circle for yes. I say a little prayer to my spirits; my ancestors, the ones that watch over me. I move the crystal slowly over the map. I'm aware of Melz and the other girls doing the same; I sense their competitiveness; there's some jostling for a good position.

I travel the crystal on its bronze chain unworriedly down the coastline from Tintagel, past Port Isaac and Polzeath. I watch as Melz's hand moves up towards mine from the far tip of Cornwall, the southernmost end of the Greenworld: Porthcurno, St Just, Zennor. Our hands meet and our gaze locks and I can't look away. I can't hide the way I feel and I know it must be glowing in my look. Melz's eyelids flutter and her pupils dilate; in slow motion I watch her lips part slightly. It feels as though there's just us in the room and I lean in just a little more towards her -

until Lowenna clears her throat.

"Hm. Anyone found anything?" she barks and Melz looks away, blushing, sitting back on her heels.

"Sorry, I... er.. I didn't get anything. Someone else should have a turn," she mutters, avoiding my eyes now, and the others crowd around the map. I watch as Demi twirls her tourmaline crystal somewhere down the south coast.

"He's here!" she crows, and I stifle a smile as Lowenna leans over her outstretched hand and encloses Demi's wrist in her meaty fist.

"Try again dear. I can see you circling it," she says, and we watch as the chain slows to a halt. Rookie mistake from the Redworld girl; Demi catches my half-smile and scowls at me. I close my eyes and try just once more, my hand above the map, the chain of the pendant looped in my fingers. I let my receptivity spread, poised, relaxed. Nothing, nothing. Moors and standing stones. Grass, trees, forests. And, then, something. A pathway through the trees. A boy, kneeling in a small clearing where hawthorns make a circle: a thick-trunked yew at the northern edge. He has his head bowed, hands clasped together. I have a brief vision of a figure standing in front of him: his God, Lugh, crowned with antlers, with a hand of light touching Danny on the shoulder. And then, a shadow obscures them: a man's figure that kneels next to Danny and whispers in his ear.

I open my eyes. Lowenna looks over. "Find something?"

"A forest. I saw him there, praying to Lugh. And then… a man next to him. He was in shadow. I couldn't see who it was,"

"You don't know which forest?"

"No. A circle of hawthorns with one yew tree. I don't know where that is,"

"No. Me neither," she sighs. "He's good enough at psychic protection to evade us. Still…" she frowns.

"What?" Melz looks at her mother.

"No, it's… It's just that Roach is still out there, you know. Weakened, but the gangs are growing. They'd like nothing more than…" she breaks off and looks away.

"Should we go and look for him? We could search the forests," Melz sits back on her feet like she's ready to jump up and go any second.

"No. I need you all here," Lowenna says abruptly.

"But..." Melz looks like she's about to go off on one but Lowenna glares at her.

"No. He's safe. If he wants some time out in the forest with his God, that's up to him. He'll soon come back with his tail between his legs," she says, dismissively.

"But I really think he should be here," Melz tries again.

"I've wasted enough of the covenstead's time on Danny Prentice," Lowenna snaps again. "Now. Village protection. Eyes closed, everyone; chakras open,"

The girls exchange glances. Would we be as disposable? It's fairly clear that there's not a lot of love in Lowenna for any of us that make mistakes. But none of us say anything: we're too afraid.

She leads us through another round of psychic protection for the village: re-energising the circle around the perimeter, creating the energetic dome of protection around Tintagel. I sneak a look at her under my lids, and though her words are calm and measured, her expression's afraid. She's losing control, and it's terrifying her.

CHAPTER TWENTY-ONE

When you cut Mother Earth, you bleed.

From Tenets and Sayings of the Greenworld

More and more of them arrive every week. Envirowarriors. Shell-shocked, dirty, thin; cowering at any loud noise, not seeming to care about anything apart from having got away from the war. Some of them make camp on the village green, preferring the company of the other Enviros, even over their own families sometimes.

We set up a special healing clinic in Merryn and Rhiannon's house with temporary, thin beds taking up the space in the two living rooms. The room's back to normal, like the earthquake never happened: trinkets replaced, rearranged; candles dusted off and burning again. Biba helps us. Merryn's been her unofficial foster mother, healing her gently with time and tea and talk. Biba still refuses to talk to me, but I'm glad to see she looks healthier. Not so thin or haunted.

"It's going to take some time for her and Sanj to bond," Merryn murmurs to me as Biba takes a pile of fresh sheets into the next room. "So Lowenna suggested she stay here for a bit where I can keep an eye. I mean, really, he's a stranger to her at this point," she clicks her tongue in that motherly way she has. "Anyway, it's nice for me and Rhi. Not like we're ever going to have kids, though we thought we might adopt one day if we were needed,"

I nod, holding the two edges of the clean sheet, waiting for her to shake it out from her end so we can fold.

"How is she, though? In herself?"

Merryn shakes her head.

"Not great. But she'll survive. She's a tough little thing," we fold the sheet and put it on the nearby sofa, taking another one from the pile of freshly washed ones. "She talks sometimes, mostly to Rhi. They've bonded over books," she smiles affectionately. "Rhiannon reads to her at bedtime. They're on *Animal Farm* at the moment,"

"Going hard on the dystopia,"

Merryn raises her eyebrow.

"Seems relevant,"

"When does she see Sanj?" I take another two corners: shake, shake; fold, fold. The rhythm of the work of our grandmothers.

"He pops in a couple of times a week. He's sleeping in the tents on the green with the others," she takes my side of the sheet from me and folds it herself. "They're family to each other at the moment, the Enviros. That needs time, too. Eventually they'll go back to their lives from before. Ten years is a long time,"

"I guess so,"

We fold in silence. There's a knock at the door and we hear Biba open it. Sanj's voice in the hall; I can't hear what they're saying but Merryn and I can both hear that they're both stilted, nervous.

"Finish these, can you? I'll go," Merryn steps out into the hall and I listen as she ushers Sanj into the treatment room.

"I don't need all this healing," there's a creak as he sits on the thin bed. "My leg's getting better. The rest'll just take time. I don't know why I came," his voice comes through the wall. I imagine Merryn's kind but no-nonsense expression, and hear Biba padding upstairs. She'll avoid me until I leave.

"Well, the thing is, my lover," Merryn's voice

chides Sanj "Your leg needs help, just like you do. And you might have forgotten about the need for energy healing after severe trauma, but it's pretty essential," there's a silence; Merryn's probably lighting some incense. "Now breathe, and relax,"

I smile to myself. Sanj is getting mothered whether he likes it or not. I close my eyes and enter the flow of Merryn's magic as it fills the house.

CHAPTER TWENTY-TWO

Borage cup (for love)

Juice of one lemon, 2 tablespoons honey, 3 young borage leaves, borage flowers, violets and elderflower cordial, wine.

Add lemon and honey to 2 pints boiling water, dissolve and chill. Add leaves and flowers and a splash of elderflower cordial and chill for another hour. An hour before you need the potion, mix the herb lemonade with ritual wine and leave to steep in a cold place. Strain out the leaves. Decorate with flower petals.

From: The Common Herbal

We have to wait until after esbat to go back to Mount Shasta; the first night there isn't anything on the coven calendar we all have to be present for.

"What did you tell Lowenna?" I ask Melz, who has the hood of her long wool cloak pulled down over her eyes.

"Out with Rain and Macha, doing moon meditation," she mutters. "You?"

"Herbal revision. I'm up in my room for all they know,"

"Risky," Melz flashes me that rare wicked grin from under her hood.

"Yeah, well. Couldn't think of anything else."

"Not like you to unimaginative, Sadie Morgan, Priestess of Fire," *Is she flirting with me? OH MY GODDESS.* I try to look unbothered, but my heart starts racing again.

"Catie? What was your excuse for coming out?" Melz knew Catie in Glastonbury. A bit of me hates her for knowing Melz before I did, even though it's hard to be jealous around Catie, who's one of life's sweet souls.

"Gone for a walk," she shrugs. "It's all right. I go for a lot of walks,"

The girls are setting up the space in the light evening - late May's not the best time to do anything secretive at night, but we just have to deal with it I guess.

"Lowenna'd burn us in a wicker rabbit at Midsummer if she knew what we were up to," I mutter.

Melz laughs despite herself. "You have a sick sense of humour, d'you know that?"

"It's how I'm still alive," I clear the grass of twigs

and bits of past rituals, so we don't trip over anything when we're going into the portal.

"Shitty thing," she frowns as the candle in its glass jar goes out in the wind.

"Not like you to swear," I raise my eyebrow at her.

"I'm anxious. You bring out the swears in me,"

"Charming,"

"You going to be all right to do this tonight?" she says, not looking at me, watching the milky light bloom in the glass.

"I'm fine," We're disobeying Lowenna again, and we're all on edge about it.

She nods, not convinced, but she knows tonight's our best chance.

"Okay. I'll be with you, so if you feel... I dunno. A lack of confidence, whatever, just... I'll be there, okay?"

"I can focus. Don't worry," I make myself sound less worried than I am. Lowenna's still the High Priestess. She's my fellow Fire Priestess of Brighid. I don't want to lose my chance to finish my training even if my feelings for

Melz are one billion on the bunnies-and-baby-chicks-riding-on-rainbows measurement device.

"If you're sure," Melz can tell I'm in two minds.

"Goddess! I'm sure! All right?" I raise my voice and the other girls look up; Melz's expression hardens.

"Fine. I was just trying to be nice," she snaps.

"Melz, I'm…" I'm instanty sorry, but she waves her hand dismissively.

"It's fine," she snaps, and looks at the circle Catie, Rain and Macha have laid out with stones. "It'll have to do," Melz narrows her eyes at the mainland. "Macha. Open the circle and call the quarters,"

Horseface Macha, teacher's pet, looks smug as she starts circling the rough area of the portal with a cup, trailing a line of the Cornish seawater in front of her, then her fingertip along the earth, then a small smoking censer, then a shrouded lamp that keeps our being here secret. She calls to the powers of each direction in a low voice to protect us and lend us their power; we need all we can get tonight. I strayed onto Mount Shasta by accident, once - this time, there are two of us and we're going to do it on purpose.

That's the plan, anyway.

Melz nods at me curtly.

"Ready?"

I take a deep breath.

"Yeah,"

She draws the opening symbols and the portal bulges into life; a huge orange-red light energy. We better hope no witches are watching Tintagel Head tonight. She takes my hand and we walk in together, concentrating on losing our outlines, on becoming less defined, less real. It feels good to lose myself like this. Part of me would like to always be half a girl, a ghost; inbetween worlds with Melz forever.

CHAPTER TWENTY-THREE

Is dá bhfeicfeá barr an tsléibhe
nuair a bhíonns an ghrian ag éirí
Níl duibheagán sa spéir ann
ná gangaid ins an ngaoth.
Tá an broc ar thaobh an léanna ann,
tá an sionnach rua ar na péaca
Tá an giorria ag boc-léimneach
le pléisiúr insa bhfraoch.

How grand to see
the mountain top at sunrise;
No cloud in the sky,
no venom in the air,
The badger in the meadow,
the fox on the peak
And the hare leaping for joy
in the heather.

From: Barr an tSleibhe, a traditional Irish song

When we walk out onto the mountain, they're waiting for us; a crowd this time, old and young, with the same brown skin and black hair as the girl. Ki'putska, the Fox.

"By Brighid, it worked," Melz breathes to me as our bodies re-solidify outside the portal. It's a strange mix of feeling physically normal, but also feeling completely wrong too - being called back by the portal, back to where we belong, or towards death.

"Thank Brighid," I mutter, feeling nauseous.

Ki'putska smiles and steps forward, holding out her hands to me.

"Fire Mistress. You returned. Welcome to you,"

"Y..yeah. Hi,"

It's disorienting coming through the portal and it's freezing here too. Damn. Forgot that. I can feel Melz shivering next to me in her Greenworld dress and cloak. But Ki'putska drapes furs around our shoulders; it feels soft against my cheek and helps guard against the wind on top of the mountain.

This time there's a big bonfire instead of the small campfire she sat by last time, and it's surrounded by tons of folk. They're all dressed like Ki'putska, in furs and with the soft leather boots strapped around their legs; lots of them have symbols and flowers and animal images painted on their foreheads and faces.

She ushers us over to the circle of villagers, some

beating drums softly, some singing. They nod and smile to us, and immediately I can feel the magic they're weaving with their song; the drumming is that kind of trance-inducing rhythm that blurs the boundaries between the worlds and takes you into dream, into the astral, place of magic. We sit down and huddle gratefully into the heat of the bonfire.

"May I present my mother, Sa'maka - in your language, White Fir. And my father, Ya'nni. Salmon," Ki'putska bows to her parents just next to us, who nod to us respectfully but stay watchful.

"Your journey blesses us," the woman, Sa'maka, says. She's our height and no bigger built than us, but her face has the weathered look of a woman in her 40s that isn't afraid of hard work; she could be a Greenworld woman.

"You must eat and drink; keep your energy high in the circle, especially having come through the connection place," Ya'nni offers us both a cup of something that steams in the cold mountain air but smells herbal; on the tray are also things shaped like biscuits. I stuff one in my mouth gratefully and sip the drink; it warms me immediately. Melz does the same and I can see a tiny bit of colour return in her cheeks. Ya'nni is a warm, secure presence, dressed in furs like his daughter. I relax a bit and gaze into the fire.

The song around the circle grows; an earthy chant from the mountain beneath us, woven with the fire and the cold mountain air. The rattles and drums that the men, women and children play steep the air with magic. I can almost see the strands of previous chants and drumbeats in the air; through the rock and snow and earth, connecting everything, connecting us.

Sa'maka takes Melz and my hands.

"I am the shaman of this tribe. My daughter is the shaman in training." She smiles at Ki'putska, who sits quietly next to us, listening. "Always for us it is the mothers that train the daughters in the ways of the wise. This is the same with your tribe," Melz nods.

"Our witches are usually women. But not always,"

"Ah, yes. The boy who is also a wise one. He is the third with you," I wonder how much she knows about Danny, about us. "He is troubled,"

"Will he heal? Will he... I don't know. Get better?" Melz asks.

"It is unclear," Sa'maka stares into the fire. "But you will need his wisdom for the work that is coming," the drums beat in a similar rhythm to the one we use: BAH-buh-buh; BAH-buh-buh. "All around the world there are tribes. Those that hold the power and knowledge of their ancestors. They keep the wisdom even though the ones around them deny it,"

"Er… yeah," I exchange a glance with Melz.

"But there is a network of the wise ones. Do you know that?"

"We have The Book of Portals, if that's what you mean? I mean, that's what we call it. My aunt, a witch in the next town to us. She keeps a kind of psychic contact with energy centres around the world. Tracks which ones are okay, which ones are blocked or polluted. More and more, these days," Melz says.

"That is so," Sa'maka sighs. "We are also in contact with the communities around these places of power,"

I turn to Melz.

"Why aren't we, then? I mean - we know about the portals; Tressa does that work, tuning in with the others around the world. It seems weird that we wouldn't have been in contact with other Greenworld-type communities before now, if there were any," I pull the fur around me as a harsh wind blows over the mountaintop. The singing continues quietly around us.

"You desired solitude. Your community separated from the outside world. But you were never alone. The world includes other peoples like yours. It was a choice," Ya'nni says.

"It was the wrong choice, then," I say shortly. "Goddess. I can't believe how shortsighted they've been. We could've been learning from each other all this time,"

Melz looks into the fire.

"Maybe they did know. But you know mum. It's just the kind of thing she'd keep to herself,"

"Do not judge your forebears too harshly. They did what seemed right to them to protect your way of life. To make a new world for their children, for you. The world around them seemed a terrible place at the time. It requires great strength to withstand the horrors outside and not close your door to them." Sa'maka smiles kindly.

"She's right," Melz shrugs. "It is what it is. The

important thing is that we're here now," she looks back at Sa'maka. "So what's going to happen now? Why are we here?"

Sa'maka passes us the herbal drink again.

"We have all seen it," she says, as we drink. "There will be a congress. A meeting of the heads of all the countries in your big city. Of all of our communities, your Greenworld is the closest one to it. You will be the catalysts of our combined force. Yours is the action that will kindle the fire across the world. You will make them understand."

"Make them understand what?"

"The answer. The gift that we have been preserving for them all these years, whilst they were fighting their wars. Our natural wisdom. But also, the energy centres. How they can be used. Ki'putska gave you the writings."

Melz takes the scroll out of her cloak.

"We didn't understand them," she confesses, spreading it out on the blanket.

"We hoped you would understand," Sa'maka

frowns. "This knowledge has been sleeping in the world for years already," she points to the diagrams. "It looks more complicated than it is. For years, as well as preserving the culture of our Shasta ancestors, we have also held some of the old knowledge of the invaders. The colonists that took our land. Some of the knowledge was good. One scientist had an idea for free energy many years ago. Our best shaman-scientists have been working on the theory for generations,"

"Scientists?" Melz and I exchange glances. "We... we don't embrace the sciences in our culture. They're patriarchal and anti-knowledge. Anti-goddess," she explains haltingly.

Sa'maka frowns harder.

"Then this may be hard for you. We thought, perhaps, by giving you the scroll, that your thinkers would understand, and be able to help,"

"No. We couldn't make much of it,"

"But... your culture. In your country. You had the knowledge as well as us. The books. The advanced sciences," Sa'maka looks confused. "We researched this. And with your philosophy, now, of respecting the earth, like us, like all indigenous peoples; you should be our partners in this work. We need your help to bring the knowledge into the hands of the people of the world,"

Melz looks embarrassed.

"The Greenworld burned a lot of books. Science and technology, among other things," she says quietly. "But you have to understand. We - our mothers - they saw all that as the cause of everything they wanted out of. Science was killing the planet, with the war for fuel. Pesticides killed the bees. Genetically modified crops poisoned us. Medicines contained hidden mind-controlling chemicals. We…"

"Do you really believe that? About medicines controlling people's minds?" Ki'putska frowns.

"Yes," Melz says, sounding less sure than she should. "That's what they told us,"

Sa'maka nods understandingly.

"All these things have been expressed as concerns here, too. But when we chose to be separate, we took the best of everything with us. We could not ignore the progress that had happened, whatever the area of study. Fortunately, among the Shasta were scientists that wanted to serve our Great Mother in the way that they knew best. They spent years building and researching, and combining their experiments with the natural energies of this place, with the wisdom of our ancestors. They are shaman-scientists. They walk with knowledge and power in the upper, lower and middle worlds,"

"So - they know what this means? They know how to make portals provide us with power? That's real?"

"It is real," interjects Ya'nni. "I have seen it,"

"So Roach was right," Melz raises her eyebrows at me. "By Brighid,"

"Maybe. But I don't think he was really going about it in the same way as the Shasta," I snap. There's no way I'm assigning any glory to that man. Ever. "I mean, I'm assuming they haven't killed anyone in the pursuit of their shamanic science,"

"So how does it actually work?" Melz peers at the scroll then back at Sa'maka.

"It is enough to say that the power of the energy portal can be powered by certain 2symbols that affect energy in different ways," Ya'nni says, his wise, lined face lit with a calm smile.

"And you… this network of other communities… You think we're supposed give this information to the government? They'll never listen to us. They spread rumours about us being terrorists so that the folk outside the Greenworld don't know the truth." I protest, looking at Melz for help.

"They will listen," Sa'maka's voice is deep and contemplative. "And your battle will be at home, too. With your loved ones, who may not all understand. Nonetheless, you must do this. For all of us. The communities are dying. We are struggling to maintain the energy centres. More and more of them are shutting down," the singing continues around us, holding us here like a charm.

"But what do we do? In practice, like?" I ask.

"You, the three marked ones, must show them." Ya'nni says, taking up his hide drum and starting to beat it softly, faster now. Buh-buh-buh-buh-buh, Buh-buh-buh-buh-buh.

"How?" Melz asks, leaning forward intently.

"Connect to an open portal. It should be the one of the Heart at your place of Glastonbury, for it is one of the major centres. The three of you together will be able to connect to it from wherever you are in the world. The three of you have the power to dream together. The power to co-create in the dream world. With the right training, you could be the shaman-scientists, like the Shasta,"

Sa'maka tops up our tea, and I drink mine instantly; I can feel myself becoming mistier, thinner. I need something to keep me here just a little longer.

"And, say we can do that. What then?" Melz drinks her tea.

"You take them inside it. The politicians. And I will coordinate the rest of the communities. The rest of the active centres. We will meet you in the place between worlds, and show them the network of all the portals linked together. They will see for themselves. Then, together, we will activate the portals. The shaman-scientists are ready. The nonbelievers will see the power that has been around them all along," Sa'maka says.

"That sounds sort of... huge," Melz says. "You think we can do that?"

"We must," Ya'nni says, drumming softly. "It is time,"

"They don't believe anything without proof. What they think is proof. So proof they will have. The time for hoping they will develop faith is over. There is no time for that anymore," Sa'maka adds.

"And when is this supposed to happen?" Melz asks.

"The war is over. There will be an emergency meeting about fuel, in your country. All the leaders will come. Soon, in the next few months," Sa'maka grabs both of our hands. "This is our only chance. If we don't try, the world will be plunged into darkness,"

Melz makes a doubtful face, but I shake my head. This makes sense.

"She's right. The numbers of refugees coming to the Greenworld are just going to increase if the Redworld continues to be uninhabitable. If we can give energy back to the world, they won't need us as much. We can still teach them about living on the land. And if the government has a new source of energy for folk, that can only be a good thing. You told me about the crime bosses in the Redworld. They profit mostly from protecting the rich who have fuel, and policing the poor that don't. A new fuel source would stop all that,"

Melz looks out across the bonfire, at the circle of the Shasta folk, drumming and chanting.

"How are we going to get mum to let us do this, though? Getting politicians on board? That means we have to go to London. Get to whoever's in charge there now. There's just no way," she's doubtful and I don't blame her. It's a crazy big ask.

"There are those that will resist change. You must step into your destiny," Sa'maka says, as if it's simple to defy the Head Witch of the Greenworld and sashay into Westminster with the promise of magic fuel.

"I don't know if that's my destiny," Melz sighs.

"Your path is to lead. You know that," Ki'putska breaks in. "Both of you, with the other one, the boy. You all have marks. You are all special. We have seen it in the fires many times,"

"We don't know that at all!" I interrupt. "You might. It isn't as clear to us,"

"I… I don't know if I can do that," Melz stammers. "It's too hard,"

Sa'maka looks piercingly at her, and at me. The

drums and rattles stop abruptly, but the circle continues a low, lilting song without words.

"Then we are all doomed," she says quietly. "You have to believe. Your goddess is the Crow, yes?"

"Yes," Melz meets Sa'maka's eyes.

"The crow follows the sound of battle because it knows it will find meat. The crow follows the predator and waits for it to kill the prey, then feasts."

"So?"

"So, Crow Priestess, the battle has been fought in Russia. There are wounds exposed; the soldiers limp home. The war is over, but the nations have not decided what to do next. They know their society is about to fall apart. You must take advantage of this moment. You pick the meat from the carcass so you live to fight another day," she holds Melz's hand and looks into her eyes imploringly. "You must be strong, Crow Priestess. And do what you know you have to, no matter how difficult,"

Melz looks down. I know what she's thinking. What we're all thinking. If we do this, she has to betray Lowenna.

Sa'maka moves her gaze to me.

"The three of you are the key," she repeats.

"There might be a problem with us being... err, there being three of us," I hate to say it, but Danny's the unpredictable factor in all of this. If the whole world's depending on the three of us to co-dream the Glastonbury portal open, then we're in trouble. Because we have no idea where he is.

Ki'putska leans in and takes Melz's hand and mine.

"This is important. You must be totally united or the centre will not hold for the rest of us. Know this," she says, her brown eyes earnest.

"We'll do our best. Don't worry," Melz smiles, and I'm not sure where she's getting her sureness from. But I can feel the faintness that comes of being on the wrong side of the portal taking over my body. I lean into her. She puts a protective arm around me.

"I don't feel so good," I murmur into her shoulder. "I feel sick again," the horizon sways like a door in a breeze; I blink hard a few times, try and refresh myself. It kind of works, but I can feel the pull of the portal, strong, like spirit hands on my energy, pulling,

pulling.

"It's time for us to go," Melz hauls me up and I can feel an unsteadiness in her too, but she hides it better than me. We bow to Sa'maka and Ya'nni, and to the circle.

"Many blessings to you all. Thank you for your wisdom and hospitality. We'll think hard about what you've told us," Melz says.

"Be blessed," they bow to us. I hold Melz's hand and we walk back into the portal, handing our furs back to Ki'putska.

"You will succeed, Fire Priestess and Priestess of the Crow," she calls out after us. "The Great Spirits will be with you; and we will see you inside the centre of all things, in the place where the great energies meet. We will know when it is time. We will see you there!"

We walk into the energy tunnel, and enter nothingness. Just for a moment, I think how peaceful it would be to stay here forever; not to have to face what we have to do. For that brief moment when our molecules aren't quite together, and outlines are hazy and reality's suspended, all I want is to pull Melz down the corridor, away from life, and into death. The pull of dissolution here is so strong. But we can resist it. We must.

CHAPTER TWENTY-FOUR

A mother's love, the strongest bond

Of earth and rock, stone and pond,

Teach the mysteries of fire and water,

The lore of wind and air and storm.

Teach them to your son and your daughter.

A mother's love, wisdom reborn.

Verse from 'A Mother's Love', from Prayers and Songs of the Greenworld

"I thought she was up in her room," I hear Lowenna's voice in the kitchen as we let ourselves in the front door; I shut it behind us quietly and motion to the girls to be quiet. "In fact, quite a few of the girls are out. You know teenagers. You've got to give them a bit of freedom every now and again," she continues. Melz raises an eyebrow.

"As if," she whispers. We're all just about to disappear upstairs when I hear mum's voice.

"I'll wait," she says, and I stop dead, one foot on the bottom stair.

Biba told me mum had escaped the village after Danny tried to kill her. After I ran away.

"It's been a long time, Linda. Where've you been?" Lowenna asks guardedly. There's a silence and then a sob. Lowenna must have handed her something, probably a tea towel to blow her nose in, because then she says "No, keep it. I've got others,"

I didn't think I'd see her again. I don't know why. Maybe that I didn't expect her to survive outside the village; we've hidden inside it for so long, from him.

"I stood trial, but they judged that I had already shown enough remorse, and I'd lost Sadie, and that was punishment enough. They let me go, but I'm banished from the village." Mum's voice is low and tired.

"That doesn't seem very harsh punishment for murder," Lowenna says, drily. "It's almost as though they don't really mind that you did it,"

"Maybe they don't. They've refused to have witches in charge now. You know that, I suppose,"

"Yes," Lowenna says shortly, and there's a silence then, until I hear another sob; mum's crying.

"I'm... I'm so sorry," she splutters, but Lowenna's quiet. "Please, Lowenna. I've come to ask for your forgiveness,"

"And for somewhere to live, presumably," Lowenna's voice's hard; she isn't moved by the tears.

"Well... yes. But I'll understand if you say no. I'll... leave for the Redworld, I suppose,"

I peek through the crack in the doorframe and watch as Lowenna gets up from the big carved wood covenstead table and starts pacing the kitchen.

"D'you understand the position you're putting me in by coming here? You're not just another refugee. You're a witch killer. It's hard enough having Sadie here, but at least she's got the brand, and she didn't kill Zia herself. But it's still an uphill struggle, constantly having to remind folk that it wasn't her fault. That she wasn't in it with you. If you're here with her, what does that look like? Like I condone what you did. That's what," Lowenna snorts and kicks the side of one of her overstuffed easy chairs in frustration. "You shouldn't have come, Linda. I really don't need this right now,"

"Please. Please, forgive me. I regret it. Every

moment, I regret it. But you must understand… why I did it…" mum's trying to control her voice, I can tell, and I remember this pleading tone. Remember hearing it as a child, when dad - Roach - was shouting at her, slapping her, telling her what an idiot she was, how short sighted. That I was gifted and she had to let him train me, make me realise my potential. She'd sob and cry out then, beg him not to take me away, I guess into the forests, into the wild, just with him. Not to hurt me. To hurt her instead. And then the slap of his hand on her face, the thump of his fist on her body, then silence, and tears.

"I know what he did to you, Linda. To both of you. But that doesn't give you the right to take a life. A witch's life. Zia's life. She was your friend, once. My friend," Lowenna's voice cracks. I see the back of her greyed yellow hair and the top of her sun-faded red kaftan as she goes to sit back down at the table with a sigh. Mum sits opposite, and shock reverberates through me when I see her face. She's so much older, all of a sudden - she's lost weight and her skin's grey and lifeless. Her eyes are shadowed and tired and she slumps forward in her chair, dishevelled.

"I know that. Don't you think I know?" mum cries out, reaching out to grasp Lowenna's hands on the table, but Lowenna pulls them away. "Please. It all happened so quickly. I... I followed Sadie. She's been going out at night and not saying where. And she was different, holding herself differently, she was secretive. I thought she was seeing him. Roach. I thought he'd got her, entranced her finally with his magic. I was frantic with worry. So I followed along behind her, to Zia's house. And when I saw them together in the garden, in the circle, everything came back. I was blind, I was deaf, everything just... just faded away except for Roach and all the times he... he hit me, hurt me, threatened me. All the times he frightened Sadie, and I tried to protect her, gods know I did, but I didn't do it well enough, and there she was, with Zia, and it just... I don't know. It just happened,"

Lowenna gazes at Linda for a long time.

"Murder doesn't just happen," she says, finally, but I know that's not true. Sometimes folk do things that they didn't know they would, or could. Sometimes darkness spills out into the world and there's nothing you can do about it. Because you've nurtured that darkness for so long, grown it carefully, slowly, and one day you realise it's a monster you can't control. And it goes into the world, and it kills and claws and eats.

"I didn't mean to do it," mum looks down at the table. "Please. I just want to see Sadie. To tell her. Try and make her understand,"

"I don't know if she will. Zia was her initiator. Her mentor. Luckily I've taken over her training. She has the mark of Brighid. Did you know?"

Mum's eyes widen in shock.

"A witch-brand? Like him?"

"Not like his. The same as mine,"

"What does that mean?"

"There's three of them now. Sadie, Daniel Prentice, Demelza. Like me, Zia and Radley. Two priestesses, one priest of the mysteries. Brighid, Morrigan and Lugh. The next generation,"

"To do what? The Greenworld's fracturing. Gidleigh's in a state now. They don't want witch rule," mum sniffs.

"No, well, you must be happy about that," Lowenna sneers. "All that hard work on your part to turn the villagers against Zia. Well done. You succeeded. Perhaps not in the way you intended, but you did it,"

"I told you. That wasn't me. He... he made me do that. Sow discord. He said if I did he'd leave us alone. I had to," mum pleads. Her whole life, she's been on her knees to one person or another. I'm never going to be like that.

"You always had a choice," Lowenna snaps, because for her, there has always only been one choice. The Greenworld, over everything.

Mum stands up and pulls up her old brown cotton blouse. I remember the white scars on her back; I'd see them when I was young if I caught her getting changed or, in the summer, lying on the grass in the garden, she'd sometimes roll onto her front to sun her back if she thought I was playing inside, so I wouldn't see. But I saw.

"This was my choice. What I took from him, all those years. You'd do the same. Would you let anyone do this to your daughters?" mum asks in a low voice. "If that was the choice: taking the belt on your skin or seeing it on theirs, wouldn't you bow your back every single time rather than see them hurt?" Lowenna looks at the scars for a long moment, then bows her head.

"Of course," she murmurs.

Mum lowers her top and sits back down.

"I'd kill to keep Sadie safe from him. Can you blame me if I didn't understand? If, for that moment, this was all I could see and feel? This pain, this fear? It was a madness. I know that. And I'm sorry. I'm so very sorry, Lowenna. But I was protecting my girl. I always have. I always will,"

I feel the tear slip down my cheek.

"Mum," I push the door open and go to her. I feel her fragility, feel her flinch as I hug her, and despite everything, she's home to me, the only home I ever had. I let the tears come then and bawl into her shoulder as she sits at the table, stroking my back.

"I'm sorry, I'm so sorry," I cry, choking on the bloody taste of the tears and the phlegm in my throat. And I'm crying for Zia and the horror of what mum did, but I'm also crying for every time I heard the impact of Roach's flat hand on her cheek. *I'll never let you go*, he'd whisper to her. *And one day she'll have the gift like me, and she'll be mine then.* But I wouldn't go with him; I knew I had something in me, but I wouldn't let him see it. Not ever.

But I also cry because maybe if I'd done what he

wanted he wouldn't have hurt mum.

"It's not your fault, love. None of this is your fault," mum breathes. "It was his. And now it's mine,"

And we both sob into each other, and I know where true power comes from, then; it's in my heart, my full heart; the heart that can forgive mum. And I realise what a beautiful and terrible thing love is, all at the same time.

CHAPTER TWENTY-FIVE

General salve for colds

1 part coconut oil, three quarters of a part grated beeswax, half a part olive oil, 35 drops eucalyptus oil, 30 drops peppermint oil, 15 drops lavender oil, 15 drops rosemary oil, 10 drops camphor oil.

Melt the oils and beeswax together. Stir in the essential oils. Pour into containers and allow to set before capping. Rub under nose, on chest and feet for colds.

From The Common Herbal

"We have to try it this way first. If we can go to them, make them see our point of view - it's easier than us turning up without warning at this energy conference thing, whenever that's going to be." Melz pants out as we make our way over Dartmoor; past the grey granite pushing up through the grass, past the streams bordered by trees with gnarled, twisting roots and covered with hanging yellow-green moss.

"What about Lowenna?" I ask her again. Melz'd come into my room the night before last night - Saba's old room - and woken me up. I'd been dreaming about her so it was, err, shall we say *slightly jarring* to wake up with her earnest face pressed up to mine. *We need to go. To the*

Redworld. Tonight, she'd hissed at me. *I've been thinking and thinking and I can't see another way.* Obviously, I'd complied.

"We'll have to deal with that when we get home," Melz says flatly.

"That'll be nice," I don't mean it to sound sarcastic, but it comes out that way.

"You got any better ideas, genius?" she snaps back.

"I didn't say I did,"

"You agreed to come," she gives me her spiky stare and looks away.

"I know, I know. I'm not saying I don't agree. I'm just saying…"

"What?"

"Goddess. Touchy,"

"Go on. I'm sorry," she sighs. "I just feel guilty, that's all. I know it's for the best, but believe it or not, I don't like disobeying mum,"

"No, I can see that. I don't either," I try to pacify Melz. "I'm not exactly happy about leaving Linda. Mum.

She's only just got to the village,"

"How are you feeling about that? Must be weird,"

I blow out my cheeks; exhaling, my breath makes a cloud in the cold morning air.

"It is weird,"

"Anything else?"

"Good. It's good to know where she is. That she's okay. There's a lot for us to talk about,"

"Sure,"

"Mums are tricky," I say.

"Hmmm," she's noncommittal.

"Hmmm like you agree, or hmmm like this is the end of the conversation?" I peer into her face.

She mimes shooting herself in the head.

"*Hmmm* like there's no point talking about this any more because it won't change the fact we have to face her when we get home, and *hmmm* I think I'm going to scream if you don't change the subject. Say something Sadie and make me laugh,"

"*Something Sadie?* What am I, your comedy puppet?"

"You said it," she grins, and there it is again: the sun after the rain; that changeability.

"Oh, do kindly bugger off,"

She laughs. "That's more like it. I like sweary Sadie,"

"Shitty sweary Sadie? Fuck me. Thanks,"

"You're my sweary entertainment,"

"Sweartertainment. Good to know,"

We plough on again in more amiable silence for a while, and as we reach the top of a hill, the sun breaks over the horizon. She takes my hand and we stand there, bathing in the new sunlight.

"You know I'm glad you're here, don't you? Seriously. I wouldn't be able to do this without you," she says, and, oh, it's like butterflies implode my energy field and her smile's the sweetness of blossom and lilacs and lemonade and summer.

"I know," I say, and her hand fits mine perfectly and I grin like an idiot, not caring, feeling sorry for anyone who isn't with the person that makes them feel magically and wholly alive right now, feeling lucky, like I won something, and here I am with my prize.

I look down at our interlinked hands. Could this actually be something? And as soon as I encounter that thought, and as wonderful as it feels right then, a shadow of mistrust comes over me. I pull my hand away.

I don't want Melz to stop being perfect, which she will inevitably do if I get to know her. If I peek underneath the magic, underneath the mask of the perfect witch and the cloak of the goth enchantress, maybe I won't love what I find there. Even the beautiful, magical, powerful (and no doubt emotionally unavailable) Cleopatra was just an ordinary and disappointing woman under that heavy makeup and righteous jewellery, even with her *infinite variety*. Love's tricky. *Love, but not the now and forever kind with chains around your vagina and a short circuit in your brain. I'd rather be alone.* Like Rita Mae says in Greenworld-approved *Rubyfruit Jungle*. Though, to be fair, I think she was talking about loving men. Much more likely to short-circuit you in all areas. I think that was an electrical term. Anyway.

Melz looks down at my hand when I take it away, but doesn't say anything.

We walk on for hours until we find the nearest road, through the Redworld border, which Melz says is a lot easier to get through than it was before. We don't see any dogs; the soldiers we do see at the checkpoints just wave us through or ignore us, sitting inside the flaking painted huts, staring gloomily out of the windows at nothing. When we put the last once-electrified fence behind us, which now has large holes in it so that we walk straight through, we watch as a group of maybe ten Redworlders carrying bags slip through the same gap.

"Heading for the Greenworld," Melz inclines her head and I watch them: exhausted, thin, sad in the midmorning chill; the sun didn't last long.

"They just keep coming," I say as I watch a mother help her young child past the rough edges of the fence.

"Yep,"

"They're not going to stop coming, are they?"

"No. Not unless they feel safe in their homes. Not unless they understand how to live like we do, with no power, no money. But that's going to take years." She hands me a bread roll and I tear off a corner hungrily.

"D'you think that'll ever happen? That they'll be able to live like we do?"

"It's possible. Anything's possible," she looks up at the sky and rubs her arms. "Like the sun actually coming out from behind those clouds. That'd be nice. I'm bloody freezing,"

"Yeah, but is it likely? Stopping the Redworlders, I mean. We're always freezing,"

"Ah. Well. *Likely's* a very different proposition to *possible*,"

"Hmmm," I chew my roll. We get to the side of the road and sit down, waiting for a ride. I stretch my legs out onto the side of the earth verge. We wait, sitting companionably on the side of the cracked black road on yellowish grass until a truck comes, heading the right way. We wave at the driver and he stops; we approach the front of the thing, huge, metal, stinking of fumes and petrol and rubber.

"Can you take us to London?" Melz shouts over the coughing, chugging engine. The driver peers down at us through the open window and hikes his thumb at us, beckoning us in.

"This is crazy. D'you know that?" I mutter to Melz as she climbs into the cab next to the driver, and I slam the door behind us.

"I'm the Crow Priestess, remember? I hunt the predator," she whispers back at me. Like that explains everything, which it really doesn't, actually, but never mind.

The driver looks us both up and down unpleasantly.

"Not often I get two young ladies in my cab," he leers. "Where you 'eaded then, my loves?"

"Westminster," Melz smiles dangerously. "So don't spare the horses, will you, my good man," and she waves her hand unobtrusively, and I know she's casting a protection sphere over us both, and maybe adding a little Melz the Red Witch glamour of some kind into the mix because the driver sits up straighter, wipes the leer off his face and presses his foot down on the accelerator.

"Certainly, madam," he says, his face blank, and she settles back into her seat and closes her eyes.

"Wake me up when it's time to eat," she says, and falls asleep, leaving me clutching the door handle in terror as the road unravels under us, faster than I ever would have thought possible.

CHAPTER TWENTY-SIX

A Brighid, scar os mo chionn
Do bhrat fionn dom anacal.

O Brighid, spread above my head
Your Mantle bright to guard me.

Chant for Brighid, from Greenworld Prayers and Songs

"Next,"

A bored-looking female soldier inside a toughened glass box beckons us forward from the line.

"We want to see the Prime Minister," Melz says loudly, her Cornish *rrr* reverberating around the walls of this once-polished, now chipped-at-and-generally-misused stone room. Some of the armed guards at the end of the rows turn around to look at us. Bullet holes sprinkle the walls liberally.

"Lower your hood please, Miss," the soldier has black rings around her eyes; it must be tiring, sitting in that box all day. I wonder how long she has to sit there. Maybe she never comes out, there's just a tube up her arse and a feeding tube from above and she'll sit there until she dies and then they'll wheel another one in.

"We want to see the Prime Minister," Melz repeats, even louder, keeping her hood around her face.

"I need you to lower your hood, Miss. When you approach the box your face can't be obscured," the soldier orders. Melz steps forward, over the red line painted on the concrete floor. She pushes her hood back from her face and presses her nose up against the glass. As she does, an alarm goes off and a red light starts flashing in the room. The guards run towards us.

"Tell her Demelza Hawthorne's here to see her," Melz shouts as she's grabbed by two black-garbed soldiers, masked and in riot gear. "She'll want to see me, I promise,"

Another guard grabs me and pushes me against the wall next to Melz. I feel him cuff my wrists, and then the point of a gun in my back.

"Are you sure this is going to work?" I hiss at Melz, but she smiles back.

"Of course," she whispers. "They have to ID us if we display threatening behaviour. Omar told me. They won't necessarily believe I'm Demelza Hawthorne just by me saying so. And once they ID us, she'll want to see us. The Prime Minister,"

"How do you know that?"

"Trust me. She will,"

"Are you sure? They could just throw us in prison and be done with it!" I grimace as the guard yanks my handcuffs. "Hey! That hurt!"

"Shut up," he says, and I feel him separate my fingers and press the end of my index finger onto something hard and cold. There's a beeping noise.

"No record on Standard Identification," another guard says, behind me. I watch as the guard holding Melz presses her fingertip onto a grey metal pad with a glassy panel; it makes the same beep.

"We're not on your records because we're from the Greenworld," Melz says, projecting her voice so it bounces around the cavernous walls; the long queue of folk lining up to talk to one of these soldiers in the toughened glass boxes are watching us now. "We don't have any certification. I'm Demelza Hawthorne and this is Sadie Morgan. We're Greenworld witches from the Tintagel covenstead. I demand you take us to the Prime

Minister *right now*," she's using her magical command voice, and it's working because I catch a confused look from the soldier holding her to the one behind me.

"Maybe we should just take them," says the obviously weaker-minded one holding me, but the other one frowns.

"That's not procedure. Have we got the up-to-date Radical ID kit down here?" her soldier asks mine.

They make us stand with our backs against the bullet-pitted wall. One of them goes to the soldier in the glass box and speaks to her for a minute; he returns with a bigger glass-screened metal thing. *Radical*, like it's amazing, or *radical*, like we're dangerous radicals? It is, I presume, the latter.

"Stand still and look at the box," he says, and holds it in front of our faces: Melz, then me. A blue light stings my eyes; I try to keep them open. The soldier turns the device around and looks at the screen for a moment, then back at us. His expression only shifts slightly, but I see it. Whatever that thing is, it's verified who we are. Goddess knows how, mind.

"It's them," he grunts to the other one. "Enact

protocol 137,"

What the fuck's Protocol 137? I guess we're going to find out soon enough because my soldier yanks me around by the handcuffs again and pushes me forward.

"Move it, Greenworld," she mutters, and Melz's guard pushes a transparent screen down over his face; I'm guessing mine has too from the slight echoing bounce of her voice.

"Where're you taking us? What's Protocol 137?" I shout, but there's no reply, just a nudge in my back with the business end of a gun.

"Trust me," Melz whispers as they push her in front of me and make us walk single file across the room; the Redworlders in the queue behind us watch us with wide eyes. Dangerous criminals, we must look like. Dramatic ingenues, shadowy bitches. I kind of love it just for the sheer drama. If you disregard the potential mortal peril, it's like we're in a Greenworld-approved novel about witches being persecuted by The Man. I glare theatrically at the Redworlders as we pass.

"We'll eat your BABIES!" I hiss at them, just for the fun of it, and laugh as two of the tatty Redworld women hold their tatty children to their thin legs as we're dragged past. They deserve to live in hell if they're that stupid.

"Not helping, Sadie," Melz mutters.

"Whatever. SORRY! We won't really eat your babies!" I call out over my shoulder. "We'll just indoctrinate them with our feminist matriarchal plutocracy!"

"Shut up," the guard dragging me whacks my head pretty hard against a set of double doors. "Greenworld slag,"

How beautifully they talk to women here.

CHAPTER TWENTY-SEVEN

We are called the Greenworld as green is the colour of life, regeneration and purity.

From: Tenets and Sayings of the Greenworld

The guards march us through a scuffed white door and down a long wood-panelled corridor, then down another identical one, and another.

"D'you know where we are?" I whisper to Melz, not like she would, she's never been here either, but some reassurance would be nice; however, her guard turns around to glare at me.

"No talking!" he barks, all muscle and uniform. We march on, into the building, up steep stairs and through narrow walkways until we stop at a door. He raps at it with his heavy glove.

The door's opened by another soldier in black, wearing sunglasses even though the light inside's dim: as I go in I realise it's dim because the window has been painted over. Brief specks of light stream through the tint spots where the paint's flaked off.

"Enter," a woman's voice commands.

The Prime Minister - that's who I hope this is, and well done to the Redworld at least for having a woman in power, or in the role of pretend power, anyway - sits at a large wooden desk. Behind her, bookshelves lined with green and red leather-bound books; a floor lamp in the corner casts a weak, flickering light on the room, smaller than I'd have expected.

"Sit down," she points to the two seats in front of her desk. Melz takes one and I take the other, warily. The Minister looks us up and down, one by one, and nods to her guard. "They've been searched?"

"At the point of detainment, Madam," he barks. *Good doggie, now roll over.*

"Detainment?" Melz glares at the guard and then the woman behind the desk. She's delicate like a sparrow, dressed forgettably in grey and blue Redworld clothes, trousers and a shirt. Not a physically large woman like a lot of the witches, our powerful women, who are stout, loud, sometimes rowdy. "We're here by choice. You're not detaining us. You can't detain us. If we want to leave, we'll leave,"

"It's a technical term," the woman snaps at Melz. "I appreciate that your visit is... - she coughs - "a diplomatic one, Miss Hawthorne," she waves her hand at the guard. "All right. Leave us,"

"Regulations say I need to stay," he rebuts but she raises her eyebrow archly.

"I make the regulations here, Officer. You will wait outside. I think I can cope with a couple of teenage girls," She reaches into a drawer and places a handgun on the desk. "All right?"

"As you wish, Madam," he nods and leaves the room.

"They're very committed, the security services," the Prime Minister smiles. "But sometimes I think they're a bit overprotective. I mean, you girls aren't here to hurt me, are you? Because that would be terribly unfortunate. For you, I mean,"

Melz glances at the gun, and I know she's assessing its weight and maybe she's thinking about how she'd hold it to the woman's head and pull the trigger as revenge for all that misinformation she's spread about the Greenworld all these years, but she smiles into the Prime Minister's grey eyes instead.

"Thank you for seeing us," she says politely as if

we've popped in for tea and a bit of fortune telling. *Cross my palm with silver.*

"Of course. I couldn't very well refuse Demelza Hawthorne an audience. And your friend is...?"

"Sadie Morgan. I'm a witch, too," I hold out my hand for her to shake it but she eyes it coolly instead.

"Indeed. At Tintagel?"

"Yeah,"

"I see. I'm Felicity Blunt. So to what do I owe the pleasure?"

"We need to talk to you about the energy portals," Melz reaches into her bag for the scroll from the Shasta, folding it open onto the table. "We've thought long and hard about this, but it's time to share this knowledge with you."

"The what?" the Prime Minister's tone changes; momentarily, she sounds confused.

"Energy portals. They're the solution to the energy crisis," Melz repeats. "I know you don't know what they are. But I can explain,"

"Portals?"

"Yes," Melz gets out a world map of Lowenna's she stole before we came. She's marked on the locations of all the Master Centres, and as many of the smaller ones as we know about: Tintagel, Scorhill, The Twelve Apostles in Yorkshire, Newgrange in Ireland, the Ring of Brodgar and Callanish in Scotland. "Look. Each one is a centre of huge natural energy, and we think we know how to use them. To provide energy to the world. To everyone,"

Felicity Blunt glances at the map and then at us, frowning.

"This is what you've come here for? To show me a map and an old manuscript?" she picks up the scroll and peers at the formulas and symbols. "What is this?"

"I told you. If you'll listen, I can explain," Melz is trying to be patient, but patience doesn't come naturally to her and it's an effort.

Blunt scans the scroll disinterestedly and drops it onto the desk.

"I thought you'd come to negotiate," she says, leaning on the desk with both hands and looking at us both keenly. "We know the Greenworld is under some -

ah - internal stress. Aren't you here to talk about rejoining the UK? Making the Contract of Separation void?"

"No," Melz exchanges a glance with me. "No, definitely not. Is that what you want?"

Blunt drums her fingers on the faded green leather top of her desk, looking at us speculatively.

"Off the record, I know that the Cabinet would be receptive to the idea. Under certain circumstances,"

"Why? I thought you were happy with the way it is. You tell everyone we're terrorists, we pretend you don't exist," I snap at her. She turns her grey eyes on me.

"Perhaps. Perhaps not. The war in Russia is over. Even the Generals admit there's no point in having a war for something that doesn't exist anymore. And when people hear that, they're going to panic. Blame us, even, for a costly and overall unsuccessful war," She gets up and walks around the desk to our side, and sits on the edge. "Also, the government needs to reclaim power over local governance. With the war on, we devolved authority to local security services to keep order. But that has been plagued with… issues, recently," she says, frowning. "We need something to encourage the people. Give them hope, and bring them back on our side. Empower them to challenge local security where necessary."

"But you've spent all these years telling them we're criminals!" I raise my voice, incredulous. "We came to offer this way we can help you. We're not here to fight crime for you!"

"We'll pardon you for all your acts of terrorism if you'll work with us to reclaim power. The people are restless. They're rioting. We can't control them anymore. Whole cities are inaccessible. We can't let private security run things anymore. Between you and me, they've made a bloody awful job of it," Blunt says drily.

"Isn't that your fault for contracting out law and order to criminals?" Melz glares at the Prime Minister sharply and I know she's talking about Bran Crowley, her old lover in the Redworld. He spun her some poor-me tale about being a boy from the wrong side of the tracks and crime being the only path available to him. *As if.* He enjoyed it, that's what I think. And he manipulated Melz so well that now she doesn't trust her own feelings anymore, which isn't great when I'm trying - very, very unsuccessfully, appallingly in fact - to make her fall in love with me.

"It was a mistake. I'll admit that," Blunt lowers her eyes for a moment. "So? What do you think? Come back to the UK. All is forgiven if you help us," she steeples her fingers together and studies us. "And I assume you're both here representing Lowenna Hawthorne. Why didn't she come?"

"Of course," Melz lies. "She asked me and Sadie to represent her. She's not well,"

Blunt raises an eyebrow.

"Nothing serious, I hope?" her tone implies the opposite.

"No." Melz says shortly. "But I can safely say that I'm representing the covensteads and Lowenna Hawthorne when I say that we don't want to be under your rule. Ever. But we do want you to recognise the portals as a power source. For everyone's sake," Melz says.

"And if I do entertain whatever it is - this notion you have about energy centres? What do I get?" Blunt asks.

"By Brighid. Isn't a solution to the world's energy shortage enough?" I stand up. "If you're not interested we'll go. Come on, Melz,"

"At this stage all you've done is shown me two pieces of paper. Excuse me if I don't applaud your remarkable ingenuity just yet," Blunt drawls. "I'd say it was me that was offering you a lot more than I'm getting. We can help you restore order in the south west. Eradicate the gangs you have down there. And that will leave room and resources for thousands of the poor. You have resources in the Greenworld we don't have anymore. Fuel, agriculture, clean water. We're going to need that for the people,"

"How are you going to help us restore order when you can't stop your own folk rioting?" I pick up one of the expensive-looking pens from the leather-covered desk and uncap it, twisting it in my fingers. Blunt gives me an annoyed glance but doesn't comment.

"The war is over. The army will come home. We've lost a… proportion of the infantry, but there's still more than enough to restore order throughout the country."

"A proportion. Thousands, you mean," Melz interrupts.

"There are always high casualties in a long war," Blunt gazes at the corner of the room, unreadable.

"But we don't want that. You're not sending soldiers to the Greenworld. And, unless I'm very much mistaken, that's not going to work with your own people either. They're rioting because they're sick of totalitarian control. It doesn't matter if it's the army or private security services," Melz stands up. "And if you think you can scare us into opening our borders you're very much mistaken. Don't underestimate our power. We came here to share something with you. A way to end all wars for fuel. A way to sustain life for the future. And you won't even listen!" she leans over and bangs her fist on the desk and the Prime Minister jumps. "Don't you think we would have come here if it wasn't really important? Why would we risk it?"

Blunt stands up to face Demelza Hawthorne in all her war goddess glory; Boudicca come back for what's hers. They stand eye to eye for a moment.

Blunt drops her gaze first.

"Fine. If it'll make you more receptive to what I'm offering, tell me about these portals," she catches Melz's wrist. "Convince me. But if I listen to you, you listen to me. Okay?"

"That's all I ask," Melz returns Blunt's stare

steadily, then sits down and reopens the scroll on the desk. Blunt sits on the edge of her chair, watching Melz's face as she talks. The light streams through the tiny specks where the paint has flaked off the windows onto us, like the tiniest shards of sun through clouds.

CHAPTER TWENTY-EIGHT

We signed the Contract of Separation with the Redworld in 2025. They required the document, not us. We did what we needed to for independence.

From: Greenworld Governance: Rules for Utopia

They send a ministerial car to take us somewhere overnight. The guards march us down from Blunt's office to a quiet walled-in courtyard where a massive, long black thing's waiting to swallow us like the proverbial python. I've never actually seen a python, they're not exactly native to the Greenworld, but snakes are holy to Brighid. And obviously we know about the sheer volume of snake mythology connected to the various goddesses of antiquity, representing female sexual magic and empowerment. Kundalini yoga, anyone?

The snake told Eve to eat the apple. Goddess knows she wouldn't be the only woman not to be happy (or indeed *vag-a-hoop*) to lie under Adam and make babies for the rest of her natural life. Lilith was Adam's first wife and was made into a demon for not wanting to assume the missionary position; there's a famous painting of her naked with a python curling around her. If you're going to be the woman embracing a snake, I guess you might as well go all the way and be naked doing it too.

(Admittedly, I'm digressing now. Shit, how meta-contextual and joyously FEMALE).

We climb into the car's slippery leathery interior. Even though we were in that truck on the way down for what seemed like hours, when the car starts up, I still embarrass myself by yelping a bit. Melz laughs, suddenly, and the weirdness of being in this foreign, inhospitable place dissipates, after a long and generally pretty horrible day.

"Sorry. It was… just, your face was…." She breaks into gales of laughter again as the car moves and the vibrations under me intensify. "You made this noise… eeep!" she does a fair imitation of it, I suppose, and goes off into giggles again, leaning into the shiny interior, shoulders shaking. "Oh… I've never… hahaha!" she lies weakly against the sofa-type chair inside this long beast of a car and laughs herself silly.

"You quite finished?" I don't know whether to laugh too or be cross, even though I know she isn't really laughing at me; it's a kind of release. Melz laughs so little that I don't want to stop her. Even at my expense.

"Sorry. Really." She clears her throat.

"It wasn't that funny,"

"I know. It's just tension. I've been wound up for days." She wipes her eyes. "You made a noise exactly like an aroused rabbit,"

"How do you even know what that sounds like? What are you, like, a rabbitophile? You get turned on by bunnies?" It's nice to talk normally just for a minute, even if we're in a car owned by an evil government being ferried to an unknown location.

"I'm a witch. I know everything," she smiles at me. "Didn't you ever have rabbits as pets? Ours used to go at it, like, all the time."

"Lovely. Rabbit sex is one of my all-time favourite topics,"

"What? It's just natural. Then when they had babies and the babies grew up we'd have rabbit pie,"

"Ugh! You ate your pets?"

"Law of the wild, Sadie. Rabbit pie tastes good," she grins and reaches for my hand. "Thanks for today," she strokes my palm softly. "For everything. I couldn't have done it without you,"

"It's okay," I can feel myself blushing at her casual touch, so I gaze out of the window. "Sorry about the baby eating thing. I just wanted to wind them up. Ignorant Redworlders,"

"Don't worry. We were being what they wanted us to be, though. The evil Greenworld witches,"

"I'd hope that they could see the obvious satire of the situation,"

"Hmmm. I think you're overestimating your comedic gifts a little,"

I hold her hand, and we both watch as a dark, street-lit London passes by the black-tinted windows. The lights flicker just like they do everywhere in the Redworld.

"Goddess. There's so many people," Melz leans past me and I catch her scent; slightly sweaty, slightly incense-tinged.

"*Maybe the only beauty left in cities is in the oil slicks on the road and maybe there isn't any beauty left in the people who live in these places.*" I quote Rita-Mae. Melz looks at me quizzically. "It's from a book I like," I say awkwardly.

She leans back and puts her head on my shoulder; I hold my breath involuntarily.

"What's it called?" she asks sleepily. "The book?"

"Rubyfruit Jungle,"

"Oh, right. Greenworld-approved," she smiles up at me faintly and yawns. "I never read it. I'm more of a poetry reader myself,"

"You like poetry?" I did not know this about her, and I think immediately about the poems about her scrawled in my Greenworld Journal.

"Her languid lips are sweeter than love's who fears to greet her; To men that mix and meet her, From many times and lands." she murmurs, opening her eyes and meeting mine. I try not to gulp but I can feel the blush creeping up my neck.

"What's that?"

"The Garden of Proserpine. One of my favourites,"

"Proto-Anarcho-Pagan poets. We did them too. In school," it was one of the few parts of school I liked. Shakespeare, Milton, Swinburne, Byron, romantic poets who liked nature. All men, but, to be fair, at the time most potential female poets were a tiny bit busy with one hand up a chicken's backside and wiping shit off a screaming kid with the other - or, were a little distracted from the higher pursuits of poetry what with being sexually assaulted, denied education or suffering from debilitating illness on a regular basis. Of course, there was the odd rich woman who could write, like Christina Rossetti or Dorothy Wordsworth or Mary Shelley. They just got other women to do the raw chickens and the shitty kids for them.

"I'm so tired," she says quietly. "I feel like I could sleep for a hundred years,"

"Like a princess in an old story," I murmur, looking at her black hair. It needs a wash and the plaits are starting to come loose, but it's still beautiful because it's part of her, the girl who feels, to me anyway, like she has everything good in the world folded up inside her. That it isn't that Shasta scroll that will save us, save me, but her. She smiles up at me and raises her eyebrow sardonically.

"Those princesses had to be woken with a kiss from a prince. I think I've had enough of princes to last me a lifetime. Or Kings of the Underworld,"

She never talks about Bran, but I know what he was to her, if only for a short time, and I know about

Tom, and that's two boys, two young men she's loved, and again like a thousand times before, despair slices my stomach and intones *she will never want you Sadie Morgan.*

"Fair enough," I smile, and she gazes up into my eyes for a long moment, and *damn* I want to kiss her, but then she sits up and clears her throat and the moment's over.

"Blunt told me this car's taking us home tomorrow. To the border, anyway. She offered to take us all the way but I didn't think that would be a good idea. Arriving in Tintagel in this,"

I gaze out of the window as we pass an alley inbetween the tall, dirty buildings; a fire crackles at one end and shadowy figures huddle around it. I'm glad I don't have to travel back through the Redworld on foot again.

"Good," I say.

A few minutes later the car approaches a black metal door set into a tall red-brick building. The gate rises slowly and the car drives in slowly and stops in the dark.

CHAPTER TWENTY-NINE

In the process of becoming the Greenworld, we created a manifesto: philosophical, represented by Tenets and Sayings of the Greenworld, and practical, represented by our Covenstead Regulations and Greenworld Governance: Rules for Utopia. The creation of a new state is ideological and practical: utopia needs a clear plan. It is not enough just to desire disconnection.

From: Greenworld Governance: Rules for Utopia

The car doors open automatically. A metallic-sounding voice emanates from somewhere inside the car. EXIT THE VEHICLE PLEASE.

As we step down out of the car, a blue light blinks on. We're standing in a high-ceilinged concrete room. There's nothing else here apart from the long black shiny car, us, and the driver, who sits motionless behind the steering wheel.

Almost immediately another door opens and a smartly dressed woman apears: black dress, hair pinned up neatly, indeterminate age. She nods to us.

"Girls," she says, coming forward and shaking our hands. "Welcome to the facility. Follow me to your rooms,"

We follow her, our boots squeaking on the rubber floor.

"Where are we?" I ask, peering up at the black cubes that swivel in our direction as we walk past.

"Closed government facility. We use it for visiting guests, sometimes other things,"

"Other things?" I ask, kind of not wanting to know.

"Prisoners under house arrest," she says, pleasantly, like that's an okay thing to be.

"That isn't what we are, though, right?" I look anxiously at Melz but she shakes her head.

"No," she says decisively and takes the small rectangular card the woman hands us as we stop outside two identical silver doors.

"I'll collect you to take you back to the car in the morning. In the meantime, you're free to explore the facility. You can order food from your rooms. The rooms have a connecting internal door if you want to socialise with each other. Please be aware that all telecommunications devices are automatically disabled on entry to the facility,"

"All right. Thanks," I say, wondering what she knows about witches and how we really don't need telecommunications to talk to the witches back home if we want to. Not that we do, on this occasion.

We open our doors and she nods, watching us go in. As soon as I close the door behind me I see what must be the interconnecting door and snick it open.

"Melz?" I peer into a room identical to mine - plain white walls apart from the same British flag, the red, white and blue that looks so alien compared to the Greenworld's black background with the white diagonal cross - the ancient Kernow flag, with the triskele in green in the centre. I can't see her and feel a stab of panic. Has she been taken, what have they done with her? But then I see her reflected in the mirror on the back of the main door. She's sitting on the edge of the wide white bed, shoulders slumped. I go in, wary.

"Melz? Are you okay?" I sit down gingerly beside her. She turns to me and the tiredness and sadness in her face ages her for a second. She looks like she's lived a whole life, not seventeen years. I smile hopefully at her and she smiles back, a small smile, but enough to chase the shadows away.

"I'm all right. Tired. I just want this to be over. I want to go home,"

I never see Melz like this; she's always the warrior, always the saviour of others, including me, more than once. Or she's the beautiful, glamorous witch. I guess that's what turned me on - the idea of her, rather than who she really was. But now, here she is, weak and tired and unimpressive. Here, instead, with a dirty face and bags under her eyes, is a real girl that still warms my heart; a real, sensitive girl who's tired and needs a friend.

And I'm terrified by that, because icy enchantresses don't need anyone. But tired girls do. And that means I can't continue to be the novice; the one that takes direction and strength from Melz all the time. I have to step up and be prepared to be the strong one sometimes. Can I do that? Do I want to?

"It'll be okay. Somehow. I believe it will," I take her hand and squeeze it. She smiles absently and squeezes it back.

"You're good at that,"

"What?"

"Believing. You've got this… this fiery strength. Maybe it's the Brighid thing,"

"Maybe. Redheads, though. We're feisty,"

"That's true. You are," We sit there companionably in the quiet for a minute, then she sighs and lies back on the bed. She leans on her arm and holds out the other hand to me. "Come here,"

My heart starts pounding agan - seriously, I might have some kind of arrhythmia - and my mouth goes completely dry. Perfect.

I take her hand and lie down next to her; on our backs we look up at the blank white of the ceiling. She turns her head on the pillow to face me.

"Thank you. Again. For coming with me. I don't think I'd have had the strength to do it on my own," she touches my cheek; her touch's completely hypnotic.

"I'd do anything for you. You know that," I croak, wishing my voice would come out seductively, but my nerves are so jagged I can hardly breathe. I don't know if I have the courage to kiss her again. It didn't go so well last time.

"I know," she breathes, and half-sits up, leaning toward me, then hesitates. The rough cotton of her off-white blouse pulls against her breasts as she leans, outlining their beautiful, achingly perfect curve. "I don't want to... I don't want to hurt you," she murmurs, but hurt seems like the last possible emotion right now with the chance of her so near and it's now or never so...

So I pull her down to me and kiss her. And I'm kidding myself, thinking *you can never hurt me, I love you, I love you*, but the truth's that I know she has all the power in the world to destroy me if she wants to. I know it. But I don't care. Demelza Hawthorne can destroy me if she wants to, but it'll still be worth it for this kiss.

I lose all sense of the rational world, *bye byeeee, see ya, it's been a blast, old life*. I'm all sensation against her rough lips; I'm alive in a way I've never been before - not with Danny, not with any of the other boys I've kissed. My whole body's like a struck bell, chiming a sweet, deep, true note. I can feel the kiss in my heart, in my lips, most definitely in the blessed orifice of ye goddess; I can feel our energies meshing and remaking, making something new, that combination of the two of us that tastes different, smells different, is something new and powerful and untried. This is the only moment I ever want to be in, the only state of being, and every other moment in my life pales compared to this; everything else has been the road leading here, everything else was filling time until we were here together, now.

I'm all the love poems I've ever read: the half-forgotten verses float to the surface of the shared sea of emotion between us and weave themselves into a bridge between our minds and hearts. *She walks in beauty like the night of cloudless climes and starry skies, and all that's best of dark and bright meet in her aspect and her eyes.* I open my eyes and pull away from her slightly, away from her parted lips and her half-closed gaze.

"I've never known anyone as... as beautiful as you," I say, but real words can only fail in this shifting sea-place where feeling can't be contained by anything as simple as a nonsensical collection of letters. She smiles but says nothing, taking my hand and placing it on her heart.

"I... I think I... " she stops herself. I catch my breath. *What?* But then she frowns and pulls away.

"Beauty is deceptive," she says, blankly, looking away. "Anyway, I'm not beautiful."

"You are. Beautiful; magical," I lean in to kiss her again but she pulls away.

"Please, Sadie. I'm so messed up. I want to… I like you, but…," she gets up and stands with her back to me, looking at the window which isn't really a window because the glass is frosted and there's a wall immediately behind it. How irritatingly symbolic of this moment.

"You don't understand. I'm bad, Sadie. You don't want me. You wouldn't, if you knew,"

No, I'd want you if you'd murdered the entire population of earth. I'd want you if wanting you meant I'd have ten years less to live. Don't tell me what I want and don't want.

"Is it because… because we're girls?" it seems unlikely, given our upbringing, but maybe that's what's troubling her.

She snorts softly.

"No. It's the ideal, isn't it? No greater love and all that," she semi-quotes the Greenworld tenet.

"Well, it might be the ideal, but that don't necessarily mean you can make yourself fancy girls,"

"That's not the problem, Sadie. Okay, I've… been

involved with boys before, but so have you,"

"It wasn't like this with them. I didn't... I didn't feel like this," Danny didn't make my pulse race and every single other crappy romantic cliché under Brighid's golden sun. "You don't... want me that way, then?"

"No, it's not that. You know it's not that,"

"Dunno anything right now," I mutter, hating the sulk in my voice but unable to stop it.

"Well, it isn't, let me tell you," she says, sharply.

"Tell me, then. I'll understand. I'm here for you. Now. Please. You can trust me," I try to keep the desperation out of my voice.

I'll do anything. If there's any chance at all that she loves me, I'll wait for her until death, after, even, to hear her finally say it.

I want to tell her now, to tell her over and over again *I love you, I love you,* I feel like I'm about to explode with it, with the not-saying it, but I know I can't.

"Is it Bran? D'you still love him?"

"No." her answer's flat, dead.

"You did love him, though," I know she did, and he's a threat lurking somewhere out there. Maybe one day she'll go back to him. To her King of the Underworld.

"I thought I did. Once. But..."

"But?"

"He's dead, Sadie. It doesn't matter now. Nothing matters now,"

"I didn't know he definitely... I mean, I know what you told us about what happened..."

"He's dead. He was electrocuted. I watched as his hair caught on fire." Her tone's icy now, but I know the horror she's trying to control; I can't imagine the awfulness of seeing that. Seeing anyone die that way, but especially someone you thought you loved. "And I know. I just know. I can feel it. He's passed," I watch her back, at the window. Straight and poised, strong, but her voice breaks as she says it.

"I'm so sorry, Melz," I stand there behind her, not knowing what to do - whether to try and hold her again or not. She bows her head and stifles a sob.

"I thought we were alike. We had our darknesses.

And then I realised how far down that path he'd gone, and I ran away. But I thought I loved him for a while. I loved him even though he was... was murdering people. What does that make me? What does that make me, Sadie?" and she starts sobbing, huge, screaming sobs that shake her and now I have to hold her; I turn her around and wrap my arms around her and she wails into me, hard and full of pain.

"You didn't know, Melz. It wasn't your fault," I hold her tighter, as if I could keep her from falling apart. I know how that feels.

"But the curse. I killed Bali and Skye, too. So I'm the same as he was,"

"You're not the same. You're good. Amazing," I don't want to comment on the curse thing. We don't speak about it in the coven.

"No. I'm a dark person, Sadie. Not bright and alive like you. The curse I did, after Tom died. On Bali and Skye. I burnt what was left of it, with the Morrigan... but I don't think it really left me. The shadow of it." She pulls back from me and takes in a few desperate, deep breaths. "I have to deal with that every day. Sometimes I feel as though I might..." she lets out a long, jagged exhale. "Some days I want to just put an end to it. Myself. Everyone would be better off,"

"Melz! Don't say that. Please, by Brighid. No!" I can feel the tears falling down my cheeks; she's breaking my heart; I don't want her to feel like this, ever. Because I know what despair is, and I never want her to feel half as awful as I do when it comes over me, relentless, sick and yellow. "Please promise me you won't do that. You won't do anything stupid,"

"I can't promise you anything. That's why you shouldn't... feel that way about me," she wipes her eyes and looks at me dully.

"I can't help the way I feel," I say, quietly, brushing my tears away.

"I know. But... I just can't. Okay? Please understand," she smiles sadly, and looks away, at her feet. This is the end of the conversation, and she's pushing me away.

"All right," I'm defeated; there really isn't anything else I can say or do right now.

"You better go to bed. Long journey back tomorrow," she says, turning back to the window, and her tone's detached and sad, and I can't believe that we're here, together, alone; that we know we have feelings for each other, but that nothing's going to happen. And I hate that darkness she's in, then, hate it madly and beyond reason and I want to get into her head somehow and set everything on fire, to clean it all out once and for all so that Melz can love me, so that she can love again, so that she can be free.

"All right. Night, then," I say, willing her to turn around, willing her to have a change of heart, willing her to do anything but stand there with her back to me, but she doesn't turn around.

"Sleep well, Sadie," she says softly, and I go to the door between our rooms and pull it shut, hard.

"Goddamn it," I hiss, leaning against the heavy wooden door, letting the tears come.

CHAPTER THIRTY

You, lost from the start,

Beloved, never-achieved,

I don't know what melodies might please you.

I no longer try, when the future surges up,

to recognise you.

From: Beloved by R M Rilke

I couldn't sleep, and when I did, I kept waking up from bad dreams: Melz slamming a door in my face, Melz shouting at me, Melz flinching as I touched her shoulder. All great.

So, I'm writing. Balm for a tortured soul, catharsis for pain; something positive you can do when life is shitty. The page is always there for you. I write about the kiss. I feel like I'll always be writing about that kiss from now on.

I'm the night, I'm the fire, I'm the rain.
I'm dreaming of you again, always dreaming,
From one edge of the world to the other and between;
Dreaming when I'm kissing you it's crystalline,

WILD FIRE

The kind of kiss that bends the world in half,
And recombines the fractured stars to make your epigraph -
Reconnects your carbon to the sun,
And mine to yours with burnt red-black hair: make it so, so it is done,
So will it ever be. Someone will chant that over and over, softly,
In a shadowed differential plane,
As we kiss that crystalline kiss again and again and again.

I'm just trying to work out if the last line reads right - it needs more, it's not the end by any stretch of the kiss-fevered imagination - and is *epigraph* right? Isn't that when you die? No, that's *epitaph*. What's an epigraph? I'm chewing the end of my pencil when there's a loud knock on the door.

I run to the connecting door, the kiss still lingering on my lips and on my mind, thinking it's Melz, that she's had a change of heart, but as I look in she's still curled up in a ball at the far edge of the big white bed, covered in the white quilt. I realise the knock's coming from the main door to my room, and open it; a young woman stands there with a shiny gold trolley.

"Breakfast," she smiles and wheels the thing in. "Shall I leave this there for Miss Hawthorne too?"

I pull the connecting door closed.

"No. Please take hers into her room," I say, and the girl nods cheerily and takes one set of plates from the tray, lays them out prettily on the table in my room and wheels the rest out. I hear her knock on Melz's door, and Melz stumble out of bed.

Melz. Too difficult. Too soon. I need to prepare my heart for another day with her. I can't be as exposed again. I close my journal, eat mechanically and then get into the huge gleaming white cubicle which I assume's some kind of Redworld standing-up bath, surprising myself with the hot water spraying out of the tiny holes in the ceiling as I twiddle the knobs. Hot water, not lukewarm or cold. I can stay in here for as long as I like; no-one to bang on the door because they need a wee; no black line painted on the bath to regulate the amount of water used. I use all the soaps and products on the little shelf, amazed at how quickly the soap foams up and at the strong floral smell of it all. Under the stream of water, I visualise my heartbreak washing away down the plughole; a muddy stream of hurt and hope. It helps a bit, but not loads. I've still been rejected. I still hate that.

About an hour later, the woman that showed us to

our rooms comes to get us. I'm ready, now; Melz opens her door and joins us in the hall.

"Morning," she says, avoiding my eyes, but I smile warmly. She's still my friend and I still love her. I can't stop loving her just like that, even if I want to.

"Morning,"

"All right, girls. Follow me," the woman leads us back down the winding hallways and stairs and we come to the garage where the same long black car's waiting for us, the faceless driver, dressed in black, ready behind the wheel.

"Thanks for... err, having us," I'm not sure what to say to her but the woman smiles briskly and sees us into the car.

"Safe travels," she says. The huge metal door rolls up again automatically and we're back onto the London streets, in the daylight this time. Melz is silent, and so I watch the city as it passes, at once grand and tall and beautiful, and at the same time filthy, disorganised and swarming with desperate-looking folk.

"I'm glad we're going home," I murmur into the silence, and look over at Melz, but she's looking away from me. She wipes her cheek and her shoulders are hunched. Is she crying? I can't tell, but I leave her be.

We've been riding in silence for over an hour when out of nowhere, there's a jolt and a screech of brakes. The car skids sideways and screeches to a stop; the seatbelts hold us back but I feel my neck snap forward and back, feel the belt dig into my shoulder like my dad's hand used to. I pull away harder, instinctively, but the belt holds me and I feel that sick yellow panic welling up inside me. *Oh no. Something bad. Something bad's coming.* I feel myself cower, get smaller, in readiness for the panic attack. The taste of salt water, the pull of water on my lungs. Breathless.

Both of Melz's hands grip her belt and she's pale, even paler than usual, if that was possible.

"What the bloody hell was that?" she shouts; I sit back and the belt goes back to normal, letting me move. I unclip it and feel the relief wash through me; I rub my shoulder where the black woven material feels like its bruised my skin. So many bruises, so many years, all layered on top of each other. I feel the panic recede slightly; enough for me to tap on the black glass partition between us and the driver. "Hey. Hey! What just happened?"

There's no answer, but the driver's door opens with a muted click.

"Stay here. I'm going to see what's up," Melz opens her door and steps down.

"Melz! Don't!" I cry out after her, feeling like she mustn't leave the car, or something terrible will happen. That the ground's writhing with monsters. I lean out of the open car door just enough to watch her walk purposefully to the front of the car.

"Think I hit something," I hear the driver say. Then he tells her to get back in the car. She refuses.

"Let me see," Melz's voice is imperious.

"Get back in the car, please, Miss," the driver's tone is respectful but firm.

"What did you hit?" I hear her ask, ignoring him. I know she isn't going to back down. I take some deep breaths and step out of the car, almost expecting to see the road rear up at me with fangs and scales, but it stays mundanely grey and in its place. I feel sick. The panic starts washing over me. I don't want to be here, I don't want to be anywhere. But I make myself move.

We're alone on a dusty, cracked, grey road that runs through dark fields; in the oak trees by the side of the road I can see the outlines of crow nests like balls of black wool on the bare branches. I hear distant bird calls as I walk carefully around the car. We're still in the Redworld but this part, wherever we are, is dead quiet. I try and take some deep breaths, but fail, and end up panting.

"Where are we?" I ask the driver. I can see myself mirrored in his black sunglasses, and note, again, the lack of badges or identification on his black military-style outfit. No idea who he is or where we are. My panic rears like a frightened horse: I feel cold. He could do anything to us out here and nobody would know. Oh Goddess.

"Get back in the car please, Miss," he repeats to me, looking around him warily. He undoes his jacket; there's a gun tucked into his waistband. I hold onto the car for support.

"Not until you tell us where we are and why we stopped," my heart's beating crazily. I lean against the car. Breathe in, breathe out. It's okay. All I have to do is exist right now.

"Wiltshire. Just went over Salisbury Plain. You need to get back in the car. I got orders to keep you in the car at all times," He could have orders to kill us out here, and nobody would know. *Shit, shit, shit.* I know he's got a gun, but I need to see what stopped the car. I peer around us: fields and trees in all directions. No other cars. I walk myself around the back of the car, holding onto it. Slowly, the walking and the breathing is calming the panic. Melz follows me.

"Hey. You okay?"

"Panic attack. It's going, I think,"

I take some more deep breaths.

"Mum said she was treating you for those,"

"Yep"

"What can I do?"

"Just stand next to me for a bit,"

She grabs my hand, and I feel her warm reassurance flow through me immediately.

"Healing energy," she smiles. "Just take your time. It's fine,"

"Miss! Get back in the car, please. I got orders," the driver says again, coming around our side of the car. I realise then he's scared. He hasn't arranged this.

"My friend is having a panic attack. Relax," Melz snaps at the driver, queenlike. "We'll get back in the car when we're ready and not before. She needs fresh air,"

He prevaricates, not looking sure. Looks around us balefully.

"Just a minute, then," he mutters, and goes to the front of the car, looking down at something on the road. I squeeze Melz's hand. I'm coming back to normal.

"I'm okay. I'll be all right," I still feel sick, but there's something weird about this situation. "What did we hit?"

"Let's look," Melz keeps my hand in hers. "Probably a pheasant or something. Stupid birds,"

We walk around to the front of the car. A raven lies dead on the road in a pool of blood.

A raven. One of the Morrigan's messengers. Melz gasps and kneels down next to it, cradling the bird in her arms, stroking the thick feathers around its broken neck.

Ravens don't live in open fields; they nest high up in mountains, in dense forests or on coastal cliffs. Not here with the sweet-voiced birds of the fields. Their deep croaks are for harsher places.

Is it a sign? The driver, following us, recoils when he sees the raven.

"What're you doing? Is it dead?" he asks, stepping backwards.

Melz hugs the bird to her and looks up at me, wide-eyed.

"A sacred bird. A messenger," she breathes.

I kneel down next to Melz and run my finger gently down the bird's back, feeling a quiver of life left. My hands start to heat up, and as they do, my panic goes altogether. "I've never see a raven before. It's beautiful," I whisper.

"It was more beautiful when it was alive," Melz snaps.

"It isn't dead yet. Not quite," I murmur.

There's a silence on the fields; the birdsong has stopped; not even a leaf rustles. The Morrigan has sent a message, or a warning, but of what?

Whatever it is, I can stop it. I can turn bad luck around. I can bring the raven back to life. I take the bird from Melz gently, and bow my head.

"What are you doing?" Melz hisses, but the soul of the bird is still nearby. I can feel it. It's only just begun its separation from the body. I start to keen into the wind, a wordless song, a song for the raven's soul. At the same time, the healing flows from my hands and into the bird's inert body, knitting its bones back together. No-one taught me the song. I've been singing it ever since I was a child. Melz and the driver watch and listen, the wind stills, and it feels as though the oaks watch and approve.

I reach for some words and speak them firmly into the morning air.

"Great Healer Brighid; Queen of Fire, give life to this bird of wisdom, so it may rise anew to serve you. Bless its body. Fill it with your wild spirit, your wild fire, so it may soar another day. You are the fire that moulds the sword and the flame that purges the body. Great Brighid, hear my cry."

I sit back on my heels, still holding the bird, and

feel its presence return, slowly. Slowly, the raven becomes a raven again and not a dead thing, not a clump of feathers. It grows heavier with life in my hands; the heat of healing intensifies until I'm sweating in the cold morning air. I feel Brighid with me, around me like a blue cloak, healing, burning death away. *Not today, not now,* She says. *This was not its time.*

The raven ruffles its feathers and *quorks*. I open my hands, and it hops onto the ground, then into the grass at the side of the road. It *quorks* again, and we watch as it rises up on the air into a tree.

I raise my head and look back at Melz and the driver, who are standing respectfully behind me.

"It's done," I say, and stand up. "We can go,"

"You just… what did you just…?" the driver takes off his sunglasses and I see that his eyes are brown, with lined skin that make him look kind.

"I healed it," I look up at the raven in the tree.

"That's impossible," he says, following my gaze.

"No, it isn't," I sigh. Even seeing something with your own eyes isn't enough for some folk.

"I..." he looks around suddenly at the sound of voices from further down the road, and suddenly the wonder on his face's gone. He pushes his glasses back on and pushes Melz and me into the car. The engine screams alive and we pull away violently; as we accelerate, something thuds into the toughened black glass behind us, then again. I hear the driver swear in the front of the car.

"Shit! What...?" I try and look arund behind us, but it's hard with the speed of the car pressing me back into the seat.

"What was that?" Melz scrambles around in her seat and peers through the tinted window. "There's a group of folk throwing things at the car!" she cries and I crane around to see. Five people standing in the middle of the road behind us, scruffily dressed. It's hard to hear what they're shouting over the revving of the engine and through the thick doors and windows as we speed away.

"What are they saying?" I ask Melz, who's watching them intently.

"Take the power back," she nods as we lose sight of them over the next hill. "I've heard it before. In Glastonbury and York,"

"When you were in the Redworld, before? Was that what they said to you? They wanted to take your power?" I shiver and turn around in my seat.

"No. Not mine. Theirs," she nods to the shadow of the driver in the front seat.

"They want to take their own power back?" I'm confused.

"No, well, kind of. I think it's more that they want power back over their own lives,"

"They're revolutionaries, then? Resistance?"

"Maybe. There were riots when I was here. More and more people getting fed up with the way things are,"

"Blunt mentioned that,"

"She should have seen it coming. You can't treat people like animals and expect them to take it. Not that we'd ever treat animals that badly. But they would. They do,"

"I guess so. So you think this resistance's getting bigger?"

"Maybe," she frowns. "The irony is that it works

against us, in a way, now. If we're going to work together with Blunt…"

"We didn't agree that we would. Only teach them about the portals,"

"I know. But that involves cooperation. I just want to make sure that any resistance movement understands what we're doing and doesn't make it difficult for us. We might look like government stooges from the outside, if we do this,"

"I guess we have to play our hand as best we can. Get the job done and then get the word out. Let them know we're helping them by helping Blunt," I say.

"They might not see it that way. Bran's idea was always that I could somehow empower the poor directly. Teach them a new way of living. Overpower the toffs at the top,"

"We need to talk to all the global leaders. We can't just go in there and smash everything up. As tempting as that would be. I mean - we need the world on side. And the only way we get to the global leaders is through Blunt," I counter.

"I know," she picks the skin around her fingers.

"It's going to be a tricky line to tread. Blunt, the covensteads, the resistance. Not least getting mum on side as well,"

"I know,"

"How are we going to do that?" she pulls a long strip of skin off from beside her nail and I watch as the blood oozes out from the pink skin. She sucks her finger, frowning.

"I've literally no idea," I say, helpfully.

"Me neither,"

There's a silence as the road races by.

"Why do you think She sent the raven?" I break the quiet. She looks out of her window, her bloodied finger playing with a button on her white blouse.

"I don't know," she says. "It's not always clear why She does what She does. A message, though. A warning," but then she looks at me, and smiles. "But you healed it. You brought it back to life,"

"I've always… ummm… well, I've always been able to do that. Birds and small animals,"

"You never told anyone?"

"No,"

"Why not?"

"I didn't want dad to know." I look at my hands. I felt like they were treacherous, before, always trying to betray me. Dad, him, Roach, looking for the slightest hint that I had power, all the time. Testing me. *Can you move this without touching it, Sadie*, he'd say, putting a book in front of me on the table. *Can you tell what I'm thinking. What did you dream, Sadie, what did you dream, tell me your dreams*. Even when he'd been living in the forest with his men for ages, he wouldn't give up on me, not for years.

She watches my face as if she can hear my thoughts, takes both of my hands in hers and kisses them. *What? Mixed signals, Demelza.* Then she looks guilty, like she ate an extra slice of Yule cake when no-one was looking. It's nice to think I might be the sweet thing she's tempted by, but I really might be over-analysing. It's probably me making a few innocent kisses between friends more than they are. I should be cool with that. I shouldn't care. But, by Brighid most holy, I do care.

"Well, he's not here now. That's a wonderful gift,"

"We can all heal," I'm deflecting her praise and I don't even know why. No, that's a lie. I don't want to talk about him.

"Not like that. I mean, I learnt it, like everyone. But I don't know if I could bring an animal back from the edge of death. So quickly, too,"

"It's just one of those things," I shrug.

"Don't downplay it," she says, giving me her piercing *I'm-your-mentor* look.

"I… I find it hard not to. Because I'm so used to hiding it… from him,"

"I understand," she says, and gives me an awkward hug. When I meet her eyes she gives me an odd look I can't quite decipher, and there's a pause where I want to lean in and kiss her again. Then the moment evaporates, and she pulls away from me, looking away.

"You shouldn't hide what you are, Sadie. Never hide what you feel," she says to the darkened window of the car. The hypocrite.

CHAPTER THIRTY-ONE

A particularly persistent man came to ask Brighid's father and her brothers to give Her to him in marriage. They approached Brighid with this proposal and once again She refused, for She wanted to found a healing centre to take care of the poor and sick. One brother said "What good is that pure eye in your head if it's not looking across the pillow at a husband?"

This angered and humiliated Brighid and, sticking Her finger in Her eye, She pulled it out of its socket and let it lay hanging on Her cheek by a few sinews. Upon seeing what She was willing to do to fulfil Her convictions, Her father and brothers promised that never again would they press Her to marry and they would respect and support Her decision.

From The Book of Brighid, Greenworld Prayers and Songs

When we get home, Lowenna's waiting for us in her kitchen, laying out her tarot cards. An almost-empty glass of wine stands on the carved covenstead table. She barely looks up as we come in. *Shit.* My stomach turns over in dread.

"You're back from your travels, I see," her tone's flat and she continues turning out cards, laying them one on top of another. Melz looks at me; we knew we'd come back to this. *We'll tell the truth; there's nothing else we can do*: we agreed it in the car. But now, the simplicity of telling the truth feels tangled and hurtful.

As we got out of the car at the Greenworld border, the black-uniformed driver had handed us an envelope. Inside was a personal letter from Felicity Blunt, detailing everything we'd talked about. We'll be allowed to attend the fuel summit and address the delegates, but we have to agree to help Blunt house Redworlders in greater numbers on Greenworld land, and work with her to overturn the private security services; help put the state back in charge. We'll be responsible for teaching Redworlders how to live more sustainably in their own communities. In return, she'll help us work with the gangs to find peace, support our witches' governance of Devon and Cornwall and revoke our terrorist status. We'll stil be the Greenworld, but the border will come down. *We will encourage respect instead of division,* Blunt finishes the letter. *You have my word.*

Melz puts it down on the table in front of her mum; Lowenna's eyes flicker over the Ministerial crest and Blunt's name on the envelope.

"She wants to make a deal. Integration back into

the Redworld with no charges for any of us if we can help them out. It's all there. They'd want us to educate the public about how to live off-grid,"

"Would they now," Lowenna murmurs, and turns over a final card. Death. She snorts and pours herself another glass of wine, emptying the bottle.

"Mum. Say something," Melz touches Lowenna's shoulder, but she shakes it off. "I think we have to consider it. Reintegration. On our terms of course, but..."

"Don't touch me," Lowenna stands up and goes to the cupboard under the sink, pulling out another bottle. She uncorks it and brings it to the table. "I suppose I should be used to being betrayed by my daughters by now," she glares at me. She's drunk. "And you. Sadie Morgan. Fire Priestess that you are. You'd go anywhere she told you to go, I know that. But don't you have any loyalty? If not to me, then to Brighid?" she shakes her head and slumps back in her seat.

"Of course I do. But, Lowenna, you can't pretend this isn't happening. The Greenworld's fracturing, more every day. The Redworld's suffering. We've seen the other portals in the world, some of them anyway. There are other communities, other resistances. They have the keys to…"

"Salvation?" she interrupts me. "Salvation *was* the Greenworld, you stupid girl. Are you naïve enough to believe you can change the Redworld? It's too far gone. If I could cut this land off from the putrid land on their side I would. Cast us into the ocean," she gulps down half the wine in the glass and sets it down unsteadily. "You went there with your open hearts and your progressive ideals and see what you came home with," she picks up the letter and spits on it. "Lies and half-promises. That's all you'll ever get from them,"

"Listen, mum. We have to make them see. It's our only chance," Melz pleads.

"Don't be stupid. We're safe here," Lowenna slurs, and Melz reaches to take the glass out of her hand.

"You've had enough," she says, but Lowenna pulls the glass away and it falls over, out of her reach, spilling the red wine over the cards like blood. She screams weakly.

"Oh, look what you've done!" she picks up the cards hurriedly and wipes them on her skirt, the wine leaving darkish stains on the shapeless light green hemp-cotton skirt, one of the particularly ugly ones Tintagel women wear; Merryn makes them and they're even more hideous than the creations we had back in Gidleigh.

"Mum, come on, we have to talk about this!" Melz yells back. "This is too important! You can't sit here drinking and pretending everything's okay. It's not okay! We've got this one chance to make positive change in the world. In the world outside here, outside our covensteads. We can't pretend what's happening in the Redworld doesn't have any effect on us. It does, and it's getting closer every day!"

"Go away, Demelza. I won't be lectured by my own daughter," Lowenna pours herself another glass.

"No, mum. You have to talk about this!" Melz shouts, getting in her mum's face but Lowenna pushes her away and throws her wine glass at the wall, where it shatters.

"I don't have to do anything! How DARE you speak to me like this! Your own mother, and High Priestess! I have absolute authority here. In this house, in the covenstead and in the Greenworld. You'll be punished for going behind my back to that... that... SNAKE! Blunt! She's spread lies about us happily enough. Terrorists, that's what they call us! Why would you go to her? Why would you betray me like that? Betray all of us? Everything I've fought to protect all this time? WHY?" she screams at us both, and Melz steps backwards, and her face clouds over. It's that same expression she had at the beach with Danny when she mocked him. That same shadow.

"Because I've had enough of this shit. You're just some sad, used up has-been that can't even cast a circle right anymore. Ever thought all this might be your fault? If you were more powerful, maybe Roach would never have been able to attack us in the first place?"

I gasp. That's going *way* too far. But Melz carries on, like she's possessed. "Look at you. Can't keep a coven together. Can't keep your own daughters from deserting you. Can't keep a man." She lunges at her mother and stands until her face's almost touching Lowenna's. "Old. Dried out and useless. It's over, mum. Your time is up,"

There's a shocked silence; Melz would never usually be so cruel. Brutally honest, sure. Plenty of that. And we haven't talked about anyone's time "being up". We disobeyed, we did what we thought was right. This is the part where we have a big heart to heart and at the very least find a compromise. Isn't it?

"Melz, come on, that's enough," I take her hand but she shakes it free.

"No, Sadie. She needs to hear this," she stares her mother down, something I've never seen anyone do.

Melz reaches forward, aiming for her mother's neck. Lowenna's eyes widen as Melz's fingers graze her throat. What the fuck is she doing? Lowenna draws back instinctively. The shadowy expression covers Melz. She's someone else; herself, but not. It reminds me of Danny, that day on the village green in Gidleigh. He wasn't himself when that cloud of thick, dark energy took him over.

Melz's fingers curl around Lowenna's rough amber necklace: the sacred possession of the High Priestess. She turns her wrist; her fingers make a fist around it. "You're not in charge anymore, old woman," she says flatly. Lowenna stands wordless, her mouth open in shock. I feel like this isn't really happening. It's surreal.

"But…"

"But me no buts, mother," incredibly, Melz's mouth twists into a smile, but it isn't a happy one. "This is a revolution. I'm taking over the covenstead,"

"What? We haven't discussed this! Melz, come on!

This is madness!" I try to keep my voice level but this just got very weird very fast.

"Shut up, Sadie,"

I'm instantly crushed. I'm so shocked that I freeze and don't know how to reply.

"Take over? You don't even know what you mean by that." Lowenna sneers at her daughter. "I made everything! The Greenworld, the coven. I made *you*, By Brighid! You can't just take over,"

"You should know what I mean. Covenstead rules say that if three or more members of the coven have serious concerns, they can depose the High Priestess," Melz enunciates clearly. "I'm a good student, mum. I know my Covenstead Regulations,"

The creak of the kitchen door makes us all turn around.

"I do, too," Saba steps forward into the kitchen; looks at us and then at the wine-soaked tarot cards. "You're going to have to catch me up, girls; I feel like I've missed something of reasonable importance," she says, one eyebrow raised.

CHAPTER THIRTY-TWO

To revive a patient suffering from exhaustion or depression

In cases of shock, stress or nervous debility, nervine tonics strengthen and feed the tissues directly, easing anxiety and depression – Damiana, Skullcap, Vervain, Wood Betony.

From: The Common Herbal

"Bersaba! Thank Goddess you're home. Your sister's gone mad," Lowenna stumbles over a wooden dining chair and imprisons Saba in her sweaty grip. Saba makes a face and pulls away.

"You been drinking, mum?" she screws up her nose in disdain. Lowenna grimaces.

"That's not important. Your sister says she wants to take over the covenstead," she turns to Melz. "If you need two others I don't know where you're going to find them. Danny's away, Goddess knows where. And the trainees are mine. They need me. I'm the founder, I'm the source of all knowledge. I initiated them and I can banish them if I want to," she clicks her fingers. "Jusht like that,"

If only the trainees knew how precariously their membership in the coven was balanced.

"Are you serious about this? Deposing Lowenna?" I ask Melz.

"Dead serious," she looks at me dispassionately.

"But... you can't. Come on," I hold out my hands to them both. "You both have to see sense. Lowenna, I'm deeply thankful for your training and all the care you've taken with me. But Melz is right. The earthquakes are just going to get worse, the world's sick. We can't just sit here and ignore it."

"I'm your High Priesthtesh, Sadie Morgan. You'll ignore whatever I tell you to ignore," She's really drunk. We shouldn't be having this conversation with her like this.

"No, I won't. Melz - come on. Lowenna's your mother. High Priestess. Head Witch of the Greenworld. I mean, I don't really know if you've thought this through," I grab her hand, hoping my touch will bring her back to earth somehow, from this madness, but she shakes her head.

"No, Sadie. I have. And you know I'm right. She's

either with us or against us. Do you really want to carry on, blind and deaf to what's going on around us?"

"No. But there has to be another way," I plead, knowing there isn't. Knowing that neither of them will back down.

Saba watches us, her eyes flicking from her mum to her sister to me. At our linked hands.

"I came with a message," she says, thoughtfully. "From Tressa at the Archive. It seems that Sadie and Melz have been journeying through the portal, out to the other side. Mount Shasta, right?"

"Yes. Twice, anyway. That's how we know about the way to use portals for energy. The Shasta told us,"

"Tressa thought as much. She says to tell you, mum, they're right. Tressa's been talking to the Shasta for a while now, though she's never visited. She communicates psychically. She taught me how to do it last time I was there. She says, if they've shown you the way, Sadie, then you have to take it. You have to do it. It's your duty. And there's more. Six portals across the world are blocked - that we know of. Big ones, in populated areas. That's six communities suffering. That has to be rectified, and Tressa thinks whatever they've told you - that's the way to do it,"

"Duty! It's their duty to obey *me*. Never mind Tressa," Lowenna says petulantly, like a child having her toy taken away as punishment.

"Why not? She's as good a witch as you. She's your sister," Saba argues. "At least she's not mad with power. At least you can have a decent conversation with Tressa without her storming out. She's serious, mum. The Boscastle coven will support Melz." She looks at us again and rolls her eyes. "And I do too. Despite the fact that she annoys the crap out of me." She looks at Melz, and you can see how alike they are, despite Melz being dark and kohl-ringed, and Saba honey-blonde and sunny. "You want to take over the coven, Melz?"

"I think it's for the best," says the dark-shadowed twin.

Saba sighs.

"All right, then. I agree. That's what you need, right? The agreement of another witch?"

"I need two," the twins look at me. Melz's eyes are full of passion; Saba watches me impassively. "Sadie. Please," Melz pleads. "You know it's the only way. The

Shasta told us,"

I'm not sure that this was exactly what they told us, but I can't refuse Melz.

"All right. I'm with you," my heart's beating in my mouth, in my ears.

"Mum, you're out," Melz says, a look of dark triumph on her face.

I cringe, looking at Lowenna as she lowers herself into one of the easy chairs and starts to sob drunkenly. Saba cradles her mother's faded yellow hair in her arms and holds her as the tears rack her whole body. The kitchen's filled with a sickening cloud of grief.

"You can't! You can't do this to me!" Lowenna cries; snot coming from her nose. It's horrible to see her like this, but she's been losing power for a while and she knows it. What I don't want to say is *who'll train me in the ways of Brighid now? Who'll teach me the fire chants and the healing and the customs of the hearthfire?* Because I want to be the Priestess of Brighid I know I can be. Saba catches my eye and looks pointedly at the jars on the shelf containing sedatives.

"Sadie. Put the kettle on for a tea, will you?" she

says lightly, but her eyes tell me different. *Make her something to knock her out.*

You have to let the old go to embrace the new, that's what they taught us at school. It's all a cycle: birth, growth, death, birth again; the three spirals of the triskele, the triple moon, the three faces of the Goddess. I put the kettle on the hearth to boil and crumble some dried herbs into a cup: valerian, hops, lemon balm. I look back over my shoulder and watch Lowenna as Saba strokes her hair, awkwardly.

"You can't do this to me. The covenshteads won't allow it," Lowenna mumbles as I hand Saba the hot cup.

"Here. Drink this, mum," Saba coos. "We'll talk about all this tomorrow."

Lowenna drinks a little. Melz stalks around the room restlessly, like a cat. I catch her eye and frown at her.

"More," Saba tips the bottom of the heavy clay mug up so that some of the tea spills down Lowenna's shirt. She coughs, but Saba smiles and offers it to her again. "It'll help," she smiles, the good daughter, and Lowenna drinks again. Saba hands the cup back to me and watches as Lowenna closes her eyes. Gently she lays her mother back in the easy chair and turns to Melz and me.

"Okay," she says. "We've got until she wakes up to come up with a plan, because she's going to be one severely pissed off and very powerful witch when she wakes up,"

"I'm taking over the coven. That's all there is to it," Melz blurts out. "She'll see sense,"

Saba snorts.

"She will NOT see sense and you know it, Melz. She's so pissed right now she's not even going to remember this conversation when she wakes up. Don't be so short sighted. Do you really think Lowenna Hawthorne is going to just hand over Tintagel to you?"

"She has to. It's the only smart way forward,"

"That doesn't matter. You know mum. Her way or nothing. That's why I went to Tressa."

"I thought you went off in a huff because mum chose Sadie over you. And you shouldn't have destroyed the measures,"

"Didn't you see them, though? Plaited together with all our hair and blood? I'd had enough of her controlling everything. Never giving us any freedom. That's why I left." Saba runs her hand through her own tawny gold hair; her expression's haunted. "Turns out that I wasn't the only one that felt like that, though. Tressa hasn't been happy with the way the Greenworld's been developing for a while, she says. Apaprently it's about half and half across the covensteads - half of them want a change. That's a lot of witches,"

"Okay, well, that's good, isn't it? I've got half the Greenworld on my side," Melz shrugs. "Done deal,"

"It's not a done deal. Don't be stupid. Don't you see? This is about way more than Tintagel. It's the whole Greenworld. If you take over here, you take it all. Zia's gone. Mum's the first and only head witch. Yeah, about half the witches might not like the way she's done things recently, but that doesn't necessarily mean they'll stand up against her, or give you the rulership. You're still only 17,"

"I don't *want* to fight her. She's my mum. But I will," Melz says, looking at the sleeping Lowenna.

"Well, if you want to take over, you're going to have to fight," Saba says grimly. "Because she's not going down without a scrap,"

CHAPTER THIRTY-THREE

There is a line of succession for Head With of the Greenworld, and it rests within the training circle of the Five Hands covenstead in Tintagel.

From: Greenworld Governance: Rules for Utopia

We half-drag, half-carry Lowenna's dead weight up to her room.

"At least wait until she's awake. Talk to her about it when she's herself," I pant as Melz draws pulls open Lowenna's bedroom door and picks up an oil lamp from the floor outside. She lights it from a candle in the hallway and puts it inside the room. Inside I recognise Lowenna's signature chaos - used teacups, puddles of underwear on the floor, piles of dusty books.

"No way. She can read our thoughts and she's very persuasive when she wants to be. I'm not giving her that chance. We need to keep her out of the way until I've had a chance to talk to all the covensteads. If I can get them all on side, it doesn't matter what she tries to do. But at the moment, she's got too much support," Melz says. "This is the only way. I've been struggling with the idea, but now it's clear,"

"You didn't say anything," I accuse, feeling hurt that I don't know everything she's thinking. I thought we'd got close, but Melz isn't that open to me, it seems.

"I wasn't sure about it until now. Seeing her drunk. She's lost control," Melz avoids my eyes.

The thing is, she's right. Lowenna isn't leading effectively. But what Melz is planning is a coup, pure and simple.

"Goddess," Saba says, as we heft Lowenna's sleeping body onto her bed. "We can't leave her up here too long, though, right?" she looks at Melz, who's pulling the bedclothes back over her mother.

"Sure," she says, but I get the sudden feeling that's a lie. We're in the dark, but just for a second I see that shadow pass over Melz again, as if she were standing under a tree at sunset and the shadows of the branches stroked her face; only, instead of stroking, this shadow looks like clutching fingers. "When she wakes up, I'll give her the strong sedative. I'll make sure she goes to the bathroom and has something to eat before she goes back down. But that'll only give us another ten hours, twelve at best. We've got to work fast. I want to be able to talk to the covensteads first without her, otherwise we don't stand a chance,"

Lowenna shifts in the bed and sighs in her sleep. Saba shakes her head.

"I don't know if she'll stay asleep that long," she says. "She's pretty strong. Even drugged, she'll work out we've done it. She can lucid dream. She might be able to, I don't know. Communicate with the other witches somehow, even if her body's here,"

"Then we shouldn't be wasting time standing here chatting. Come on," Melz says, and stalks out. Saba raises her eyebrow at me.

"You're prepared to follow her into this? Demelza doesn't do anything by half measures, you know. She's like mum that way," she warns.

"She's doing the right thing," I say, not at all sure about that, and walk past her to the stairs.

"Let's hope so," Saba pulls the door shut behind us and follows me down.

CHAPTER THIRTY-FOUR

Community, family, covenstead. All one and none separate.

From: Tenets and Sayings of the Greenworld

Melz doesn't waste any time inviting the heads of the thirteen covensteads of the Greenworld to meet at Tintagel. She goes back down to the kitchen, writes the names of all the heads of the thirteen covensteads on a piece of paper and holds it, one hand underneath, one hand over, and raises her energy; when she feels the power high within her and around her, she starts talking, sending the message to the other witches.

I watch her from a corner in the kitchen. I want to support her, and I will support her, but basically it's really not okay that her mum's upstairs, drugged, while she does this.

It's more complex summoning Omar.

Immediately after she sends what Lowenna jokily calls *bush telegraph*, Melz and I walk out to the perimeter of the village; she ties a red scarf to one of the tall wooden posts supporting the barbed wire fence at the north side; silhouetted in black against the setting sun, she looks like a girl from a Russian Communist poster. We studied them at school as part of a rare historical unit: *Redworld Patriarchy: Politics and Propaganda,* where we surveyed 2000 years of Western democracy, theocracy and feudalism. The Russian Communist posters were the least of it, mind you: the worst were the commercial adverts of the 20th and 21st century: naked women advertising toothpaste, By Brighid. Ugh.

She climbs back down the shallow steps carved into the post and I reach out to steady her as she gets off; she holds my arm briefly and then pulls away.

"We should do all four points," she says, squinting up at the last trails of the setting sun and wrapping the other three scarves around her right hand like she was going to shove her fist through a window any minute. The tension's baking off her, heat off rock on a summer's day.

"Is he going to see these, though, if he isn't around? No-one knows where he is. He could be anywhere," I peer up doubtfully at the frayed red cotton flapping in the evening breeze.

"I don't know. But we have to try. Come on," she says, her mouth set in a grim line.

We tie the other two scarves at the rough east and south points of the boundary and end up at the Witch's Gate on the west side of Tintagel, a huge wrought iron gate Omar built years ago when he was part of the original Five Hands: Lowenna, Zia Prentice, my mum, Linda Morgan, my dad and Omar. In the new dark of the evening, between its bars, the stars are starting to sprinkle the early summer sky. Past the boundary, the waning moon is rising between the two wide black posts. It's a beautiful thing, the gate, although the tops are spiked and nowadays it's always kept closed.

"Once it was always open," Melz speaks abruptly into the night. "It was symbolic. The place between us and spirit; it used to be the place we honoured the dead. But then the gangs came," she goes to a little shack next to one side of the gate and opens it, pulling out a small ladder and propping it up against the gate; the iron doesn't move as it takes Melz's weight. "We still used to come out here every now and again to do magic. Protection, mostly; sometimes banishing," she reaches for the top of the gate on tiptoe and ties the scarf, then climbs down and looks at it speculatively.

"You're right. The scarves aren't enough. If he's around Gidleigh or in the Redworld he's not going to know we need him. We need to summon him," she says, and points at the iron ribbon design that threads through the bars on the gate. "He made this. This is his place. He protects the Greenworld and he always will; I know that even if he doesn't, right now. He'll come if we call,"

She takes the ladder back into the shack and I hear her moving things around.

"Dunno if he will. Since he lost Zia…" I call in after her. I think of the way we all watched him mourn that day at the funeral, when her body was buried in the middle of Scorhill circle on Dartmoor. The way he knelt at her grave and his big shoulders heaved, shook with the pain of losing her. Since then, he hasn't been around much.

Melz comes back out holding a blackened abalone shell bowl, some glass storm lamps and a wrinkled brown paper bag.

"He will. Give us a hand," she says, handing me the lamps and going back inside for two more. She comes back out and crouches down, lighting the creamy coloured candles inside the lamps with a match.

I light the two lamps from one of Melz's lit

candles and sing the Invocatoin to Brighid. Melz bows her head respectfully as I sing. We place the lamps at the cardinal points: north, east, south and west.

"Do you really think he'll come?" I ask again.

"He's done what a bear does when it's hurt. Gone into the forest to tend its wound alone. But bears always protect their loved ones. He loves Danny. He'll come. Help me,"

From her bag she pulls out a chunk of chalk: the witches get it from the East Devon coast at Beer and Lyme Regis and use it for ceremonial workings. Chalk runs through the Greenworld and the Redworld - it's made of compressed fossils, a link back to the planet's deep past when the ocean covered this land. So, in a way, using that chalk grounds us back to the herstory of this land-before-it-was-land: to the ocean, the Mother of us all, both spiritually and practically. All life began in the ocean, and it's those remnants of early life we use to stake out a protective circle sometimes, like we do now. Zia taught me that.

Melz draws a large circle on the dry dirt ground behind the gate with the chalk, and a pentagram within the circle, points touching the outside.

"We've got to get his attention," she says.

She walks round the outside of the circle clockwise first with the chalk, re-marking the circle, drawing it in darker. *I cast this circle with earth.* Then, with the shell bowl in which burns sage and pine. The clean, sweet smoke fills the night air. *I cast this circle with air.* Then with one of the candles; *I cast this circle with fire,* and then water from a small bottle of fresh sea water. *I cast this circle with water.* Then she calls in the quarters, loudly and confidently calling to the spirits of each direction to lend us their power and protection.

She invokes the Morrigan to bless the space: the Queen of Dreams, Goddess of the Night.

"Great Morrigan; Phantom Queen; Possessor of our psyches, our deep powers, of the water; of the moon that inspires our dreams and governs the astral realm. Please be with us to summon Omar Blake," Melz nods to me and I call down power from the stars and into my third eye chakra; then up from the ground and into my centre.

"We call to Omar Blake. Lead his eyes to Tintagel; Omar Blake, hear our call," she says, and draws his name in the dirt three times with the chalk. Then she starts singing the lines engraved on the Witch's Gate: *Strong is the fortress, early and late; Iron are the bars on the Witch's Gate. Keep out the evil and keep in the good; honour the power of the wild and the wood.* I join in, and Melz adds two last lines: *Listen to us Omar, and come when we call; We need your strength for Danny, we need you for us all.*

We sing over and over, shaping a pile of the dirt into the rough shape of a man inside the circle. When it's defined enough, Melz cuts the end of her thumb open with her athame and drips three large drops of blood onto it.

"Phantom Queen, awake Omar Blake from his grief. I need him to find Daniel Prentice; I need Daniel Prentice to come to us; to do the magic You require to heal the Greenworld and the Red," she calls out. "We will sit vigil until morning; we will empower the call until the light, so that Omar Blake may hear us in his dreams and awake with new purpose," she says.

I didn't know I was in for an all-nighter. It's fine, I guess. Any chance to be alone with Melz, right? But she's not herself. There's a humourless focus about her that I don't like. And I'm uncomfortable with what we're doing. Even if Saba says its what half the Greenworld wants.

I'm not sure they'd approve of a drugged High

Priestess and an underhand coup.

We sing some more and Melz's three blood spots dry on the man-shaped dirt mound. She reaches for my hand.

"We need to channel the energy for as long as we can, into the dawn," she says, and when her skin meets mine I feel the shock of her power, of the intensely high vibration of her, of her aura and skin.

"If you're sure," I say, and I don't just mean Omar.

"He'll come," she sounds sure. I hope she is.

CHAPTER THIRTY-FIVE

You didn't know

what was in the heap. A visitor found

it to contain beggars. They sell the hollow

of their hands.

From: Beggars by R M Rilke

I wake up in incredible pain. I can't feel my right leg at all and my neck's at a weird angle. Sitting up slowly, wincing, I realise Melz's lying along my right side, snuggled into me for warmth like a cat. I stroke her hair gently, smiling at how knotty it is; how I can see her tawny roots coming through under the black henna; how, like always, Melz's hair always seems to need a wash. But even so, she's lovely in the dawn light; half a frown on her sleeping lips like she's disapproving of someone in her dream; the pink of the dawn casting a rosy glow on her cheek. The shadow has gone; I'm hugely relieved. Maybe all this can stop being so insane and life can go back to normal.

I look up through the bars of the gate and see Omar's back sitting up against the gatepost.

Or, maybe not.

I nudge Melz reluctantly.

"Mmmmph. No," she says and rolls over so her arm's over her eyes.

"Melz, wake up," I tap her on the shoulder gently. "Come on. It worked,"

"Wha. No. What?" she rolls onto her back with a huff. This girl isn't a morning person.

"Omar. He's here," I whisper. She sits up, then groans.

"Oww. My back's killing me," she rubs her shoulder with the opposite hand and peers at the gate where Omar's recognisably bulky figure is leaning against the post.

"Goddess. That worked faster than I expected. We were supposed to stay awake, though," she looks at me accusingly as if I was in charge of sleep and time and the whole temporal realm. "You shouldn't have let me nod off,"

"I didn't do it on purpose!" I protest. "Should I… dunno. Go and poke him?"

"I guess," she shrugs.

I hang back.

"You should do it. You know him better than I do,"

"I don't know him that well," she snaps.

"You rescued Danny with him,"

"Well, he lived in your village, like, all your life," she counters, and I realise even though we were both happy to summon this man, , to invade his dreams and make him come to us, walking miles through the night - neither of us are that keen on actually waking him up. Seems rude.

"He didn't *live* in the village. He visited. Are you shy?" I smile and poke her in the side. "I never thought I'd see the day. The great Demelza Hawthorne, scared of talking to an oaf like Omar Blake,"

She giggles, despite the situation.

"Shut up, you idiot" she pokes me back playfully. "I'm not scared,"

We're interrupted by the sound of Omar clearing

his throat.

"Oaf at your service, girls. You called?" he says, standing at the gate, unsmiling.

He must be almost seven feet tall; a huge, craggy mountain of a man; an inch of black beard covering the lower half of his face; still bald-headed, his head must be the one place that isn't covered with tattoos, tracing their black language across his dark brown skin.

Melz scrambles to her feet.

"Omar. Sorry about that. We... we were just having a laugh. Thanks for coming," she tries to smooth her crazy, matted hair down on the side she's been sleeping.

"I couldn't very well refuse, could I? When the Priestess of the Morrigan calls, you come. I learnt that from..." he stops, unable to say her name. "I learnt that a long time ago," he says instead. "D'you want to let me through?" he nods to the gate. "Not that it isn't nice to see it again. Probably weathering better than I am,"

Melz scuffs Omar's name in chalk out with her boot and looks at me meaningfully; I bend down and collect the man-shaped pile of bloodstained dirt carefully in my hand (that we miraculously managed not to roll on in the night) and scatter it unobtrusively at the boundary wall, murmuring thanks to Brighid and Morrigan, while Melz rummages in the shack for the key to the gate.

It creaks open when she turns the ornate black iron key in the lock; Omar pushes it hard, scraping the dirt underneath into a half moon. This isn't a gate that has been opened very often in the past years. I can't help feeling there's something symbolic about Omar pushing it open. Sometimes the old ways have to be forced to change.

"Good to be back," he raises a sceptical eyebrow as he looks around at the Tintagel inner boundary; the wide dirt pathway that surrounds the village. Scruffy, less tended than it used to be. More kids come out here at night now to hang out instead of going to the community singalongs or the mystery plays. He nods at me.

"Sadie Morgan. How're you enjoying Tintagel?"

"It's all right, thanks,"

He nods, not taking his eyes off mine.

"Heard your mother's made it here too," his tone's even, measured, but I can feel the tension underneath it.

"That's right," I say shortly.

"Can't imagine she's going to be very popular in the village," I don't blame him for hating mum: the woman who killed the love of his life. I wonder if he blames me too.

"It's going to take time," I say, shortly.

"No shit," he retorts. "I don't want to see her. Okay? Not yet. I don't trust myself,"

"Of course," Melz nods placatingly. "That's totally understandable,"

"Yeah. Well. What can I do for you, then? I'm hungry, Melz. Can we take this somewhere there's food?"

"Sure," Melz pulls the gate closed again and locks it behind us. I hand her the lamps from the ground and she locks everything away in the shack and pockets the key. "Come on. We'll go to the community café."

Not home. We're not going home because Lowenna's still out cold on her bed, out of the way while Melz executes her plan.

"Fine," Omar rumbles, following her into the village. "I'm starving. Any chance of a wash too?"

"Anything for you, Omar, you know that," I hear Melz's voice soften as I follow them. "Now. About why I asked you to come…"

She'll get her way. She always does. She learned from Lowenna.

CHAPTER THIRTY-SIX

Save it, hive it, share it.

From: Tenets and Sayings of the Greenworld

The covenstead witches start to arrive midmorning. Melz looks worriedly at the sun in the early June sky. It's been fourteen hours already since we drugged Lowenna.

"I hope they get here in time. I need enough of them on side. More than half," she smiles and nods to two witches taking off their robes. Saba comes to stand next to us.

"She's asleep again. Woke up this morning when you were still out. She was hazy about what happened last night but she was talking about some of it. I made sure she had a wee and some breakfast, then I gave her the same as last night. Should keep her out of the picture for a few more hours," she says in a low voice, out of the corner of her mouth, cloak-and-dagger-style.

"Hope it's enough time," Melz murmurs back. "It's going to take a while for the rest to arrive. The ones that have to come from Penzance and thereabouts aren't going to make it in time,"

"Then we deal with who we have," Saba smiles her sparkling smile at the other witches, not looking at us. "It should be enough,"

We're at the village hall, not in Lowenna's house where the covensteads usually meet, sitting around the big wooden table with the pentagram carved in its centre.

"What did you tell the trainees?" I direct my question to my own shoulder, not making eye contact.

"Woke them up early. Said Lowenna was sick; not to be disturbed. Sent them out foraging for ingredients for a healing tea," she smiles vaguely at the old stage at the front of the hall. "Told them that's why we had to meet here. Give her some peace and quiet,"

"What'd you tell them about why we're meeting in the first place?" Melz murmurs. "They know this isn't in the calendar,"

"Didn't say anything. That they'd find out at the meeting. They're trainees. They don't have to be told everything upfront,"

"Fair enough,"

The women gather in the old hall for the next hour, gossiping affectionately. Melz paces the hall, welcoming folk in, but I know she's counting. Estimating how many'll want to hear what she has to say; how many'll stay loyal to Lowenna. And all the time with the knowledge that Lowenna might wake up any moment, might, even in her dreams, know what we're plotting, wake up and bust this meeting. I start to sweat. Every time the heavy wooden door to the hall creaks open, all three of us jump.

Eventually Melz clears her throat and asks them to sit down in the circle of old plastic chairs we've pulled out of the cupboard. One day, all that'll be left of this village will be a stack of these bloody chairs with the O shape cut out of their backs. Maybe future generations or new races of humans will revere them as ancient, holy artefacts and, wrongly, extrapolate that they were in some way vital to the way that we interacted with the truths of our universe.

Nope. We sat on them and lost the feeling in our arses. That was it.

"Thanks to you all for coming at such short notice. Blessed Be," Melz welcomes the other witches with the usual greeting. "I'm afraid that my mother won't be with us today, for reasons you will soon come to understand. You know my sister Bersaba, and this is Sadie Morgan. She's a branded witch," Melz introduces us and I know she's expecting the looks and the whispered comments to each other when she says my name.

She's nervous. Me being here could go either way, because they all know what mum did. These witches knew Zia Prentice well. "Sadie. Show them the mark of Brighid," she intones, and so I lower the collar of my top and reveal the triple moon, seared mysteriously onto my skin. There's a few indrawn breaths. Murmurings.

"She has the brand," Saba takes my hand, and you could knock me down with a feather. I guess she might not like me too much, but she's chosen Melz over Lowenna and it seems I go with Melz as a package deal. "With Danny Prentice, that makes three. The three brands in a new generation. Historically, the branded ones have been the ones in charge. Chosen by the gods to lead,"

There's some exchanging of glances at this. They're wary. They don't know me, and what they do know isn't that great.

Tressa Hawthorne, Melz and Saba's aunt, stands up and clears her throat. She's wearing old pre-Greenworld denim dungarees and her grey hair's short and practical. She wears the triskele symbol on a silver chain around her neck. We don't have silver to make jewellery with, but sometimes folk melt down old things they might've had and remake them; it's a witch's craft, as Brighid's patroness of smithing - hers is the fire that transforms, hers is the power that remakes.

"Welcome, Sadie. Blessed Be," she says, perhaps deliberately setting the tone, leading the rest of the witches.

"Blessed Be," I say, and Tressa smiles kindly at me.

"We're fortunate to have another branded witch in the covensteads. I understand you're training with Lowenna as a Priestess of Brighid,"

"That's right," I say.

"And where *is* my sister?" Tressa asks, and the murmur goes around the group again. But it's Saba that answers.

"That's what we need to talk to you about," she says. And she tells them all about my journey to Mount Shasta, and the scroll, and what we believe about Danny, Melz and me. About our meeting with Felicity Blunt and the deal she's offered us.

"We believe we need to address this energy summit. All the world leaders will be there. It's our only opportunity to be able to show them all, at the same time, what a force for good the portals are. What they can do,"

"What *can* they do?" one of the other witches shouts. "I mean, we know what they are. But all this about the scroll and using it for fuel. We never knew about that before,"

"No, well. It's… experimental," Melz says. "Sadie and I … glimpsed its potential when the Shasta explained the process to us. But we need Danny to be able to complete the process. Complete the circuit, if you like,"

"So you haven't actually done it yet?"

"Not completely. No," Melz faces the crowd down as best she can, but it puts her in a weak position to say *here's what we need you to believe, but the thing is, I'm not absolutely sure that it works.*

"By Brighid! How d'you expect us to go along with this?" the same witch asks incredulously.

"I need you to have a little faith," Melz shoots back, sharply. That wasn't the way to go with this crowd. They don't like her tone, and Melz isn't great at public relations.

"So where's Danny?" Tressa asks. "If he's such a vital part of all this he should be here, surely,"

Melz clears her throat.

"He's gone. We think to the gangs," she says. "Omar's gone after him. We need him for this, but we also can't wait for him to get here. The summit's in a week. So, Omar has my orders to bring Danny to London. Whatever it takes,"

"What will you do if Omar can't find him? Or if he refuses to come?" one of the other witches asks.

"He won't fail. He has the God on his side," Melz says. There's a lot of raised eyebrows - it isn't exactly the most watertight of answers, even for witches.

"But there's another reason I wanted to talk to you all. Together, as Greenworld covenstead leaders. I want to talk to you about..." but she doesn't get to finish what's she's saying because there's a crash and the doors to the village hall are thrown open, and Lowenna strides in, wild-haired and furious.

Shitting hell.

"She wants to betray me," Lowenna shouts over her daughter and her voice fills the hall like angry bees. "She wants to betray all of us; the Greenworld itself where she's known nothing but love and truth and fairness." Lowenna strides through them, making way for her in the same redundant way you'd make way for a charging rhino (I've seen them in books); she's coming through, regardless.

"So let's see her try, shall we, ladies? Because it really isn't fair unless you give your opponent a fair turn," She squares up to Melz, who stands her ground as best she can and returns her mother's stare. "Go on, then, Demelza. Tell everyone what you propose. That you want to take over rule of the Greenworld from me. That you and your fellow witches have just *drugged* me for a day and a half so that you could organise this little shindig without me being here!" There's a combined indrawn gasp from the assembled witches, who've never known drama like this. "Go on, then! Amaze them all with your grand plan!" she folds her thick, muscled, shawl-covered arms across her chest and waist, one eyebrow raised.

Now I see exactly where Melz gets that expression from.

Melz turns to the witches, who are mostly looking extremely uncomfortable about this whole situation, with the occasional face expressing a kind of delighted disbelief.

"I'm sorry to say that's true, about the... err... sedative. But I knew I had to get you all here, and I wouldn't've been able to do it with mum around. I called you all here because I feel that the direction we're going in, in the Greenworld... it's..." she stumbles on her words and it isn't surprising because Lowenna's aggressively penetrating gaze and sneer would put anyone off.

Melz clears her throat. "It's wrong. Mum...Lowenna has been an incredible Head Witch. She and the original Five Hands - Zia Prentice in particular - invented the Greenworld; they built it from nothing into a whole community - into everything we have today, and I'm... I'm grateful for that. Of course I am," Melz stops to draw a breath; she balls her hands into fists like she always does when she's nervous.

"Well then? Why are we here?" Lowenna barks. "Come on, Demelza. You've got the floor for once. So use it," the challenge's in Lowenna's eyes. She's not a mother now. She's a High Priestess, defending her turf.

"I... I..." it's hard, so hard, what she has to say

next. Because even though Lowenna has no qualms about putting the Greenworld before her family, Melz does. But she has to say this, now, in this moment, or everything we believe we have to do will be lost. So I feel into the earth and draw its energy up through me as if I was a tree taking nourishment from the ground, and I pull down the power of the stars and the sun above me, and I feel Brighid's holy fire growing within me. Her fire's transformative and healing; it doesn't come from fear or hate or envy; it comes from love. And love is the most savage power in the universe.

I visualise that power, that fire, streaming from my heart to Melz's; I imagine her bathed in fire, burning away her uncertainties, her fears. I imagine the fire burning away everything but the truth, the message that's in her heart and her throat, waiting to be expressed. And I give her the fire of passion; the strength to say that truth loudly and with force and pride.

"I..." she looks at me as the energy hits her; I know that they all feel it; as witches we're all used to feeling energy shifts like this. I let my head fall back on my shoulders and feel the hot exhilaration flow through me; it's not mine, I'm only the channel. It grows and grows; I spread my legs to stand in a star position, supporting my body. I push it out of me, to her.

"I believe it's time for a change," Melz's voice drops a note into a more comfortable tone, and gets louder. Her voice fills the corners of the room. "I believe that fear is not the path for us to tread anymore. Because that's what our separation is. Fear of contamination. Fear of association. Fear of our own insecurity in the face of opposition. Fear that, if challenged, our philosophies, our way of life, might not stand up to scrutiny," I nod imperceptibly to her. *Go on*, I will her. *Say what you have to say.*

"I believe in the Greenworld. I believe that what we have is right and good and beautiful. I love Brighid. I love the Morrigan. But times have changed, and we must change with them. The Redworld is in crisis. The war for fuel is over and there's nothing left to burn anymore. Even the fracking sites are closing, one by one,"

One of the witches in the circle snorts.

"I don't give a stuff about the Redworld, my lover. That's why we're on this side of the border and they're on that side. See how they likes it now," she says.

"But we're in crisis too. Greenworld villages are

opting out of witch rule. Redworld refugees are swarming here across the border, that border you've got so much faith in. In practice, soon, it won't be the Greenworld anymore, no matter what you think or what you do, because there will be more Redworlders here than you anyway. And some of them might be all right with you being in charge, but some of them won't. Some of them just want food for their families and a roof over their head. And who are we to argue with that?"

Melz sweeps the room with her gaze. "Wouldn't you do the same? Isn't it unfair to deny help to the people that need it just because they made the mistake of being born on the wrong side of the border? Because they believed the lies their leaders told them about us? I've been to the Redworld. People are just the same there as they are here. Good and bad. We have the opportunity to be the better people here. We have the opportunity to step up and extend the hand. To reach out and help the poor and the homeless and the starving, just like Brighid does,"

I feel the thrill of her words as she speaks them. Now comes the hard part.

"How very inspiring," Lowenna says drily. "And please tell the group what your plan is, Demelza. To make everything so wonderful and new again," she turns to the other witches. "She wants to make a deal with Westminster. Felicity Blunt and that bloody lot of traitors and liars. She's already told them about the portals; she'll give them to the Redworld,"

There's a huge commotion. *You can't do that, that's wrong, that's against the Constitution.* I hear all of those things, and I see worry and fear and anger on some of the faces. And standing over them all, Lowenna smiles.

CHAPTER THIRTY-SEVEN

Ronsoera Brighid
sech drungu demna
roroena reunn
cathu cach thedma

Save us Brighid
From hordes of demons
May she win for us
Battles of every hardship

Prayer to Brighid from Greenworld Prayers and Songs

"Look at it this way," Melz shouts over the melee; I'm still sending her energy but I can see she's getting tired. "It may not have been the right time to reveal the portals before. I think we were right to keep them a secret. But the fact is that they're not a secret anymore anyway. When I was in the Redworld, in Glastonbury, last year - Bran Crowley knew about them because of Roach. That was our plan. That the Redworlders should know about them," she scans the room.

"At this stage it makes the most sense for us to manage them - but they have a potential to serve humanity - the whole of humanity, not just us. And I think that if we can start that process - work with the Redworld, not against it - then we can move forward. It's not sustainable for us to live independently, on our own, anymore. That option doesn't exist," she looks around the room. "We're not dealing in utopias anymore. There's no ideal situation here. And I still believe we can be magical. Live magical lives. Maybe the real magic is healing the Redworld,"

There's a moment of quiet, and I jump in before Lowenna can.

"We need a vote. On two counts. One, Demelza Hawthorne as High Priestess of Tintagel. Two, agreeing to talks with Westminster,"

Melz nods.

"Over my dead body!" Lowenna thunders. "Neither is a question for vote OR discussion!"

"Well, actually, they are, Wenna," Tressa stands up and faces her sister. "If Demelza has two witches in agreement, under Covenstead Regulations she's within her rights to challenge you for leadership. Do you, Melz?"

"Sadie and Saba support my claim," Melz says smoothly.

"No!" Lowenna looks desperately at us both.

"Saba! Sadie, please!"

"Wenna. You made the rules," Tressa says, gently.

Lowenna opens her mouth but no words come out.

"But... I..." she stammers. She meets my gaze. "Sadie. Please. I haven't finished your training. Don't betray me,"

My stomach turns. I know I'm betraying her. But I know this has to be done.

"Let's have a show of hands. First, all those in favour of an agreement with Westminster. It doesn't mean we're going to lie down and take shit from them. We go, but on our terms. Hands up in favour; Demelza and Lowenna, your votes are exempt,"

Hands go up. Who knows if it's enough. I follow Tressa's eyes as she counts: eighteen.

"Hands up against?" she nods her head again and notes down everyone's names under their vote. Some covensteads have more than one witch.

"How many?" Lowenna looks around the room, at her betrayers.

"Fourteen," There's a silence. Tressa holds out her notebook to her sister. "Here. See for yourself," Lowenna takes it and stares at it blankly, then looks around the room.

"Have I really failed you that badly?" she says to the room, and most of them avoid her gaze. "Anyone? None of you will talk to me? Isn't anyone going to say anything?" she shouts, then, but no-one answers.

"We've voted, Wenna. We'll do as Demelza suggests and go to Westminster," her sister says firmly. "Now, we can vote on the role of High Priestess of the Tintagel covenstead, which by extension also means Head Witch of the Greenworld,"

But Lowenna shakes her head.

"No. I'm not going to be embarrassed any further. It's clear which way the wind's blowing. You can all fuck off." She stares aggressively at Melz. "You think you want to be High Priestess? You're welcome, you ungrateful little bitch. Good luck. You'll need it,"

She looks around the room.

"Anyone that believes in the Greenworld, come with me now. I'm going to Zennor and Gidleigh and any other of the ignorant little villages that think they can do without us. We'll show them what it means to have a witch in charge," she growls, and strides out.

A couple of the other covenstead leaders follow her, along with Demi, who throws us a scornful look, and Merryn and Beryan and Rhiannon, heads bowed. We watch them go, and no-one looks at anyone else, because we know that it might've been necessary, but it isn't a victory.

"That's that, then," Saba mutters. "Doesn't feel right," she says, and looks to the floor.

"That's it? Melz's High Priestess now?" I didn't expect that. Nobody did. Tressa looks devastated. She looks exactly how we all feel. She nods, and turns to the remaining witches.

"We'll initiate Demelza as Head Witch at the next full moon. Then, all of you - you'll need to get the word out to your covensteads. Tell them everything. If Lowenna's going off on her own, that's up to her. I want nobody to be in any doubt. She's deserted us,"

The remaining witches nod, still uncertain. Not sure they've done the right thing. Maybe they wouldn't have voted to Melz as High Priestess. We'll never know. Tressa hugs Melz.

"I'll be here to help you, dear. But don't worry. You've been training all your life for this. It just happened a bit sooner than anyone expected," she looks up at me over Melz's head. Assessing me. Looking me over. "And you. Sadie Morgan. You're ready to help Demelza? Both of you?" she looks at Saba.

"We're ready," Saba's eyes are fierce.

"I'm ready," I say. Sometimes life makes a decision for you. The dice have fallen.

CHAPTER THIRTY-EIGHT

All loves are great, but the greatest loves are motherhood and sisterhood, whether a sister from the womb or a sister of the soul, a blood mother or the Great Mother of us all.

From Tenets and Sayings of the Greenworld

I'm sleeping in Saba's room. I took it while she was away, and there's no room for me anywhere else. She's lying diagonally across the other bed, the more comfortable one. I sigh and kneel down in front of the thin, hard camping bed on the other side of the room and move my stuff, which has been thrown there without much care. It's been a bad couple of days and all I want to do is get some sleep. Get some oblivion in my veins.

About ten minutes after I've got in bed and I've finally found a vaguely comfortable position on the cardboard mattress, Saba sits up in bed.

"Goddess. Could you make any more noise?"

"Sorry, I thought you were asleep," I mutter.

"Well, I'm not,"

"So it would seem,"

There's a silence where I can feel her staring, even though I doubt she can see me in the dark.

"You were his girlfriend. Back in Gidleigh,"

"Whose?" I ask, although I know. I've been waiting for this.

"You know who,"

"You're talking about Danny, I assume,"

"That's the one,"

"Not really. A lot's changed since then," I say, quietly.

She laughs, but not for amusement.

"Yes, it has. What was he like with you?"

"What d'you mean?"

"I mean, did he tell you he loved you, was he sweet to you, did he make you laugh? Were you the most beautiful girl on earth?"

"I don't really know... he made me laugh. He could be sweet. But we didn't love each other,"

"Oh, and you know what that feels like now, do

you?" she might have supported me in front of the crowd, but it's just us now and she's going for the jugular.

"As much as you do," I counter. Saba doesn't like me, that's not news.

"You don't know anything about my love life!" she snaps, but I do - I know what Melz has told me, that there was her childhood sweetheart Tom, and then Danny, and they were in love with her at the same time. Then, when Tom died and Danny left, she turned to their childhood friend Ennor to keep her warm under the covers on cold Cornish nights. Which was practically like incest, as far as Melz saw it, but I don't say any of that, because why feed a fire that doesn't need feeding?

"Sorry," I say instead, and the uncomfortable silence grows in the room like a weed again.

"You've got close, then. Since I've been away. You and Melz,"

"I s'pose," I'm guarded.

"I know you're lying there, thinking about her," she says, harshly.

I feel myself blush; I'm sure-to-goddess grateful

that the lights are out.

"Shut up. I have no idea what you're talking about," I say, as dismissively as I can.

"You shut up. Don't lie to me. As if it wasn't obvious enough in your face, earlier. I can practically hear your thoughts. *Melz Melz Melz. Ohhh, Demelza. I love you.* It's radiating off you like stale sweat and it's DISGUSTING!" she whispers.

"I... it isn't, I..." I don't exactly know how to respond. Witches can read each other's thoughts sometimes - Lowenna can do it and there's no reason why Saba couldn't have developed the skill. "It's none of your business what I feel. I'm not saying I do have feelings for Melz," Saba snorts derisively, and I ignore her "But if I did, it wouldn't be disgusting. There's no greater love than one woman for another," I quote the Greenworld tenet at her.

"Oh, that's not what I mean and you know it. I mean, my sister's a real witch. What are you? A pretender. You initiated yourself. You caused a Greenworld elder to die. You're tainted with Zia's death."

"Brighid initiated me," I argue, trying to keep the

petulance out of my voice, because my initation was real and beautiful. I won't let her make out it wasn't as special as hers or anyone else's. "Why are you having a go at me anyway? I thought you were on our side," I sound as befuddled as I am, frankly. I'm tired. I'm really, really tired, and I don't have the brain for this shit right now.

"Just because I agree that mum's in the wrong doesn't mean I approve of you mooning around my sister like a lovesick hare. She won't love you, anyway, don't you know that? She's broken. Tom, and Bran Crowley, they broke her heart. I know my sister. There's nothing left for you,"

The words chill my impetuous for-love-for-glory heart. How can Melz ever love me? Why would she ever want me? She loved Tom so much that she cursed the ones that killed him, and they died - not too coincidentally, jumping off Tintagel Head.

I don't know if she'll ever heal her broken heart, although I want desperately to help her try. I want to believe. I want to hold out my hand to her; for my fire to light the dark cave she sleeps in every night, beset with nightmares.

I roll over, my back to Saba. A tear leaks into my

pillow, then another. I try to control my breathing; she can't know I'm crying.

"I'm her friend. That's all," I control my voice with some effort.

"That's all you'll ever be," Saba snaps back at me. "She doesn't think of you that way, so you might as well give up. I'm her twin. I can tell,"

My heart pounds; I cry silently and motionlessly into my pillow. I know Melz's wounded. I know what old, gnarled pain feels like -my pain's so much a part of me that I'd forgotten what hope was until I met her. But somewhere on the road from Gidleigh to Tintagel, Melz brought me hope. Maybe it was the healing that poured from her hands, or the way she listened to me when I told her, haltingly, about dad. About Roach. She didn't say anything, didn't judge. Just listened. And when I was finished, she held me.

And I know she must have felt some of what I did, because our energy felt right together. It really did. It was beautiful, walking through the night together, over the moors, even though I was grieving for Zia and destroyed over mum and having to leave the village, the only place I'd ever known, my whole life; still, it was exceptional to be there, breathing in the night air with her.

So I want to believe that one day, Demelza Hawthorne will let me love her. Just let me in a little bit, so that I can warm her heart like she warmed mine that first night. So that I can make just the tiniest, new-moon-sliver of room in her heart for hope.

Saba doesn't want me to hope. She can't stand the thought that Lowenna's been teaching me the secret ways of Brighid, and she obviously can't stand the thought that her sister might one day have feelings for me too. And, apparently, she's going to pretend she's okay with me in front of Melz and bitch at me in private. So that's great.

Her words hurt, but I can't believe they're true. I won't.

I close my eyes; she doesn't say anything more. I dream of Melz, but she's far away. I'm calling to her, but she can't hear.

CHAPTER THIRTY-NINE

*Exposed on the cliffs of the heart. Stoneground
under your hands. Even here, though,
something can bloom; on a silent cliff-edge
an unknowing plant blooms, singing, into the air.*

From Exposed on the Cliffs of the Heart, R M Rilke

I wake up about 2am. It's a dark moon tonight; the night of unmaking. It's the time when things unravel, go back to source, when the tide pulls the ocean back and exposes the sand and rock underneath; the night of lost things. How deeply appropriate it was, what we did earlier, although awful at the same time. Destroying the Greenworld as we know it. *Unmake, unmake, unmake.*

I have a sudden image in my mind of Melz on Tintagel Head. I sit up quietly and hug my knees, listening to the night - a fair wind up, even though it's warmish. Windy in June. More unseasonal weather. Then I wonder. What if Melz IS up on Tintagel Head? She could have gone there. It'd be dark - dark moon's not a time to go climbing on sea-lashed rock, you wouldn't be able to see a bloody thing - but she could be there.

She is. I think she is. I feel she is. *Shit, Melz. You*

better not be.

I get up, walk as quietly as I can toward her room and poke my head inside, wanting to see her curled in a ball under the blankets, wanting her to be there. But she isn't. The blankets are rumpled but flat on the bed.

I go back to Saba's room and pull on my clothes - wool-hemp blend trousers (brown: delightful), an itchy lambswool jumper, my boots. I tiptoe down the stairs, avoiding the creaks. Pick up a lamp from beside the front door, one we use for outdoor rituals in bad weather, and light it. I'm going out to find her.

I follow the path from the house out to the boundary and let myself out the heavy gate, then past the barbed wire fence and through the energy circle. I wrap my dark coloured clothing around me and around the lamp so not to attract any attention, (although Goddess knows which overcommitted gang member would be out and about looking for witches on a night like this) being careful not to inadvertently set myself on fire. The lamp has to be lit because there's no easy way to light it when I get there without another source of fire, and I need light tonight.

I follow the faint track in the grass to the headland that leads down to the beach, and instead of climbing down the huge, heavy stone slabs, I head up the slippery stone steps that lead to the tiny walkway between the mainland and Tintagel Head, technically an island, jutting out from Tintagel and crowned with the ruins of a castle. She's up there, I know she is.

The wind's worse the higher I get. The dark moon energy's in full force: open, unhinged, velvety death pounds my senses in a kind of balletic torture. I creep up the walkway, holding on for my life. The temperature dips up here. Not freezing, but definitely less comfortable.

When I get to the top, I hold up the lamp. I see her straightaway.

She's at the edge of the cliff, black hair loose and blowing madly in the wind. The drop is unforgiving: hundreds of metres straight down into the churning sea.

"Melz! Come away from the edge!" I shout, but the wind carries my voice away and she doesn't look around. I struggle across the uneven ground to her.

Finally, I get close enough. I stretch out my arm for her and graze her cloak, which ripples back at me like a malevolent ghost. She hardly acknowledges my presence, gazing at the sea and the black night.

"This is where they jumped, you know," she says in a small voice.

"Melz!" I shout. "Come on. Let's go home!" I don't want to be here.

"No," she whispers. I can hardly hear her.

"What? Come on. Please,"

"It's not over,"

"What?"

"It will never be over!" she screams back at me. "Don't you get it? The curse. They jumped from here. Bali and Skye. I made them do it. I'm going to spend my life standing here, feeling them jump," she turns to me and holds her hand over her solar plexus. "Here. I feel it here. The terrible weightlessness. And then the fall,"

"I… I know. But you can heal. You'll heal, over time. Make amends," I shout weakly into the tearing wind, holding out my hand. "Come on. Please. Come home with me,"

She looks back out at the horizon and shakes her head.

"I can't do it. I live in the village. My whole life, I'm not going to be more than half a mile from this point. Here. Right here," she shouts back at me, scoring the ground with the toe of her boot, making a line in the long grass. "What kind of High Priestess am I going to make with this inside me? What kind of Head Witch? I was wrong, Sadie. You have to do it. Without me,"

"What do you mean?" I shout. "I'm only in training! I can't be a High Priestess!"

She leans further over the edge of the cliff, looking down into the black sea far beneath.

"Saba, then. Not me. I can't,"

"Melz! Please!"

Everything in me wants to freeze and to step back, but I force myself to stand next to her and take her hand. *Don't look down, don't look down*, I chant it like a mantra, but it doesn't work. The dark sea blooms under me.

"Go home!" she screams back at me, her face streaked grey with the tears that have made her black eyeliner run. She holds out her arms to her sides like a cross, perhaps to steady herself. She looks up at the stars as if waiting to see words printed across them; something that can give her peace.

"Melz! Please! Please step back from the edge!" I try to pull her back, but she pulls her arm away, and the wind blows in a sudden harsh gust, pushing her forward. I shout out her name but the wind steals it; spirits it away like she's hexed Tintagel Head, like she's bound all its natural spirits to be her familiars: bewitched the wind itself. In the dark her face is a skull, her cheekbones hollow, her eye sockets deep.

"Leave me alone. Let me go!" she cries. Everything in her is taut with the tension of horror and remorse. I can feel it. "I can't do it. Mum was right. I'm too messed up. I can't,"

"No. I'm not leaving you," I reach out for her but she balances on her back foot, away from me; I hear a stone dislodge and fall down the cliff; the sea swallows its impact, indistinguishable from the spray and the heave of the waves crashing against Tintagel Head.

"LET ME GO!" she screams at me then, and the force of her desolation hits me in the chest like an anchor on the ocean floor. And, suddenly, I see. Bali and Skye. Holding hands, brother and sister, going to their deaths in the deep black bitter sea. I'm watching an echo; something that happened here, but that on some level is still happening; on some kind of supernatural repeat. They both seem to pull and push the other, as if they're both trying to jump but also trying to stop the other from falling.

I can see them next to her, on the cliff. Maybe it's the depth of the dark; maybe it's the distant starlight. They're dim, like smoke, forming and unforming the shape of a boy and a girl. Their hands are on her; they clutch her face, her body. They stand behind her. They float around Melz's body.

"Come on, Melz. Just step back. Stay with me," I don't know if she knows the ghosts are there; maybe they've been on Tintagel Head since they died. Or, maybe they've been with Melz all this time. But I have to save her; have to get her off the island, and get the dead away from her too.

I reach for her again, and get a hold of her shoulder and then her arm, and as I do, I feel a rumble under my feet.

"I can't. I can't!" she sobs as I clutch at her forearm. It's fragile in my hand, like a bird's. "It's the curse. They'll never let me go and I'll never... I'll never be able to take it back," She's pale in the darkness, so pale; bruises under her eyes. It's the spirits, draining her of her strength, I know it as I squint at their vague outlines next to her. They're feeding off her energy, depleting her like vampires. The shadow that I saw on her; the darkness that I failed to see, because I loved her. Because I do love her.

"Come on, Melz, Come home. I'll help you," I hold out my hand again, and feel the earth shift now, harder, under me, as if Tintagel Head was a sleeping giant just waking up. I hold out my other arm to steady me. *Shit, shit, shit.* Suddenly, I realise what's happening. But though I want to shout at her, *it's an earthquake, Melz, quick, get away from the edge, quick, we have to get off the island*, I can't make my mouth move; in that split second she speaks instead.

"No. I'll never be free of them," she speaks dully into the night; the waves quieten in a sudden lull. "I was wrong. I can't do what needs to be done, with the portals," The wind dies and the waves hush like they know what's coming, and she looks me calmly in the eye. "I can't be the High Priestess. I'm sorry," she says, clear and cold as the water beneath, and my fingers curl around her arm tighter, but she pulls away. And at the same time the whole of Tintagel Head shakes, and she stumbles into the night air.

In the tiny quiet second, that one perfect unit of time, I hear the breath catch in her throat. I feel my spirit lunge forward to catch her, but my body stays momentarily still. I'm screaming at it: Move! Move! But muscle and bone is slow compared to spirit.

I see it in her eyes as she teeters at the edge of the cliff: I see it, the moment when she realises she doesn't want to die; that she realises it isn't too late for her, and that when death really comes, she isn't as willing to walk into it as she thought she was.

The ground gives way under her and slides like cut clay into the sea. Everything slows, even my heartbeat. Her eyes meet mine and I see terror there.

"Sadie...!" she calls out my name. Reaches for me.

And falls.

CHAPTER FORTY

For what we do for good or for ill, shall be returned to us threefold.

From: Tenets and Sayings of the Greenworld

Melz. I don't have time to shout it but her name screams through me like a sharp wind. I lunge forward with everything I have, my body as well as my magic - reaching out of myself with a red power I never knew I had, grabbing wildly at her, sinking my fingernails into her skin with savage relief.

I haul her back from the edge. I feel a stabbing pain in my back and my arms take the weight of her. Even though she's skinny and the bone in her arm is like a bird's, an eighteen-year-old girl has weight; I fall to my knees holding her, feeling her sea-spray-wet skin slipping through my weak fingers.

"Sadie. Don't let go," she pants. Her legs thrash wildly on the rock below as I hold onto her arm. *Respect Nature, for She has no respect for you*, the Greenworld tenet repeats in my mind. I taste blood in the back of my throat and hate the Redworld that caused this, made the earthquakes happen in this peaceful isle where they were never meant to.

I pray. I pray hard, desperately, to Brighid and the Morrigan and Lugh and all the witches to come and save us, because I know I can't hold Melz very long. *Please, Blessed Brighid, please help us; I can't lose her, I love her, I love her, please,* I beg with the words screaming in my mind because I have no strength or breath to say them out loud.

"Sadie! Please don't... don't let me fall," she grunts, and I can hear her feet kicking against the rock, trying to find something to grip, anything; I watch, my arms being torn from my body, as she jolts and lunges desperately to stay alive.

But I can also sense the spirits of Bali and Skye pulling Melz down, pulling her down towards the water, to be with them forever. I feel Brighid's holy fire consume me.

No. Death can whistle for Melz, but she isn't coming, not while I have a body to ruin to save her.

My hands fill with healing power. The dead raven on the road was a message for me, not Melz. Telling me that I would have to save her. That it would be up to me to heal her one day. I call to the goddess.

"Go geosnai tirte fhaire Bhride, Muid ag na-hoibre. Go ndo tinnail rabhaidh Bhride, Muid a ghiollacht tri na scaileanna. Go lasa laistigh bruane coranach Bhride, Agus ceangail muid le ne dheithe."

I feel Brighid's power fill me and, slowly, I grip Melz's arm tighter, then her shoulder, and I manage to get up on my knees and pull, and pull. I pull until I think my body'll sever in half, and then I pull past that pain, feeling my tendons pop and the nerves tighten in my back and pull right down my legs, and that's excruciating but I never break my gaze from Melz's, the fire in my eyes as hot as my burning lungs.

The shadowy shapes stay with Melz, pulling her back. They want her. Oh, they want her so badly. Their power is huge; the more they pull her down, the heavier she gets, like she's soaked in sea water. But I focus everything I have on channelling the fiery power of Brighid in me, as if I'm nothing more than a lightning rod, a rope of wild fire. I let go of fury; I let go of fear and pain. I let go of everything but love.

I pull her up, little by little, grabbing her other hand. Brighid is around us like a tower of fire now, lighting up the old stone remnants of Tintagel Castle. The dark sea lashes beneath us, pulling Melz down.

"Don't let me go," she whispers, terror in her eyes. "Please, Sadie,"

But Bali and Skye pull and pull, spiralling down and down, and I feel her hand slipping from mine. *She must finish what she started. This is the end. Let it be ended* they whisper. *We are due this. This is the curse.*

"You will not have her!" I scream at the spirit shapes, tears running down my cheeks. "Please, Brighid! Please help me. Don't let her be taken by this darkness. I'll do anything. I'll atone for her. Anything. Please!"

And Brighid's hands of fire envelope mine, and she says quietly: *it's all right, Sadie.*

I won't ever let Melz go. I'd rather go over the edge with her than let the curse have her.

The fire moves down my arms, from my hands and weaves up Melz's arms; it holds her body, and I feel the weight lessen.

I pull as hard as I can, and the fire does the rest.

Melz hauls herself back onto the ground and lies there, panting.

I want to lie on the ground and never get up again, but I can't. The island rumbles under me and I know I have to act fast.

Painfully, my arms and chest in fiery agony, I turn from Melz, lying on the ground, and stagger to where I remember the portal being. As meditatively as I can, I trace the opening symbols into the air and it blooms alive, orange-red. I cast a look back at Melz, unconscious now, sprawled on the ground, then at the spirits attached to her. There's only one place for them to go now; they have to cross over properly. This has to be over, once and for all.

CHAPTER FORTY-ONE

Lament for the life cut short,

Lament for vitality waned;

Keen for the spirit taken away,

Cry for the loss of the world.

Suggested lament for the dead (short version)

From Greenworld Prayers and Songs

I don't want to have to do this. I don't want to get close to the spirits. I don't want to feel them latch onto my energy like leeches, draining my power away.

Melz, prostrate on the grassy top of Tintagel Head, moans and turns away from them; their smoky, ill-defined fingers caress her, stroking her aura, sucking her energy; her energy centres are depleted instead of the bright and vibrant whorls they should be.

Be careful what you wish for, mum used to tell me. The same might go for *be careful of the curses you make; be careful of what you hold next to your skin*. Melz's cursed Bali and Skye and then wore that curse around her neck, feeding it every day until they died - accidentally or not. But as she fed that curse, she strengthened her link to them.

Doubled over in unbelievable knifing, cutting pain, my back and neck and shoulders on fire, I hold out my hands to the shifting, cursed spirits of Bali and Skye.

"I banish you, spirits of a curse. Leave Demelza Hawthorne. I command you! Leave this realm! Leave Demelza Hawthorne. Be gone! Go! Be gone and go! Be gone and go into the next world. You are at peace. Be at peace now,"

Nothing happens. I am not enough. My power is not enough. The spirits stay with Melz, wanting her still.

"Blessed Brighid! Please help!" I call out to Her; but the wind is the only answer I get.

I bow my head. The ground rumbles again, and I realise what I have to do.

"Morrigan, Dark Mother, Phantom Queen. Ruler of the Realm of the Dead. I command you to appear! I implore you to help your priestess! Cleanse her once and for all from these parasitic spirits. Cleans your priestess of this destructive curse! I bid you, Morrigan, Queen of the Dead, come!" I scream out into the night. The Morrigan takes souls into the next world. She rows the barge. She isn't my goddess but I hope she can hear me.

Still, nothing happens.

The spirits, half-formed, twisting, abstract, linger by Melz's inert body. My invocation isn't enough. I'm not enough. Should've known that I'd be useless. I crumple next to Melz, healing power streaming out of my hands, and crouched next to her, my forehead on hers, crying, weak and pathetic, sobbing *please help me, please help me* to anyone that's listening.

Lightning bathes the world in its shocked whiteness for one second, setting fire to a tree on the mainland. I huddle next to Melz. *Nothing, nothing, I'm nothing, I'm ruined, worthless. I can't do this.* I feel the ground shaking under me again and grasp her in terror, even though she's unconscious, still, like she's my raft. Like she can save me. The yellow sickness spirals up through my middle, ugh, no, no, no. The lightning flashes again, and the accompanying roll of thunder grumbles on the inky horizon. A summer storm.

Come on, Sadie Morgan. You know the words to call us if you really want us.

I chant the Charge of the Goddess manically under

my breath, calling the Morrigan to me. I try to hurry because this rock could move and maybe even split apart at any moment; I'm not safe here.

For mine is the secret door which opens upon the Land of Youth; and mine is the Cup of the Wine of Life, and the Cauldron of Cerridwen, which is the Holy Grail of Immortality.

I am the Gracious Goddess, who gives the gift of joy unto the heart. Upon earth, I give the knowledge of the spirit eternal; and beyond death, I give peace, and freedom, and reunion with those who have gone before. Nor do I demand sacrifice, for behold I am the Mother of All Living, and my love is poured out upon the earth.

Hear ye the words of the Star Goddess, she in the dust of whose feet are the hosts of heaven; whose body encircleth the Universe; I, who am the beauty of the green earth, and the white Moon among the stars, and the mystery of the waters, and the heart's desire, call unto thy soul. Arise and come unto me.

For I am the Soul of Nature, who giveth life to the universe; from me all things proceed, and unto me must all things return; and before my face, beloved of gods and mortals, thine inmost divine self shall be unfolded in the rapture of infinite joy.

Following that, I sing the chant for the Morrigan.

Morrigan, Ancient One; Morrigan, Dark Mother, Wise Mother

Morrigan, Shining One; Morrigan, Shape-shifter, Soul Healer

Morrigan, Sovereign One; Morrigan, Goddess of Rebirth

Finally, I feel a distinct shift in the energy around me. I keep singing, desperately, breathlessly, running the words together; *MorriganShiningOneMorriganShapeshifterSoulHealer*. Three crows alight on the rough stone of the castle foundations near to us and caw at me. She's coming. Please, let her be coming. I keep chanting. *MorriganAncientOneMorriganDarkMotherWiseMother,* and She materialises, standing over Melz.

"Priestess of Brighid. You have called me here in the middle of a great shift in the earth's energy. You are taking a great risk being here,"

"Yes... Yes, Great Morrigan. I know. But I need your help. To guide these cursed spirits into the next world. Through the portal. I can't do it alone. I have to do it for Melz... Demelza. They're draining her. I don't think she can fight it anymore. The curse. It has to be now.

Please,"

The Morrigan frowns and kneels next to Melz, her black robes swirling around her, the blue woad tattoos reaching up Her arms. Melz tries to sit up but she can't.

"You have suffered, Priestess. Sleep now," The Morrigan intones, and the air thrums with her voice. She places Her hand on Melz's forehead and Melz slumps; the Morrigan lays her down carefully on the rock and turns to me.

"We have little time," She says, and stands. The confused, clinging spirits of Bali and Sky pulse nearby: nightmares, phantoms, their faces merging and changing and melting like running wax as I watch. I can see something like a bloody stain on Melz's aura. As if she's spilled coffee on herself long ago and forgot to clean it up.

"Why did you let her do it in the first place? Place the curse? You should have stopped her!" I shout at her angrily over the wind.

"I advised against it. But she has free will, just like you do, Priestess. Demelza left Tintagel because of the curse, and experienced the Redworld. Thereby she understood the depth of the problem that faces the world," The Morrigan, tall and stern-faced, stands with her black robes pulled by the wind and looks out over the sea. "There are always consequences. I tried to tell them so many times about the drilling, but they weren't listening. They dismissed me as a bad dream, a piece of bad luck, the Redworld men that raped my body. Now they will understand," she holds out her hand to me. "But I'm afraid your border won't protect you from this earth shaking, Fire Priestess. What Man has wrought he has to mend,"

"I know. But we don't have time to think about that now," I point at the spirits. "We need to take them into the portal. Make them cross over, so they don't... infect her anymore. Whatever it is they're doing,"

"As you wish," The Morrigan walks over to the centre of the portal and opens her arms wide. She starts singing something - I can't understand it, and the wind rises - and this time it's not unseasonal weather at all but definitely the work of the Goddess, and I cower down, balling myself up next to Melz on the ground to avoid being swept off the cliff altogether. I get snatches of Her voice inbetween the gusts of wind; shielding my eyes, hearing her strange words. Gaelic, I think, but nothing I know, my gaelic's confined to the songs and chants

Lowenna teaches me as part of my Brighid training. *Na h-ataireachd ard, mo leabaidh dean suas, Ri fuaim na h-ataireachd ard, mo leabaidh dean suas,* I hear, then the wind whips around me again and all I can see are the Morrigan's lips moving as she calls the spirits to her. She's made a kind of wind funnel in front of her; commanding the elements as gods can, and the spirits of Bali and Skye are pulled towards her, making a kind of screaming, keening noise that merges with the wind. They clutch back at Melz, trying to stay with her, but the Morrigan's magic's too strong. They can't evade the Phantom Queen forever.

I shudder as I watch Her song peel them away from Melz; they are sucked in towards the Morrigan, through the wind, as if it's made a vacuum just for them. When they are close to her, She bows her head and wraps Her arms around them somehow, and the keening nose in the air stops. She nods to me and turns away, disappearing into the portal, and I know She's taking them through the portal, across the River of Death in her black barge. That as soon as the spirits enter the portal they'll be compelled by the magnetic pull of dissolution at the other end to follow Her wherever She may lead.

"Love is the greatest magic of all," She says, before She disappears. "Be good Demelza; she is a warrior that needs a rock. Together you will be an inspiration for many. Love her, as a woman, not with the glamour of the goddess; love her as she really is, flaws and beauty, and let her love you the same,"

The portal closes behind the Morrigan, and I bow my head in reverence.

I take Melz's hand in mine and feel some warmth returning. I chafe her hands. Her eyes flicker; she opens her eyes, drawing in a deep breath. I hold her hand to my heart instinctively and feel her energy returning; feel my own fiery heart warming her, burning me. The wind stills and she sits up, looking around her confusedly.

"What happened... I... I was..." she frowns, and looks to the edge of Tintagel Head. "I was hanging there. I fell," her voice's small and croaky; she clears her throat. "Sadie, I fell. I remember slipping off the edge. I... I was so...,"

"I know. Brighid gave me the strength to pull you up. Don't you remember? The Morrigan. She took the spirits. Bali and Skye. They're gone, Melz. You're free. You're free," I squeeze her hand as I repeat it.

"Free?" she repeats slowly.

"It's over," I smile hopefully into her brown eyes and watch as the confusion clears; as Brighid's fire flows through my hand and into her, charging her with a new energy. Keeping my hand in hers, she stands carefully and takes my other hand.

"You did this. I feel... I feel so different. I feel so new. Lighter. Better,"

"It was the goddesses really. I just called them, like. But we have to go. We have to get off the island,"

"No. It was you," she looks into my eyes with a kind of wonder. "I know it. You saved me, Sadie. And this..." she holds our entwined hands up to our faces; this close, I can see the energy passing between our interlocked fingers: a silvery, shifting light flecked with sparks of red and gold and orange. "This. You're healing me right now. And your heart... I can see your heart, Sadie. It's burning. The sacred heart of Brighid," her voice's awestruck, suddenly, and I can feel what she sees, but I can only stare at her, take all of her in, unbelieving that this moment's really happening; that Demelza Hawthorne's standing there with love and awe in her eyes, just for me. And I watch as it removes the last vestiges of the sticky-brown energy from Melz's aura.

I bring our hands to my lips and kiss her fingers where they interlock with mine.

"I …" *I love you.* It feels as natural as breathing, but the rock starts to crack under our feet.

Instead of kissing her like I want to, I pull her hand, hard, and we run for our lives.

CHAPTER FORTY-TWO

The moment is all we have and the one thing we cannot keep.

From: Tenets and Sayings of the Greenworld

Tintagel Head's technically an island. It was attached to the mainland once, but time made a gap between it and the cliffs, and so to get to it you have to climb a narrow and steep wooden walkway that stretches over a neck-like ridge of rock. In wet weather it's treacherous; during an earthquake it's lethal.

I pull Melz behind me as Tintagel Head shudders; the noise of the cracking and heaving rock above the crashing of the ocean is unbelievable.

"Sadie! Be careful!" she shouts as I follow the slick, mossed wooden treads quicker than I should. But then there's another sound; not rock against rock. Like creeping up Lowenna's aged stairs at night; like old wood doorframes expanding when winter comes. We run faster, almost falling, and I can see the unforgiving black Cornish sea under me, freezing and deep, wearing down the jagged rock underneath just a little more every century, but not enough to make it soft if we fall.

"Shit," Melz, ragged breathed, curses behind me. "Shit! Sadie! The walkway, it's... shit, it's coming apart, oh Goddess!"

I look back, past Melz, and see that the wooden rail and the top steps have come away from Tintagel Head and are hanging off on one side.

Respect Nature, for She has no respect for you.

I can feel my teeth biting into my lip and my neck braces as if anticipating the fall. Our feet are hardly touching the steps because the angle of the decline is so steep and there's a strange out-of-myself voice that wants to say *haha look witches **can** fly* which I hope I will live to analyse as seriously inappropriate at a later date.

Ahead of me's the twist in the walkway; the angle of the rock means there can't be a straight path down. Without being able to stop myself, I slam hard into the wood handrail at the apex of the corner.

Maybe it's my impact into the corner; maybe it would have happened anyway, but the walkway lurches away from the rock altogether, not tethered to the top anymore, and it swings us out over the black water.

Instinctively, we cling to each other, suspended for

a second above the waves. My arm's bent around the handrail, wet wood nestled in my elbow. A long crack runs up its middle; Melz's wide eyes meet mine.

The top of the walkway falls into the sea, and the bit we're crouched on veers back to the shore, creaking and drunken. I close my eyes as we drop, sickeningly.

"Hold on!" I scream at Melz. She wraps her arms around my waist; the wood splinters under my arm, and we fall.

I open my eyes just as the rocks rear up under us. There's no time for prayer or invocation: I scream *Brighid,* instinctively, like the first cry of a newborn.

CHAPTER FORTY-THREE

Enchanted thing: how can two chosen words
ever attain the harmony of pure rhyme
that pulses through you as your body stirs?
Out of your forehead branch and lyre climb

and all your features pass in simile through
the songs of love whose words as light as rose-
petals rest on the face of someone who
has put his book away and shut his eyes

From: The Gazelle by R M Rilke

We're all the blessed ones of Brighid, so the witches say; everyone in the Greenworld's under Her mighty protection. We must be blessed, Melz and me, because we're alive.

I come to with sand in my mouth and sit up, spitting it out violently. Melz's on her back next to me, eyes closed. On the short beach, miraculously, we've both avoided the rocks that you have to clamber down if you want to get on the sand, the same rocks that Danny sat on that day when he called me a slut, and the tide's out far enough for there to actually be sand to lie on.

I lean on my hand and retch; I can't get rid of the salt in my mouth, but my wrist can't take my weight so I half-fall back on to the ground and catch myself on my elbow, which also feels like it's been stretched too far: a cut of red pain slices up my arm to my elbow. Carefully, I roll over onto my other side and get into a sitting position by curling up in a ball and sitting up with steepled legs. My knees seem all right but I think there's blood somewhere - I can't see too well, but I can feel the stickiness of something on my trousers and something feels sore on my thigh. I ache all over.

Melz rolls over and groans.

"Ugh. Am I dead?" she opens her eyes and groans again. "I'm dead,"

"Can you move your arms and legs?" I turn to look at her, trying not to move too much, but even rotating my neck's painful. "Ow. Shit,"

She flexes her fingers and then picks her arms off the sand and flops them back down again, then rolls her ankles away from each other and snaps them back together.

"They seem to be functional," she sits up carefully. "I don't know how we got here. We should have landed on the rocks," she squints to our left and then up at the rock, where the remains of the walkway are hanging. She nudges a bit of shattered wood by her foot.

"We're lucky to be alive," I murmur.

"I think we had help," she mutters.

I stand up very carefully and help her up.

"I almost lost you. Twice," A part of me wants this to be a romantic moment, but I'm just too exhausted and in too much pain. "Careless, really,"

"If you will be so... so... oh, damn it. I've lost all my words. You know what I mean. Stupidly heroic," she smiles tiredly. "D'you think you can make it home?" she holds out her arm. "I'll help you,"

"I'll help you, more like. You're the one that almost died,"

"I'm fine. You were the one who took the brunt of the fall,"

"You're not fine. You were possessed by malign spirits and impelled to jump to your doom, lest we forget." We start climbing the rocks to get to the steps leading down from the village path.

"Like I said, *almost*. Didn't though, did I?"

"That's a very cavalier attitude,"

"Well, that's me. Devil-may-care,"

"He may do, but we've got other fish to fry,"

"True. I could say the same about you. Coming out here in the middle of the night. How d'you know I was here, anyway?" she gives me a hand up to the next foothold and I grimace as my elbow takes the strain.

"I just woke up and I knew,"I shiver in the cold. Wet clothes. And the realisation sinking into me quickly about what just happened. How close we came to death.

"Goddess. Anyone would think you were a witch or something,"she replies, offhand, but it's not that falling to what should have been our deaths won't stop us being witty bitches. It's more that we don't have the energy to do anything else but the comfortable wisecrack. The pithy comeback.

We're just heaving ourselves onto the top of the rocks when there's an almighty crack and a crash, and we look behind us to see a deep crack divide Tintagel Head into two halves.

"The Goddess has taken back what was hers," Melz says, wearily.

"Yup," I lean my head on her shoulder, and we watch the stone island dissolve into the sea. Neither of us says anything more. We both know what happened here, and we know that we're both still alive only by the grace of the Goddess.

Anything else from here on in will be easy, compared. Won't it?

CHAPTER FORTY-FOUR

Demulcent herbs – to soothe irritated tissue, e.g. mallow, oats, comfrey.

Combine in a tea, one tsp dried/3 tsp fresh herb, one cup boiling water per teaspoon of herb, steep for 10-15 mins / 5-15 drops per tincture if taken.

From The Common Herbal

The night after we get home - not telling anyone what happened and acting as surprised as everyone that half of Tintagel Head's missing - and definitely not explaining why we're covered in bruises - Melz holds a village meeting.

"We need the gangs on our side. We need a convoy to go to London, for this energy summit that the Shasta told us about. Omar's going to find out when it is. Get word to Blunt that we'll come to it. That we'll accept the deal. Okay?" she scans the crowd, but they've already heard about the big showdown wth Lowenna. Some of them have left already, and Melz let them go with her blessing. Most have stayed, though. It's hard to move your whole life. Most'd rather stay and make the best of things.

"We need to make our presence felt in the

Redworld. That's part of the deal. Start to show them who we really are. That we're here to help them. Blunt's idea. Not mine. But it's a good one," she says firmly to some of the expressions that could adequately be expressed as *whatthehell? The gangs? The Redworld?*

"And, if we're going to bring down the Greenworld border - eventually, not now, but one day - " - the voices bubble up in panic again but she carries on, firmly and clearly - "then we also need to mend fences with the gangs,"

Cue general havoc. She answers every single question and accusation, and there are a lot. Into the night, it goes. But eventually, the majority agree. We'll talk to the gangs, see if we can get them on our side.

I survived death twice yesterday, she says when we get home late. *Fuck me if local politics isn't worse.*

*

That was yesterday.

Today, we're getting ready for our meeting with the gangs outside the covenstead. I'll be walking onto his turf. Dad's community is the gangs. He built them up from the ground. They're his people.

I have to say something. I don't ever want to see him again, and that includes now.

"Look, I'm happy to go with you today and that, you know I am, but... not sure if I'm up to seeing him," I say to Melz's back as she's lacing up some new brown boots, her old cowboy ones having finally given up the ghost on the beach.

She doesn't reply until both boots are tied up; when she does, she takes my hands in hers.

"I can't imagine what it must be like for you, Sadie. But I need you. I'll protect you, okay? We need to go in there together. And you need to be able to show him how strong you are. That he can't victimise you anymore. You know that, right?" I nod, looking down, and she grips my hands tighter. "No. Look at me. You saved me. You healed me. You're strong, Sadie Morgan, and you're a witch now. There's nothing he has that gives him power over you except memory. 'Kay?"

I feel power flowing to me through her hands. Everything we've been through versus this? I can do it. I don't want to, but I can.

"All right,"

"For me," she moves my clasped hands to her heart. "You'll do it for me, won't you?"

"Okay. For you," I gaze into her eyes. I haven't had any chance to be alone with her since we, you know, *almost died*. I want to tell her I love her. Brighid's courage is still racing through me. This needs to come out into the open, once and for all. "Look, there was something I wanted to say. When we were up there. On Tintagel Head, and I didn't get the chance. But I…"

She smiles and reaches her index finger up over my lips.

"I know. Don't say it yet, though. Not here. Not now. It's not the right time,"

"When is the right time?" I sulk.

"When we're not about to walk straight into a gang camp. Sound fair?"

"Fine. Whatever," I walk out of the room, huffily. I know I'm being an arse but I can't help it. Her curse is over. The spirits are gone. I love her. I don't want to wait anymore.

I hear her swear and come after me. She grabs me

by the shoulder and turns me around to her.

"Fine, Sadie Morgan. Have it your way. Here and now," she says, and grabs me. Kisses me hard and deep, then just when I've caught up with the moment and start to kiss her back, she pulls away. "Okay?"

"Okay," I'm taken aback. Wipe my mouth with the back of my hand without thinking.

"I love you, all right? I was hoping to say it at a slightly more auspicious time," she raises her eyebrow. "I love you. You're beautiful, smart, magical, sweet. You're… full of beauty. It's impossible not to love you,"

I am completely without words.

"I… I love you too. I loved you from the first minute. From the dream. Even before that day you opened the door at Danny's house,"

"I know. Me too, I think. But I had to clear a lot of my head out before I could admit it," she smiles. We gaze at each other like imbeciles.

"So," I take a deep breath. Life feels as though it's restarted suddenly. The sun looks brighter. The grass, why didn't I notice how perfect it was, before? *Did I actually just think that? Unbelievably lame. Even for me.*

"So. Come on. More of this later, okay? For now we've got hardened criminals to charm," she takes my arm and propels me out of the house.

I still have no words. The irony doesn't escape me.

*

We walk into the gang camp unarmed.

Sanj and some of the enviros walk behind us. They've got guns - they refused to come without them - but Melz, Saba and I know our only chance is to go in as we are, open-handed, peaceful and ready to negotiate.

When we get through the trees and into the clearing, though, I forget about the very new and all-consuming *I love you* episode, because this is where Roach lives, and I dread him. Against this new love, the dread is even more painful than usual.

This is the main gang camp near to Tintagel: a mess of caravans, tents and small badly made shacks. They're the inbetweeners, the ones on the edge; they don't want to live in the Redworld but they didn't want to integrate with us either - for some, it's a dislike for any kind of organised community, for others, they didn't like our philosophies. And some just wanted to make trouble.

Before we left Tintagel, we sent a peace spell of healing in front of us, to make the gang folk receptive when we arrive, to make the meeting go as well as it could possibly go - but the thing is, with magic and healing, when you ask for the best possible thing to happen, you never really know what that best thing is. Sometimes it might not be all that peaceful or nice. It might be the best thing for us to come to blows with these folk for some reason. Maybe that needs to happen for them to understand what we're about, or to expend the stored up negative energy between us. So, as much as we've prepared, we still can't really predict what's going to happen.

I take a deep calming breath and chant to Brighid in my head as we approach. A group of six or so men and women forms in the centre of the clearing, casually gathering around a campfire but their eyes never leaving ours. Most of them are holding some kind of weapon: sticks, knives.

Melz walks forward and dimly I see the black shimmer of wings at her back; the Morrigan's with her. She holds her hands up so that the gang members can see she's unarmed.

"Greetings," her voice is loud, clear and steady.

"You're not welcome here," one of the men says. It's hard to tell his age because like everyone in the gangs, he's got the weathered skin that comes of living in the open all year round. He wears a tattered black jacket, mud stained jeans and has a brownish unkempt beard. "Go home, witch,"

"I will. But not before I've spoken to all of you. Where's Roach?"

They look at each other, and none of them reply.

"Where is he? I need to speak with him. And you," Melz says.

"He's not here," blurts out one of the others. "He's gone. Into the woods with that Daniel. The young witch, like you. Been gone for days now," The others shush him and glare.

"Shut up!" hisses one of the women.

"Well, maybe that will make this a bit easier for all of us," Melz says, and beckons Sanj and the enviros closer. "We come in peace. We're not here to hurt you. We want to end this war between us. We want to give you sanctuary,"

The man that spoke first laughs.

"Is that really why you came? You shouldn't have bothered, love," he taps the stick he's holding into his other cupped hand: one, two. "We're quite happy here thanks. Shangri-La, this is. Can't you tell?" I gaze around at the trampled mud, at the washing lines sagging with clothes strung between the caravans, at the thin children peering at us from behind one of the shacks.

"Just listen to what we have to say," Melz says, again, in that special tone, and signals to Saba who steps forward gingerly and shows the folk the basket of food she's brought: goat's milk and cheese, vegetables, bread, even some wine. One of the women steps forward and touches the bearded man on the arm.

"Come on, Bill. Won't do any harm to listen," she says, and nods to Saba. "Here. I'll take that," she says.

"You're making the right decision," Melz says, and she beckons Sanj to stand next to her.

"This is Sanjit Nayar. He's a Greenworld envirowarrior. So are all of these men and women," she explains. "They've just come back from the war in Russia, and we've welcomed them in Tintagel. Along with a number of Redworld refugees; you must have noticed them coming through the border. Probably you've taken in a few yourselves," Melz smiles; her voice is warm. "We want to open our doors to you as well. We'd like to invite you to leave Roach and become part of our community. I've..." she swallows and clears her throat. "I've taken over from Lowenna Hawthorne as Head Witch. And I don't want us to carry on like this anymore. Us behind the barrier, you outside it, starving. Suffering in the cold and the rain," she looks around her, and slowly a crowd's forming, listening to her. Mothers with babies, old women, old men as well as the more typical thugs and disillusioned young men I think of when I think about the gangs.

"There's a bigger threat out there. Bigger than our fight for territory. The war for fuel in Russia's over. Very soon the Redworld is going to go into crisis because there isn't any fuel left for them. We know about something that can change that. But we have to make the world leaders listen to us, because if they don't, it means chaos for all of us.

"The Prime Minister's offered us a deal. She'll let us talk to the delegates at this climate summit, when it happens, in London, but in return, she wants us to help turn the tide in the Redworld. Re-educate the folk; house some of them if necessary.

"We're happy to take you in and feed your families," Melz smiles at a small child that comes to stand in from of her, sucking her thumb and watching Melz solemnly as she talks. "But we need something from you. Numbers. Support. Vehicles. We need your strength to march with us on Westminster. If you're able,"

The woman holding the basket shakes her head.

"I don't think so, my lover. All that magic and goddess rubbish. I don't want that for my children. It's wrong. I'd rather stay here, thanks all the same,"

The basket in her hand's full of the wholesome food we grew that she'll feed her hungry children with - but I don't say anything. We need these folk.

"I'm not a fan of all that religious stuff either," Sanj says. "Never was. I was married to one of the witches; that was partly why I left to be an Enviro in the first place. Couldn't be doing with all the chanting and the solstices and the bloody community singalongs," there's a few laughs. I can tell Melz is making an effort not to bristle.

"But they're good people. They mean well. And, like Melz says, she's in charge now. Lowenna Hawthorne, yeah, she wasn't too keen on you lot. But the younger generation, I dunno," he looks at me, Melz and Saba. "They're more tolerant, maybe. There's different priorities, like they say. And it's true. All the soldiers are coming back from the war now. There's going to be more and more refugees coming this way if nothing gets done, and you won't have the option of living out here on your own. They're going to be coming and fighting you for every scrap of land. They're desperate. Even more desperate than you,"

The crowd murmurs, but they still watch us suspiciously. Sanj points to a man in the crowd carrying a young boy who has some kind of skin disorder - from here it looks like a severe case of psoriasis or eczema.

"They can help with that, you know. The witches," he bends and rolls up his trouser leg to reveal a long jagged scar. "It was infected when I got here from Russia. Ripped it open on a piece of metal. Wouldn't heal, the medics there couldn't keep it clean. By the time I got here it was in a right state. Some of the other witches put this disgusting smelling poultice on it. Kept changing the wrapping, these particular leaves, what was it?" he looks at me.

"Geranium, nasturtium and marrow leaves," I say softly. We'd change the leaves every day; they went on green, they came off black from soaking up the gangrene that'd set in Sanj's leg. But slowly, it improved. It was amazing, but Lowenna had just smiled. *Nature gives you all the medicine you need,* she'd said.

"You could help my boy?" the father looks at me suspiciously.

"I think so," I say shyly.

"Never slept through the night and he's six. Wakes up screaming, it itches so much," the father's grey with exhaustion. "We can't stop him scratching it,"

"It looks like an infected eczema. I could give you a cream. It works," I say. "Plus energy healing. I really think we could help," I smile as helpfully as I can, knowing that we could make these folks' lives better. Help them know how to get the best out of living in the wild. But we need them too. There's not enough of us to take a demonstration down to London and leave enough folk behind to care for the enviros and the refugees that're too sick or broken to come with us, and to make sure the bread gets baked and the crops get tended. More mouths to feed means more folk in the fields, more villagers being trained in farming and distilling and animal husbandry and milking.

"Won't you sit down with us and just talk?" Melz opens her hands in a conscious, conciliatory way. "That's all we want to do. To talk. And to help you,"

An old man in the crowd steps forward and takes Melz's hand unexpectedly. She flinches for a second, but he smiles up into her eyes; he's tiny, smaller than her, and his eyes are kind.

"Come on, young witch. I'll make thee a cuppa," he says, and leads her through the crowd to his caravan, a brightly painted red and blue Romany style one with steps leading up to a domed roof. He waves his hand at the crowd, some of whom are calling out in dismay.

"Ah, shut up, the lot of ye. Been a long time since witches came to talk with us. Aint ye got enough weapons between you to use if ye need to?" he offers Melz a seat on the painted steps and she smiles up at him. "And better when Roach isn't around. Ye all know he's not what he was. Gone bad, he has. He's left us. Off in the woods with the young feller doing god knows what. He don't care about us anymore," he turns to Melz. "Now, young lady. Milk in yer tea? Or something stronger?" he winks, and she gives a little laugh despite the tension of the situation.

"Errr... no milk, thank you. Just the tea will be lovely. Thank you," she exchanges a look with me and, gingerly as I can, I go and sit beside her. Saba and the Enviros follow us, making their way through the crowd gently. I take a cup of tea from the tiny man who gives it to me with a cheery nod. And we sit under the trees, and listen.

CHAPTER FORTY-FIVE

There are five things which a learned person should know about each day...

The day of the solar month, the age of the moon, the running of the sea, Without folly, the day of the week, of pure festivals, according to right clarity.

From the Saltair na Rann

"It's a high price. Are you sure it's really worth it?" I ask Melz over the fire. We're with Saba out at the deserted farmhouse on the edge of the village. Melz and Saba and their village gang used to come here, she says, before Tom died.

Melz kicks the wood at the base of the flames as she stalks around it.

"Don't have any choice. We need them. Need their trucks and all that to get down there in time. It's only a few days away. More to the point, we can't carry on like this. Them out there. Us behind the barbed wire, doing our psychic protection every day, sleeping with one eye open in case Roach decides to attack again. I can't live like that,"

"But Roach's never going to just roll over and

suddenly be friends," I hold out my hand to her to stop walking; she takes it absently and holds my fingers. "Believe me. He never gives up on anything,"

Melz squeezes the ends of my fingers and sits down next to me. Saba shoots us an unreadable look.

"I know. Unless for some reason he suddenly appears waving a white flag, we're going to have to deal with Roach. There's no way I can move forward as the Head of the Greenworld with him inciting the gangs to violence. I'm sorry, Sadie. But you know that as well as I do,"

"What do you mean? Kill him?" I trace my finger in the dirt, drawing a pentagram, a triskele, the triple moon. I keep my voice steady, but the words lick my stomach like fire. The desire to be free of him; the knowledge that it'd be wrong.

"I leave that to the Goddess. But She's shown me the future and Roach isn't in it,"

"The gangs. It seems like they're getting a lot from us and not giving a lot back," Saba says, looking down at Melz's handwriting on the pulpy handmade paper in my hand. An agreement between Melz, representing the

Greenworld, and five members of the gangs. Second tier to Roach, they said, but that was good enough.

"They only want security. It's understandable," Melz sighs.

What they want from us, in return for laying down arms, deserting Roach and coming to London to support us on our march, is their own villages. Villages where they'll have everything we have - running water, food, farms, clothes, community. But without a witch in charge. No compulsory religion. Melz managed to get them to agree that witches could live in the village and perform ceremonies, blessings, medicine, healing, counselling, all the usual stuff, but they'd just be another person whose services could be consulted if required.

"They want all the wisdom of the Goddess without giving Her the proper reverence," I shake my head. "It isn't right, Melz. You shouldn't agree to this,"

"I know it isn't. But it's the deal we have to make for now, Sadie. "Should" is a luxury. I can't afford the idealism of living in a world of "should" right now. Blunt will agree. They'll be places the Redworlders can live in, too,"

I look into the flames; the healing light of Brighid, and murmur Her prayer; I'm surprised to hear Saba echo my words. *Go geosnai tirte fhaire Bhride, Muid ag na-hoibre. Go ndo tinnail rabhaidh Bhride, Muid a ghiollacht tri na scaileanna. Go lasa laistigh bruane coranach Bhride, Agus ceangail muid le ne dheithe.*

"And where are these villages going to be?" she asks her sister. "You've got to establish rule over all the covensteads, as well as making new non-Greenworld communities. Kind of a lot of work. And that's only to start with. Then, there's being Head Witch on a day to day basis. Keeping track of everything. All those wilful witches in the middle of nowhere. Even Tintagel on it's own a massive job," she narrows her eyes at her sister.

Melz looks into the fire, moodily.

"For the gangs, I was thinking Gidleigh, extend the village out to Chagford to accommodate them if necessary. It was populated once before the Greenworld, so there's houses that can be done up, and there's good forest and farmland out that way."

"Gidleigh?!" Saba shouts. "They'll go mad. They won't want that, surely!"

"I know. But there's no witch there anyway since Zia died. The're already independent,"

"Yes, but..." Saba frowns, but Melz interrupts her.

"The people aren't going to like it? No, probably not. But I'll explain it to them simply. Either they can accept gang members into their newly independent community or they can protect themselves against them without us and without Redworld help,"

"Redworld help?" I wrap my arms around myself and peer around me at the crumbling walls; at the fragrant roses in full bloom.

"They have resources we don't. Soldiers, security. We can use that,"

"That might be unpopular," Saba warns.

"Not my problem at this stage," Melz pokes the fire viciously. "But you're right. About ruling. I don't think I can do it alone," she looks up and meets her twin's amber gaze. "But we could do it together,"

"What? Two Head Witches?"

"Two heads are better than one," Melz raises an eyebrow.

"Only if you're a gorgon," Saba mutters dismissively.

"Gorgons only had one head. Snakes for hair," Melz side-eyes me. Saba rolls her eyes.

"Whatever. Ancient herstory. Not my strength,"

"No shit," Melz raises an eyebrow at her twin.

"Shut up. Really, though? You'd rule… with me?"

"Why not? Makes sense. More stability. We're both Lowenna's blood. You're good with people. I'm good with magic,"

"Are you saying I can't do magic?" Saba pouts.

"No, you're irritatingly good at that, too. But people don't love me. They'd love you, though,"

Saba's cheeks colour ever so slightly pink and she looks away from us.

"Of course I would. If you wanted me," she says, quietly. "That's what I always wanted. From when we were kids,"

"It'll be a different experience, mind you. If we're going to help the Redworld and be more open, share our ways with them, that's a whole new type of Head Witch. We'd still need a circle of witches in the covenstead. Bring Danny in, Sadie, the three branded ones. I don't know what might happen. You up for that?" Melz steeples her fingers and looks calculatingly at her sister over the flames. But Saba grins.

"I was born ready,"

"All right, then. Co-Head Witch you are. We're going to need you to be as charming as possible,"

Saba tosses her tawny hair affectedly, on purpose, baring her teeth in an aggressive smile. "Like this?"

"No, not like that. You look like a lunatic,"

Saba shrugs. "What would you prefer? Beauty or Truth?" it's a game she and Melz used to play; Melz told me about it once. Give each other scenarios and argue out which was the better: what it looked like or what it was, really, inside. "I'm Beauty. You're Truth," she strokes her dark twin's matted black hair. "Truth isn't always attractive, but you have to like the look of something to take notice in the first place. Beauty has its place,"

Melz smiles and takes her sister's hand; something unsaid passes between them, and a tear rolls down Melz's cheek.

"I'm sorry," she says. "About everything. I messed up. I did everything wrong. I'm so sorry," Saba reaches for Melz and envelops her in a fierce, protective hug.

"You don't ever need to apologise to me, stupid. I love you more than the stars. I should be the one to say sorry. I'm sorry about Tom. I should have stepped aside. And I shouldn't have left you. I just couldn't deal with mum. And I was jealous. Don't cry; please don't cry," she mumbles into Melz's hair, and kisses the top of her head. "You're my sister. I might be a bitch sometimes but if anyone hurt you…" she trails off, and looks at me.

"Someone did hurt me," Melz says, standing back and wiping her nose with the back of her hand. "But I made sure he didn't do it again,"

Saba laughs, her eyes watery. She wipes them with her sleeve.

"I bet you did," she wipes her nose on her sleeve, and they both burst out laughing; still hurt, still teary, but laughing. "Goddess knows, you're one nasty bitch when you want to be,"

"Takes one to know one,"

"Shut up,"

"You shut up."

I hug my knees, watching them, glad they're friends again.

Saba hugs her sister one last time and nods at me.

"You're in love with my sister, then?" she demands.

I cough in the campfire's smoke.

"Ummm... wow, that's direct,"

"Well?" hands on her hips, giving me that don't-shit-me trademark Hawthorne stare. I look sideways at Melz.

"Yeah. She knows I am," I say it shyly into the flames. It's still so new.

Melz looks into the fire, smiling, and I can't tell if it's the heat or a blush on her cheeks in the night.

"You better not hurt her, then. If you do, you've got a world of pain coming. I'm warning you, Sadie Morgan. I'm warning you," Saba leans in so that her nose's almost on mine. "Forget witchcraft. You hurt her, I'll cut your nipples off and make you eat them,"

"Errrr... okay..."

What can you say to that? She gives me one second more's deranged stare, then smiles brightly and wraps her cloak around her. "Anyway. I'm going home. You two coming?"

"I guess," I stand up, but Melz reaches out for me.

"We'll follow in a while," she says, looking meaningfully at Saba.

"Fine. Love's young dream," Saba sniffs and picks her way back through the rubble to the door in the wall.

"Yeah, whatever," Melz calls back as Saba disappears through the shadowed opening, and she pulls me down next to her, by the fire, straight into a long kiss, her mouth hot against the night on our skin.

"There's no one else here and we've got a crumbling farmhouse, the stars above us and firelight for romantic staging. This is happening, Sadie," she grins, sliding her cold hands inside my cloak and unbuttoning my shirt. "We've waited long enough. But that's over now," she breathes.

Bloody hell - when Melz the Red Witch wants something I guess she really wants it. My overall temperature rises roughly a thousand times and lines of bright pink power flash and shiver into my skin where her hand makes contact with my stomach, my neck, brushing my breasts, *ohhhh goddess.*

"Oh. Right," I say, unromantically, and shit, can't I think of anything better than that? All that time writing romantic poems for her and comparing her to Cleopatra and quoting Wuthering Heights and thinking about her and me in a Greenworld-approved feminist romance. All that time imagining telling her exactly how much I love her fierce vulnerability and her bravery, about how much I love how she cares for folk and wolfishly protects them and how I can't stop thinking about her kiss, her brand of fire on my mouth, her smoky incense and honey smell.

And then no words are necessary, because we tell each other everything we'll ever need to say with our bodies, and it's beautiful and soft and hot and wet and the firelight paints patterns on her skin as I kiss and kiss her. Hours pass by - or it feels like it as we lie naked in the summer night - and time's one long extension of her mouth and her skin and the way she touches me, and finally I'm feeling her gasp under my lips and her body fill with pleasure and she cries out *Sadie, Sadie, Sadie.*

A few seconds later I'm in that same place of darkness and magic where nothing has a name and I am only sensation. I'm only kisses, only love, only hers.

CHAPTER FORTY-SIX

Cast the circle, sacred space, out of space and time,

Break the link within ourselves, to skin and hair and bone,

Let us see, grant us wisdom, Lady of Fire, Lady of Tides,

Sight be here, be with us, Brighid; Sight be here, be with us, Brighid.

Chant for seership, from Greenworld Prayers and Songs

Melz and I fall asleep under the stars.

I dream of Roach and Danny, but it isn't really a dream.

I'm in the forest, watching them. They're inside a magic circle. They've made the sacred space, and I know that they're invoking an old power into the circle, but it isn't Lugh, the god they have in common - the god they have the witch-brand for. And beyond them, superimposed between them and me, there's my memory wall, holding back the thing I don't want to remember. I cower back and feel the panic trying to engulf me, in this part-dream part-vision.

I'm remembering.

He'd beaten mum so badly that day she couldn't make him leave me alone by putting her body inbetween him and me like she usually did. And so, while she lay on the kitchen floor by the back door, eyes already puffing over - it'd be a week before she could really see, afterwards - he - Roach - had dragged me into the circle: wax-spattered cast iron candleholders at the quarters, pungent incense up my nose.

He'd held me there, on the overgrown grass in the back garden. Tested me. He'd wanted to know, all this time. *Did I have the gift?* I called out for mum, but she couldn't get to me. He'd broken her arm and three of her ribs.

This is what I never wanted to remember. This is the thing that makes the yellow sickness come. This giant spirit *thing* that had appeared. The same thing that's with Danny now as I watch, in dream. One ruined eye, a bloody, gouged eye socket. This *thing* that clung to me; touched me with its vile fingers. The thing he invited into the circle to take what it wanted from me. Seeing it again, my stomach lurches and my temperature drops, suddenly, like being plunged into ice water.

He'd said it was a test, watching me with those

cold eyes. *If you can control that thing, it'll do anything for you.* He'd stood there and watched as the thing - a sickening, coiled, compresssed energy, primal, savage - tried to get inside me. My head. My heart. Everywhere. *Control it!* Roach'd hissed at me. *I know you can.*

But I was seven years old and I couldn't *control it*. I was SEVEN YEARS OLD and I wasn't even a witch then, I was a little girl that couldn't breathe. I was a little girl who had seen her mum beaten over and over again. I was seven and my mum was lying on the kitchen floor.

It was like being drowned. I could taste salt water in my mouth and pressure on my lungs like it was pulling me under, I gasped and lunged for air, but the demon wouldn't let me go.

And so I flew away, out of my body; I watched from above as my body rolled around the circle, possessed by that thing. Watched as it threw me around like a doll, until Roach stepped in and banished it, and stood over me, disappointment visible around him like a cloud. I watched him nudge me with his foot, still safe outside my body. Impersonal, dismissive. Not even a hand on the shoulder.

Then I woke up in my body, and retched and retched, wanting to get rid of whatever that wasn't me that was still inside. *You ruined it. Stupid girl. I don't know why I bother. Just trying to empower you. My daughter. Trying to give you the opportunities I didn't have.*

Stupid girl. Stupid girl. Stupid girl. The taste of salt water.

As the same dark spirit, an old thing of the deep darkness, appears in the circle, I feel that weight on my lungs; I gasp for air. I taste salt water in my mouth.

And Danny steps back, disgusted and afraid. He knows what Lugh's and Brighid's and even the Morrigan's energy feels like, animal spirits and plant energies too, and this is none of those. It watches Danny with its one eye, until Danny swallows nervously and nods to Roach. *No, no, no, no!* I try to scream at him. *Don't let it in!* But he seems to want to. He's vulnerable; he's still not recovered fully from imprisonment. He's grieving for Zia, angry at the world; he's got no-one left to watch out for him, or so he thinks. Whatever he's been doing out here with Roach hasn't exactly been good for him. And that means it'll be easier for the darkness to take hold.

Danny opens his arms and calls it in. It's Latin, I think; the witches don't use it; it's the language of the Father after all. And the spirit goes to him willingly, drawn by his light.

But the moment that energy touches him I can tell Danny knows he doesn't want it. He flinches as the weight and thickness hits him. Melz thought she wanted to jump off Tintagel Head, but when the ground shifted under her feet, when she really did fall, she clung on to me as I held her over the edge, desperate not to die.

When the old spirit's shadow covers Danny, Roach smiles. And in my dream, I cry out.

The cry echoes in the night forest. Roach looks up, suspiciously, but sees nothing. He starts walking around the circle clockwise - deosil, witches call it - chanting the same Latin, over and over. *No!* I cry out again, but my dream-voice is a wind in the trees.

But now Roach stops his circling because there's a noise in the forest: cracking of wood and a thumping tread. Heavy feet in heavy boots.

Omar breaks into the circle of yews and pushes Roach out of the way. Roach is not as strong as he was; conversely, Omar always looks bigger than the last time you saw him.

He grabs Danny, and as he does it, the shadow

reaches for him too. But Omar won't let go, and he's yelling at Roach and then shaking Danny who's gone limp in his arms, and I can see the spirit caressing its long fingers over Danny's heart and his throat and I know that Omar has the strength to fight Roach and win, and he can carry Danny away, but unless someone banishes that old, primal power, it won't leave Danny alone. It's been called and welcomed.

In the dream, I step forward. I don't know if this is a real moment I'm in - it doesn't really matter. I don't know if Roach, Omar and Danny can see me. But I know how to shackle that beast. I even know its name; now that the memory has burst, I remember it all, what he taught me. And I'm not seven years old anymore.

I start by chanting Brighid's blessing, loudly and firmly, and I feel power start to course through me. *Teigi ar bhur ngluine, agus osclaigi bhur suile, Agus ligigi Brid bheannaithe isteach.* I reach for Danny, putting one of my hands on his heart and one on his head, and time slows down, for me at least, in the dream realm, whether I'm somehow interacting with him in real time or not, and I cry out to Brighid:

Blessed Brighid of the heavenly fire,

Blood fire enchantress, incendiary smith,

Cleanse Daniel Prentice with your merciful fire,

Banish this spirit so he may live.

Then, to the thing itself I shout:

I bind and banish you,

I command you in the Holy names of Brighid, Lugh, Morrigan;

I bind and banish you,

Obey my fiery command.

Leave this space! Leave these bodies! I command!

With Brighid's fire and Lugh's bright spear I command you!

With Brighid's fire and Lugh's bright spear I command you!

A blue-red circle of fire ignites on the scrubby grass, surrounding us. Instinctively I close my eyes against it, and though I can't feel its heat physically, and I'm not burning, every single part of me ignites with this singing, flowing power that eats me up from base to head, right up my spine as if it's the wick of a candle.

Glowing, and full of the cleansing fire of Brighid, I repeat the final part of the banishment, and draw the symbols of the pentagram, the triskele and the triple moon on Danny's heart and forehead. Brighid's fire trails from my fingertips and leaves a glowing mark on him. I push all the love I have in me at him.

The demon spirit releases Danny: Brighid's fire is too bright for it, burning it from the feet upward, finally consuming the bloody, butchered eye socket that I dreamed of for so long as a child, never sure when I would see it again, but always knowing that I would.

But now, I watch it burn, and with it I feel my nightmares burning away too until there's nothing left. All the time, that hidden memory's held me back. Filled me with fear and panic, lessened my power. And now I can let go the unconscious association between magic and pain that I always had. There was always the gift I knew I had, and there was always the desire. But there was also always a block, and I didn't fully know it until now.

Omar, Danny in his arms, turns to go; Roach, looking a little stunned that somehow his demon has disappeared, reaches out and takes a hold of Omar' wrist.

"You're not going anywhere," he snarls, but Omar's so much stronger than Roach. Once, Roach would have been about the same; a big man, tough, weathered, used to living rough. But now, he's stooped, white-haired, burn marks on his face.

Omar pulls his wrist away.

"I told you once to leave him alone, and you didn't listen," he reaches towards his belt, and I can't see what he's doing because Danny's inert body is in the way.

"He came to me, just like he did before," Roach sneers back. "I'm just doing what he wanted me to do. He wanted real power. I'm giving him it,"

"Don't give me that. You want his power on your side and you'll do anything to get it," Omar mutters.

"So what if I did? I always knew what we could do together. Overturn the witches. Rule like we were always supposed to. Reclaim the God. The old powers,"

Omar raises a bushy eyebrow.

"You're out of touch, then. They've just deposed Lowenna Hawthorne. The Greenworld's overturned itself," I wonder why Omar's telling Roach that, and then I see what he's got in his hand; see him heft the unconscious Danny over his left shoulder. Watch him adjust his balance so that his right arm is free.

His right hand.

His gun hand.

"Shame you won't be around to do anything about it,"

Omar raises the black handgun to Roach's temple and pulls the trigger.

Roach's body folds neatly to the ground in the middle of the circle. A sacrifice to the old gods.

Omar spits on the ground next to Roach's body, and puts the gun back in his belt carefully, adjusting Danny's unconscious weight so he doesn't drop him.

"I warned you to stay away from my boy," he grunts.

I wake up, crying.

I don't know if what I saw was real.

But I know in my bones that my father is dead.

h that, and then I see what he's got in his hand; see him heft the unconscious Danny over his left shoulder. Watch him adjust his balance so that his right arm is free.

His right hand.

His gun hand.

"Shame you won't be around to do anything about it,"

Omar raises the black handgun to Roach's temple and pulls the trigger.

Roach's body folds neatly to the ground in the middle of the circle. A sacrifice to the old gods.

Omar spits on the ground next to Roach's body, and puts the gun back in his belt carefully, adjusting Danny's unconscious weight so he doesn't drop him.

"I warned you to stay away from my boy," he grunts.

I wake up, crying.

I don't know if what I saw was real.

But I know in my bones that my father is dead.

CHAPTER FORTY-SEVEN

to see you: tensed as if each leg were a gun
loaded with leaps but not fired while your neck
holds your head still listening: as when

while swimming in some isolated place
a girl hears leaves rustle and turns to look:
the forest pool reflected in her face.

From: The Gazelle by R M Rilke

We chant all the way to London.

MOR-RI-GAN! MOR-RI-GAN!

HELP US TO PROTECT OUR LAND!

BRI-GHID! BRI-GHID!

BLESS OUR PROTEST, BLESS OUR LAND!

The fuel summit starts today at Westminster; leaders from all the countries of the world are coming to debate the end of the war and what happens next.

"Debate, my arse. Shitting themselves, more like," Sanj said this morning as we sat down for breakfast before setting off. *An army runs on its stomach,* he'd said, whilst frying up eggs and bacon and mushrooms; he had Saba on toast duty, two prongs in the heartfire with thick-cut wheat bread slices stuck on them. Her face was flushed and her expression was pretty unimpressed at manual labour. Ordinarily, I would have laughed. But, today, it's all I can do not to burst into tears.

I'm not sad for Roach. I won't be. I refuse. I'm not some kind of Stockholm Syndrome loser that loves her torturer (It's messed up; I read about it in a book). I'm not afraid to say that and I don't care how it makes me sound. Like a bitch? Fine, then I'm a bitch for being glad my abusive father's dead.

The tears are like a bursting dam. *Tears make us whole again*, that's what they say here. All part of the healing process, I suppose, but all I want to do is cry, and I keep having to invent excuses to remove myself from the kitchen and stick my face into a cupboard and bawl or go into the garden for some air. I'm not crying for him. I'm crying for me, for mum. For her scars and my lost childhood.

I'm releasing all the fear, all the sadness. I'm releasing the tension of not knowing where he was or when he was going to hurt us from every day of the past thirteen-or-so years.

But there's no time for my grief right now. It's crappy timing when you see your father die in vision the night before you have to save the world.

Once we're on the road, it's better. More distraction. Even so, I have to stare out of the window of the truck so that no-one can see me cry; it's still coming in waves. My neck's getting a massive crick in it but I can't take the risk of showing my tears to anyone. I don't even know why. I know I'm allowed to be sad. I know witches have precognitive dreams. And I know Melz'll want to know everything about the dream because we're desperate for Omar to bring Danny down to London; and I know she'll understand. But I still don't want to tell anyone. Not yet. Maybe I'm too used to keeping my tears secret.

She taps me on the arm.

"Hey. Hey! You asleep?" she has to raise her voice above the grumble of the van's engine so it's more of a shout. I wipe my eyes surreptitiously and turn to her.

"Just watching the road," I try out a small smile.

"It's crazy we're doing this, huh," she cranes around and waves to the rest of the folk in the back of the truck; we at least have the luxury of sitting up front with Sanj, who's driving. "Everyone okay back there?" they nod and smile back at her, still chanting.

"They've got spirit, I'll give 'em that," Sanj adds, squinting and flipping a visor down inside the window. "Think this is gonna make the splash you want it to? All these people?" he points with his thumb backwards, at the long train of envirowarriors, gang members, villagers and witches behind us, in the vans and cars and trucks borrowed from the gangs or from Omar's Redworld contacts. Hundreds of folk, squeezed in any which way.

"Sure," Melz shouts over the engine. "Not sure about spirit so much as sweaty armpits and bad breath," she says in an undertone to me, grinning, but I'm not in the mood to joke.

"They care. They know that the stakes are high. Make the governments listen to us, or what? Be plunged into the new Dark Ages?" Sanj shouts. I look out of the window again.

"How come you're so serious all of a sudden?" Melz leans in puts her hand on my arm. "Sadie. Hey. What is it? You've been quiet all day. It's not like you,"

"I don't want to talk about it," I feel another wave of tears coming; it makes it worse when you're feeling crappy and someone's nice to you.

"Talk about what? Hey. Come on. You can tell me anything," she strokes my arm; the Greenworlders and the gang members in the back of the van chant MOR-RI-GAN! MOR-RI-GAN! HELP US TO PROTECT OUR LAND! like a tribal heartbeat. *Shit, shit, shit.* The wave breaks and engulfs me again, but this time I can breathe. I can survive.

I lean on Melz's shoulder and wail like a child. She strokes my hair, gently, letting me cry. And when I have breath for words, I tell her everything about the dream, or whatever it was, and she nods, not comenting, just listening, like she always does, until I've wrenched everything out from myself that I can.

"He's dead, then," she says, taking my cheeks in both hands and leaning her forehead on mine, eyes closed. "Are you sad for him?"

I close my eyes, forgetting the jolting of our bodies together and the drying tears on my cheeks; tuning out the chanting from the folk behind.

"No," I whisper.

"You shouldn't be. You're free now. You can step into your power more than you ever have," she kisses the tears from my cheeks.

"I'm… I'm just…" I sob again; she waits patiently, stroking my hair. "I'm sad for myself. What I lost," I manage to get it ut, stammeringly.

Melz hugs me to her.

"Oh, Sadie. I can't imagine how you feel. I'm so sorry," I can hear her heart beating, my head against her chest. Her good heart; always caring, always ready to protect. "I wish I'd been there to protect you. When you were little. I wouldn't have let him touch a hair on your head," she squeezes me tight.

"You couldn't have stopped him," I sit up and wipe my eyes.

"I would. I'd die before I let anyone hurt you," she kisses my forehead, but her voice is steel.

"My knight in shining armour," I smile carefully, a small smile.

"You know how good I'd look riding into battle

for my fair maiden," she says, folding her arm around my shoulders. "Black armour, obviously. Shiny. Fitted. The boots would be amazing,"

"None of that silver shit," I wipe my nose on my sleeve. She frowns and hands me a handkerchief.

"Nope. Only, my fair maiden would be at the front of the attack anyway. Screaming obscenities at the enemy,"

Melz can make me laugh at the worst times.

"I would not!" I wipe my eyes on the hanky. "I never swear,"

"I think we're both past the point of pretending to be ladylike, don't you?" she squeezes my shoulder. She sings along with the rest of the people in the van, loud and off-key, but her arm stays firmly around my shoulders.

MOR-RI-GAN! MOR-RI-GAN!

HELP US TO PROTECT OUR LAND!

I close my eyes and breathe, letting the tears come as they need to. Tears will make us whole again. So they say.

CHAPTER FORTY-EIGHT

THE NIGHTS were not made for crowds, and they sever
You from your neighbour, and you shall never
Seek him, defiantly, at night.
But if you make your dark house light,
To look on strangers in your room,
You must reflect—on whom.

From: People at Night by R M Rilke

When we get to central London, the houses are close together and the air's grey and thick. There are so many houses.

We get out and walk at a certain point when we're not too far from the summit. The enviros and gang members drive the cars and trucks slowly in a line down the pocked London roads; we walk on either side of them, unfurling our banners in the drizzle. Blunt asked us to start educating the Redworlders, so that's what we're doing.

We chant and hand out leaflets to the Londoners that start to line the streets. GREEN ENERGY IS POSSIBLE, they say. THERE IS AN ALTERNATIVE. YOU DON'T HAVE TO LIVE IN THE DARK. We hand-lettered them all, a group of twenty of us, over the last two days, using up our valuable vegetable inks and handmade paper. Some folk snort and throw the paper onto the street, but some watch us thoughtfully as we pass. Some even smile and wave; after we've been walking for about half an hour, a group of girls Biba's age walk with us and hand out food and water from bulky bags.

"How did you know we were coming?" I ask one of them as she hands me a paper-wrapped sandwich; I take another for Melz, and hand it to her through the open side of a jeep. She's still not totally healed from her fall onto the beach; Sanj's taking a break from driving; he's walking beside me. I'm achy too but I need to walk. Quiets the mind.

The girl produces a thin shiny black plastic rectangle from her pocket. A phone. Melz told me about them.

"Word travels fast," she grins, and hands an apple to Sanj. He nods at my confused face.

"Internet," he says. "A type of communication through telephone lines. But it depends on electricity, just like everything. She must be a rich kid. Have a home generator or something, to keep that thing going. Good to know that internet services haven't collapsed yet though. Mine and Omar's Redworld contacts are online, telling their networks what's going on,"

"Er. Right," I have literally no idea what any of that meant.

"You don't know what I'm talking about,"

"Nope," I look around me at the crowds. They don't look hostile yet.

"No, well, why would you?" he narrows his eyes at the end of the street in front of us where some blue lights begin to flash. "I see they've still got enough power to recharge the batteries for those, though,"

He holds up his fist and we stop; the word goes back through the line. "We've got company,"

The police - I remember them from when we visited before - walk towards us behind riot shields that obscure most of their bodies. The one at the front consults a black device in his hand.

"Demelza Hawthorne?" he barks, and Sanj undoes his gun holster, all casual, as the blue-suited, black-booted riot-masked man walks past us, scanning the crowd; enviros and gang members cluster up. I walk back to the jeep Melz's in and place my hand protectively on the sill of the open window; her hand reaches for mine.

"Here," she calls and nods at me, like she knows it'll be okay, but she can't know that. I mean, Blunt's made this deal with us, but we don't know if she's going to back out on it. That's why we're armed.

Either way, here she sits, Demelza Hawthorne, like Cleopatra in that perfumed barge, sailing down the Nile to Caesar or Mark Antony or whichever horny old Roman she had to get on side, only her barge's a battered army jeep that runs on biodiesel made from recycled cooking oil. But she's still a queen at the head of her tribe.

The policeman comes to the jeep; reluctantly, I stand aside.

"You're Demelza Hawthorne?" he asks, with a hint of derision.

"I am," She smiles thinly.

"I've been told you have a recognisable tattoo at the base of your neck,"

"Have you, indeed?" she answers coolly and I feel myself smirking.

"I have been instructed to make sure of your identity before I give you this communication," he replies dully and I wonder what it must be like to be the human inside that carapace, to be the soft erring flesh, the fickle heart and the changeable mind held by the rigid costume of enforcer and protector. And perhaps it isn't so different from being the witch; from being the figurehead, the one with the power. We're still people. We still mess up.

Melz turns her head away and rolls down the collar on her cream-coloured cotton shift top so that her witch-brand's visible: the triskele, blue, as if it was painted on in woad.

"This enough identity for you?" she pulls her shirt up again and turns back to his impassive mask. He nods and hands her the device. She presses the button cautiously. The screen lights up and Felicity Blunt's there, talking to us.

I jump. "By Brighid! What the…?"

"Sadie! Shhh!" Melz waves her hand impatiently at me.

"… to London. As you stipulated in your letter, I will invite you to take the floor at the summit as a special representative from the UK government, and you will share your…"

On the moving screen, Blunt stops to sip from a glass of water.

"You'll share your ideas with the delegation. I have sent a police escort to bring you to the Ministry building. They'll protect you from any potential street harassment. You may also encounter some resistance from security services personnel. The security services do not currently operate under governmental jurisdiction and are acting under the criminal remit of several powerful city figures, since this government introduced emergency legislation to re-nationalise crime protection. The police forces are on hand to help you if required. I look forward to seeing you," she pauses, and for a moment her businesslike façade drops and she smiles hopefully, honestly. "And - thank you. For making the first move, for coming down here when we refused to come to you. Thank you for persevering. You don't have to convince me any longer. I just hope you can convince the rest of the world," she nods curtly and the screen goes black again.

"So... they've reneged on the deal with the security services. Where they used to deliver law and order, now it's the police again," I watch the police men and women, metres away from us at the front of the procession. "But they're massively under-resourced. They have to be - there's been no money for policing in the Redworld for years, because of the war. That's how the security firms took over. They had the money so they paid for the privelige of enforcing whatever laws they liked,"I know all this because Melz told me. And she learnt from Bran Crowley, a criminal himself.

Melz raises her eyebrows.

"Consequence you pay for killing Mother Earth. Everything bad follows. Corruption. Greed. Disease. Crime,"

I catch Sanj's eye. "She's putting everything on the line for us. Blunt,"

"Then you better deliver," he grunts, and nods to the police escort. We start walking again, and Melz's jeep drives on slowly. I reach my hand in again through the window and hold her hand as I walk, revelling in the heat and energy that flows up my arm from her touch.

"You okay?" she asks, her voice quiet above the rattle of the jeep and the din behind us, the chanting, the onlookers shouting from the sides of the streets. Yeah, it's going to take a long time to deal with what happened in that dream, that vision. It's going to take a long time to heal, still. But I faced it. The worst thing imaginable; I faced it. And I defeated it.

"I'm always okay with you, Hawthorne," I grin up at her.

"Corny. And since when did you call me by my last name?"

"Since... now?"

"Hawthorne and Morgan. Fighting the patriarchy since 2047," she gives me her mischievious smile.

"Sounds good," I take two pre-rolled herbal cigarettes out of a tin in my pocket and beckon to one of the nine lamp-bearers walking with us. Nine devotional flames for Brighid, accompanying us to London. I hand one to Melz and we smoke in companionable silence.

CHAPTER FORTY-NINE

Brighid, bless the corn,

Brighid, bless the grain,

Blessed Brighid bless our food,

And make us whole again.

Chant for food preparation, from Greenworld Prayers and Songs

It's Midsummer. We should be preparing for the solstice celebrations at home, but here we are instead, making herstory.

A noise like a swarm of bees approaches and intensifies; I look up and see a vehicle of some kind floating in the air above us. A blurred circle at the top, a shape like a wasp with a long tail underneath. It hovers over us and I drop down onto my knees, cowering.

"What in Brighid's name's THAT?" I yell, and Sanj hauls me up.

"Helicopter. Don't worry, it's the army. I mean, DO worry, but it's not unusual. They're just watching us,"

"Oh. Well, that's all right then," I put my hands

over my ears and we walk on in silence until they helicopter flies off.

"Good to see they do have some armed forces left," Sanj muses. "They didn't all get sent to Russia to die for nothing," he spits on the ground. "At least I chose to go, stupid as it was. They didn't have any choice, those poor Redworld bastards. The Enviros thought we were going over there to sabotage a fascist military. Not a load of terrified, out of condition, underfed civilians,"

"Weren't you terrified too?" I ask.

"Course I was. When I got there and I realised what was really going on. By then I was there and it was too late. We were in a ton of shit. I couldn't desert the rest of the Enviros. They all had families they should have been with, too," he looks away and coughs.

"You missed him, then. When you were away?"

"Who?" Sanj frowns at me.

"Danny. When you were away. Didn't you miss him? And Biba?"

"Course I did," he mutters, and takes a drink of water from his bottle.

"Why did you go in the first place?" it's something kids like us have never been able to understand. Melz's dad went too, off to the war, to be an Envirowarrior. Like anything was better than sitting at home with women, farming and singing and praising the Goddess.

He sighs.

"You wouldn't understand," he says.

"Try me."

He puts his bottle back in the loop of his frayed leather Enviro belt then looks at me.

"Your dad left you. That why you want to know?"

"No. I know why he left us. And we never wanted him back,"

"Different case, granted. Radley was always a mean bastard. Never knew what your mum saw in him,"

Me neither.

"So? Why did you go?"

Sanj looks back at the crowd behind us and then at the deepening rows of folk watching us from the sides of the roads.

"Zia always said that she thought there was no colour in the Greenworld. She thought her and her friends had created this wonderful utopia where everyone was loved; everyone was safe. And it was good. It was beautiful and peaceful and all of the things she wanted it to be. And she was a beautiful woman. Strong, sexy, intelligent, wild; I wanted her as soon as I saw her,"

I look away, feeling my cheeks flush.

"But look behind you. At the Greenworlders. Not a very mixed bunch, are they?"

"No," I know that. I know how folk used to talk about Danny and Biba at home in Gidleigh, sometimes - some of the bitter old folk but some of the kids, too - they'd heard their parents talking about Danny and Biba's brown skin and black hair, calling them names, and repeated it at school. And it didn't matter that Danny's mum was the Head Witch, didn't matter that their mum made the rules. To some folk she'd always be the white bitch with two brown kids and somehow that was cause for alarm.

"No. So it was partly that. I would have been able to cope with that, though, and I could have put up with Zia defending it, her precious Greenworld. But she never defended me against them. Even when the kids got older and they were old enough to understand what folk were saying to them at school, in the street; here and there: they weren't quite right, they didn't fit in. Even when she brushed that off, if it'd been only that, I'd have stayed. But..." he looks away. "I regret it now. I didn't realise what it would do to Biba and Danny when I left. But, at the time, I didn't feel like there was a place for me. As a man. There wasn't anything for me to do. And all the goddess stuff. It wasn't for me."

"The Goddess is for everyone," I say, on rote.

"For you, yeah. For Zia. But not me. Maybe if there had been more empowering options for me. There's supposed to be a balance between their God and their Goddess, and I'm no expert, but there didn't seem to be. I got sick of being treated like a gardener that she'd use for sex now and again. I fell out of love. Your age, you probably think getting handfasted and having kids is some wonderful romantic adventure. Truth is, it's really bloody hard. Sorry. You asked,"

I don't really know what to say to this level of candid explanation from a parent type - except, I want to say, *I have no desire to have children at all thank you, I'm seventeen years old, I don't even know if I ever want to be handfasted.* But did Melz's dad feel the same, I wonder? Lowenna's a difficult woman to be around sometimes; she challenges, she's strong, she's formidable enough to have built a whole world, a whole community. Not many folk could have done that. And I think Melz and Saba, maybe they didn't have the most conventional childhood. Maybe Lowenna was away a lot, maybe they spent a lot of time being looked after by other people. But despite everything I think Lowenna really loves them. Despite it all, I still really love mum. Because she fought for me and protected me; because she fed and clothed me and made me believe in myself.

"Danny's out there somewhere," I look back at the gang followers that're walking alongside the Tintagel villagers, the witches, to avoid his eyes in case he might somehow detect what I know. What I saw.

"I know," Sanj is unreadable.

"Didn't you want to go with Omar? To find him?"

"He doesn't want me," Sanj says flatly. "Omar's been a better dad to him than I have,"

"I know, but you're his real dad. That still means

something. He... he needs you," I think of Danny's unconscious body in Omar's arms. *Where are they now?*

"Does it? I don't know anymore,"

"I think it does," I say.

Sanj shrugs.

"It's been too long. I tried talking to the boy but look where it got me. Ran away to Roach. Even that was better than me, apparently,"

"Aren't you worried about him?" I ask; his lined, tired face says he is.

"Yeah. Of course. But I don't have a right to be worried. I gave that up when I left," he says, and nods at another two helicopters that have joined the first. "We're getting close now. All eyes on us, I guess," he raises his eyebrows at me and drains his water bottle. "They want to make sure we behave ourselves,"

I squint up at the wasp-like machines, so loud I feel the sound reverberating in my head.

I can't guarantee that, I think, watching them track us, watching them watch us. *Until last month we were your worst nightmare, Redworld. And now you want our help.*

WILD FIRE

It's going to be quite a day.

CHAPTER FIFTY

One moment your life is a stone in you, and the next, a star.

From: Sunset by R M Rilke

We're almost there when we pass a big grey monument of some kind; some of the Enviros stop to look at it and bow their heads. But some of them spit on it.

"The Cenotaph," Sanj says as we walk past it, head unbowed, but not spitting or shouting either.

"What's that?"

"The monument for the dead in the two great wars,"

"Surely there's nothing great about war," I watch the faces of the enviros; still gaunt, even though the ones that came on the march were the stronger ones, the ones that'd been in the Greenworld longer, had had time to eat and heal a little; loads of them couldn't walk, were half dead or worse when they got to us.

"It's a turn of phrase. The world wars at the

beginning of the twentieth century. So many millions died," he mutters.

"Why are they spitting on it?"

He shrugs, scanning the crowd, eyeing up the soldiers behind the riot shields that line the streets on both sides.

"I expect they don't feel like war's so great either,"

"Those wars weren't for fuel, though. At least they were..." I search for the right way to say it.

"What? Honourable? Worthy? Don't kid yourself. Tell me what's worth killing millions for,"

"Freedom, I guess?" I think about Lowenna. About what she would do, about what she has done for the Greenworld. For that freedom to be apart from the Redworld, freedom to worship Brighid. Freedom to rule ourselves. Omar snorts.

"Freedom, right. Freedom for a while. We defeated the ones that wanted to put us in camps and starve and gas and bomb us to death, sure. And then the corporations took over and made us slaves to money. And they paved the way for the Redworld, and the Redworld sent thousands, a million maybe, to fight a pointless war a long way away from their families and their loved ones, just so that there'd be less people to oppose the powers-that-be at home. That's what you do when you want to take all the power from the masses. You make up a war. Create a bogeyman for the people to fixate on. Make them fear it so much that they love you by comparison,"

"I suppose," I say.

"Anyway. After then, that's all wars were about. Fuel. This is the last one in a long legacy,"

"At least there'll never be another one. For fuel, I mean," it's a strange kind of hope, but with no fuel left, at least that gives the world a kind of clarity. A clean slate.

He raises one grey-speckled black eyebrow and adjusts the heavy pack on his back which I know contains food but also guns and ammunition.

"Don't kid yourself. The fuel's gone, the next scrap'll be for water. The wealthy've been buying it up for years. Aquifiers, lakes, water sources everywhere,"

"Is that true?"

He smiles bitterly.

"Sometimes I'm glad I'm old enough not to have to live with it like you'll have to," he says, looking off into the distance. He points ahead of us. "There. That's where we're going,"

The building's tall, square, once-white; the road full of similarly grand, old, once-white places. We plod on steadily; there're even more black and blue-uniformed policemen in front of it with their scratched riot shields, and about ten grey vans with black-uniformed folk standing outside them, all wearing black sunglasses and carrying machine guns. Whereas there's a sense of tension with the police personnel, the black-clothed ones stand with an air of arrogance.

"Security services," Sanj nods at them. "Better be careful. They don't play by the rules," he looks at me. "Who's going to talk to them?"

"We will. Me, Saba and Melz. Come with us, though?" He nods.

"Security's pretty tight," Sanj murmurs as we're corralled outside the building: *55 Whitehall, Department of Energy and Climate Change*, which I can just make out from the rusty once-golden sign on the entrance.

I'm abnormally aware of all my senses as the four of us approach: feeling the soft chafing of the seams of the cotton trousers between my thighs; drawing the thick grey polluted air of the city into my country lungs and feel its strange, unhealthy allure, like a night with too much wine next to a black smudgy fire. I'm distinctly aware of our footsteps on the hard grey road and the rhythm of our walking, a rough march, an echoing of each other.

Sanj nods to the phalanx of security personnel that bar the entry to the building as we approach.

"Afternoon," he says, but nothing changes on any of the sunglass-wearing faces; all of their eyes are masked by mirrors. "We're here for the climate summit,"

"No entry unless you're a delegate," one of the Security services men state, emotionless and cold.

"We have been invited. Please check with the Prime Minister," Melz says, her voice seeming small inside the vaulted porch.

"We don't report to her," another security person says, with a hint of derision.

"That's not anything to do with me. We have a personal invitation from the Prime Minister. I'm Demelza

Hawthorne and this is Sadie Morgan, Bersaba Hawthorne and Sanjit Nayar,"

"I don't care if you're Mickey Mouse, love. You're not coming in," the man says, a hint of a smile playing on his square-chinned face.

The lead policewoman steps in and hands the chillingly blank, sunglassed man an envelope with an official stamp on it.

"This is an official invitation to the event for the named participants here and a public order notice to allow the protestors access outside the building. Additionally, this includes the legal paperwork for you cease and desist from all public order responsibilities," she says clearly.

He nods, turning the envelope over in his hands.

"Never was one for love letters, darlin'. All digital nowadays, 'aven't you 'eard? Message me if you wanna hook up," and he rips the envelope in half and drops it. "Not that I go for ugly bitches, mind you,"

"Sir, I repeat, step away from the doors and let the delegates through or we will have no choice other than to use force," the policewoman repeats, and takes a small black cylinder out of her belt. The security guys laugh louder.

"What're you going to do, love? Kill me with a lipstick? Don't think it's my colour," he says, unsmiling, and takes a large, long black gun from his belt. It isn't a rifle or a pistol, both of which I've seen before. This is shinier and blacker with more... bits on it.

"Fine," says the policewoman, and holds out the small cylinder and presses a button. Two black things jump out of the far end of it and attach themselves to the security man's jacket. As soon as they do, he convulses and drops his gun. Or whatever it was.

"Take cover!" The policewoman barks at us and we leap to one side of the porch, behind the black iron railing. Then the security guys start firing at the police.

Instantly, one of them's hit, despite the riot shield he holds in front of him. Those things look fairly tough and maybe they do resist bullets, but the shot still gets him in the head and he goes down, and I look away in horror, feeling like I'm going to be sick as I watch the blood pool around his head on the grey road.

The crowd watching from the sides of the road go into a mass panic; running away, shouting, screaming, colliding into each other. The police hide behind a nearby car and the Greenworlders get inside the cars and the trucks we brought with us, but the enviros and the gang members, men and women, start firing back.

The police look behind them in surprise, as they clearly had us all down as useless peacenik hippies and not a reasonably well-prepared mini militia. Which is just as well, because for their part, they seem to be pretty badly equipped - they have the little shock things and the shields, and wooden sticks in their belts - *sticks? Really?* But they don't seem to have guns, and I remember that the privately-funded security services have been running the show here for a long time; the funded-by-the-criminal-super-rich security services have all the best weapons.

The security guys are good, but the Enviros have just come back from fighting in Russia. And the gangs have some pretty modern weaponry, too - unsurprisingly, for criminals. I watch as a gang woman, about the same age as mum and Lowenna, gets something that looks like a small metal pineapple out of her bag, pull out a pin from its top, and throw it into the porch. Sanj's eyes widen and he pulls us away from the railings.

"Shit. Run!" he yells as we belt it across the road

and hide behind a truck, just in time to shelter from a massive explosion that rocks the battered metal of the truck almost off its wheels. We run and cower behind another truck's big wheels, and I'm holding Saba's hand, and Sanj's body-blocking Melz, and we're breathing in the acrid fumes of the fire and the explosive.

And in that moment I have an epiphany: I'm scared as shit, but I'm not outside looking in at myself. I'm not having a panic attack and the sick heat isn't radiating out from my middle and threatening to kill me.

I've confronted my demon, and it can't take power from me anymore.

Now, my fear's the eminently sensible zen-present-moment kind about not being shot, which, as fear goes, is completely reasonable.

We stay next to the truck until the police come and get us and walk us through the front door. I don't look at the bodies of the security services people, but I have to step over them at one point. The policewoman that handed the paperwork to the sunglassed man is leaning over his inert body, taking the envelope back from his clasped hand. She looks up and we share a smile.

CHAPTER FIFTY-ONE

*After the summer's yield, Lord, it is time
to let your shadow lengthen on the sundials
and in the pastures let the rough winds fly.*

From: Day in Autumn by R M Rilke

We're shown in to the auditorium: all the witches - me, Melz, Saba, Macha, Rain - plus Sanj and some of the other Enviros. *For protection*, he says, though we're perfectly able to protect ourselves. I know it's an auditorium because it has a sign on the door that says so. "Auditorium" apparently means "a huge room with circular seating". Each wooden chair in it has a little desk attached. On the back wall of the room there's a massive screen showing moving pictures.

"It's a TV," Melz whispers to me when she sees me staring at it, open mouthed. The explanation adds mothing to my understanding. On the screen are pictures of our convoy; words run along the bottom. UNEXPECTED PROTEST MARCH ON CLIMATE SUMMIT FROM GREENWORLD REPRESENTATIVES. More shots from the crowds, but none of the skirmish that took place outside.

"How can they not be showing the grenade hit? The standoff just now?" I whisper to Melz, but she shakes her head.

"Blunt's government must be running this station. She wants to represent us as peaceful. Remember, she wants us to reach out to the people. If she's going to introduce us to all this lot, it's not in her interests to make us look controversial or dangerous,"

"But they attacked us. We were just defending ourselves," I protest. Melz shushes me as two women in front of us look round disapprovingly.

"Whatever. It doesn't necessarily look like that from the outside. Best not to show it at all,"

The images change and another subtitle screams LONDONERS WELCOME GREENWORLD ACTIVISTS IN HISTORIC SCENES as a film showing the girls handing out food to Greenworlders plays.

"They're not referring to us as terrorists," Saba whispers. "That's got to be a good start,"

The summit's started already. A soldier shows us to some seats at the back of the hall, and hands us some papers. *International Climate Summit 2047 Agenda* it says at the top. I scan it as Saba and Sanj slide into their seats next to us.

"Goddess. They've been here since dawn," Saba says, reading over my shoulder.

"Shitting themselves," Sanj repeats. "Desperate for any solution at all,"

"Just as well we're here, then," Saba says smugly.

"Yeah. But Omar's cutting it pretty fine. We can't do this without Danny," Melz looks anxiously at the double doors we came through as if she's willing them to burst through them, waving the Greenworld flag or something.

"How do you know he'll come at all?" Saba frowns. "We have to be prepared to do this without Danny. It's unlikely at this stage that he'll just turn up,"

"He'll come," Melz says, looking at me. I know she won't say anything unless I do. Protecting me, as ever. Saba catches the look.

"Something you need to tell us?" she hisses. "We've risked our lives to be here, Sadie. If you've got information about Danny, spit it out,"

"I… I had a vision. I saw Omar find him. That's all," no-one needs to know the rest, not for the moment anyway.

"We're on in an hour," Saba holds the agenda paper in front of my face. I push it away. "They going to be here in an hour? Otherwise, we need a backup plan. I can be the third, in his place. It's the only way,"

Melz lets a long breath out slowly.

"Omar'll be here. It's destiny," Melz mutters. I take her hand.

"He's got Danny. I know he has," I rub my thumb over the back of her hand but she pulls it away and picks nervously at the shredded skin around her nails, making them bleed.

"Right. But just in case destiny fucks up, maybe we could have a backup plan?" Saba whispers testily.

"If Danny doesn't get here, then yes, it has to be you, Saba. But you're not a branded one. I don't know if the magic will work in the same way," Melz whispers back.

"It'll have to," Sanj mutters.

"I know. Believe me, I know," Melz grimaces.

CHAPTER FIFTY-TWO

Whoever's homeless now, will build no shelter;
who lives alone will live indefinitely so,
waking up to read a little, draft long letters,
and, along the city's avenues,
fitfully wander, when the wild leaves loosen.

From: Day in Autumn by R M Rilke

An hour later and they're still not here and Blunt's standing up and preparing to announce us and *oh shit we're not ready.*

Two soldiers in different types of uniforms to the ones outside (these are prettier, with gold and twiddly bits, very smart and angular, clean-pressed, like, even the trousers have perfect poker-straight creases down the middle of the blue fabric) come and whisper to us to follow them. Sanj and the enviros follow us at a respectful distance.

"They don't have to come with us everywhere, do they?" Saba hisses at me, but I shrug.

"I think they like feeling useful,"

"Spare me from the big strong men," she mutters, rolling her eyes.

"Don't be mean. He's been good so far," I mutter.

Felicity Blunt welcomes us to the circular area in the centre of the chairs.

"Thanks for coming," she murmurs, but she's looking over our shoulders to the politicians behind us at their desks. She's anxious. This is a risk for her.

"Can we go on after the next person?" I smile ingratiatingly at her. "We're still waiting for someone. We kind of need him to do this right,"

"No. We're running to a strict deadline and we don't defer items on the agenda, I'm afraid," she looks at her phone. "Two minutes. We have to start on time,"

"But…" I try to explain but she cuts me off.

"Look. I've put a lot on the line to get you here. You had time to prepare. This is it. I'm fulfilling my part of the deal. Right?" she's standing pretty close to me. I lean away.

"We'll just have to do it without him," Melz says in a low voice. "Use Saba,"

"But she doesn't have the connection. That special thing between us," I say out of the corner of my mouth.

"Yeah, well. I'd settle for functional over special right now," she blows out her cheeks, exhaling. Trying to calm the shake in her hands.

Blunt turns to the room of politicians. So many countries, so many folk - I didn't know there even were this many countries in the world. And the people themselves - I haven't seen many of their features before. I didn't realise there were so many people that looked different to me.

"Thank you for your patience," Blunt's voice is magnified through the auditorium; the blue-suited soldier taps me on the shoulder and fits some wire around my ears; a tiny piece of wire sticks out beside my chin; he drops a small metal box in my pocket, attached to the wire.

"You're all set," he whispers and I just stare at him confusedly because I have no idea what he's just done. He makes his hand into a cone and puts it to his mouth. "Microphone. Amplifies your voice when you talk," he whispers.

"Oh. Thanks," I say in my ordinary voice; it echoes around the auditorim, making everyone jump. "Sorry," I blush to the roots of my hair. *Smooth*.

"I'd like to introduce some young women from Cornwall, in the south west of England. As you'll know, for the past twenty years, the counties of Devon and Cornwall have been segregated from the rest of the country and known as the Greenworld, the result of an ideological disagreement with its originating ecopagan group, The Five Hands. Separation occurred at the end of a brief but painful series of terrorist activities on the part of the Five Hands, out of a desire to maintain peace in an increasingly volatile national crisis of opposition to environmental, fiscal and defence policies."

"We're not terrorists," Melz interjects. Her microphone's working too, then. "We never were,"

"We're not here to argue about the past," Blunt says smoothly. "The point is that I'm delighted to say that these representatives from The Greenworld, as the community calls itself, have agreed to a series of measures to reintegrate into British society,"

There's a muted but polite clap around the room.

"We haven't specifically agreed to reintegrate," Saba whispers to me, her hand covering the wire by her jaw. "She's lying,"

"She's a politician. Remember, we're here for one thing today: the portal network. Nothing else matters," Melz says, doing the same thing with the wire.

"With the end of the Tunguska conflict and the issue of international fuel poverty, it is timely that these young women would like to share some information about their ecological way of life that may inform some of your green policies going forward," Blunt continues, making it sound like we're going to stand here and talk about preserving pears by candlelight, not saving the world. Melz shakes her head gently at me, sensing my frustration. "So I will now hand over to these fascinating young people. Thank you," she nods to us, and there's a steely look in her eyes. Like *don't do anything too crazy.*

Fascinating young people. Patronising bitch.

Danny's still not here. Shit, shit, shit.

Brighid, if you can get us out of this, I'd really appreciate it.

Saba smiles at everyone in the room, turning around slowly so that no-one's spared her incendiary grin.

"Good day," her voice rings through the room, up into the far corners. "I'm Bersaba Hawthorne. This is my sister, Demelza Hawthorne. We are the Joint Head Witches of the Greenworld. These young women are our covenstead witches: Sadie Morgan, Rain Bellever, Macha Lewis. We're not here to tell you about how to live more sustainably. We can tell you that another day. Today, we're going to save your arses,"

An offended *what?* runs around the room, but Saba ignores it, raising her voice until they listen to her again.

"You've messed this world up pretty comprehensively, stripping it of all its natural resources; overpopulating it; polluting it. All the problems you have now are basically down to the fact that you don't understand how nature works. You thought you could do whatever you wanted and it'd be fine. Well, it's not fine. And finally, you've asked for help. So here we are,"

"She's not taking any prisoners," Sanj mutters to me. There's a brief silence in the room followed by a flurry of chatter as, I guess, interpreters repeat what Sadie's just said into hundreds of non-English-speaking ears.

"Nope," I grin. This is kind of brilliant.

"You can thank us all later," Saba adds, still managing to be charming in a completely aggressive way. One of her talents, I guess. "What we've come here to tell you - to show you - is that there's a way to get power from another totally sustainable natural resource."

Melz takes over, taking her sister's hand. "Across the world, there are hundreds of energy portals. A portal is the energetic link between life and death and a regulator of earthly energy. Human souls travel through the portal before birth and when they die. We've been guarding two of these portals in the Greenworld for years, so I can assure you that they do exist. Among the worldwide portals are seven Master Centres: Glastonbury, in the UK; Mount Elbrus in Russia; Lake Titicaca, Peru, Uluru, in Australia, the Egyptian pyramids; Mount Kailas, in the Himalayas; Mount Shasta in the USA. These are the largest and most important."

She gives the room the trademark Demelza Hawthorne glare.

"The indigenous peoples of every country have always known about the existence of portals, but the Redworld - most of you, here - have denied and forgotten their power, because to recognise them for what they are would be to admit that the earth was a living, breathing thing. In fact, that the earth is sacred. Holy. And that every single indigenous culture in the world, sensibly, regards it as a deity in itself. If your Redworld people started thinking about that for too long they'd start questioning why they were endangering its future, just so that the very few at the top could have more of the new thing you made your God: money,"

"And your new God, money, it pushed the old gods to the sidelines and ridiculed them. You sold your people the lie that it was more rational not to have gods, but to have things instead. Recognising the sovereignty of the earth - and truly understanding what that means, in terms of magic, in terms of natural energy - means admitting that the pursuit of money is not the truth of this life. And it's the truth you're terrified of, because it means more people like us. Awake to your shit and powerful enough to oppose it,"

Saba walks around the centre circle of the stage area deosil, clockwise, as she takes over from Melz, raising power just with her words. Melz follows her light tread. *They're casting a circle.*

"Because of your wars, your pollution, your

incessant drilling and scraping and mining and burning for the valuable natural elements the earth holds in Her Womb, some of the portals have been blocked. They've stopped working; stopped regulating the flow of life and death in this world. I'm very sorry to say that Mount Elbrus, one of the Master Centres, has suffered this fate, because of the war that has raged around it for the past ten years. But we can repair it. And we can show you how these portals can make energy for the world's population. We don't know how much, exactly. But it's got to be better than none. And we - and communities like us - we can teach your people how to live more sustainably; to cope with less," Melz's voice adopts a singsony tone like it does in circle. Casting her spell.

There's a hubbub of dissent from some of the delegates. Some stand up, disgusted, ripping their earpieces off and throwing them onto the floor. Some walk out. Arguments break out and folk shout at us in a cacophony of languages. Blunt tries to restore order, but she can't make herself heard.

"Please! Please!" she shouts, but no-one's listening.

"I think you went in too hard," Macha says, raising a horsy eyebrow (I don't know if horses even have eyebrows; I'm thinking they don't, but still. Hers are bushy anyway).

"This is what happens when you blow people's tiny minds with the Goddess, By Brighid," Saba sighs, surveying the scene. It's true. We're subversives here because we're saying what they don't want to hear. That this is all their fault.

"Patriarchy's rubbish. Look at how many men are in here, compared to women," Rain says. We're clustered in a circle at the centre of the room waiting for Blunt to restore order, but I'm not sure that she can. "It's about three quarters men. How did that happen?"

"We've got a lot to be grateful for," Melz says. "Thank the Goddess that Greenworld decision making's not dependent on these idiots,"

It's so noisy I can't focus, and the chaos seems to be coming from outside as well; it sounds like there's voices outside the room, but I can't be sure.

"Are we going to take control here, or..." Rain looks around anxiously. "I feel like this is getting away from us,"

"Yeah, you're right," Melz sighs. "I was hoping we

could play for time a bit more - for Danny - but if they're leaving, we should probably do something,"

There's a series of loud bangs outside.

Sanj looks up as a bright flash of fire illuminates the windows and a roar goes up outside. There's another bang, but this time it's the door. Melz frowns and I can tell she's expecting the blue and gold-uniformed guys to usher us out, but when she sees who's slammed the door back onto its hinges, she grins.

Danny and Omar barrel through the heavy wooden double doors, sweaty, smoke-stained and very much in the nick of time.

Another three bangs shake the room. The delegates go into full-on panic.

"What the… what the hell was that?" Saba shouts, turning her face away from the smoke billowing through the doorway.

"Bomb," Omar says, simply.

CHAPTER FIFTY-THREE

Much care must be taken when invoking the Gods within yourself and should only be tried by a senior witch with the full permission and support of her high priestess and the covenstead at large. It is vital to prepare mindfully and carefully beforehand, be rested and strong, and to ground instantly afterwards by eating, drinking and, ideally, receiving healing from another witch.

From Greenworld Covenstead Magic: A Practical Guide

"Danny!" Saba's the first to hug him; he looks a mixture of embarrassed and pleased. Melz grins; the other girls hug him too.

"Standing ovation would have been sufficient," he mutters, pushing his black curls out of his remarkable green eyes. He looks shyly at me. (Shyly! Danny Prentice was never shy).

"Sades," he nods with half a smile.

"Danny," I nod back cautiously.

"Alright?"

"Yeah. Glad you made it,"

"Got a feeling you knew I would," he says, looking away. Omar claps his hand on Danny's shoulder.

"We were always going to get here in time. Got held up outside though. It's all kicking off between the security services and the gangs. Turns out, gangs don't like Nazis in sunglasses. Who'd a thought?" he wipes his sweaty forehead, and clocks Sanj in the circle. "Christ on a bike. Sanj?"

"Omar," Sanj looks at him warily. Omar and Zia were an item before Sanj came along and then again after he left. Can't imagine they're ever really going to bond, manwise, but that's not our problem right now.

"It's been a while," Omar holds out his bear paw hand; I notice a tattoo on his arm that looks new. A woman's face. *Zia, My White Rose*, curls underneath it in a flowing script. I look away. Sanj shakes his hand cautiously.

"It has," he says, his hand a bit lost in Omar's. Melz rolls her eyes.

"Save the reminiscences. We've got work to do," she says impatiently, and, taking Omar's pistol from his belt - *that's the same one he shot my dad with, I can tell; should I feel disloyal being pleased to see him?* - she shoots it into the ceiling.

Melz, we all appreciate your focus at this emotional time.

"All right!" Melz shouts into the melee. "There seems to be a situation outside between the security services and the Greenworlders. But we'll finish what we came here to do." The room quiets; we can hear the chaos outside. More explosions flash against the windows; a couple of them shatter and the glass shards tinkle onto the floor. "We can't stop. Now is the time. Now!"

CHAPTER FIFTY-FOUR

Brighid b adach,
B·aid na fine,
Siur R g nime,
Nßr in duine,
Eslind luige,
Lethan breo.
Ro-siacht no bnem
Mumme Go del,
Riar na n-o ged,
O bel ecnai,
Ingen Dubthaig,
Duine ·allach,
Brighid b·adach,
Brighid b·adach

Invocation to Brighid from The Book of Brighid, Greenworld Prayers and Songs

The power comes very quickly, like the gods were waiting at the corners of the room, counting down the minutes until they were asked to intervene.

The five of us join the circle, holding hands, ignoring the battle outside. We start to dance, around, around, in a circle, raising energy. As we dance, we chant. *Cast the circle, sacred space, out of space and time; Break the link within ourselves, to skin and hair and bone; Let us see, grant us wisdom, Lady of Fire, Lady of Tides; Sight be here, be with us, Brighid; Sight be here, be with us, Brighid.*

The energy spools into the circle, fast and hot. I feel Brighid's presence almost immediately, surging through me, strength and victory and magic; the whole room's lashed with psychic energy, leaping and devouring like fire. The politicians watch, caught in the energy: although they may not be able to see it, they sense it. I've never felt any power as intense as this outside a portal; the combination of the three of us, together: the branded ones, blazing like midsummer bonfires, magnetising the whole room.

Melz and I know what the plan is, but we had to resort to giving Omar a letter for Danny explaining what we had to do, and hope that was enough in the event that we didn't get to talk to him before this - and we didn't, so it's just as well. I hope he remembers everything, but he's not so great at the books - always the one capering about at school, or skiving off, or doodling big-titted girls in the margins of his copy of his Reflective Greenworld Journal.

Now that we can feel the energy racing through our bodies, our auras, now that the whole room's a charged battery, we have to guide this group visioning. We have to create a group hallucination and connect to the Glastonbury portal. No pressure or anything. We stop circling, centring the energy.

"Find Glastonbury Tor with your mind," Melz instructs, raising her voice against the shouting and banging outside. "Imagine walking up its grassy hill; circle it in a spiral like the priests and priestesses before you. Feel the wind around you. Notice the smell of the grass, the birds flying overhead,"

Closing my eyes, following her voice, I'm there immediately; it's easy, like viewing the picture on one of those TV screens, because the energy's so high already and we're feeding off each other, too: a group visualisation's pretty powerful. The ground's tussocky like the moor, but it's warm and the sun's beating down on my bare shoulders and the wind's blowing my hair into tangles. I can't hear the fighting anymore. Everything's peaceful.

"Now. We meet at the top of the hill. Join hands," she says, and as I imagine us doing that, my perception shifts from a vivid visualisation to reality, and I'm really there, holding Rain's hand on one side and Danny's on the other.

"Don't let go. We're co-visualising now. Co-dreaming, like that time in Russia," Melz says. "Rain and Macha, follow what we do. We need to extend the circle energy to include all the folk in that room, and bring them here. Then we need to open the portal, but I'm going to project the symbols mentally rather than direct them with my hands, because I think if we let go of each other, we might lose the connection. Okay?"

"Okay. And then, when the portal's open, we should be able to go in together, and the Shasta'll take it from there?" Danny asks, and catches my surprised expression: surprised that he's paid attention, I guess. "I am actually a pretty good witch, you know, Sades," he raises his eyebrow.

"Didn't say you weren't," I counter.

"Yes. That's the plan," Melz's brow crinkles. "If we can maintain this energy. Okay. So, none of us have done anything like this before, but I suggest we visualise our circle getting wider and wider, and imagine all the politicians standing around us, here on the hill. But we've got to start with calling in the gods,"

I nod and begin the call to Brighid, singing it in Gaelic.

WILD FIRE

Brighid b adach, B·aid na fine, Siur R g nime, Nßr in duine, Eslind luige, Lethan breo.
Ro-siacht no bnem, Mumme Go del, Riar na n-o ged,
O bel ecnai, Ingen Dubthaig,
Duine ·allach, Brigit b·adach, Brighid b·adach.

Glastonbury's one of Brighid's holiest places, even though it's in the Redworld. Before the tower that used to be on top of the hill collapsed, there were engravings of Her on it, Melz told me once.

Bright orange, yellow and red explodes at the centre of our bodies in ever-expanding waves; we are the fire circle, the heat of our combined power, and it radiates out from us, out, out, out, further and further. Rain and Macha echo my chant, and Melz and Danny chant their own words to call in the Morrigan and Lugh, their own incantations, meshing with mine.

The words appear in the space between us, in the air, ghostly grey and then darker, black, red and yellow, merging to create new words, new things. My words are red, for fire and love and healing; Melz's are black, for night, crows, death and regeneration; Danny's are golden, yellow and bright for the sun, day, life and joy. I watch as his chanted words, the same as on his witch-brand, come alive and swim away from his skin and into the mesh like floating dust motes in the sunlight; *I am the spear, the slingshot, the smith, the poet, the warrior, the magician, the gift; the trunk of the tree, the arrow of war, the movement of time, the lover at dawn. I am the sun, the heat of the day; the might of the land; the great bird of prey.* And from Melz, the Chant for the Morrigan we use to invoke Her - *Morrigan, Ancient One; Morrigan, Dark Mother, Wise Mother, Morrigan, Shining One; Morrigan, Shape-shifter, Soul Healer; Morrigan, Sovereign One; Morrigan, Goddess of Rebirth.*

And over and through all of us, the song that's been playing in my mind ever since my initiation at Scorhill circle: *Three to bind, to open, to see, the power in them as within thee.* We start to chant that instead, our voices slowly coming together into a new rhythm, with a new refrain at the end: *Dark Mother, Bright Spear, Queen of Fire, come!* over and over - to the Morrigan, the Dark Mother; to Lugh, the Bright Spear, and to Brighid, the Queen of Fire.

When They appear behind us, the power of three deities is so intense I almost let go of Danny's hand, but he grips me tightly and presses his thumbnail into my palm as if to say *focus*; he consciously takes deep breaths through his nose, and I do the same. Better.

"Blessed Brighid, Lugh and Morrigan; thank you

for being with us in this holy space," Melz cries breathlessly into the charged air. "We ask for your help in bringing the consciousness of the delegates at the climate summit here, in health and peace, to witness the power of the portal; please help us keep them here with your great power. So mote it be!" she shouts, and we hold our linked hands up to the sky.

"You honour us with your invocation, Crow Priestess, and your intention for this revolutionary action," Brighid is as tall as a tree, blue robes flowing, her face painted with blue woad and her red hair tangling in the breeze like mine. Her voice is deep and bell-like. She passes a giant hand over our circle.

The Morrigan is just as tall, white-haired, black-skinned, with the triskele painted in white on Her aged cheeks and forehead. She is in the black robes of Her Crone aspect, patterned with silver crescent moons and skulls.

"We bring the power of life and death to your circle, knowing that they are one," She calls, and her spirit-crows fly above us, making a circle of wings and beaks.

Lugh appears in his aspect as the young warrior: he wears an antler head-dress, and there is a yellow sun painted on his bare chest. His legs are clothed in leaves.

"Blessed be the vision of the new generation. Blessed be the fruit on your trees. Blessed be your rivers and seas. Blessed be your resolve. Blessed be your clean air. Alight be your holy fires," he intones, and power flashes through me like lightning, from the top of my head, through my fingertips and hips and the soles of my feet, and the circle explodes out beyond us, and the politicians start appearing, more and more, ring by ring, until they're with us, looking around them in confusion.

Melz nods, feeling the increased drain on our energy, even though the gods are helping us hold all these folk here in a weird transport-hallucination-group vision. I know she's projecting the opening symbols into the portal because almost immediately it blooms into life, a gigantic cerise-pink-red heart-shaped portal. Instead of going into it one by one, the whole thing envelopes outwards and engulfs us, swallows us up like that exotic plant that eats insects that I can't remember the name of right now. And there we are, a whole village-sized gang of displaced souls, right at the edge of oblivion, at the border between life and death, inside the feathery softness of the pulsing light portal.

Ki'putska, Sa'maka and Ya'nni are waiting for us, just like they said they would be; to say I'm relieved is the biggest understatement in herstory. They bow; we bow our heads in reply.

"You're here," Ki'putska grins happily. "I knew you'd come," she looks around in awe at the hundreds of delegates, all in a kind of daze, watching us.

"Do they know where they are? What's happening?" I ask, looking around concernedly. "I mean, I don't want them to be, like, disturbed by all this,"

"They will experience it as a vivid dream. But they will remember," Ki'putska says. "Our shaman-scientists are ready," she breathes. Sa'maka starts to sing.

This is the time of listening to our ancestors' wisdom.

It is the time to realize that all that is, is sacred.

It is time to light the beacons; to power the world with fire.

Gods hear me... Animals heal me.... Ancestors grant me peace.

Gods, spirits, ancestors, land. I honour you. Ho!

As she sings, the three shaman-scientists, brown skinned and black-haired like Ki'putska, Sa'maka and

Ya'nni, wearing the same silver jewellery, the same leather clothes, are doing something weird. Making strange movements with their hands, bringing them to their bodies like fluttering birds, pressing them up to the sky, then shaping a spiral together, round and round. As we watch, it gains an outline, a colour, a sense of mass: as tall as me, glassy; beautiful, catching the pulsing light of the portal and reflecting it back at us. Moving, slowly and now faster. They're singing something much stranger, underneath it all; sounds and words none of us Greenworlders understand. The energy spiral glows into a deep red, like a lamp when you turn the wick.

I feel the Gods behind us, their huge presences framing our magic, the power streaming from them almost incomprehensible, almost too much to bear. I know that the forms of the black crone, bright warrior and flame-haired, woad-tattooed giantess are only masks for these vast sources of universal power that we call Morrigan, Lugh and Brighid; they're ancient natural phenomena, just like the oceans and the stars.

Energetic paths start to open around us, into other portals at other locations; the power of the spiral thing's linking them all up, I guess - opening some that haven't been open for ages and blowing open some that're blocked. And as the paths open up, more tribes, more guardians join our circle. And every time a portal opens, the shamans travel to it and create another red spiral, and another. Red for blood, red for fire.

We watch as the smoke-belching towers of a power station explode as one portal opens; as a landslide buries a factory next to another sacred site. And as each portal opens, their light shines back at us and into the room, like beacons being lit. Like Midsummer fires, Brighid's fires, glowing and burning and remaking across the world. And along with each portal, a new figure to the circle; a new guardian, their spirit body joining hands with us; folk of all races and cultures. Soon the circle's 20, then 30 strong, all chanting *Gods hear me... Animals heal me.... Ancestors grant me peace.Gods, spirits, ancestors, land. I honour you. Ho!* our voices louder and louder.

In the circle, we watch in awe as pure, unfettered fiery power streams between the portals, flowing like a river.

As the shamans place the final spiral in the last Master Centre, Elbrus, the ground beneath us shakes.

"The Fire of the World," Ki'putska breathes, and the rumble increases under our feet.

"What's it going to do?" I whisper to Melz, who shakes her head. Mount Elbrus is the only Master Centre that's been blocked, because of the war that's raged around it for the past ten years.

And as if it doesn't want to make us wonder any longer, the volcano erupts.

CHAPTER FIFTY-FIVE

Let's not forget the music, either,
that soon had hauled him
toward absence complicated
by an overflowing heart...

From: Fire's Reflection, R M Rilke

We're not actually standing in it, obviously, so we can watch from a distance as the black smoke plumes out from the top of the mountain, followed by what must be molten rock, which spurts after the smoke like... well, I can't compare it to anything, actually. It's exactly how you'd expect liquid rock to behave.

"Goddess," Saba breathes, and it's probably pretty much anyone can think of as we watch the full force of fire transform the landscape. Fire can even melt rock. Relentless, wild heat of such a terrifying temperature that, if it melts rock, it must vaporise a body. I gaze into the heat haze that seems to emanate into this between-world place we're in; it's harder to concentrate, harder to breathe. The chanting grows louder and louder and the power streaming through from the gods is so intense I don't feel like a human anymore at all; I'm not even a mind, I'm a breath that cycles in and out, panting, I'm a tight cone of air in two aching, red hot lungs.

Midsummer fire: I suppose you could say it was appropriate.

I start to feel faint and loosen my grip on Danny's hand, but he squeezes my fingers and I try to concentrate again, but it's too much, and like the minutes before falling asleep when faces and images and nonsense words flash into my mind. Behind my eyes, I see an immense face form in the plateauing explosion that's Mount Elbrus right now. Brighid's face. The lava's her red hair, streaming out into the blackened, sooty sky; the smoke morphs into the shape of a triskele, then the triple moon, her symbols. Now it's Brighid's face again: Her eyes glow and from Her open mouth comes the pent-up scream of the damaged portal wailing back into life, refusing to be tortured anymore. I hear the same scream coming out of my throat, out of the depth of me, and everyone else. Screaming, deranged, holding nothing back.

It reaches deafening, and the Brighid of the volcano, the Fire of the World, appears to stand up and raise Her arms to the blackened sky. Light flows between Her hands and condenses into a ball, into a sphere of zigzagging, momentous energy. She bends and places the ball - the width of the base of the volcano - into the ground, into the earth, and lines of fire - lines of white hot energy - stream out from it in all directions, and I know instinctively they're going to the other Master Centres, linking, connecting the circuit again; and then, from there, to the smaller ones, and then, like the irrigation tracks we have in the fields at Tintagel, out across the land, reviving it, healing it; restoring the natural energies throughout the world. And She places Her palm on the ravaged earth there, which is nothing but broken ground and mud. Her mouth moves as She blesses the land. And then, She reaches out Her massive hand for me.

And when She touches me, I know that She also touches every single person on Earth. For that moment, I am Her, and I am humanity. I see everything: rivers, cities, deserts; children, grandmothers, Redworlders, soldiers, even the rich in their gated fortresses and palaces. And I know that they each feel this shift in the world; this sudden return to what it must have been like, once, before war and separation, loneliness and hate. We are all connected in that one moment. Connected to the earth, to each other, to life itself.

But, no, that isn't it. The realisation comes to me; I hold my hand over my heart. *We were always connected.* In that intense moment, every human on earth realises the lie of separation. Every human knows Brighid intimately, because they are Her and She is them. And in that moment, I am everyone and I see everything. And that includes Lowenna.

She's deep in converstion by a hearthfire, Demi and Merryn and Rhiannon and the others with her, and some other witches. One of the other covensteads. I know it all; I see it all in that moment. She's there to try and get their support, and maybe it isn't going so well. They want to know why Saba and Melz have left, and Lowenna's holding it back. I can see worry and resignation clustered in the corners of the room like webs.

In that one red-gold moment, Lowenna drops to her knees in front of the hearthfire. For Brighid has always been her goddess, and she knows Her voice as well as I do. I watch as the light streams through her; as light zings between all the witches in that room. Lowenna bows her head. "My goddess. My goddess, forgive me," she whispers, wide eyed, because she sees our circle, and understands. "I didn't realise. Forgive me. I was afraid,"

But Brighid puts Her bright hand on Lowenna's yellow hair, and there are no words that need to be said because love is in that touch. Pure love and pure joy.

And elsewhere, in the billions of hearts that awake and minds that are suddenly elevated by Brighid's touch, I see Mum. She's in our Lowenna's garden, crouching down with a watering can by the water butt, filling it up. She was never very green-fingered, like it was another way she could show her disapproval of the Greenworld, but she's started doing odd jobs where she can. I think it soothes her.

When the moment hits her, her eyes meet mine. She drops the watering can and stands up, seeing me, seeing Brighid, I'm not sure. Her hand goes to her heart, and a smile breaks over her face. She reaches out for me. "Sadie," she says, simple and pure. "Come home, Sadie. I…I…" but then her smile turns to a kind of wonder as Brighid's heavenly fire envelops her like it does everyone in that moment. And she finally gets it, the magic she's pushed against all these years. Maybe even when she was part of the original Five Hands she never felt this. Lowenna and Zia were the mystics, the witches. Mum was the academic, the idealist. *Mum.* I want to go to her, hug her. *Home. I want to go home.* "Sadie… Oh, my Goddess," she falls to her knees, and I know the awe and joy that's cleansing her heart, because it's in me too, like being an entire ocean, deep with unceasing magic.

"It is done," it might be Ki'putska's voice and it might be Brighid's; maybe it's mine, I dunno. There's a lengthening of the moment, a time where there is no time, and I stretch away from Mum, up to the stars, and I feel what Brighid feels. I feel Her, I am Her, wide as the sun, the Mother of Stars, the Mother of Fire; the wild fire of the universe.

And I am full of what She is full of, and it's this: the undeniable, expansive fire of hope.

I return to my own body and look down. A red spiral has appeared on my skin, over my heart. Melz looks down at her own heart and sees the same thing.

All of us have received the mark of Brighid. Every single human being on earth. I know it like I know my own name.

CHAPTER FIFTY-SIX

Badb and Macha and Anand, of whom are the Paps of Anu in Luachar, were the three daughters of Ernmas the she-farmer.

From: Lebor Gabála Érenn, or Book of Invasions

When I come to, I'm lying on top of an unconscious Danny in the middle of the conference room and everything's crazy: Chaos, meet your try-harder sister, Oblivion. Half the politicians are running around with a kind of fervent zeal in their eyes because *WOW they've seen something they couldn't quantify with maths or whatever and WOW it's changed their lives and WOW they have to do something about it RIGHT NOW* and half of them are groggily sitting up like me probably thinking *shit I feel like death warmed up.*

The large TV's back on, showing the crowd outside the building. I roll off Danny's stomach and hug my steepled legs to my chest which I remember is always a good thing to do if you've suffered shock. Melz sits up behind me.

"Goddess, I'm definitely dead this time," she groans.

"Shitty afterlife, then," I hug her awkwardly to my

knees. "You all right?"

"That's not comfortable. Yeah. Okay," she breathes, pulling away but reaching out for my hand instead.

We gaze up at the animated screen above us. Words scroll across the bottom of the screen. END OF THE WORLD AS WE KNOW IT? RIOTS ROCK WESTMINSTER. SECURITY SERVICES USE EXCESSIVE FORCE.

It's apocalyptic. Fire blazing everywhere. Grey vans overturned, on fire. Bodies in the street. My stomach turns.

"Oh, shit. Oh, goddess. No," I murmur. It didn't work. Everything I saw was some kind of hallucination. I feel cold to my bones.

"But they protected us. Our people. They gave us the time we needed," Melz wraps her arms around me and holds me into her neck, her shoulder, as familiar dread engulfs me. *Not a panic attack, please. Not now.* "It's okay. It'll be okay. I promise," but it feels like she's trying to reassure herself and not just me.

At the bottom of the screen, the text scrolls

swiftly.

ENVIRONMENT SUMMIT CONTINUES IN LONDON. GREENWORLD PROTESTORS SURROUND WESTMINSTER. CONFRONTATION BETWEEN POLICE AND SECURITY SERVICES.

"Playing down the gang involvement. Interesting," Melz says, watching. "That's the government's propaganda. Look. They're going to put any blame onto the security services, not us,"

"We haven't done anything wrong anyway," I mutter into her shoulder.

"I know. But they could have said that if they wanted to, and they didn't. Most people aren't here. They don't know what's going on, really. They could say we were an evil Greenworld horde setting fire to government buildings," she points at the screen, and her jaw drops. "Holy shit. Look at that,"

People are arguing and pushing and shoving in the street, suddenly all of them (and I mean ALL) stand completely still. Statue-still. Their faces go utterly blank. Some of them sway on their feet a little bit then, and something must happen to the camera or something at that moment because the screen goes black.

And when it comes back on, everything has changed. Just like it has here in the room.

People are smiling at each other. Hugging. Looking dazed, crying, sitting down shakily on the pavement and looking around them with new eyes.

When a woman with a scoop-necked t shirt walks dazedly past the camera, I see the red spiral over her heart. And, in the chamber, I watch as Felicity Blunt frowns absently and unbuttons the top two buttons of her blouse. By her expression, I know what she sees. So it is real.

"Shit. The camera must have been on a delay or something," Melz watches with me. "It's all a few minutes ago. Must be,"

The words scrolling at the bottom of the screen change.

INCREDIBLE SCENES AS GREENWORLDERS CREATE A BRIDGE OF TORCHES DOWN THE EMBANKMENT. JOURNALISTS AND PROTESTORS REPORT STRANGE EXPERIENCES.

The screen cuts to the river next to the Houses of

Parliament - I know what they are, I've seen them in a book too. The screen shows one Enviro in tatty clothes lighting a candle in a small lamp like the ones we have at home, an old dirty glass with the stub of a candle inside. Another enviro's handing out lamps from a box in the back of one of the vans we brought. And slowly, beautifully, against a red sunset, a line of light reaches down the river and across the bridges as the Redworlders join in. A line of fire, mimicking the portals, like beacons themselves, but instead of place to place, it's person to person - hand to hand, heart to heart. Midsummer fires.

I can see it in their eyes as they pass by the camera; joy, relief, a glow they didn't have before. People are showing each other the spiral marks they have over their hearts. A mark on humanity that this magic has been done; that it can never be undone. That nothing will ever be the same.

THOUSANDS OF LONDONERS JOIN HISTORIC GREENWORLD DEMONSTRATION. The subtitles roll and the politicians inside the conference room watch, and smile. And suddenly, a gust of air and not smoke blows through the window, and with it, the sound of voices. Singing, not shouting.

Imagine no possessions
I wonder if you can
No need for greed or hunger
A brotherhood of man
Imagine all the people
Sharing all the world...

It's an old song but I recognise it; sometimes mum sang it. We stand in awe as the outside voices wash over us. Danny buries his head in his knees but I know he's crying; exhaustion, sorrow, hopelessness, hope, everything: he looks up and I watch the tears spill down his cheeks. Sanj fights through the chaos to get to Danny; he wraps his son in his weary arms and they crouch there together, finally, powerless against the upswell of power in the song, in the moment. I watch as Sanj bows his head to rest on Danny's shoulder. *I'm sorry; I'm so sorry* I see the words pass from father to son.

Omar stands tactfully off to one side, watching, sad. He knows better than anyone that the path to Danny's heart is a rocky one. But I know all about rocky paths, and I know they can lead to beautiful places. And as I watch, Danny pulls away from Sanj, walks over to Omar, takes him by the top of his huge arm and leads him over to Sanj. And he makes them all hug, together. It's awkward at first, in that straight alpha male way, but then they really feel it, and there's some hearty back-slapping that makes Melz grin at me and I roll my eyes a bit. But I'm happy for Danny. He gets a family again, maybe. I don't think it's what any of them ever imagined, but a family is a family, whatever it looks like from the outside. For Biba too.

After they've nodded to each other and hugged and back-slapped some more, Danny disentangles himself from Sanj and Omar and walks over to us, not meeting our eyes.

"Alright," he nods, and gives us a flash of that old Danny grin I thought I'd never seen again. He's felt Brighid just like we all did, in that moment, and maybe Her healing gave him what he needed. Maybe Lugh's energy is truly back with him again, too. I hope it is. "That seemed to go all right, as saving the world goes,"

"It'll do. Minus marks for lateness," Melz grins at him, unexpectedly twinkly.

"Demelza Hawthorne. Please don't flirt with me in front of your new girlfriend. It's embarrassing for everyone," he grins at her, and it's a huge and sudden relief to know that whatever happened between them, it's over.

His expression softens and he holds out his hand to me. "Sadie? I'm so sorry. For calling you those names, that day on the beach. And for everything else. I didn't mean it, really I didn't. I was just... I wasn't me. Okay?" he looks at me from under those long ladykiller eyelashes, and it really is him again. That sweet, silly boy that was my friend. Who is still my friend.

I take his hand, and pull him in for a hug.

"I know. And you know I love you. Just..." I pull back, worried. I do love him, as a friend. I always will. He sees my expression and laughs. And I know it's for our benefit, because I know it still hurts that we chose each other and he's alone.

"Do me a favour, Sades. There's a world of Redworld girls out there now, just dying for a piece of this," he runs his hand through his dark curls. "Go and be in love. Gods know it's all too much bloody talking and staring into each other's eyes anyway,"

"You'll find someone, Danny. When you're ready," Melz says quietly, seriously, and her eyes flicker to Saba, who's hanging back, letting us have this moment. "She'll be there. The right girl at the right time,"

He shrugs, studiously not looking at Saba even though I know he knows she's there. It's all bluster. We all know he's broken. But we also know he'll be okay.

"Maybe. Not for now, though," he looks around us, at the growing chaos. Puts his hands over his ears. "But I do think you're going to have to take charge, witches of the new aeon. Like, now,"

"You're in this too, Dan. You're one of us," I murmur as Melz takes a deep breath. He reaches for my hand and squeezes it. "*We* have to take charge. Together,"

I pull him forward so that he's standing with me, Saba and Melz. The other trainees (I guess they're not trainees anymore) Rain, Macha and Catie stand behind us with Sanj, Omar and the other Enviros.

I look back and catch the message on Omar's lips. *We've got your back.*

"All right! Can I have some quiet please?" Saba bangs on the nearest desk and enough of them shut up for a minute so that she can shout over them.

"Okay. Calm down. Anyone would think it was the apocalypse," she shouts, smiling. Amazingly, a few of them laugh. God, but she can be charming when she wants to.

"Thank you. I think we can all agree that was… well, I don't know what that was. Something all of us will remember for a very long time," she holds her arms out to them all. "Thank you. Thank you for being here, for seeing, for listening. For *feeling*," she points to the red spiral over her heart. "We are all connected. We always were, but this will be a reminder. For all of us. Forever,"

"Your people out there want something real from you now. You've just seen the power you can harness. You've seen the natural power of the portals. That's our future," Saba speaks clearly and loudly, her voice reaching to the back of the auditorium.

"Whatever the portals can give us, my people are willing to help you make the transition to a new life. And the people in the communities in your own countries, the indigenous communities, the ones with the wisdom, they'll help you, if you honour them. Embrace the Old Ways, the old rhythms of the year; we can teach you how to farm again, how to live a different way. You'll survive. It'll be tough, but it'll also be honest," Melz turns to Danny. Nods imperceptibly. "Say what you need to say," she says in an undertone. "We're the three branded ones. This is your moment as well as ours,"

She turns back to the room.

"Among the witches of the Greenworld, there have always been three that were chosen to do the work of the Gods. Daniel Prentice is the one of us that has the most powerful vision, and the deepest connection to our god, Lugh, the masculine principle of light and growth in the universe. In time, he will help us build a new world by visioning it and leading us towards it. Sadie Morgan," she smiles and nods to me, as I look away, embarrassed, "Sadie is the great healer, and brings the fiery power of Brighid to the world. And I am the mystic, the diviner into the dark. I know and love the darkness, and by loving it, transmute its power. As representative of the god, Danny must speak here and now, too,"

He looks panicked, and his voice wavers.

"Umm. Yeah. The masculine…. It's been sick. That's what I want to say, I guess," he looks at me; I smile supportively and start sending him energy, silently calling it down from the stars and up through the ground. "Hm. So, in our world, the god gives us light and growth, but in your world, expansion - you know, that kind of limitless thing, like everything would last forever - caused war and collapse. But in our world, the god didn't have the power that he should have, either," I know Danny's thinking about Roach; about Lugh's power that went dark in the Greenworld. And he's warming up; my power, Melz, Saba's, it's all helping him.

"So, yeah. That's part of it, I think. Balance. For us and for you. The people, out there, they can feel the change in the world already. So... listen to your people. Listen to what they want," Danny's voice deepens and widens, louder, filling the room now. "Honour the vision you've had. Feel the love of Brighid, of the gods. Feel the fire inside you. We can make a new future. Together. The healing's happening. Let's vision the new world, now. No Greenworld, No Redworld. Just us, together. Responsible. Clean. Honest. Balanced,"

There's something different now, a power shift again in the room. With us all standing together, I can see what Danny's seeing in his mind's eye. A green world, uncomplicated and real. It looks like the Greenworld, but the ideology's simpler. Books aren't burnt. Technology is there, powered in clean ways, and operated by people connected to their hearts and the earth. It's a future where we know what and where we are, and act accordingly. As a part of an ecosystem, as people rooted in our own individual and collective power. This is Danny's power, supported by us, alive and awake at last. Channelling and co-creating the vision of life that we can all see with him; everyone in this room, the people singing outside.

And now, the song comes inside the room, and all the delegates start to join in. And it is as if Lugh's bright spear has cut through the fear and the strangeness of the past hour, and now we are changed forever, but still just simple humans, holding hands, singing an old song about a new world. *You may say I'm a dreamer. But I'm not the only one. I hope someday you will join us; and the earth will be as one.*

Melz turns to me, brings my hand to her lips and kisses my palm, looking into my eyes.

"I love you," she shouts over the hubbub in the room, and my blood sings and my throat constricts with sudden tears.

"I love you too. More than anything. Anyone," I shout back, and I hold her and kiss her deep and hot for the red witch she is; strong enough to hold my fire without being burnt; the underworld girl that needs a flame in the darkness. Her lips are full, brushing against mine, again, again, setting off star explosions behind my eyes, her fingers tousled in my hair. She smells of incense and sweat. I can't stop kissing her; I never want to stop. When I'm touching her I feel right, connected, to her and the moon and the sea and the earth all at once, and her kiss tastes of smoke and honey.

Felicity Blunt bangs a hammer onto a piece of wood for silence; her voice rings low and clear in the strange new world we find ourselves in. Melz pulls away gently from my lips, smiling that wicked, incredible siren smile, and touches my lips with her fingertip.

"Later," she whispers. "Tonight's for you, Sadie Morgan. Right now I have to go and save the world,"

"Did you really just say that?" I murmur; even though her lips are slick with my kisses and mine crave the addictive touch of her tongue. "Who says that?"

"Warrior Queens," she kisses my top lip. "And poets. *Her languid lips are sweeter than love's who fears to greet her.* Proserpine, remember,"

"I remember,"

I close my eyes and reach for her kiss again, thinking of my own words. *Dreaming when I'm kissing you it's crystalline/The kind of kiss that bends the world in half*

Melz traces the outline of my lips with her fingertip instead of kissing me, and looks away to the audience, taking my hand in hers instead. "Patience, Sadie Morgan, Queen of Fire," she whispers, tickling my ear, sending tiny lines of electricity down my arms and legs.

I have no patience when it comes to restoring the electric connection of our bodies together; no patience at all. But even I can accept that a fragile world peace is at least some competition for kissing. Though, still, I'd have Melz's kisses over peace and take my chances in an apocalyptic dystopia if it absolutely had to be a straight choice.

"Bersaba. Demelza. Over to you," Blunt calls, and the politicians, some still sitting at their desks, some crosslegged on the floor, but most of them listening, now, quiet themselves as Saba stands up, holding her sister's hand. "We're listening,"

Reluctantly, I let go of her hand, knowing that I'll never lose it again. My Warrior Queen, my love. Glorious, the fiery queens of a new aeon, Saba and Melz take the floor.

THE END

ACKNOWLEDGMENTS

I took the chant *Teigi ar bhur ngluine, agus osclaigi bhur suile, Agus ligigi Brid bheannaithe isteach* from p93 of Gina McGarry's *Brighid's Healing: Ireland's Celtic Medicine Traditions*, Green Magic Press, 2005.

I also used Lunaea Weatherstone's excellent *Tending Brighid's Fire: Awaken to the Celtic Goddess of Hearth, Temple and Forge* (Llewellyn Publications US, 2015) as general research and specifically used her call to Brighid on her p133.

Na h-ataireachd ard, mo leabaidh dean suas, Ri fuaim na h-ataireachd ard, mo leabaidh dean suas are lines from the old gaelic song 'An Ataireachd Ard', which translates as *The surge of the sea, my bed make up, behind the sound of the sea.*

The Greenworld Invocation to Brighid is taken from *Dánta Ban: Poems of Irish Women Early and Modern - A Collection* by P.L Henry, Mercier Press, 1992.

Sadie writes poetry as part of her connection to Brighid, who, along with fire, smithcraft, love, hearth and healing, is a goddess of poetry and the arts. Therefore I also included some excerpts from one of Sadie's favourite (and very romantic) poets, Rainer Maria Rilke.

The crowds outside the environment summit sing *Imagine* by John Lennon, (Apple Records, 1971)

More information on the Shasta Indian Nation can be found here: http://www.shastaindiannation.org

I have referenced various elements of Wiccan and magickal ceremony, such as Doreen Valients and Gerald Gardner's *Charge of the Goddess* and the overall sense of the *Lesser Banishing Ritual of the Pentagram,* although these processes aren't quoted in full because of space, and their probable impediment to the flow of the story. In the case of the use of the LBRP, I have amended it for the girls' purposes in freeing Danny. The Greenworld witches have their own traditions that are informed by, but don't always precisely replicate, traditional theory.

I first found the concept of energetic portals in *A Little Light on Ascension* by Diana Cooper (Findhorn Press, 1997). There is some disagreement about where the definitive Master Centre portals are, so I took the seven main generally agreed global energetic centres as Mt Elbrus, Mt Shasta, Mt Kailas, Glastonbury, the Pyramids, Uluru and Lake Titicaca from http://www.wakingtimes.com/2013/07/25/earth-chakras-the-7-key-energy-vortices-of-mother-earth/. I added Mount Elbrus for story purposes, though Elbrus has a deeply mystical heritage.

ABOUT THE AUTHOR

Anna McKerrow is the author of the Greenworld trilogy: CROW MOON, RED WITCH AND WILD FIRE. She has also published four volumes of poetry and taught creative writing in adult education before becoming a children's books reviewer.

Anna is an eclectic pagan witch with particular interest in tarot, the dark feminine, sacred landscapes, healing, herbalism and shamanic practices.

Find out more about Anna on www.annamckerrow.com, and on Twitter and Instagram @AnnaMckerrow

Printed in Poland
by Amazon Fulfillment
Poland Sp. z o.o., Wrocław